Frederick Locker-Lampson

My Confidences

An Autobiographical Sketch Addressed to my Descendents

Frederick Locker-Lampson

My Confidences
An Autobiographical Sketch Addressed to my Descendents

ISBN/EAN: 9783337010843

Printed in Europe, USA, Canada, Australia, Japan

Cover: Foto ©Raphael Reischuk / pixelio.de

More available books at **www.hansebooks.com**

MY CONFIDENCES.

AN AUTOBIOGRAPHICAL SKETCH

ADDRESSED TO MY DESCENDANTS.

BY

FREDERICK LOCKER-LAMPSON.

Hoc est
Vivere bis, vitâ posse priore frui.

Cecy est un livre de bonne foi.

Ce ne sont mes gestes que j'écris; c'est moy.

SECOND EDITION.

LONDON:
SMITH, ELDER, & CO., 15 WATERLOO PLACE.
1896.

NOTE BY EDITOR

THIS volume was written by Mr. Locker at different periods during the last fifteen years of his life, and was in type at the date of his death, which happened at Rowfant on May 30, 1895.

Amongst the short biographical sketches there was included one of the late Lord Tennyson; but Mr. Locker, shortly before his death, gave this sketch to the present Lord, who will include it in the forthcoming biography of his illustrious father.

I have added the Appendices, for, though they relate to Mr. Locker's great-grandfather and grandfather, they describe traits of character as noticeable in Frederick Locker as ever they can have been in John or William.

AUGUSTINE BIRRELL.

LINCOLN'S INN:
January 30, 1896.

THE AUTHOR'S APOLOGY FOR HIS BOOK

I HAVE printed the following pages and directed them to be put into the shape of a published volume because I am anxious (a whimsical, foolish anxiety, some may think; but this I cannot help) that, if any descendant of mine, in days far distant, should chance to inherit, or at all events to show, some portion of my fondness for family records however simple, for ancestral anecdotes however slender, he or she should find something to gratify their humour saved from the fire-grate and the paper-mill. I cannot trust my frail cargo of memories to oral tradition. Could I have done so, the world would not have been affronted with even this semblance of publicity. Between me and posterity there stands bold and erect a generation which has not inherited my tastes, which does not share my backward-going thoughts. It is, indeed, a most impartial, a most unprejudiced generation. When I point, in my library, to the memoir, still in manuscript, of their grandfather, written in the clerkly hand of a Privy Councillor no less eminent than the late John Wilson Croker, this generation eyes the pages suspiciously. 'Is it Literature?' it inquires; and as I am unable to give the assurance it demands, the poor memoir remains unread by them. I cannot show this indifference, nor could I ever have made such a demand, for I feel as if I would give up a good deal to know even as much of my grandfather's great-grandfather as I do of my own, who lived in Gray's Inn in 1723, and nursed the scheme of producing an edition of Lord Bacon's works; and I wish I knew more of my grandfather, who was shipmate, correspondent, and friend of Nelson. I am not inclined to insist upon the facts that the edition of Lord Bacon never appeared, and that my grandfather was not himself the hero of Trafalgar. I am well content to range with humble livers, provided I am allowed my share of humble memories.

However, it is useless to quarrel with one's immediate descendants; besides, I have an immense admiration for mine. But in this little matter I cannot trust them: they would make havoc of my hobby. I hardly know which is the more trying to me—their languid endurance of a family story, or their inaccurate repetition of it.

Such being the case, my duty to that unknown

and shadowy being my fancy depicts, who may hereafter, in his voyage through immensity, reach earth's human shores, and for his season be fond of the things I have been fond of, and be interested in his ancestors for no better reason than because they were ancestors, presses somewhat heavily upon me, and I have thought it right before I push off those same shores to bury for him a little heap in some place where he may be likely to find it.

I have accordingly selected from my papers the following memoranda, or sketches, which make no pretence to be of general interest. This is a volume which it will be found exceedingly easy to leave alone; an old book-collector like myself thinks none the worse of a volume merely on that account. But as a book-collector I am able clearly to perceive that my best chance of accomplishing my purpose is to bury my treasure in print. A well-bound book mocks at Time. How few books are read, and yet how the world is full of them!

At all events, I have now done all I have strength to do—more than most men would think worth doing at all. But if, on some far-off day, any honest man or quick-witted woman of my stock, either here at home or in some part of the world we have already left off calling New, should chance upon this book of mine, and, seeing within its pages a familiar name, pay its price and carry it home, a little interested, and be pleased to read it indulgently and with the faintest tincture of gratitude, my cold shade (can I answer for it?) will be satisfied, and seek no further reward for his labour whilst alive.

ILLUSTRATIONS

THE FIRST PORTRAIT OF FREDERICK LOCKER

AGED THREE

BY MISS CHARLOTTE MILNES (1824)

MY CONFIDENCES

Preliminary

Rowfant: August 10, 1888.

I have often wished that I had kept a journal, as, if I had done so, I think it would have been interesting to the children, and perhaps to those who may come after them, for to them only it would have been addressed; but it is too late: I am fast growing old. Now, on this fine afternoon, far away from the distractions of the town, my thoughts my only company, when the woods are wearing the silence which August brings with it—now, as I look back, that gigantic and ever-growing monster, The Past (distance, middle distance, and even foreground), is an indistinct blur. In the dim vistas of memory, as a city that is dissolving into space, my life seems like a dream, lagging, yet fleeting; so vague that it might almost have been lived or dreamt by somebody else—a vision from which it is hopeless to rescue aught worth preserving. Sometimes I half wish—only half—that I could live it over again, and moralise the experience.

Vesper admonuit, and in the face of what I have just said I will try to gather up a few of these far-away echoes of my vanishing *Atlantis* —the old times, the trials, the compensations. There is an excitement in hunting a recollection, even though it may elude us. There is nothing more agreeable than talking about oneself : of all luxuries, it is the most enticing and the cheapest. May those that come after me not resent that I so indulged myself! There is another satisfaction. The little pleasures, now looked back upon, seem so passing sweet—and the minor miseries have become altogether amusing.

I never had a good memory. It was always weak, and often treacherous ; it is now weaker and more perfidious than ever.

I believe it was at Greenwich Hospital, and in 1821, that the person whom I have known for so many years as *myself* first came into being. I do not know this as a positive fact, but I accept it as the wisest people accept a good many things—on authority. And let me say that I showed my sense thus early in life, and my appreciation of Horace's dictum, in the selection of my parents—for my father was a singularly upright and able man, and had considerable mental energy ; my mother, of whom more hereafter, had a remarkable attractiveness.

I have a distinct idea that as a little fellow I was made much of. For some time I was the youngest of the family, as Algernon was more than five years my junior. There were the usual tussles over Noah's Arks and for possession of the rocking-horse. I believe I was a cry-baby and mamma's darling. There is a humbling tradition that when Edward or Ellen teased me I ran to my mother. Whom have I to run to now?

One of my earliest recollections is a large mezzotint engraving which hung in the nursery, Puck on a Toadstool, after Joshua Reynolds. This print was said to be the image of me; it is thought like my daughter Maud, who is aged three years and a half.

I was pretty, and said what prejudiced people considered *funny, freakish things*, with little, eager glances; so much so that when I was not more than six years old my father, whose family geese were not swans, was struck by it, and took me in the yellow-bodied 'charrot,' hung high in air, to De Ville, the craniologist and lampmaker in the Strand. The sage discovered that my 'bump of gaiety and wit' was markedly developed. However this may have been, I do not think any record is preserved of my *bons mots*. But I was a pretty boy with an inquiring mind. I suppose it is not conceited to talk thus, especially as all is so changed. Past sixty, I am now a grizzled and discreet old fogey; moreover,

> At my back I alwaies hear
> Time's winged chariot hurrying near,
> And yonder all before me lye
> Desarts of vast Eternity.

And yet, perhaps because my mind may have aged more slowly than my body, I do not always exhibit that sobriety which is naturally looked for in elderly people. Perhaps this levity may be accounted for by a certain rigidity in some of my surroundings (a salutary environment); but, after all, it is not much more than a meek protest.

When I was approaching fifty I had a more than usually acute attack of dyspepsia. On my partial recovery my aspect was more hungry than before; I had always been pale, but now the pallor was marked.[1] But my appearance up to the present time has not been repulsive, and for this I thank God.[2]

[1] Last year Alfred Tennyson, speaking of my personal appearance, said 'that I looked like a famished and avaricious Jew.' Now I demur to this. I confess that I have tried to cultivate that fine old gentlemanly vice, but entirely without success. I have never got beyond a timid and pitiful parsimony. It is only fair to add that he also said that, in his portrait by Millais, as rendered by Barlow's print, he himself was something between 'a prig and a scarecrow.' Now that is perfectly true.

[2] ''Ealth, after personal appearance, is the greatest blessing as is,' as the barmaid said.

I mention these trifling details as I wish to be 'an honest chronicler,' and to give a correct idea and faithful account of myself; and I hope that you kind people who have lived with me will again recognise me in these chapters, and not find anything incongruous between that which you may remember of me and that which I have written down here, and that you will be able, as it were, to bind me up in my book. At the same time I ask you to think of me as benevolently as you can, to make excuses for my weaknesses—physical, intellectual, and moral. I know them well—nobody knows them much better than I do; and you cannot read these pages, and between the lines, without discovering most of them. *Liberavi animam meam.* I speak seriously and sorrowfully when I say—

> Be kind to my Remains, and, oh! defend,
> Against your judgment, your departed friend.

But to continue. I was a well-built child, and fairly well grown; nervous, however, and highly sensitive. Both as child and boy I had a curious affection, from which my mother and one or two other members of her family have suffered. It generally assailed me when I was in repose and alone, indoors and out—a strange sensation, as if invisible or ghostly wheels, or something like them, were rushing round or about me. The sighing of the wind in the trees, the droning of bees, or any faint sound, lent itself to and intensified the feeling; whereas a boisterous bluebottle at the window-pane at once dispelled it.

It was an uncanny visitation: it justified all my phantom terrors. But luckily it only lasted a minute or two; it would come and go, and come again. However, by rousing myself and speaking aloud, or moving about quickly, I was able to exorcise the fiend. At night it once or twice mingled with my dreams, and then it became a nightmare of brimstone horror. It proved to be merely a nervous disorder, and I have long since outgrown it.

I had a decided objection to ghostly rooms, or to passing down ill-lighted passages where bogies might be suspected of lurking, only waiting their opportunity to pounce out. I do not remember the time when I was absolutely free from such tremors. I always had them; they took substance from the japanned perforated rushlight of my nursery, and from a hundred other things. I had them *last year*, at dusk, in the spectral gallery at Cobham. I might have them now. I could write a succubine chapter, and call it 'Gobliniana,' which would surprise you. Yet nobody knows this. Why, it would astonish my wife! My childhood was embittered by stories of the Press-gang; I had panics that some day I should commit a murder and be hanged. I dare say most children suffer thus; but, mark you, my misery was not the crime, but the gallows.

Besides this, I suffered from nervous exhaustion, cerebral lassitude, and a most delicate stomach: I hardly ever did or ate anything unusual without being unpleasantly reminded of it. I inherited this infirmity *ab incunabulis*;[1] it lay down with me, and *when my mother rocked me, she rocked my discomfort also. I slept with it, and no sooner did I open my eyes in the morning than it woke also. As I grew this small misery grew and strengthened with me, till it became a large one.* It was present at my baptism.

I was baptised in the drawing-room at Greenwich Hospital by my godfather, Shute Barrington, Bishop of Durham. After the ceremony (for me a novel and possibly exciting one) the Bishop, in his usual stately[2] manner, as has been described to me, for it is beyond the period of memory, presented me with a handsome Testament, illustrated, and bound in dark blue morocco, gilt; and the instant it was placed before me I was incontinently sick over it. In after-years I well remember the shame of being shown this precious volume, and that it

[1] I hope my children may not inherit this infirmity, or any of my regrettable defects of character. We do not really hate our foibles and vices till we recognise them in our beloved offspring.

[2] I am told that he was a stately *little* personage. It is to him that my father dedicated his *Lectures on the Bible*.

ever bore the disfigurement of that early catastrophe. Thus my introduction to the sacred writings was not auspicious.

As a consequence of this feebleness I used soon to get weary and restless; and, *à propos* thereof, there is a tradition that when I was about five years old I was promised a delightful row in a wherry (the Thames flowed under our windows). The day for its realisation arrived; we took our seats, the boat put off from shore; but I had not been ten minutes afloat before I turned to my mother: 'Mamma, why do people get tired in boats?' This feeling and this sort of sentiment have more or less troubled me through my whole life.

My father was short, clean-shaved, had a neat and active figure, and a nose that would have satisfied Mr. Walter Shandy himself. I have a lively recollection of his bright eyes, intelligent and homely face,[1] his blue coat and gilt buttons; also that we children were very distinctly afraid of him.

[1] There is a portrait of him in the Painted Hall of Greenwich Hospital, but it is of my *Sunday* father. I wish I had one of my *everyday* father. The Lockers were a homely-looking race. Uncle John Locker, who was very ugly, used to say that you could not widen the mouth of a Locker without injury to his ears. One day at Malta, at the dinner-table, he asked a stranger, who had just landed, to take wine, expressing his pleasure in seeing him there and his obligation in these words: 'Yesterday, sir, I was the ugliest man in all Malta!' Tradition says that the man did not resent this speech, so I presume my uncle, with all his impudence, had some social tact.

We scuttled away if he came into the room where we were at play, for he was strict, had a quick, decided manner, and a rather irritable temper. Though benevolent, he seemed a little hard. For instance, if, as any boy might, I knocked down a wineglass, or stumbled over a footstool, he would say, with surprise, 'Can't you navigate, sir?' Or, conversing with visitors, he would suddenly wish to refer to some book, and would call me to him, would describe its aspect, shelf, and position on that shelf. He would go through this swiftly, clearly, succinctly, and then send me off headlong to fetch it.[1] I used to go in a tremor, for I was short-sighted, and hardly ever could find his book, and I dreaded the flouts which, I believe, were as quickly forgotten by this dear father as they were hastily uttered. He would say and do things, little things, which no woman would have said and done if she had been a man. There was very little of the woman in my father; but—and in this respect he was like most women—he could not tolerate falsehood, cowardice, and low descent. However, perhaps I may be unjust in all this, for in John Wilson Croker's manuscript memoir of my father he speaks warmly of his perfect temper. I know he did his best to instil into us a love of truth and a respect

[1] Now and then I propose to send my children on an errand, and apologise for doing so. They accept the apology, but they do not go.

for manliness. Perhaps we children tried him; perhaps the failure of memory, which was so soon to overtake him, may have already begun.

I think my father had a certain inability to make allowance for the shortcomings of those about him. Then he was a rigid moralist, and we know that in most societies such people are square pegs in round holes; but at the same time he was *exceedingly* agreeable. He had an alert and versatile intellect, an essentially picturesque mind and eye. A decidedly playful vein ran through his talk, and he was amused with trifles. We children, who reluctantly started for a walk with him, generally returned having much enjoyed it. He was a brisk walker, and I well remember my mother's usual parting injunction: 'Don't drag the children.'

My father was an accomplished draughtsman: one of his excellent sketches, the 'Castagno di Cento Cavalli' on Mount Etna, made under the influence of Paul Sandby or Thomas Hearne, hangs in my dressing-room at New Haven Court. My father often quoted Johnson, the lines on Levett, and 'Swedish Charles,' Marlborough, and Swift. He shared the Bolt Court Sage's affection for tea, quoting Virgil's 'Te veniente die, te decedente canebat,' as he drank it.

Knaves respected my father, and fools thought they did so. He was very humorous up to a certain point, but perhaps he had a foible which is not valued by anybody—he was prone to improve the occasion. Perhaps that was a part of his fun. When I was about twelve or fourteen years old I said something about something or somebody that he did not quite like, and he replied, with a touch of asperity, 'You should never jest on serious subjects.' 'But, papa, if I don't do that, what am I to jest on?'[1]

I am ashamed to think how much nonsense I have talked in my day, but I hope I have not thought nonsensically—that 'I wear not motley in my brain.'

My father corresponded with the distinguished clergy of his day: Macneile, Melvill, Chalmers, &c. Bishops valued him as a lay adviser. I have confidential letters addressed to him by Blomfield, the Sumners, &c. He expanded in the society of intelligent elderly ladies.

I hope what I have said here and in other places will not weaken the impression which I have endeavoured to convey. I am proud to have had such parents.

[1] This loses in point, as I have forgotten what the joke was; but the impression of my father's *rigidity* remains.

My Family

Rowfant, 1888.

My dear Children,—I find, from a memoir written by my father in the year 1823, that the family of Locker (said to be of foreign extraction) was seated for several generations at Bromley in Middlesex, where they possessed considerable property until it was forfeited by their devotion to the Stuart cause. So late as the beginning of the present century the family chronicle records the birth of a son, *Charles Edward.*

Stephen Locker, my great-great-grandfather, and John Locker, his son, were barristers, commissioners of bankrupts, and clerks to two City companies—offices which in those days were held by barristers. My grandfather, Captain William Locker, was born in 1730, in the official house of Leathersellers' Hall, Great St. Helen's. His father, the aforesaid John Locker, a man of sterling probity and recognised learning, was educated at Merton College, Oxford, and afterwards occupied chambers at Gray's Inn where once resided Francis Bacon; and the zeal and delight with which John Locker there studied Lord Bacon's writings gave a bias to his future life, for in maturer years he prepared a very fine and complete edition of the philosopher's works, which, at the time of his death, was almost ready for press. His papers passed into the hands of Dr. Birch and Mr. Mallet, and when, in 1765, the work appeared, my worthy ancestor's labours were amply acknowledged in the preface.

Mr. John Locker was one of the original members of the Society of Antiquaries, and he is thus referred to in Johnson's 'Life of Addison:' 'It is related that Addison had once a design to make an English dictionary, and that he considered Dr. Tillotson a writer of the very highest authority. There was formerly lent me by Mr. Locker, clerk of the Leathersellers' Company, who was eminent for curiosity and literature, a collection of examples selected from Tillotson's works, as Locker said, by Addison. It came too late to be of use to me.' I may say here that I am distantly connected with Addison on my mother's side.

John Locker married Elizabeth Stillingfleet, granddaughter of the Bishop of Worcester, the families having been previously related. He died in 1760, and notices of him may be found in Chalmers's 'Biographical Dictionary' and Nichols's 'Literary Anecdotes.'[1]

About the time of John Locker's death, and indeed afterwards, my family were much indebted to Mrs. John Locker's brother, Benjamin Stilling-

[1] Also in the *Dictionary of National Biography*, vol. xxxiv.

fleet, the philosopher and poet; he showed them no little kindness. This eminent man had graduated at Trinity College, Cambridge, and, having no profession, spent much of his life between Felbrig[1] and Piccadilly. Stillingfleet was curiously accomplished and singularly agreeable. He cultivated the society of those learned ladies, Mrs. Montague, Mrs. Talbot, and Mrs. Elizabeth Carter, and always made his appearance at their gatherings in a full suit of dark brown, a wig, gilt sword, and buckles; also stockings *of a bluish grey*, by which last portion of his attire the notable coterie especially distinguished him. In consequence of this recognition the wits of the time, perhaps rather irreverently, dubbed them the 'Bas Bleu Club,' and it is thus that the phrase 'Blue-stocking' has become a cant term for learned ladies generally. My father's

[1] Felbrig is a fine place, and now belongs to Mr. Ketton. His accomplished sisters have lately shown me a pane of glass in the window of a room which formerly was called the 'North Parlour,' but which is now used as a store-room, on which Benjamin Stillingfleet had scratched the following lines. They are addressed to a Miss Annie (Lammy) Barnes, the clergyman's daughter. Some graceless person, possibly a rival, had added the word '*Fool*' under Stillingfleet's signature.

'Could Lammy look within my breast,
She'd find her image there impressed—
In characters as bright as here
The letters of her name appear:
And ever, like them, shall remain
Till time shall break my heart in twain.

'B. Stillingfleet.'

venerable friend, Hannah More, in her giddy youth, wrote what I have been told is an amusing poem under this title. The volume is at Rowfant. Benjamin Stillingfleet died in 1771, and was buried in St. James's Church, where my father raised a monument to his memory.

My grandfather, William Locker, left Merchant Taylors' School to go to sea; had fifty years and more of active service; was severely wounded in a gallant fight when first lieutenant of the 'Experiment' (see the picture, of which I have a duplicate, in Greenwich Hospital commemorating the victory); served with Lord Hawke in the ill-starred 'Royal George,' and also under Lord St. Vincent at Quiberon. When my grandfather commanded the 'Lowestoffe,' a youth of eighteen, one Horatio Nelson (a name to conjure with) was his second-lieutenant! Cuthbert, afterwards Lord, Collingwood, also served under him in the same vessel.

We know how Claudio had looked on Hero with only a soldier's eye, that liked, but had a rougher task in hand than to drive liking to the name of love. It was so with my grandfather. For some time he had felt a sincere affection for Lucy, the only child of Admiral William Parry; but, being devoted to his profession, he had abstained from making any special advances. However, the time came when his ship was paid off, and it ended by his winning the fair Lucy for his wife. Her mother was the daughter of Commodore Charles Brown, Commissioner of the Navy at Chatham. Brown had served as commodore, second in command under Admiral Vernon, at the capture of Porto Bello (1739). It is recorded that when the Spanish governor came off to the 'Hampton Court,' and tendered his sword to Brown in token of submission, Brown very properly declined to receive it, saying he was 'but second in command;' and he accordingly took him in his boat to Admiral Vernon, to whom the surrender was due. But the Spaniard was obstinate, and declared that if it had not been for the insupportable fire of the commodore he never would have yielded; on which Vernon, turning to Brown, very handsomely presented the sword to him. I still possess this Spanish sword.[1]

At this point I am constrained to give you a little letter, the fair copy of which, I presume, found its way to Lucy's future husband. Maids, in modesty, say 'No' to that which they would have the profferer construe 'Ay.' Lucy Parry would seem to have been demure in her letters, but as Lucy Locker she had a gay and airy spirit.

[1] Many and varied medals, both in silver and copper, were struck to commemorate this victory, several of them combining portraits of both Vernon and Brown. Brown's portrait is at Greenwich Hospital. My father used to say that he had a *disinheriting* countenance.

1770.

Sir,—It has given me real concern not having it in my power to answer your letter till this day, which is the first I have been able to hold a pen. The favourable sentiments you entertain of me, and your kind wishes, claim to have my most sincere thanks; but as I have been bless'd with the best of Parents, who's care and affection for me has been far superior to my merrit, 'tis impossible for me to think of any alliance without their entire consent. I look upon that as the only means by which I can make them a proper return for their goodness. Should your wishes meet with their approbation, mine will undoubtedly follow; but if, on the contrary, they disapprove, I must entreat you to think no more of this affair. Perhaps I have been too open in giving you my sentiments so freely, but I cannot think of deceiving —— (*sic*) to whom I esteem myself so much indebted.

I am, Sir,
Your much obliged, humble servant.
[*This draft is not signed.*]

Captain Locker.

In 1792 my grandfather hoisted his flag as Commodore at the Nore, but soon afterwards, his health giving way, he was appointed Lieutenant-Governor of Greenwich Hospital.

Sir John Jervis won his famous victory on February 14, 1797; and it is interesting to us to know that, even on that eventful day, he found time to write the following letter to his old friend:—

'Victory,' Largos Bay:
February 14, 1797.

My dear Locker,—I know you will be desirous of a line from me, and though I have not time to give you anything like detail, I cannot resist telling you that your *élève* Commodore Nelson received the swords of the commanders of a first-rate and an eighty-gun ship of the enemy on their respective quarterdecks.

As you will probably see Mrs. Parker, give my love to her, although unknown, and say 'the junction of her husband [afterwards Sir William Parker] with the squadron under his command I must ever consider the happiest event of my life.' Say everything kind to your young men, and be assured

I am ever truly yours,
JOHN JERVIS.

Lieutenant-Governor Locker,
Greenwich Hospital.

It should be remembered that Vincent was a stern old Berserker. Indeed, some of his acquaintances said that he had a tongue like a cow—that there was a rough side to it as well as a smooth one.

Hawke, Jervis, and Nelson had a peculiar respect and affection for my grandfather, who, I cannot help thinking, must have been a very lovable person as well as a gallant seaman.[1]

I will here give the copy of a letter that Lord Nelson wrote to him not long before his death.

Palermo: February 9, 1799.

My dear Friend,—I well know your goodness of heart will make all due allowances for my present situation, and that truly I have not the time or power to answer all the letters I receive at the moment. But you, my old friend, after twenty-seven years' acquaintance, know that nothing can alter my attachment and gratitude to you. I have been your scholar. It is you who taught me to board a Frenchman by your conduct when in the 'Experiment.' It is you who always said, 'Lay a Frenchman close, and you will beat him;' and my only merit in my profession is being a good scholar. Our friendship will never end but with my life, but you have always been too partial to me. Pray tell Kingsmill that it was impossible I could attend to his recommendations—indeed I had (not being a commander-in-chief) no power to name an agent—and remember me kindly to him. The

[1] January 1891.—In the Guelph Collection, now open, there is a picture by Rigaud, lent by the present Earl Nelson, of Nelson when he was made a captain. It belonged to my grandfather, and afterwards to my father. In this collection may also be seen a watch that my grandfather bequeathed to Nelson.

Vesuvian Republic being formed, I have now to look out for Sicily; but revolutionary principles are so prevalent in the world that no monarchical government is safe, or sure of lasting ten years. I beg you will make my kindest remembrances to Miss Locker and all your good sons, and

Believe me,

Ever your faithful and affectionate friend,

NELSON.

Lieutenant-Governor Locker.

My grandfather died at Greenwich Hospital in 1800. On the day fixed for the funeral Lord Nelson came down to the Hospital, and followed the remains of his old friend to Addington (Kent) churchyard, where they were laid beside those of his ever-lamented wife, who died as early as 1780.[1]

I give the copy of a letter which Lord Nelson

[1] To-day (June 28, 1890) Jane and I went to see Mr. Hewlitt, at Wrotham, and took the opportunity of visiting Addington church and churchyard. There is a tablet to Admiral Parry in the church, and a monument to Captain Locker and his wife in the churchyard. She was only thirty-three when she died, and the following lines are on the obelisk :—

Sincere, and undisguised by Art,
Blest with the kindest and the tenderest heart;
With unaffected pride and graceful ease,
With every virtue, every power to please;
With every requisite for social life,
The warmest friend, the prudent, virtuous wife,
Here Lucy lies (Divine assurance given)—
Such worth we know must meet reward in Heaven.

(*Feeble verses.*)

wrote to my uncle, John Locker, the day after my grandfather's death.

December 27, 1800.

My dear John,—From my heart do I condole with you on the great and irreparable loss we have all sustained in the death of your dear worthy father, a man whom to know was to love, and those who only heard of him, honoured. The greatest consolation to us, his friends that remain, is that he has left a character for honour and honesty which none of us can surpass and very, very few attain. That the posterity of the righteous will prosper we are taught to believe, and on no occasion can it be more truly verified than from my dear, much-lamented friend; and that it may be realised in you, your sisters and brothers, is the fervent prayer of,

My dear John,
Your afflicted friend,
NELSON.

John Locker, Esq.

Also a letter to Emma Lady Hamilton.

My dear Lady Hamilton,—It is now six o'clock, and I dread the fatigue of this day, being not in the very best of spirits; and believe me when I say that I regret that I am not the person to be attended *upon* at this funeral, for, although I have had my days of glory, yet I find this world so full of jealousys and envy, that I see but a very faint gleam of future comfort. I shall come to Grosvenor Square on my return from this melancholy procession, and hope to find in the smiles of my friends some alleviation for the cold looks and cruel words of my enemies. May God bless you, my dear lady, and

Believe me, ever your unalterable

NELSON.

Saturday morn.

My father, Edward Hawke Locker, included a graphic sketch of my grandfather in his 'Memoirs of Naval Commanders,' of which that good man, the late Charles Knight, selected a portion for his 'Half-hours with the Best Authors.' The sketch is excellent; it is well worth reading; indeed, it is literature.[1]

William IV. and Queen Adelaide would sometimes come down to Greenwich Hospital, for Sunday divine service, if the day happened to be the anniversary of any important naval victory. On one of these Sundays, perhaps about 1833, the royal party visited the Painted Hall, attended by that distinguished seaman, Sir Richard Keats, the Governor. The King stopped before the portrait of Captain William Locker, and, turning to Sir

[1] Printed in the Appendix.

Richard, said, 'There's the best man I ever knew.' It was known that many years before, when the King was Prince William Henry, my grandfather had had the temerity to reprove him for swearing, at which accomplishment his Majesty was first-rate, even for an admiral.

I say again, there is no doubt my grandfather was a very lovable man as well as a gallant seaman.

My father was the youngest son of Captain William Locker. He left Eton to become a clerk in the Navy Office; thence he was soon promoted to be Under-Secretary to the Board of Control for the Affairs of India, and afterwards to the Board of Naval Inquiry. In 1804 he was appointed *Civil* Secretary to the Fleet, under Admiral Viscount Exmouth, in the East Indies, and thence, in the same capacity, to the Mediterranean.

In 1813 my father, in company with Lord John Russell (afterwards Earl Russell), made a rather memorable tour in Spain, of which he published an account, illustrated with his own excellent sketches. This tour had a special interest, as the Peninsular War was then at its height; and my father was the bearer of important despatches from Lord William Bentinck to the Duke of Wellington.

In May, 1814, my father was charged with

another interesting mission, this time in H.M.S. 'Curaçoa,' Captain Towers, to Elba, where Napoleon had just arrived from Fréjus after his abdication; and he published in that noteworthy magazine, 'The Plain Englishman' (vol. iii. p. 475), an account of his interview with the ex-Emperor at Porto Ferrajo.[1]

Porto Ferrajo: May 8, 1814.

We had scarcely anchored when Captain Usher came on board from the 'Undaunted,' to welcome our arrival; and we were soon surrounded with other boats from the shore. After some time spent in mutual inquiries, Captain Usher pointed out to us Napoleon at a distance amusing himself in a boat, and he left us to announce who we were. He soon returned in company with Colonel Niel Campbell, the British Commissioner appointed to attend the Emperor from Fontainebleau, who brought a message from the ex-Emperor, inviting us to visit him on shore.

We landed immediately, and Colonel Campbell accompanied us to the Hôtel de Ville, which serves for the temporary residence of Napoleon. On the way he pointed out to us a house at a little distance which is fitting up as his future residence. Nothing can be more mean and ill-furnished than

[1] See also a paper in the *Century Magazine* for March 1893, which gives Admiral Sir Thomas Usher's account of Napoleon at Elba, in which Mr. E. H. Locker is mentioned.

his present abode. The apartment into which we were shown was small, with no other furniture than two or three chairs.

Count Bertrand, who still retains the office of Grand Maréchal du Palais, received us with much politeness, and prepossessed us with his pleasing address. We were also introduced to some of the inferior officers of the Household. The Count soon quitted us to announce our arrival to his imperial master, who at the moment was waiting in a little room within. Our curiosity was now raised to a degree of intensity. We were separated by only a door from the once *great Napoleon*, the boast of France, the scourge of Europe! Presently the door opened, the man entered, and, with a slight bow, came forward to receive us, and with much apparent good-humour.

The Grand Maréchal presented us in form, and we were received very graciously. Napoleon inquired as to the length of our passage from Genoa, the name and force of the frigate, and asked a few other trifling questions; he then looked towards me, as though ready to receive my communication. I then delivered to him . . .

. . . .

I next presented to him a copy of the Convention for the cessation of hostilities, which had been signed at Paris on the 23rd April after his departure. He read it eagerly, and I watched his countenance with great curiosity as the several articles passed under his eye. During this time his features betrayed considerable emotion; and when he came to that passage which denoted that the French frontier was now to be restricted within the limits which existed in 1792, he looked up with an expression of much surprise, repeating 1792 with great emphasis. He made no other comment sufficiently loud to be audible. While Napoleon was thus occupied, of course every eye was fixed intently upon him.

The address and appearance of Buonaparte were certainly attractive, more especially when we consider the circumstances under which we saw him. He was dressed in a plain uniform of green faced with red, waistcoat and breeches also green, with Hessian boots and spurs. A silver cross of the Legion of Honour hung at his breast, with another small Order which I could not make out. He is short and somewhat fat: his height, as he stood facing me, apparently not more than five feet five or six inches. His hair is black, and cut quite short; he is rather bald, and wears no whiskers. His complexion is a clear brown, without any colour in the cheeks; but though sallow, his appearance is quite healthy. He takes much snuff, and moves with quickness. His features are well formed; and I should call the head altogether handsome, if it were not too large for his body, and the neck too short. His general aspect has more an air of *bonhomie* than I expected. There was a tranquil serenity in his look, which exhibited no traces of the anxiety he must have lately suffered. His smile is very pleasing, and his voice not disagreeable, excepting his laugh, which is singularly discordant, almost a *neigh*. I imagine his face must have been more handsome before he acquired his present *embonpoint*; and this also deducts a good deal from the gracefulness of his figure, to which, whatever elegance it might once have possessed, it has now no pretensions. It has more the appearance of feminine softness than of muscular activity. His person in general appeared perfectly cleanly, his hand white and delicate; and his limbs have that roundness of form which does not become a man, and especially a soldier.

After some pause, he renewed the conversation by asking for news. I gave him all the public intelligence which had reached Genoa previous to my departure, avoiding as much as possible such details as might bring back painful recollections. He expressed great sense of Captain Usher's attention to him during his passage from Fréjus, as well as since his arrival at Porto Ferrajo. I stated that one of our cruisers would be allowed to convey the

Princess Pauline to Elba. This seemed to please him exceedingly, and he spoke of it with much sense of acknowledgement. He showed great anxiety for his sister's recovery, whom he stated to be in very delicate health.

Napoleon spoke of the extreme difficulty of the English language, saying that, though he had at length acquired the power of reading it readily, he could never overcome the harsh pronunciation. I asked him if he understood it when spoken. He said, 'Only sometimes,' and bid me speak a few sentences deliberately, saying as I went on, 'Ah! that I comprehend well enough,' and immediately gave the interpretation in French; but he added, 'When you speak to each other I am soon bewildered—your words are all confusion and discord to my ear;' and shook his head, saying, 'Ma foi, c'est une langue barbare.'

In the course of my replies to his inquiries concerning the present state of affairs on the Continent I referred more than once to the peculiar situation of the Neapolitan territories, and was struck with the apparent indifference with which he treated the subject, seeming disinclined to talk of Murat, about whom, independent of relationship, he could not but really entertain much interest, on account of his proximity to Elba.

After this a long silence followed, during which

he appeared to be lost in reverie. He then suddenly recollected himself, and, after speaking apart to Colonel Campbell for two or three minutes, he came forward and asked us to dine with him; which of course we accepted, although we had already dispatched our dinner before we entered the Port. It was now past six o'clock. Dinner was immediately served in an adjoining room of somewhat larger dimensions, tawdrily fitted up with looking-glasses, &c., and a sort of throne erected at one end of the apartment. The guests consisted of the Austrian Commissioner, Baron Köller, Colonel Campbell, Captain Towers, Captain Usher, Count Bertrand, General Drouot, and myself. The dinner was very good, but not in any manner remarkable. The service was of silver, made very light, being a part of his camp equipage. The coffee service was of Sèvres china, and the whole was marked with the imperial crown and the letter 'N' beneath. Buonaparte ate with a good appetite, almost wholly in silence, while the Grand Maréchal was very attentive to his guests. When the dishes were removed, Napoleon began to talk freely, and put us all at our ease by the readiness with which he engaged in conversation. Like all other men of eminent ability, his manner was plain and unaffected. His inquiries were chiefly directed to continental intelligence. When I came to speak of

Spain, his countenance showed much surprise on learning that Ferdinand VII., on returning from his long captivity in France, had shown spirit enough to halt at Valencia, with a resolution to refuse the acceptance of the new Constitution established by the Cortes. As he was accompanied by the Duke of San Carlos, he was doubtless well informed of the democratic views of the *Liberales* in that assembly; and I mentioned that General Elio,[1] on his arrival at Valencia, had openly declared his resolution to support the King in his prerogative.

Napoleon did not seem to have heard even the name of this officer, and asked what I considered the general disposition of the troops in the South of Spain. In answer to this I observed that hitherto the Spanish army had expressed the fullest determination to support the new Constitution, but that of course Elio had ascertained the disposition of his own troops before he ventured to take the part of the King. On which Buonaparte remarked that unless Ferdinand secured the army *generally*, he would bring inevitable destruction on his own head; that he should conciliate no other class of his subjects—the mass of the people were not worth his attention; all his power must depend on the troops. This observation was quite consistent with

[1] Lately executed.

the maxim upon which he himself had uniformly acted, and to this alone he owes his extraordinary elevation. He never seems to have looked to the people for his support; and Colonel Campbell told me that not long since Napoleon explicitly avowed this maxim in answer to the urgent solicitations of his Ministers, when the Allies passed the French frontiers. Their entreaties were received with his usual obstinacy, and he replied: 'Non, jamais je ne ferai ma cour à la nation.'

He next asked me what arrangement the Allied Sovereigns designed for Beauharnois (late Viceroy of Italy), and if I knew where he then was. Of their ultimate intentions I could say nothing, beyond what was contained in the Treaty of Abdication, by an article of which they engage to give him a suitable establishment *out of France*. I informed him of the armistice just signed with the Viceroy of Mantua by General Bellegarde, which has established tranquillity for the present in the North of Italy. The surrender of Genoa did not seem to surprise him; but he seemed very little disposed to talk of anything in which Murat's co-operation with Lord William Bentinck's forces was at all concerned.

I found he had heard no particulars of the battle of Toulouse, nor of the sortie from Bayonne, with which I now acquainted him. He expressed great concern at the unnecessary bloodshed which had ensued for want of proper intelligence of the cessation of hostilities at Paris, by which all this slaughter might have been spared.

The Emperor then mentioned that, in his impatience for some intelligence, he had opened a communication with Piombino on the opposite coast, and hoped soon to obtain through that channel some regular tidings of public occurrences. He jested, with much apparent good-humour, about his present humble dominions, comparing them with the empire he had just lost; talked of obtaining the sovereignty of the little islands of Pianosa and Monte Christo in addition to that of Elba, and seemed pleased to learn from Captain Towers that there was good water to be found on both of them.

We spoke of the difficulties which occurred at Genoa, and others of the Italian ports, in consequence of the alarm which had been excited by the plague at Malta; and as there was a vessel now in the port just arrived from thence, I said his communications would be greatly interrupted unless he could furnish me with some written documents to authenticate the healthy state of this island. He immediately acquiesced in this proposal, and directed General Drouot to prepare the requisite certificate of health. The conversation then turned on the Barbary States. He expressed great anxiety respecting them, lest some attempt should be made upon him by the Tunisian or Algerine corsairs in the present weak state of the island. He said that he looked for his safety entirely to the protection of the British cruisers, and hoped that the 'Undaunted' would not be withdrawn from Elba.

We sat some time after dinner, though little wine was drunk, and scarcely any by Napoleon himself. Ice and coffee were then served; and soon after he rose from the table, and we all followed him into the 'Audience Chamber' (as I found the next apartment is designated). Here a circle was formed, and he renewed the conversation for a short time, saying something to each person, as though he were once more holding his *levée* in the Palace of the Tuilleries.

I took the occasion of some inquiries about our ship to inform him of my intention to quit Elba the next evening, or the following morning, on my return to Genoa, and requested that I might be allowed to bear any of his commissions for the Continent. In return he invited us all to breakfast with him to-morrow morning, saying we must not leave him till we had seen his *dominions.* Of course we were delighted with the opportunity of hearing more of his conversation. He proposes to employ to-morrow in riding with us through the island, and finishing the day's amusement by dining at Porto Longono, on the opposite side of the island. About nine o'clock he took leave of us, and withdrew to his own apartment, leaving us highly gratified by his gracious behaviour—so unlike the impressions with which we had approached him. It may well be supposed that all the time he was present my observation was fixed on everything he said and did and looked with the deepest attention. It was quite evident to me that this unusual courtesy was assumed as a necessary policy; for he allowed that our naval force was his principal security against the Barbary corsair, and he must have felt it to be his interest to ingratiate himself with those about him, whom he regarded as so many spies on his conduct.

However, the effort of keeping up this sort of conversation with us was not always successful. He relapsed now and then into fits of thoughtfulness, during which he occasionally lost that singular command of feature which I had heretofore heard described. In such moments of forgetfulness his countenance showed that his mind was busily engaged elsewhere in matters of far deeper interest.

He avoided, with great dexterity, all allusions to those wonderful changes which have so lately occurred in France, referring only to such transactions as were necessary to obtain the information he required. It may be supposed that his guests were equally anxious to observe a similar forbearance; and this produced some embarrassment in maintaining the conversation and in framing replies to his numerous questions.

Considering the tremendous plunge which he had just made from an imperial throne, a throne surrounded with all the pride and splendour of military sovereignty, to the paltry mansion of the Mayor of Porto Ferrajo; that he had suddenly exchanged a crowd of abject Ministers and a body-guard of marshals and generals for the company of half a dozen foreigners in an obscure island—when all these violent contrasts are remembered to their full extent, his present self-possession surely affords a wonderful proof of the versatility of his mind and the firmness of his resolution in bearing up against a reverse of fortune so sudden and so complete. Nothing but a latent, though sanguine, hope of restoration could account for this extraordinary equanimity.

To a man of Napoleon's temper and disposition, I can scarcely conceive any exertion more irksome than this of playing the agreeable to persons like ourselves, whom in his heart he must have regarded with profound contempt and dislike; and I apprehend that a British officer, of all others, must have been the object of his implacable aversion.

E. H. Locker.

I must apologise to my readers for having admitted so serious and interesting an episode into my trifling little volume.

My father married my mother in 1815. If you read this memoir you will find her often mentioned. She was the daughter of the Rev. Jonathan Boucher, an excellent divine and distinguished philologist. Mr. Boucher spent several years of his quite early manhood in America, and there made the acquaintance, and indeed the close friendship, of General George Washington. When, however, the troubles began which ended in the independence of the colonies, Washington and my grandfather took opposite sides, and their friendship was suspended. My grandfather was an uncompromising loyalist, and preached boldly against the revolutionary doctrines, and by so doing he often ran no small risk of personal violence. His last sermon, preached at Annapolis, with pistols on his pulpit cushion, concluded with the following words: 'As long as I live, yea, while I have my being, will I proclaim, "God save the King!"' At length he was compelled to return to England. I have several of Washington's letters to my grandfather, which I lent to Thackeray when he was writing 'Esmond.'[1] Jonathan Boucher was a member of Nobody's Club, and enjoyed through life the cordial

[1] This is the fact, though no doubt the letters were more useful for the 'Virginians.'—[Ed.]

acquaintance of many leading men of learning and science, and he was always ready with pen and purse to forward the interests of his native Cumberland, which, although he had been so long separated from it, he loved with an intense local patriotism. He died vicar of Epsom in 1804. There was much to admire in his character.[1]

In 1819 my father was appointed Secretary, and not very long afterwards Civil Commissioner, of Greenwich Hospital. One of his many interests there was the foundation and formation of the Royal Naval Gallery.

My father was the intimate friend of several distinguished people. As regards one of them I quote John Gibson Lockhart's own words: 'He was an old and dear friend of Scott.' You will find the account of his balloon adventure, with other small matters concerning him, at page 62.

In 1832 he commenced a biographical history of the Navy, especially as connected with the gallery at Greenwich Hospital; but failing health warned him to curtail the work to one volume

[1] Notices of Mr. Boucher may be found in the *Dictionary of National Biography*, Allibone's *Dictionary of English Literature*, Chalmers's *Biographical Dictionary*, and *Memoirs of William Stevens* by James Allan Park. In 1793 it was arranged that Mr. Boucher should be consecrated Bishop of Edinburgh in the hope of making the communion more intimate between the Episcopal Churches of Scotland and England. Mr. Boucher visited Edinburgh, and all arrangements were made, but at the last moment the scheme was frustrated.—EDITOR.

quarto. My father died in 1849, and was buried in Iver churchyard.[1]

This is a very meagre account of my dear father. He was able, attractive, and high-minded, and he did many things that showed him to be so. I have not space to enlarge on his fine qualities, but that he had them you may take my word for it.

There is only one other member of that generation of my family of whom I should do very wrong not to make mention—that is my father's second sister, Elizabeth. She was very dear and very little: we have a tradition that as a child she was so short that she could walk under the tables! She grew up (if such growth could in reason be so described) to be very sweet-tempered and exceedingly agreeable, full of good sense, and consistently religious. She was her father's child.

> A soul so charming, from a stock so good—
> Her father was transfused into her blood.

She may be said to have been gay without levity and serious without gloom.

[1] There is an inscription to my father under the second bay of the arcading on the south side of the Dean's Cloisters, Windsor Castle. It was put up in 1850 by the Rev. E. Canning, and it runs as follows: 'Sacred to the memory of EDWARD HAWKE LOCKER, ESQ., late one of the Commissioners of the Royal Hospital at Greenwich, who resided from 1814 to 1820 within the precincts of these Cloisters, and to whose active benevolence and persevering exertions during that short period the inhabitants of this town are indebted for the establishment of the Savings Bank, Dispensary, and National School. He died October 21, 1849, and was buried at Iver.' Edward and Ellen were born in the Cloisters.

We have a portrait by Lemuel Abbot of Lord Nelson, taken shortly after he lost his arm at Teneriffe. It was painted in my grandfather's apartment at Greenwich Hospital; and I have heard Aunt Elizabeth describe that she was allowed to help Nelson on and off with his gold-laced coat before and after each sitting. My aunt died full thirty years ago, and many excellent family anecdotes deceased with her. She never married.

My Father and Mother

Dear Children,—I should like to give you a short account of my father and mother. I have often wished I could draw portraits of them, finished and at full length, for indeed they were worthy of it; but I cannot. I can only give a distorted sketch. My mother was nearly sixteen years younger than my father, and though up to the age of sixty he was a singularly active man, she was that, and more. She was fresher in feelings and mind and ideas; for though he was brisk in his movements, he was rather antiquated in his dress; and though lively and picturesque in talk, he was rigid, not to say rather prejudiced in opinion. I have now pretty well made up my mind that all superior people are prejudiced. In 1809 my father returned from India with his natural hair as a pigtail; and it was characteristic of him that he could not be persuaded to surrender that obsolete decoration, so Uncle John, the wag of that generation of Lockers, came behind his chair at dinner and cut it off. We have a slight sketch of him as a little boy, cocked hat in hand, trying to capture a long-winged swallow. Fancy one's father having worn a queue and a three-cornered hat, and having been so sanguine.

My mother was exceedingly handsome. Tall and slight, she had a remarkably graceful carriage, a natural dignity of manner and movement; and this description held good when she was more than sixty years old. She had an innocent, anxious face. She told me that she was very timid as a girl, and that when first married to my father she was afraid of him. She often suffered from nervous lassitude, which made general society, especially in the evening, irksome to her.[1] But, independently of that, her thoughts and desires centred in home, with husband and children.

[1] Unlike Sganarelle's master, my mother could hardly be described as *impie en médecine*, for she was one of that numerous band who are infatuated with amateur physicking. She was deeply read in Graham's *Domestic Medicine*. Her favourite nostrum was mustard-seed, swallowed whole. She was an inveterate experimenter in patent drugs; but this was nothing to what she at last came to under homœopathy, infinitesimal doses, and a colossal faith.

However, she took the liveliest interest in many things—a simple, womanly interest. Hers was a

> delight in little things—
> The buoyant girl surviving in the wife.

My mother often gave me accounts of her early days in the Epsom Parsonage: of the stagnant monotony of existence there, and how at one brief interval it was curiously quickened by the arrival of a number of French refugees. Among them came several Catholic priests, seeking advice and assistance. These refugees were not allowed to live near the coast.

One of the seculars, a Monsieur Chabot, was too thankful to remain and give French lessons. He was as lean as St. Thomas Aquinas after a vigil, and his bows and his snuff-box were memorable. There was also a Monsieur Jerduke, 'conceited and absurd, a dressed-up horrour,' who taught dancing. My mother would describe with a simple complacency her Oldenburg bonnet and 'jaconet muslin;' also her skill in the minuet. 'You know that the minuet is a Court dance; it is in a slow *tempo.* Instead of making a decided step after the first step, I used to fill the pause by raising and sinking my instep, arching it like an egg, so as to glide into the second. Then there was a great art in giving, and even in withdrawing, the hand, the head being turned gracefully: "vous allez à droite, vous regardez à gauche, vous allez à gauche, vous regardez à droite." It was very elegant,' &c.

My mother was swayed by her feelings and sentiments more than by any intellectual and logical conviction. She was not what is called 'a superior person.' Early in her married life she became acquainted with Mrs. Shore, a warm-hearted, friendly matron. However, this Mrs. Shore, though in her own way peculiarly fond of the world, held strong Evangelical views. I think she placed religion on a false basis, and her 'religiosity' had a baneful influence on my mother, and weakened her influence for real good. Strange to say, my father was also slightly infected by it. It was a point with Mrs. Shore that dancing and playing at cards were not compatible with salvation. She had very decided opinions, and, as we used to say in the City, she was well 'posted-up' in the designs of Providence. I lay many of the miseries of my early school-time at Mrs. Shore's door; but still there was a good deal for which I alone was responsible.

There is no power on earth to compare with the power of religion, but it comes to us in various guises. In those days there were no peculiar Ritualistic genuflexions; introits, ciboriums, monstrances, were unknown; there was none of that sniffing after incense now so common. The High Church party were as unlike that of to-day as it is possible to imagine, but still religion was a great force.

'Length begets loathing.' I well remember the sultry Sunday evenings when my mother would carry me off to an ugly little pepper-boxed temple, with its tin-kettle bell, where we simmered through Mr. Shepherd's long-winded pastorals. The mean, cramped, white-painted pew; the faint and unpleasant odour of Mr. Shepherd's large flock (how he collected it was a mystery), made the worthy man's weariful discourses—doctrine, reproof, instruction, and dubious grammar—still more irksome.

I was very docile, and I have remained so. I am told that the devout Papuans perform their religious rites standing on one leg. If ever my lot should be cast among these simple people, I should be glad to oblige them. I used to be sorry that I did not care for going to church, and I was sorry not to be more sorry. Do not suppose, however, that I approved or approve of a sabbathless existence; but at that time my ideas of heaven were a good deal mixed up with Mr. Shepherd's sermon-house, and such-like.

We have good authority for asserting that piety enjoineth no man to be dull; but still let us be grateful that woman is a church-going animal. My father was as regular an attendant as my mother; however, as we went, I have heard him more than once quote these homely lines, which amused him, and still cling to my memory:

'Tis said, by men of deep research,
He's a good dog who goes to church.
I hold him as good, every bit,
Who stays at home and minds the spit;
For tho' good dogs to church may go,
The going there don't make 'em so.

My dear mother did everything for the best, but I think she lacked judgment; yet I hardly ought to say this, for she was often placed in positions of peculiar difficulty, and acquitted herself admirably. There is no doubt that she was sometimes unwise; however, it was usually about matters of slight importance. The fact is, that she leant upon others, and looked to them for guidance and support—which was the more unfortunate as she was not always discriminating in the choice of her advisers. But who is?

For some years we had a very tall and very gaunt Irishman, a pensioner, who assisted in the stable, cleaned shoes, went errands, and occasionally got drunk. He had valuable qualities; but he was a talebearer, and my mother gave ear to his insinuations against the other domestics. I can see them now. Scene: Her sitting-room. There would be a knock and a 'Come in.' The door slowly opened, and a shaggy head was thrust in, shaken bodingly; this was followed by the upper half of a long, navy-blue-clad body; then the figure raised its hands and eyes in mournful and minatory fashion, and in the direction of the servants' quarters. My poor mother could not resist this dumb show; it was always, 'Come into the room, Malone, at once, and shut the door.' Then would begin, 'Och, mistress! thim chatin' sarvints,' &c.

There were difficulties, not seldom of a ridiculous kind, the absurdity of which she was the first to appreciate. One of her peculiar attractions was her simple enjoyment of a joke against herself. My mother was as merry as a grig. She had a delightful laugh. As I have said, we were very proud, but rather afraid, of my father. No one liked a jest more than he did, but it was not the same thing. And I am afraid she spoilt us, for when he was angry she would often and often stand in the gap while we rallied behind her. She had as much of her children's confidence as parents can well have. How little that really is! She was very unselfish, entering heart and soul into our fun and amusements, and even sympathising with our minor follies.

Alas that we should get the fairest love at a time of life when we are so little able to comprehend it!

We had less jollity than most families, but we had more jokes. We used to make a good deal of fun, and of a graceless kind too, of a clerical relative of my mother. We gradually built up a fable, which at last even she half accepted as fact, that he was needy and greedy, combining the self-indulgence of a Rev. Charles Honeyman with the want of accuracy of Ananias; a dissembler, whose sole affections were centred in beer and all kinds of shellfish, especially oysters—the world was his oyster; that he wrote little books with goody-goody titles. One of them, 'Manna in the Cloister,' Arthur renamed 'Oysters on the Sideboard.' I hardly ever set eyes on this interesting relative of mine, but I have a boy's recollection that he was smooth, sleek, and sonorous; that he turned out his toes with a strut; and that there was a plaintive pietism in his sermons, aimed at nothing. This was all the direct pabulum we profane jesters had to go upon; but then, as time went on, our good mother provided us with plenty more. She revealed it as a warning. From her we learnt that, though he was painfully impecunious, he did not subsist on dew, like the grasshopper; that he did not make a sin of abstinence, but, on the contrary, that he was exceedingly self-indulgent.

> Oh! what may man within him hide,
> Though angel on the outward side!

We thus made up our minds that our cousin was altogether a better *mussel*-man than Christian, and that his wife, though partial to fine garments, was halting in grammar. He had fallen in love and married shortly after his ordination; hence the following lyric (a flirt ecclesiastic) of that date. You will see that, like his quill, he was a bit of a goose. I only give the first and last stanzas :—

Love is but a gentle creature,
Innocence in every feature:
    Flora, kiss the boy!

. . . . . .

Sweetly smiling, faintly flushing,
Then, to hide her own cheek's blushing,
    Flora kissed the boy!

Fitful efforts were made to get him a living, and at last, much to our surprise, one was secured. Then, with a wider sphere of uselessness, began other troubles—meddling parishioners and malevolent churchwardens—troubles in which our mother took a lively, but at the same time a highly critical, interest. She told us everything that happened, and whenever a poem could be squeezed out, a joke cut, or a caricature drawn, she was always ready to applaud.

A family jest loses its zest when the domestic cork is withdrawn, so I will cut mine short with a light and fleeting poem composed before I was twenty. It is not so ribald as some ; it comprehends several of our poor gibes, and it had the merit of giving my mother irresponsible delight. I hope my juniors are not imitating my pernicious example. I am a good subject for their mockeries, but, though I do not deserve it, I advise them to forbear. Indulgence in ridicule tends to harden the heart, and is one of the *mala mentis gaudia*. Full well do I know that my cousin comes out by no means the worst in this very graceless chapter.

THE OYSTER-POUCHER

One afternoon, in sandal shoon,
Along the wayside bleak
A palmer grey did wend his way,
A pilgrim passing sleek.

No cockle-shell adorned his hat,
That long had served him well;
He carried in the place of that
A native oyster-shell.

He knock'd at the Archbishop's gate;
His Grace observed the knock.
'Who at my postern knocks so late?'
''Tis Poucher,' cried the Cock.[1]

'And what does Poucher want with me—
The selfish (shell-fish), pouching knave?'
'Your Grace, he hath stept in to see
If you a living have.

'The varlet swears he has not touched
An oyster for a week;
He says, tho' frail, in bitter ale
He never dips his beak.'

[1] The Archbishop's butler (a rogue).

'Saint Broderip!'[1] swore the Archbishop,
'His brass, I won't endure it;
My crosier to a crumpet-top
I'll let him starve a curate.'

'Oh, mercy!' cried the oyster-man—
'Our lot, have mercy on it;
Of food bereft, we've nothing left
But Susan's 'andsome bonnet.'

'More shame to you. Go, live by rule—
Live so you'll never need.'
Says Poucher, 'I am no such fool—
I live by Rule[2] indeed!

More shame unto thy pointed toes;
I've heard the ugly news:
To make a dash you spend the cash
Subscribed to make the pews!

Your vices shock your worthy flock;
For you I've no remorse, man.'
'About the pews,' thus thinks the Cock,
'I'll run and write to Horsman.'[3]

'Begone apace!' went on his Grace;
'My mood is not for giving.
Small need, d'ye see, to come to me
When Rule provides a living.'

Says Poucher, 'Tho' I ne'er shall strut
A rector or a vicar,
You cannot blight my appetite
For oysters or for liquor.'

I now return more especially to my father and

[1] My father's lawyer, who had been at Eton with him and the Archbishop, where the latter, on account of his complexion, was called '*Crumpet* Sumner.'

[2] The well-known *écailler* of Maiden Lane. Last night Godfrey and I ate oysters there, after seeing Irving in *Macbeth* (January 5, 1889).

[3] A Radical M.P. who attacked the bishops.

mother. My mother took an interest in all kinds of people and things; she had a warm sympathy, which made her popular with many whom my father would not tolerate. He was much more exclusive; for though simple and natural, and even playful, he was seldom familiar. Fastidious in the selection of his acquaintance, he could not brook underbred people. My mother was more tolerant and more of a latitudinarian than my father, though, according to their lights, both were equally religious. I hope I am not wronging my mother, but, for instance, as regards smuggling, whether it were books or lace—whatever it might be—my mother smuggled with infinite relish, and with no after-qualms, whereas the idea of smuggling was abominable to my father.[1]

We cannot all be friars, and various are the ways by which God conducts the humble to heaven; but in the days I am treating of a good many of the more orthodox members of the Church of England held

[1] On the other hand, things amused my father which pained my mother. My father had a horror of Voltaire (at whom with infant eyes he might have gazed), Tom Paine, and Henry Brougham, and so had my mother; but I remember my father allowed himself to be tickled by Voltaire's complaints of the way in which he was perpetually being persecuted by people to whom he was a perfect stranger, but who believed in his infallibility. A credulous, sceptical burgomaster wrote asking him whether there was a Supreme Being, and, if there was, what were His intentions; also, whether he might consider his soul immortal. The funny part of it was that the inquiring burgomaster wrote in hot haste: he asked for a reply by return of post. My mother did not like this.

a sure and certain opinion as to eternal punishment. They were jealous of the dogma being questioned, and this grew into their having a distrust and curious dislike of people whose minds were in suspense on the subject, and who indulged in etymological reasoning about αἰών and its derivatives—almost as if they suspected such people of a desire to deprive them of their just rights and natural privileges. This belief and this feeling have long existed.[1] My mother suffered much anxiety from the thought that perhaps some of those whom she most dearly loved were in danger; at times she was very unhappy. She plied us with tracts, and hung texts over our bed-heads. Daily and for years the question, worked on perforated card in coloured worsted, 'Do you ever pray?' was present to me. Surely, if the half-articulate cries of poor suffering creatures are prayers to the ears of Heaven, few of us are altogether prayerless. During early-middle life my mother went very far indeed, for she believed that only a few people would be saved, that the road to everlasting punishment was extremely broad and very crowded; yet,

[1] 'To preach long, loud, and damnation is the way to become popular. We run after a man who damns us, and we again run after him to save us.' Selden says this, and Selden was a good man and a Sussex man. A dignitary of the Greek Church ventured to question this dogma, and the historian who records the event gravely remarks: 'His congregation, justly incensed, tore their bishop to pieces.'

wonderful to say, she did not seem dissatisfied that her children should increase in number. I believe she consoled her benevolent self, in an illogical way, with the idea that her acquaintances'—Mrs. A.'s, or Mrs. B.'s, or Mrs. C.'s—numerous broods would probably be all lost, and that the necessary average would thus be kept up. What made it most curious was, that the natural woman was strongly opposed to all this. However, it was only during her last years, long after she had completed the work of making me thoroughly, I might almost say permanently, unhappy, that she changed her opinions. She *did* entirely change them, and probably, like many other good people, would have argued as unreasonably on the one side as she had done on the other. My mother had always had a strong human feeling, and this broadened as she aged. I well remember, when her poor speech was affected and the range of her vocabulary very much restricted, her saying that, such was the infinite mercy of the Eternal, she firmly believed that every human being would ultimately be saved; and then she haltingly added, 'Yes—even—Lord—Hertford!' Just at that time Lord Hertford was the typically wicked nobleman; and my dear mother had a great interest in and consideration for the aristocracy of her own country. My mother's worldliness was one of the many forms of her ingenuousness.

My father was very unselfish—a most liberal man in his acts; and I may say that my mother was equally so. During the last two or three years of her life she gave away all her personalty. She was full of sensibility. With considerable capacity for enjoyment, there was a curious little vein of cynicism running through her nature, which gave it a delightful flavour. I never knew any one quite like her in this respect. I wish I could really describe her, for her memory, apart from affection, is very fragrant to me. She was an innocent Bohemian, and ought not I to have been a happy son?

I could mention many anecdotes characteristic of my parents, and of their relations to each other. Here is one.

My father was sometimes led, through momentary irritation, to take people to task in a somewhat intemperate way, and afterwards he was sorry for it. My mother regretted this failing. One evening he happened to return from London after the west gate of the Hospital had been shut for the night; and he told her that the warder, a boatswain's mate of pensioners, had questioned his right to enter, not recognising who he was—in fact, had been very disrespectful—probably rather tipsy; but that he (my father) had given him a piece of his mind which he would not forget in a hurry, &c. On this the demon of mischief entered into my mother, and prompted her to indite a letter, supposed to come from the recalcitrant warder, in which the said functionary expressed great regret for what he had done, &c.; that if he had only known, &c. But the letter concluded with a few words to the effect that he could not help thinking my father, as a Christian gentleman, had been rather harsh, &c. My mother wafered and despatched this letter, and then entirely forgot it. I am afraid she was too much accustomed to such pranks.

The next morning, just as they had finished breakfast, the butler opened the door, and said that a pensioner had come by appointment to see my father. Even then my mother did not call to mind the letter she had written. My father glanced at her, as much as to say, 'I wish to see him alone.' So she got up and left the room. But as she was closing the door she heard my father say: 'I have sent for you about that letter, and to tell you that I regret——' In an instant my mother knew what was coming. She put her head into the room in an agony, and said, 'C'est moi qui l'ai écrite,' and then withdrew. It is presumed that on hearing this my father turned to the warder and said, 'It is all right, I will see you another time,' for the man left the house almost immediately afterwards. My father never afterwards referred to the matter. I think the story shows that he was really a good-tempered as well as a good-natured husband and father. Ellen and I were then sixteen and fourteen years old, and she was my mother's trusted confidant throughout the whole affair.

'Tall men are like tall houses—often poorly furnished on the top story.'

My dear father was below the middle height, and, as I have said, a rigid moralist. One day, when I was quite a small boy, I was walking with him in London, he leading me by the hand, and we met a certain Sir Joseph Greensides, a very tall and a very big man, with red whiskers standing out like the wings of a cherub. Sir Joseph stopped, and spoke a few words, and I noticed that my father gazed up at him with a keen expression of distaste. When they parted my father looked down at me with a sardonic smile, and said (as if he were taking me into his confidence), 'That's a nice little infant, eh?' After a minute he added, and with energy, 'He's a jobber!' and then he said no more.

I could not have been above nine years old when this happened, yet I have never forgotten it. I was in awe of my father; but somehow, even then, it occurred to me that he might not have spoken quite so strongly if the old boy had not been quite so big.

Sir Joseph was a rich man, and he was a jobber. It was bruited abroad that he had married a woman even richer than himself. Now people, especially if they are impecunious, resent this. Sir Joseph had not felt—as he ought to have done—how highly indelicate, in fact, how unfair, it was for any one to marry money who did not actually need it. He has long since gone over to the majority. Some people called him Sir Joseph Redsides by reason of his whiskers—a circumstance hardly worth recording. *Basta!* Here I kick him out of any further notice in my memoir.

My father considered it a serious disadvantage to have a short-sighted footman. When he was at Madras, nearly eighty years ago, he happened to be dining out, and wore, as was usual at that time and in that climate, a white jean jacket. After the meal was over one of the servants walked round the table, picking up the remaining fragments with a steel-pronged fork, and he stuck the cruel weapon into my father's honest, sunburnt fist, which rested on the tablecloth while he was conversing. The short-sighted man mistook it for a piece of brown bread, and confounded the sleeve of his jacket with the tablecloth.[1]

My father wrote two or three biographies for

[1] To my surprise, I have just found an incident similar to this in Sir Jonah Barrington's *Personal Sketches*, published in 1830. There the victim is stated to have been an Admiral Cosby. If Sir Jonah is right, it only shows how treacherous are our recollections, as I seem to remember that my father mentioned this misfortune as having happened to himself. *Et voilà comme on écrit l'histoire!*

'Lodge's Portraits.' He had a regard for Lodge, who was Norroy King of Arms, and for his sister, who lived with him, I think in Bloomsbury Square. She was plain, but had a charming figure and a fitful pleasantry. One day, as she was walking near their house, she heard manly strides behind her, following her. The individuals gained upon her, got alongside of her, and then one of them, having peeped round her poke-bonnet, ejaculated in a tone of deep disappointment as they fell back, 'Extrornaryornary' (extraordinarily ordinary), 'by Gum!'

We often walked with my father on Sunday afternoons. He was intolerant of *endimanché* young men. If we ever saw any such poor fellows, walking three or four abreast, smoking pestiferous cigars and looking slangy or overdressed, but apparently happy, he would mutter 'Blackguards!' and hasten his steps; but he had his indemnifications, for when he met a modest-looking servant-girl, hymnal (Plymouth Collection) and prayer-book in hand, on her way to church (or its alternative), he was as much edified.

In 1837, during one of our walks near Mottingham, we saw from afar a poor wretch, by name Cocking, launch himself from Green's balloon in a parachute of his own contrivance. The machine collapsed and turned over and over, Cocking clinging to it. He was killed on the spot. The ascent had been made from Vauxhall.

My dear Children,—Some day you must pay a visit to Greenwich Park, so interesting for its huge cedars and Spanish chestnuts in ruin. I mean to go there once again before I flit; *ibimus, ibimus!* Let us go together, and follow wherever our vagrant fancy leads. How often, as child and boy, have I loitered in its ferny solitudes, and listened to many a warbled 'Ben mio te vedo,' and the amorous reply, 'Si tu mi vedi, vieni a me.' It was my father's habit—it was almost a matter of conscience with him—if he did not ride, or go to London, to take a constitutional round the wall that girdles the amenity of this delightful little park. His walk was by Maze Hill, and so round to Croom's Hill, but he sometimes varied it by ending at Maze Hill. I took the very same walk (by Croom's inspiring steep) the other day. I had not done so for thirty years. I passed through London Street and Stockwell Street, which were full of ghosts, but I looked in vain for a familiar, or even a transmitted, face. The town looked meaner and poorer, and incomparably more squalid; but the Hospital, disencumbered of its enclosed gardens, was more than ever imposing. Of course, certain changes had wrought themselves into the Blackheath landscape, but not so very many; the Park wall looked several bricks lower than it used to do; the once primitive path was paved with asphalte; neither of the windmills was standing; nearly all the gorse was gone; and where were the donkeys? Even the gravel-pits did not look so cavernous as of yore. On the side facing the Heath, the only mortal I met was a simpering lass, reading a comic paper, and pushing her charge in a perambulator of the period.[1] The season was adverse to cricket, but there lay the stretch of turf on which, day after day, the renowned Felix (Mr. Wanostrocht) used to educate his band of little pupils in bowling and fielding, and his famous cut to point. The old houses on either hill seemed many degrees smaller and meaner; there was nothing palatial about anything. Even the Ranger's Lodge, with its legendary royalty and homely pomp, was not the pile of memory: it had a shrunken aspect, as if the rooms might be dark, not to say poky. But it was early spring; the east wind was raging in Chesterfield Walk, and everything seemed blighted.

These anecdotes connected with my parents, and these few lines about Greenwich and its park, are a page of that interesting story-book called 'Auld Lang Syne,' which records and recalls the fragrance of pleasant summer—ay, and pleasant

[1] There is nothing more beautiful in nature than a woman with a child in her arms. An experienced nurse dandling a baby is a pretty sight. Conceive if Raphael had had to deal with the perambulator!

winter—days; days that seem more engaging as they fade into the forgotten. 'Le meilleur ami à avoir, c'est le passé.'

My father was circumspect, and, in a sort of way, a straitlaced and proper person; yet in the course of his life he did one or two things which seem foreign to that character. I do not know who was the human being who, more daring than the original navigator of Horace, first ventured into the upper air, but my father was the second Englishman who did so. In the year 1802 he paid a considerable sum of money to go up in a balloon with Garnerin, to the imminent peril of his neck; and on May 1, 1821, he went to see the Cato Street conspirators hanged—to the more than imminent peril of their necks. I give his account of it:

'You will be surprised to hear that I witnessed the execution of the conspirators this morning before Newgate. Yesterday I entertained the scheme from a desire to see how such men would behave. I was in a window right facing them, and saw the whole. It was an awful sight.

'These wretches died quite regardless of religion, and firm to the last.

'Ings gave a shout to the populace when he mounted the platform, and Brunt nodded and smiled, first at some of his friends, and then at his coffin—the five coffins being placed in a row.

None of them spoke, and the others showed no fear. When all were tied up the drop fell, and they died easily. After hanging about twenty minutes they were cut down and placed one by one in their shells. A surgeon (masked) coming forward and cutting off in a minute the head of each in succession, not a drop of blood followed, owing to the strangulation. The executioner held up the heads successively, saying, "This is the head of Arthur Thistlewood, a traitor," &c. They were all removed by nine o'clock.

'The populace was quiet, but cheered them on their first appearance, and hooted the surgeon each time he came on the scaffold to take off the heads. There was no quartering, &c. Mr. Cotton, the clergyman, tried in vain to engage their attention. Davison, the black, alone made him a bow on first coming up the ladder. I am very glad I went.' [1]

As regards the balloon ascent. In those days it was by no means so ordinary an affair as it is now; so I think my father's exploit was more adventurous, and his curiosity more rational, than at first it might appear. He was not vain of the feat, and even at the time seems to have wished to escape notoriety, for in the 'Annual Register' for 1802 it is stated that he made the ascent under the

[1] For another view of this transaction see the appendix to George Borrow's *Romany Rye*, p. 358.—EDITOR.

pseudonym of Brown. That large family has much to answer for. The conclusion was not the least interesting part of the adventure. The balloon alighted in a field near a high-road in Essex; the aëronauts were in difficulties, and made signals to a passing post-chaise. It at once stopped; the occupants leaped out, and ran across the field to render assistance. One of them was a young cavalry officer, returning from foreign service, just landed at Harwich on his way to London. Then there was a sudden recognition and exclamations. 'What! Edward?' 'William?' The officer was my father's eldest brother, just arrived from India. They had not seen each other for years!

I give here a copy of a characteristic letter from my mother, Eleanor Mary Elizabeth Boucher, written when she was about twenty. You must remember that she was the simple daughter of a quiet country parson of the last century, writing to her mother, whom I can just recollect as a severe old lady, and whose black bombazine embraces I was sufficiently dutiful not to resent.

Harley Street: September 3, 1814.

My dearest Mama,—My first letter from hence must surely be to you, and most happy am I to say that I arrived quite safe here last night between seven and eight o'clock. I will begin with my history from the beginning and go on regularly.

Thursday evening, M. A. [her half-sister, older] departed for Sorrell on horseback, escorted by Thompson Wright and Guthrie *à pied*. We proposed if seats were vacant in the traveller [stage-coach ?] to travel all night, and arrive in London as yesterday morning; but alas! all were full. But at the very moment a returning *chay* passed by. This we seized, and it conveyed M. A., T., and I to Leicester, where we slept till half-past four, when we seated our *carcases* in the post coach. Tommy was the quintessence of civility all along; but long before we arrived at Seagrave[1] I felt a painful aversion to him—why, then I knew not, but I thought him old-maidish, self-sufficient, and arrogant to me, though all attention. I do not commonly take dislikes, but so it was. Well, at Seagrave it grew desperate, for he was so dreadfully officious, and talked and gave his opinion on all subjects so like a man of forty, that I completed my aversion. G., save this failing, liked him, and thought as he grew older he might improve. It went against my stomach to be even civil, and I fully expected he would spite me when we were travelling together. However, to divert my mind after parting with my dear M. A., I condescended to talk to him, and we started politics. I found he was a hideous

[1] Robert Burton, who wrote *The Anatomy of Melancholy*, held the living of Seagrave till his death in 1640.

democrat. He abused in most scurrilous terms all the first men in Church, State, and Law, and even dared to speak harshly of Mr. Park [her and my father's friend, afterwards Judge Park]. All this I could not bear. I was, however, very cool, and gave him very severe reproofs, so much so that I thought he must hate me. I looked dreadfully grave and majestic, and whenever he thought he had said a clever thing, and laughed heartily, I turned graver still, and sometimes, indeed full five minutes after, I would ask what amused him. In short, the whole way a smile never illuminated my countenance, and I hoped I had humbled him ; but you will hear. On our arrival at Islington he got a coach, and we departed, bag and baggage, for Harley Street. In the coach I begged we might settle accounts. My share was 6*l.* After this I began to thank him for his attention to me, which, I must confess, was very great, and I never should have done without, toad though he was.

Well, the polite manner I was obliged to assume on the occasion made him presumptuous : he dared to seize my hand by main force, and, notwithstanding my frowns and entreaties, the monster —kissed it !

I was angry, and loftier than ever. Well, just before we arrived he had the impudence to ask and to endeavour for a kiss. This I successfully resisted, and by way of punishment coolly wished him 'good-bye;' but still, should you ever see him, thank him for his civilities to me; and in the journey he was very respectful. He is a *backbiter!* and gave his opinion about people above him in so decided and pert a manner that I cannot bear him; but he was too much satisfied with himself to see my contempt for him.

Butler and footman came to hand me out. These, with the grand hall, must have knocked him down. However, I left him, for Mr. and Mrs. Foreman met me in the hall. The latter gave me a kiss; former longed, I saw, but *wifey* was by. However, both received me most kindly. As far as I can judge at present, my dear mother may make herself happy about Ellen, for I see every prospect of the greatest kindness. They enquired particularly about you all, and asked several questions about Elizabeth. I retired rather early. My apartment is *magnifique*, &c. Dearest Mama, keep up your spirits. A thousand thanks to my dear Mary for her letter; 'twas indeed an unexpected pleasure. God bless you all! I would not send this scrawl, but you will expect it.

Ever your loving daughter,

Eleanor Mary Elizabeth Boucher.

To Mrs. Boucher,
Coledale Hall, Carlisle.

Mr. and Mrs. Foreman were on the wing for Paris, and took my mother with them. She returned thence with a short waist, a full sash, and puffed sleeves, and, being very fascinating, my father at once fell a victim to her charms. They were married on February 28, 1815, after a six weeks' acquaintance.

My mother had many and deep sorrows: the death of two of her sons in the army in India; then my father's long, anxious, and melancholy illness and death; and lastly, the death of Bertha, who was all-in-all to her. This tragedy [1] occurred in July 1853, and was a terrible shock to my mother, for immediately afterwards she had a stroke of paralysis, by which her mental powers and faculty of speech were permanently affected. However, she partially recovered, and lingered on till March 1861. She died at Exeter, and is buried at Iver in Buckinghamshire. She had more than once expressed a wish that when she died she should be laid among the very poor, and her wish was remembered. During the last two or three years of her life, when at Edinburgh and elsewhere, she found comfort in visiting the cemeteries, some of which are beautiful. She went to one or other of them almost daily, to meditate, in devout submission to the Divine will.

[1] Bertha Locker was burnt to death whilst on a visit to Paris. She was then twenty-two years of age.

She had a filial trust in God. I have some of her letters written at this time, which are singularly touching. Mighty is the power of motherhood, and yet few of us seem to realise that we can never have but one mother!

While we are yet together we cannot help behaving as if we were never to be separated; and, as a consequence, there are thoughts which torment us as we sit by a lonely hearth, thinking, with a yearning pain, of the dear ones that are gone. Our faults rise in remorseless judgment against us, that while they were yet with us we did so little for them. And where is the atonement? My dear father and mother! I am cut to the heart when, through these long, dim years, I again seem to see your kind faces, and think of your great virtues, your much affection, your manifold chagrins, your heavy sorrows, your tragical afflictions, and then of the small comfort I must have been to you.[1]

I wish I could see you, were it only to say one word, and to kiss your poor faces. Troubles came upon you, the income diminished, health failed, and your children, if not a sorrow, were a burden. I fear I was a disappointment to you. You both died in peace. But the end must be tragical, whatever

[1] She was very generous. She said after I was grown up, 'Fred, you have never spoken to me in a way a son should not speak to his mother.' It was her 'Yet never heard I once hard speech from thee.' (December, 1888.)

gay comedy there may have been in the first flush of life. Age came, and sickness—twilight, and the inevitable night. We must all cross the black river with the languid wave; we must all die, we must all die alone! My dear father was so high-minded, so able, so upright. My dear mother was so devout, so unselfish, so dear. As I write their clear voices seem to ring out of the silence of the past; but it is too late. I was often graceless in spirit, if not in manner and behaviour; now it is too late, too late. But things past redress are not with me past care.

I will here give a fragment of a letter, dated May 1827, written by Edward Stanley, Bishop of Norwich, the father of my brother-in-law (Arthur Stanley, Dean of Westminster), to his wife, that 'friend of his bosom and prop of his heart.' The manuscript is to be found in the volume of my parents' correspondence, where also are letters from Blanco White (Doblado), half a Spaniard by descent, and once so well known at Oriel, who possessed what Renan has aptly called 'la grande curiosité,' and to whom they were both much attached; Southey, Croker, Sir Robert Peel, Sir Walter Scott, Hallam, Macintosh, Milman, Lockhart, Mountstuart Elphinstone, Dr. Chalmers, and many other interesting people.

'I went down to Greenwich on Sunday as soon

as I had deposited Bella and Arthur in Audley Square, after escorting them to the Catholic chapel; but how to speak of Mr. and Mrs. Locker and their children in terms sufficiently high is difficult. To begin with their rooms. They are lodged on a first-floor, with bedrooms above, in one of the wings of the Hospital, overlooking the river, which is, as you may recollect, a moving panorama of shipping of every variety, seen to the greatest possible advantage. On a deep crimson-coloured paper (just the tint you like) in the drawing-room and dining-room are hung a choice collection of drawings and paintings, the intermediate room being a library, filled up with books, in oak shelves, in a style and manner most enjoyable and comfortable. He is about my age and size, and, I may add to you (but far, far behind do I tread in his steps), of somewhat the same character. His whole soul is energy and vivacity, cased in a body quick and active. He is secretary[1] to the establishment of the Hospital, which gives an influence of which he avails himself for the best purpose; and the changes he has effected and the visible good he has done speak volumes in his praise. That he is a man of admirable taste and a lover of art everything about him proves. Upon all subjects he can speak much and well, and his acquaintance is, at the same time,

[1] My father was afterwards appointed one of the Commissioners.

general and select. His situation as secretary to admirals on foreign stations has given him knowledge of the world, and nothing has passed before him unobserved.

'If you wish to see a school in perfection, follow him to that which he has, if not founded, at least superintended till it became what it now is.

'One thousand children, under perfect discipline, are educated and prepared for the sea, &c.

'She [Mrs. Locker] is the counterpart of him—as much zeal, spirit, and good sense. If I might breathe a fault, it would be to say that there might be a slight tendency to Evangelicism; but this, which is weakness and folly in others, in them becomes a virtue which I deeply respect, if I cannot adopt it, for it exists with such good feeling and judgment that nothing objectionable can spring from it. Taking him altogether (and I speak it to you with a confidence with which I can only speak of it to my own heart), I consider him as what I might have been had my life been passed under similar circumstances. But what he now is I never can be.

'They have four children, but I only saw two of them, the eldest being a girl [these were Ellen and myself]. They are quite beautiful, and their manners like their countenances. In a week I should have loved them like my own.

'From all I have said you may fairly infer that they are taken with me. I believe and hope they were, for there was not a subject started on which my opinion was not hailed with surprise and apparent delight, as coinciding with their own. They will form prominent guests in the parties I have formed for meeting in another world.'

I wonder the Bishop did not remark on my mother's good looks.

Greenwich Hospital and our Apartment there

How graphic in our literature are some of the descriptions of places! They are delightful. Cobbett has given us not a few of them. There are little finished pictures of Boston, in America, that linger in the memory. I have not been at Olney, or Bemerton,[1] or Hawsted, and shall never go there, yet they are very visible to me. I have not visited at Blakesmore, and do not exactly know where Blakesmore is; yet it seems strangely near, and I have a particular feeling for its family portraits, its faded tapestries, and even for certain tarnished gilt-

[1] I have now seen Bemerton (1892).

leather battledores. It is a country mansion familiar of the imagination, and I am satisfied. I may say that I have my own visions about certain places, and have no desire to undo them.

If such is the case as regards what one has not seen, how much more endearing is the sentiment for those nooks and corners where one's early days were passed!

Combien j'ai douce souvenance
Du joli lieu de mon enfance!

I have this deeply rooted affection for Greenwich.

As I have already said, my father had been Civil Secretary to the Mediterranean Fleet, and ended by being a Civil Commissioner of Greenwich Hospital. I was born and brought up there; and you should know that our apartment was in the east wing, facing the Thames, and corresponding to the Governor's quarters, and that it was commodious, airy, and very pleasant. I will now describe it. The principal rooms were on the first floor. The kitchen, &c., nursery, and attic bedrooms were on the *mezzanine* above. We had three large windows, with heavy bar-sashes, fronting the Thames, and six, equally large, looking into the Grand Quadrangle.

The drawing-room, a corner room, faced both square and river; the library and dining-room had only the river view—and all were *en suite.* On a wet afternoon my father would open the doors between these three rooms, and so get a 'quarter-deck walk' of some length.

The drawing-room was papered with a thick crimson flock, and was well covered with water-colour drawings in neat carved and gilt frames, a collection of which you will appreciate the interest when I tell you that it included excellent specimens of Thomas Lawrence, Wilkie, Prout, Edridge, Girtin, Turner, Alexander, Chinnery, Paul Sandby, Hearne, Nicholson, Cipriani, Cozens, and Lady Farnborough (Amelia Long). It was a harsh necessity that, after my father's death, obliged us to part with these.

The library was the centre room, with one large window. Its walls were almost entirely occupied by high bookshelves, unglazed. The exception was over the chimney-piece, where there hung a very agreeable little oil-picture, hemmed in by books, of Eton and the Playing-fields, and Windsor towers in the distance, by John Varley. This landscape, in my recollection, seems hardly less shadowy than the real view from the window. On the tops of the bookcases there were three or four busts indicative of a Tory bias.

The dining-room had a paper almost similar to that in the drawing-room, and there hung our oil-pictures—portraits of Lockers and Stillingfleets and Parrys; of Nelson, Exmouth, St. Vincent, Barrington; Captains Pole [1] and Sir William Montague, John W. Croker, and Lord Prudhoe. There were one or two naval fights; there was also an admirable picture, by Hogarth, of David and Mrs. Garrick. This picture is so lifelike that as little children we were afraid of it; so much so that my mother persuaded my father to sell it to George IV. Garrick is seated at a writing-table in the act of composition,[2] gazing up, rapt, smiling, and absorbed; and Mrs. Garrick has stolen behind him, and is in the act of twitching the pen out of his fingers. Most of these oil-pictures are either at Rowfant or Newhaven Court.

It was a Philistine age, but this apartment was furnished in excellent taste. I especially remember a Reisner marqueterie table; also an ancient buhl chest of drawers, and an old lac screen, scarlet with glass panels.

A long gallery ran through a good portion of the apartment; it was embellished by a very pretty pair of marble statues after the antique.

[1] Sir Charles Pole, of Aldenham Abbey. His daughter, who inherited Aldenham, married Mr. William Stuart. There is a good picture of my grandfather, in uniform, at Aldenham; it is by a well-known painter, Gilbert Charles Stuart. Old Boswell, my grandfather's shipmate and body-servant, is said to have pronounced this portrait a success, 'particklar the buttons.'

[2] Garrick is writing the prologue to Foote's comedy of *Taste*.

There were two staircases to the mezzanine, which, as I have said, contained the servants' quarters and the kitchen, &c., also the nursery (known as 'Powder'em Castle'!). Its three small windows were close to the ceiling—two of them long and narrow, the third, a very small oval, not quite so high; so, though the room fronted both river and square, there was no look-out. Well do I remember the bliss of being held up to the oval, and my first sight of sky and ships. There was a closet by the door, deep and roomy, where toys were kept, and lost, to turn up again after what to us appeared long years of deprivation. My mother was Sabbatarian—strictly so—and these toys were generally locked up on Sunday, though now and then some were reluctantly permitted to us, on account of the hardness of our young hearts. Missionary Lotto had not then been introduced. I remember a rent in the old faded and patched Turkey carpet, which I did my best to enlarge. I have already mentioned a large mezzotint engraving of Puck seated on a toadstool, which hung on the wall; and beside this, in a recess under one of the long narrow windows, stood a pair of common white plaster casts, after Canova, of almost naked children, for which I had a deep admiration. I think they must have been very pretty. They were about eighteen inches high, seated on low pedestals, with one leg drawn up. One was 'Reading,' and the other was 'Writing.'[1] I should have said that on the principal floor, besides the three sitting-rooms, already described, there were six bedrooms and a schoolroom (called the 'skullery').

The apartment was reached by a private stone staircase from Queen Anne's Square, into which square three of our bedrooms looked.

I have here given a prosaic, almost an upholsterer's, account of this apartment, yet to me it is an abode of memory and sentiment, quickened and glorified by affection. It is mysterious and shadowy, and yet it seems very real. Sometimes I see the magic words 'Greenwich Hospital' in the newspapers, but what is said never carries any significance with it. Greenwich has become a mere suburb of London, like Peckham or Holloway.

It is a question whether Greenwich Hospital ever existed as I fancy it did, and, if so, whether it has not all faded away. Sometimes I feel that I might go down to Greenwich and still find it there!

I must say yet a few more words about my much-beloved Greenwich Hospital. Early attachments remain ever faithful and dear, and I have

[1] I have just been looking at the first edition of Lamb's 'Album Verses,' and am pleased to see a pretty little woodcut of 'Writing' which decorates the title-page. It is pleasant to think that Lamb and I at any rate had one taste in common. (1891.)

faint visitings of nostalgia when I think of my home there[1]—the snug little nest where my affections were fledged, the squares and colonnades that were the playground of my boyhood, the terrace, the 'five-foot walk,' and the abounding river. One of my earliest recollections was the men, mysterious in their enormous boots, who, with a toothless rake, as the tide receded, cleared the mud from the shore immediately in front of our windows. Then, on wintry mornings there were the river-pilots and longshore men, in their row-boats at anchor, taking a fisherman's constitutional ('three steps and overboard'), and with shrugged shoulders promoting circulation by beating their arms across their chests. I remember the familiar sounds from the craft in mid-stream and the cheer of the early colliermen as they weighed anchor. I fancy I still hear the not specially melodious quarter-to-eight bell, which awoke me as its *squilla di lontano* called the pensioners to breakfast. How my heart, or my fancy, still yearns at the recollection of those sweet sounds! I suppose the sailors still cheer and the

[1] 'Four ducks on a pond,
A grass bank beyond;
A blue sky of spring,
White clouds on the wing;
How little a thing
To remember for years—
To remember with tears!'

bell still rings. Why should they go on when I am no longer there to listen? Then there was 'Cats' Square' (Queen Anne's), so called by us from the many cats that assembled in it. It was also there that, at whatever hour of night or very early morning you happened to be about, you were pretty sure to find one or two pensioners taking a quarter-deck walk together, doing as they had been accustomed to do when keeping watch at sea; also a certain corner in one of the colonnades where I played thousands of games of fives with Hobbes, the little sentry;[1] then the superb chapel, and its sleepy services, and an indescribable and penetrating atmosphere of 'fust,' which was present wherever the pensioners congregated. This reminds me of the pensioners' wards, which, as children, we visited with fearful joy, but at the same time with a half-realised disgust—a desire to hold our button-noses. The odour abides with me yet. I remember the figure-head of Anson's ship, the old 'Centurion,' in the Anson Ward, and my father's excellent verses thereon, which I give here:

[1] He did not seem to follow the ball: it was the ball that seemed to follow him. He was very adroit.

'LINES

ON

The Lion Figure-head

OF

H.M.S. "CENTURION,"

NOW IN THE

ANSON WARD,

GREENWICH HOSPITAL.

BY AN OLD SEAMAN

'Introduction

'On a visit of King William IV. to Greenwich Hospital His Majesty went into the Anson Ward to look at the lion-head of the "Centurion" man-of-war, in which ship Lord Anson sailed round the world in 1740–44. This relic had stood for many years in front of an inn at Goodwood, Sussex, from whence His Majesty caused it to be removed, first to Windsor Castle, and since to Greenwich. One of the old men who stood near the King had written some lines on the occasion, but, as he did not presume to offer them to His Majesty, we now present them to our friends as a testimony of his loyalty.

'THE FIGURE-HEAD OF THE "CENTURION."

'What cheer, my messmates? Ah! you stare indeed.
But I'm a Lion of true English breed,
A vet'ran sailor, past my hundredth year,
And well deserve a berth in Greenwich tier;
For I with Anson sailed the world around,
Firm to my post, and ever faithful found.
Astride the bow I plough'd the foaming deep
(Drench'd with the surge) and watch'd the dolphins leap.
In fight or flood I led my Commodore
Through perils dire and seas untried before;
With him I brav'd the battle and the blast,
And mock'd at fear while others stood aghast.
Proof against famine, pestilence, and pain,
Death o'er my head still shook his dart in vain,
While many a comrade found a seaman's grave
Beneath the dark, unfathomable wave.
My chief was brave and wise, but lov'd the pelf:
He always took the *Lion's share* himself
When he divided prize-money or ransom;
To me, at least, such conduct was unhandsome;
For Paita's burning ruins could have told
His dear-bought plunder of Peruvian gold;
And when at length we took the rich galleon
He gave me neither dollar nor doubloon.
Yet I ne'er growl'd, like discontented railers,
Greedy to share that bane of English sailors,
But well deserved, when our long voyage was o'er,
A kinder fate than to be turned ashore.
Hard was the wrench that tore me from my ship,
Launch'd as we were together from the slip.
How many dismal years have rolled away
Since I was doomed to premature decay!
In utmost need, without a friend on earth,
Forced on the King's highway to gain a berth,
I took my stand beside a village inn,
For no kind shelter could I find within:
Like a sheer hulk, of adverse winds the sport,
Fix'd on a shoal when close in sight of port.
Though my old crippled limbs scarce hung together,

I stood exposed to every change of weather,
And, uncomplaining, bore my landlord's prate,
The ostler's daily jest, the boors' debate.
To me no voice in soothing accents spoke,
On me the traveller cast his passing joke.
Like a scathed oak, alone I with'ring stood,
The sole survivor of my parent wood.
At length my Sov'reign Master saw my plight,
Felt my disgrace, and vowed to do me right.
Aboard the "Windsor Castle" I was drafted,
And seem'd on Glory's heav'nly pinions wafted;
For, introduc'd among the Lions there,
I gain'd respect from lords and ladies fair.
But when my damag'd timbers were survey'd,
Alas! my upper works were found decay'd.
Our Royal Admiral, on this report,
Pronounced that Greenwich was my proper port,
Order'd me here—and now, safe moor'd at last,
I rest from all my strange adventures past.
O for a voice that patriot hymn to sing,
"God save my country! and God bless the King!"'

Some years ago this figure-head was removed from the Centurion Ward to the Royal Naval Asylum, and there, being again exposed to the weather, it fell to pieces. I wish I had heard of the condition it was in, as, for the sake of the verses, I should like to have bought it.

Among other recollections are Tom Flanders, a pensioner, *vif, mâle, et flamboyant*, whom we called 'Harry the Eighth,' and who made me a beautiful ship; and Fitzgibbon, who played tunes on a very squeaky fiddle; not forgetting the quaint forms, and music as quaint, of the drummer and fifer who at sunset during the summer months marched round the Grand Quadrangle. The four grass-plots of this emplacement were held very sacred: a pensioner-sentry with a powerful voice was stationed in the middle to warn off the holiday-makers. I can hear him now, as he bawled to the townspeople and cockneys, 'Git off the grass there, will yer! git off the grass!' *A propos* of this, at least forty years ago I was crossing from the Opera-house corner of the Haymarket to Cockspur Street, when a Greenwich pensioner, in his three-cornered hat and knee-breeches, attempting to do so, was driven back by a carriage, and was within an ace of being run over. On seeing this, a man who was passing, and who evidently remembered how he had been snubbed at the Hospital, yelled out, 'Yah! get off the grass there!' I felt pretty sure I was the only bystander who understood and enjoyed the full force of the sarcasm. Then there was the union-jack that waved drowsily over the Governor's quarters, but which now and again would fight madly with the frantic north-westers, and which vividly recalled to our tender minds the terrible tradition of a certain old pensioner who, on being sent to free the flag that had got entangled, was cruelly caught up by it and hurled headlong over the parapet to his death. I must not omit the dismal Isle of Dogs, at that time with hardly a habitation on it; Gallows Point and the neighbouring marshes, mysterious wastes, whose shores were fortified with black mud, and the carcases of drowned dogs, hideously swollen, among the ooze. I have a dim remembrance of the body of a pirate being pointed out to me, gibbeted on the edge of the horizon in his rusty chains; but perhaps in this I deceive myself, or was deceived. Then there were strawberry-feasts and Christmas-trees, bonfires and birthday-keepings—hot elder wine and such wassail—each new pleasure a bright little bead to string on memory.

Then came, as I grew older, sculling and sailing where the anything but silver-streaming Thames flowed on and widened past Woolwich to Erith and its broad estuary. There was also the long-looked-forward-to annual regatta for Greenwich watermen, to which, weeks beforehand, my father's old friends, Lord Prudhoe and Captain Orlando Felix, were seriously invited from London, and to which, as a matter of course, they often came; and cricket on Blackheath; also Greenwich Fair (with its merry-go-rounds, three throws a penny, the iniquities of Mr. Punch, and a learned dog that could shuffle and cut)—a sanctuary for ill-manners, and altogether a less holy gathering.

Beauty was there, but beauty in disgrace.

Also Greenwich Park! Well do I remember my frolics there—hunt the handkerchief with the dryads of the grove, hoydens with wind-blown skirts and rebel curls, and all their laughing graces, so hard to be entirely approved of. Pleasant is the balm of recollection!

The Painted Hall was always an interest, my father having had so much to do with its foundation and formation. I can recollect sitting to Mr. Briggs, the Academician, for my portrait in the large picture of George III. presenting a diamond-hilted sword to Lord Howe.[1] I am perched on the poop in a crimson tunic.

Lord Prudhoe was of a playful disposition: though a sailor, he pretended that he did not know a ship's stem from her stern; he talked of commanding a 'Patagonian line-of-battle brig.' He was tall and fair, and wore his hat just a little bit on one side.

Captain Orlando Felix (afterwards General Orlando Felix) was short and slight, and rather an exquisite, who went in for doing the correct thing. He composed verses.

Felix was also jocular, and, in spite of an attractive stammer, would pretend to be a showman in Wombwell's menagerie. He made us all laugh with such nonsense as the following:—

[1] I have a handsome sword that Admiral Howe gave my grandfather, and which is at his (Lord Howe's) side in Briggs's picture. The Howe family still possess their splendid 'presentation sword.' The peer who now owns it does not keep it at his side: he always keeps it at his banker's.

'Walk up, ladies and gentlemen. Walk up, and see my most extrornary little hanimal, the Manshoot Monkey, which came to this country on the bottom crust of a twopenny loaf, the crumb of which served him for his prowision during his woyage. There was two of these extrornary little hanimals. King George had one, and I had t'other, but hisn died; and he comes to me and he says, says he, "I say, Tom, give us your monkey." "No," says I, "King George, no! I'll see you blest first, for you sees as how I gets my livin' thereboy."'

Prudhoe and Felix travelled together in Egypt in 1827, and published a startling account of the magic which they witnessed there.

I remember, about 1841, hearing Elizabeth Fry, portly, debonair, and drab-coloured, address a ship's crew from the deck of their vessel on the eve of its departure for the Niger. Her quaint Quaker personality is admirably preserved for us in George Richmond's drawing. In her youth she had been a 'wet Quakeress,' gay and laughter-provoking, fond of song and the dance; she rode to hounds in a scarlet habit, and walked to meeting in scarlet shoes. A warm-hearted woman, with much vigour of character, she had an enormous natural benevolence.

At that time the Hospital grounds were divided

into gardens—now all swept away—gone like one's own youth. We had two, one of them of a fair size for a walled garden. To my childish recollection it was immense, and to me it is still a garden of memory. There vegetables grew, and fruit sometimes. It contained a pavilion of pleasure in the shape of a very earwiggy summer-house. The seats were not comfortable: if they were not damp, they were dusty. But with what precious associations are they not fraught! Why may not I go and sit there now? I remember a certain chickweedy tank where we thought it probable that large fish might still be lurking, and a leaden cistern with a delightful ball-cock. The gravel-walks had snug box-edgings, where we taught the gay nasturtium to wanton. Suburban bees hummed among the blossoms, which were none of your Maréchal Niels and Jacqueminots, but only a few garden weeds, extraordinarily sweet, as is the recollection of the strawberries, golden pippins, big bushes of lavender, sceptral hollyhocks, cabbage-roses, larkspur, 'old man,' dog's-grass, and bachelor's buttons. They could not have been of really much account.

Then, close to our apartment was the smaller garden—a sort of yard which had erst been a garden, with one solitary tree crucified to the wall: a tree that never bore, but which we gazed at with a hope long deferred, for we were told it was a nectarine—

the only green thing left 'to mark where a garden had been.' This yard was called the laundry-garden, and was sacred to a washerwoman, or rather a succession of such. It was from this *caro luogo* that we became a nuisance to the neighbours. We lighted bonfires there, dug caves; kept rabbits, fowls, pigeons, and guinea-pigs, called after the characters in Walter Scott's novels; also dogs, a donkey, and even a pony. The donkey was christened Strawberry, the pony Rough and Tough. When Strawberry presented us with a foal it was called Dustyfoot. A sorrel pony that my mother drove, and which was kept at the stables, was Alasan, and Blunderbore was the name of a series of my father's hacks.

Ellen had rather a well-stocked poultry-yard. Among other varieties, Dorkings with five claws, and a curious breed of white-booted bantams; but she was not a successful henwife. She was imposed upon by fraudulent dealers and ill-advised by *doctrinaire* dabblers. Once, for economy, and by the advice of a Mrs. Pawsey, *femme alors célèbre*, she fed her cocks and hens on paddy (rice in the husk), and in consequence half her stock became stone-blind. Hens are about the most wayward of created creatures. Sometimes nothing on earth will persuade them to sit; pluck out their under feathers, and whip them with stinging-nettles—do what you will, it is of no use. Again, at other times they are so broody that you may kick them off the empty nest, and they are on it again before your back is turned; they refuse to be disturbed. Ellen had many such monomaniacs to contend with. Then there were pestilences—successions of such: pip, roup, gapes, and an obscure disease called bumblefoot. These destroyed what the paddy had spared, the white-booted and all. Poor Ellen!

Father Thames flowed on the other side of our wall. There watermen, jacks-in-the-water, mudlarks, and other nondescripts congregated and loafed, leaning against posts, with their hands in the pockets of their stiff and tarred trousers, smoking when they could, and using the energetic language of imprecation when they could not. During the pestilences the poor child, shedding tears as big as decanter-stoppers, would go round the yard, gather up her dead, and fling them over the wall. She collected them many times, but threw them over only twice; for the second time she did so these men of Belial, when they saw the corpses coming, shouted to each other: 'I say, look out! Here they comes again! I'm blowed,' &c.

All this seemed funny enough to us boys, yet I fear it will not seem so to any one else; however, I give future possible generations of Locker the chance of a smile or a yawn. But what is the use of appealing to posterity? No circumstance or story is the same after a lapse of time; even the tellers are not the same interpreters.

Last, but not least, certainly biggest, I must not forget Argus, a huge black and white Newfoundland dog. He was the *flos canum*, whose affections we faithfully returned. The faithful beast entered into all our sports. He was very fond of looking on at battledore and shuttlecock. He might have described us as Luath did his playmates:

> The young anes rantin' thro' the house—
> My heart has been sae fain to see them
> That I, for joy, hae barkit wi' them.

A butcher's dog in the town, and the cats in Cats' Square, were his only ill-wishers. Like his namesake of the 'Odyssey,' he fawned with his tail and laid down his ears when approached by those he loved; and probably the ancient Argus, when he came out of Ionian waters, had exactly the same curious and thorough way of shaking himself that our Argus had when he came ashore from the Thames: he wrung himself dry, gradually, from nose to tail. After our sports he would lie with his eyes half closed, snapping lazily at the flies, or fall asleep at his enormous length on the hearthrug, and dream. Many were the phantom Toms he hunted there.

In those days Dr. Coke, R.N., was chaplain of the Hospital—a Churchman of the tawny port-wine school; an ecclesiastic, and nothing more; one of those perverse divines who prefer absolute unbelief to spurious orthodoxy. He was a kindly but choleric old boy, with a sanguine complexion and roomy boots. Ellen, at that time quite a little girl, mounted on Strawberry, often went off for a ride with him; and most amiably would he draw rein and wait for her whenever her steed lagged behind, which it not seldom did. I have said that Dr. Coke was choleric; but he had a kind of sensibility, for he could never read the parable of the Prodigal Son, that most beautiful of all parables, without shedding tears. However, as an instance of his spiritual aridity, on a certain occasion he was called in to minister to one of the captains who, on his deathbed, was perturbed as to his ghostly welfare. Dr. Coke comforted him by saying, 'Don't concern yourself about *that*, my dear sir—that's *my* affair!' So much for Dr. Coke. I will not suppress a story about this or some other old sea-captain. He had a faithful servant called John, who invariably provided a penny roll for his master's breakfast. One morning the breakfast-room bell rang, and his master groaned, and said, in an agitated voice, 'John, I'm very ill. Go for Doctor Dobson; this is probably the beginning of my last illness.' 'Indeed, sir,' said John, 'I hope not. What is it, sir? What does you feel like?' 'I am very bad indeed,' quoth his master; 'I've entirely lost my appetite, John—*I can't get through my penny roll!*' 'Eh!' says John, much relieved, 'when the baker came this mornin' all the penny rolls was gone, sir, so I gave you a twopenny roll.'[1]

Once on a time I was mad about domesticated animals, and now the taste has almost died out of me; my owls are but the languidest dregs of it. I was also devoted to squirts, pea-shooting, and bows and arrows—in fact, to everything that propelled; and to an enormously heavy rifle, a reluctant weapon, into which you pounded a greased bullet. I wonder I never slaughtered anybody. The laundry garden was the scene of most of my exploits.

These are my reminiscences, with which the reader, if ever *he* has been a boy, will be able to sympathise.

At last, one day, all at once I found myself grown up, a curly-headed youth, occupied with and arranging my costume to the exigencies of the hour. Then there were picnics in the neighbourhood; *coketeerings* in Greenwich Park; flirtations on the river, our home-returning lit by the rising moon

[1] My only excuse for such trivialities must be—

> Discit enim citius, meminitque libentius illud
> Quod quis deridet, quam quod probat et veneratur.'

and the risen stars, 'Moony tides swelling to roll us ashore;' strawberry junkets at Mottingham Moat, where the grass grew so green and all the orchard-trees had whitewashed stems; dances on Blackheath, at which certain Custs, Legges, Newdigates, Rogerses, Hislops, were prominent, and for all of whom we had a regard; dances in the Artillery mess-room at Woolwich; posy-sending, verse-making,[1] and all the requisite equipments of chivalry. An idyllic time! Yes, for there was a certain Miss Adelaide Amy Trefusis, of Ferrer's Court, St. Mary Cray. This young lady—she was not nineteen—was gently born, and nearly connected with the ancient family of Darell, who, I believe, are still pleased to pronounce their name Dorell. But I must not thus linger over the prelude to a melancholy story. Well do I remember Miss Trefusis—her sapphire glances, her dimpling smile, her winning English face—and my first introduction. I stood before her a rude, unfinished creature, awkward and sheepish, struck dumb by triumphant and ravishing beauty.[2] *Mine eyes were not in fault, for she was beautiful;* not tall, *she was just as high as my heart.*

[1] It was about this time that I developed a taste for poetry—for Campbell's odes and Cowper's short poems; the *Rejected Addresses*, Swift's *Baucis and Philemon*, &c., and Goldsmith's 'Retaliation' and 'Haunch of Venison.'

[2] 'Love taught me shame, and shame, with love at strife,
Soon taught the sweet civilities of life.'

There are tragic intervals in all our young lives; at any rate, so it seems at the time, whatever it may seem afterwards. I was in love, that May-day of the heart, when hope is at its highest.[1] I had been looking forward to meeting her at a ball, a garrison 'hop.' I had nourished myself with the brightest anticipations. I felt that this ball would be the crisis of my career, perhaps of my very existence. You must remember I was very young: I was only eighteen. I arranged to go, though the doing so would entail a serious personal sacrifice; but I rejoiced to make such a sacrifice. Hobbledehoys, as well as men, vainly struggle in the meshes of their destiny; for, though I set out, I was delayed: agonising entanglements, maddening obstacles, held me back. Heaven and earth declined to interfere, and the powers of darkness prevailed. I was so late that, as I stood at the front entrance, tore off my coat, and flung it in the face of the astonished doorkeeper, I beheld Miss Trefusis over the heads of the arriving and departing guests. She was descending the steps towards the banqueting-chamber, to the music of 'Le Remède contre le Sommeil.' My absence had not troubled her. She had been speedily accommodated with military consolation, for she was on the scarlet-and-gold arm of my rival—an old man of about five-and-thirty!

[1] Francis Bacon said, 'Hope is a good breakfast, but a bad supper.'

She appeared to be replying in an animated manner to his idiotic remarks. Of course she looked beautiful. The sight of her innocent happiness in being so lovely was torture to me. *She never cared for me!* I tried hard, but I was not able to approach her—'she *never* cared.' Then, all at once I felt giddy, faint, with sharp internal discomfort. It nearly doubled me up. It was the result of harassment and prolonged perturbation of spirit. I dragged myself into the crowded supper-room, where, above the babblement and *brouhaha*, was a confounded rattle of crockery, a sardonic clatter of knives and forks. I crawled to a chair. I drew into a corner. There was an unwieldy waiter. 'Quick!' said I, 'get me some brandy, quick!' He was deliberate. I thought he would never go, and then I made up my mind he would never come back. When he returned, it was with negus. Poor wretch! he became tiresome with his unfruitful, undesired attentions. 'Try a leetle mossal o' biled fowl,' &c. I remember everything. He was old. He had eyes bleared and mournful, weak legs, white cotton stockings, and a joyless smile. I should have pitied him, if he would only have allowed me to do so, if he would but have relieved me of his presence; however he hung over me,[1] and half poisoned me

[1] 'Ce gros butor de valet!' who picked up Mademoiselle de Briel's glove.

with the odour of onions; and all the time my internal discomfort went on to the falsetto of fiddles and the flight of champagne-corks.

I do not know why I describe all this; it is not from thinking I can interest you. 'Ask my pen. It governs me, I govern not it;' it impels me. Who dares to say that those people are the happiest who have their troubles in the morning of their days? I am still conscious of those onions!

By this time I had become completely hemmed in by the feasters and philanderers. Miss Trefusis may have been within a few yards of me; but, for aught it availed me, she might have been at Jericho. The whole affair was a very carnival of mockery. I could not escape from my corner. My chance was gone, and, as it turned out, for ever! Beautiful Amy! what has become of you now, now that I can no longer sun myself in your blue eyes? And what—what has become of me—of me as I was when I did so?

She was fair, with fair hair. She wore a frock with a black velvet body and fluffy muslin skirt. She was adorable. If she ever violated our conventionalities, it was done charmingly, triumphantly. I used to wonder that saucy words could ever come out of so sweet a mouth. They say that Pity is akin to Love, though only a Poor Relation; but Amy did not even pity me. There is a remedy for everything except Death (Death itself is a remedy), so the bitterness of this disappointment has long passed away; it belongs to a far-off period—part of a former state of existence. Love's torments have become a tender souvenir; but even now I think of her. In memory I still gaze upon her, and with a pensiveness that is inseparable from retrospect. *Lost was she—lost! nor could the sufferer say that in the act of preference he had been unjustly dealt with*, but the maid was gone!

Women have been my worst and best educators.

You see my morbid feelings and malaise were ever present, though more concealed than they had been, and took the keen edge off my social enjoyments.[1] At last my boating and ball-playing youth was at an end: the scenes of my life changed from Greenwich Hospital to London—'London, that is to me so dere and swete, in which I was forthgrowen; and more kindly love have I to that place than any other on Yerth'[2]—

Fumum et opes, strepitumque Romæ.

I became a coxcomb and an Admiralty clerk, having lodgings in Southampton Street, Jermyn

[1] 'As there gleams in the thyrsus that bacchanals bear,
Thro' the bloom of a garland, the point of a spear.'

[2] Chaucer's 'Testament of Love.'

Street, and afterwards in Bury Street, till I married; but I am anticipating.

1893.—My two sons will soon be young men, and I do not wish them worse luck than to win the friendship of two chaste, intelligent, and fairly young married women; and if my sons fall in love with these ladies, so much the better, say I.

The society and influence of such women are more valuable to a very young man in forming his character than the experience of men and all the pedantry of books.

Schooldays

I will now go back to the winter of 1826–27, when I was between five and six, and paid a long visit to my dear Aunt Mary. A childless woman with a motherly heart, who was 'born under a charitable star,' she lived a life of affection and beneficence at Carlisle with her mother, Mrs. Boucher, and a short distance from another very ancient female relative, whose name I forget, but who had a prehistoric reputation for great beauty, and passed a humdrum, hidden-away existence in a house all by herself, like a shy old tench year after year growing fatter and sleepier in its stagnant pool.

I can remember that we indulged in the comfortable joyance of tea and crumpets, the inclination for which still remains with me. They made me very happy. However, although I was a great darling, and could freely appreciate translations from the ingenious M. Charles Perrault, these kind folk did not fail to discover that I was slow at book-learning; but I was not the less beloved on that account.

On my return home my own people also found out, notwithstanding my golden curls and bump of gaiety,[1] that I was not nearly so apt at lessons as Edward or Ellen.[2] My A B C was a burden; I

[1] I have a kind letter that my father wrote me, dated January 1829:—'Yesterday I dined with Mr. Croker at Kensington Palace, where I met Theodore Hook, a great wit, who has the same-shaped forehead that Freddy has. Do you think that Freddy will be a wit, too? I trust not, for it is a great snare,' &c.

I remember Theodore being pointed out to me at a fish banquet at Blackwall. My father once took me to breakfast with Mr. Rogers, an ugly little man, a wrinkled Mæcenas; and Mr. Luttrell was there in a brown coat, also rather little and ugly; and as my father was there too, I suppose there were three of them. Mr. Rogers was calm and kind: neither then nor afterwards did I detect any of that quiet venom for which his particular friends were pleased to give him so much credit.

[2] I see by my father's diary that on July 19, 1828, he took Edward, Ellen, and me to Bruges, to see Aunt Lucy, the nun. We were abroad about eight days. I remember the field of Waterloo, and my immense weariness during the night journeys in the diligence (I had a serious illness after I got home). I was so small that at the English convent they easily passed me through the *guichet*. When the nuns got me on the other side there was no end of kissing and hugging. I remember that the Nun pressed all sorts of parting gifts upon us, and when my father protested that we had no room for more, she said, offering some gift of slenderer dimensions, 'Well, only this; it isn't so big as a bee's knee.' I had never heard the simile before, nor have I since.

read very imperfectly, and could not spell. This inability continues. They also discovered that I was exceedingly spoilt; so I gradually sank into disgrace, my curls were sacrificed, and eventually, on August 19, 1829, I was marched off to a preparatory school on Clapham Common kept by one Miss Griffin. There I was rather miserable—most probably much my own fault. My father says, in a letter to my mother now before me: 'Clapham, April 29, 1829.—Fred, notwithstanding all Miss Griffin's pains and all our remonstrances, is as idle and as reluctant as ever, and cannot read even tolerably, though almost eight. He is now at my side as I write this melancholy report.'

As far as my memory serves me, I have a child's impression that Miss Griffin had all the qualities of a kitchen-poker, *except its occasional warmth*; that her deportment was frigid; and that she had a kick even in her caress, was severely Calvinistic, and had a proper sense of the importance of veracity. At that time the first (the doctrine) was a terror to me, and my preternaturally keen instinct for self-preservation made me regard the last as an impossible virtue. I am more reasonable now.

I remained about a year with Miss Griffin, and was then (1830) sent to Mr. Barnett, of Yateley, in Hampshire, a clergyman who took five or six pupils. There is a passing allusion to this Orbilius of the birch in the fourth, sixth, and ninth stanzas of my lyric, 'The Jester's Moral.'

My brother Edward had been with him; and Henry and Robert Cust, George Windham, and two sons of Sumner, Bishop of Winchester, were my schoolfellows.

I hated, feared, and almost despised Mr. Barnett, but I loved his wife—as far as I had capacity for such a feeling. My heart goes out to her with a tender recollection as I write this. I believe she was a sensible and motherly woman; but she had wretched health; and I think that even she, at last, rather gave me up as a not satisfactory little boy. Old Barnett used to grin at me despitefully as he drew his switch out of his desk. Even in those moments of supreme terror, I remember I was curiously interested in the quantity of gold in his gums.

It is painful to remember, it is impossible to forget, that I used to steal Mrs. Barnett's jams and pickles; I cut off and appropriated the shiny black buttons of Mr. Barnett's ecclesiastical gaiters, made free with his lozenges, and ruined his fishing-tackle. But, be it also remembered, I was not more than nine years old, and he thrashed me unmercifully with the buckle-ends of my own braces. Curiously enough, I remember he wore none; and yet I was very young to be so suspended. All this I recollect with a penitent self-pity.

I had threepence a week pocket-money, but as I smashed a pane of glass a few days after my arrival, and glass was dear in those days, my allowance was stopped to pay for it. I now realise that my grief was aggravated by a vague sense of injustice.

In spite of what the phrenologist had asserted, I had always been rather queer, and morbid, and introspective; but about this time these tendencies had become more apparent. At school, I would get away from my playmates and sit alone, while they jeered at me for doing so, and said I was mad. Poor little wretch! I did not know whether I was mad or not; I only felt I was not such as they were—that I was inferior to them. I was short-sighted, which placed me at a great disadvantage. Even at that time I lived in a little world of my own—the dells and valleys of dreamland, where my blue devils danced very funnily, but in an elfish sort of way. There seemed to be a quiet inner chamber to my being, to which my shrinking spirit retired.

I mention these peculiarities in case hereafter any of my blood, having inherited them, should think too much about them, and so give way to weakness.

Yes, before I was nine years old I had become pretty well acquainted with the raw-head-and-cross-bones feeling. Even then a mystery and a burden oppressed me; my companions seemed phantoms; time, space, everything, was a phantom. And yet I realised my isolation—that I was myself, and could not be any other than myself. I used to wonder—as others have wondered—when everybody had left a room, when the room is empty, what became of that room. Even when one is grown up one cannot help thinking oneself the pivot on which everything turns. Surely, we say, there will be a difference when we slip away: Piccadilly will not be quite so crowded; surely we shall take something with us.

The sense of tears in mortal things and of the transitory nature of everything took, and has ever since kept, possession of me. The Veiled Figure with his reversed torch was a presence, though a fitful one and a shadowy.

It must not be supposed that these ideas passed distinctly through my young mind, but the effect of them was such as I have attempted to describe.

I had never heard of Moschus, but the little child even then would have been able to appreciate the heart-piercing pathos of that passage where the poor heathen contrasts the revival of the woods and fields after seeming death with the sleep of man that knows no waking.

Ah me, the mallows, dead in the gardens drear!
Ah, the green parsley, the thriving tufts of dill!—
These again shall rise, shall live in the coming year.

But we men in our pride, we in wisdom and strength—
We, if once we die, deaf in the womb of earth,
Sleep the sleep that wakes not—sleep of infinite length.

And yet there was a mocking spirit in my sad thoughts. And you, my dear son, or son's son, who may kindly read these pages, must understand that, with all this morbidity and inclination for reverie, I was in some ways an exceptionally lively little boy, interested in many things. The child was father of the man in his appreciation of jest and whim and nonsense, and yet in having an imperfect sense of the ridiculous.

But to return. I remember Mr. Barnett had two horses, called *Dactyl* and *Centum*. I used to think how odd it was to give such senseless names to animals with the same number of feet; but I suppose the names meant more than I knew of. However, I was afraid to ask. I do not think I cared much for the Sumners. Windham was the eldest brother of the present Lord Leconfield; everybody liked Windham. Harry Cust was a daring boy. You will be able to appreciate the tether of his audacity when I tell you that he once made old Barnett an apple-pie bed! I do not remember if he was severely punished for this. I was the youngest of all.

We much affected a wheelwright's shop, with its pigsties and straw beehives—a drunken-looking row; there rusty iron, tin pots, naves of wheels, and ancient litter lay about, also a grindstone; and there was a sawpit, where we hunted the stag-beetle. All these were owned by one Barlow, an inveterate Baptist, whose Christian name was Isaac; he had two sons, Moses and Aaron.[1]

Eight or ten years ago I was staying with Sir Edward Hamley at the Staff College, and we walked over to Yateley. The schoolhouse had been pulled down; modest daisies and buttercups were springing where erst the gaudy Kidderminster had flowered; but still there were the tree-girt meadows, the deeply rutted lanes and abounding hedgerows, the cress-set rivulets where minnows darted, and a hazel copse where millions of primroses grew unmolested. This last was the spot where old Barnett had employed *me* to cut his switches, but where also were sounds and sights still pleasant to remember; for it was there that I used to hear the blackcap warble with sweet but inward melody,

> And thro' the hazels thick, espy
> The hatching throstle's shining eye.

I missed the gipsy encampment and the village pound, but there were the same old footpaths through the same old fields. With difficulty I identified

[1] See my poem, 'The Jester's Moral.'

two neighbouring patches of straw-thatched and whitewashed cottages which lay nestled in little gardens with sweetbriar hedges; and there the frugal bee still improved her hour. While I was looking about me, upon whom should I come but Aaron Barlow himself, still a hale man, but ingloriously mute, and bent with toil. To my young eyes he had seemed oldish half a century before. I think I was a trifle interesting to him. How far more interesting was he to me!

It was curious how that sight of Yateley Common brought back an afternoon of little-boyhood. I had been moulding clay and making little bricks, and after I had put them in the sun to dry I remember I read a chapter of 'Sandford and Merton.' The surrounding landscape, the birds in the near orchard answering each other in their songs, the four Russian sailors in Spitzbergen, the row of little bricks, and my own feelings, all united and mixed, were vivid as if it had been yesterday.

We used to angle for little coarse fish at a neighbouring watermill. This sport was about the only pursuit that brought Mr. Barnett and me pleasantly together. The rod he then brandished had no terrors. I remember the panting pulsing of the machinery, the huge cobwebs made white with floating meal, the dripping wheel, the river banks, willow-fringed, and the leap of the fish.

Sometimes we heard the 'View halloa!' and fell in with Sir John Cope's hounds. Our pets were high-shouldered hawks and lop-eared rabbits, pigeons, and that disappointing little animal, the guinea-pig. Then there was the usual bird-catching and bird-nesting, but I never could make up my mind to rob a bird's nest.

I recall the village shop, kept by one of the churchwardens, where mops, cheese, gunpowder, ribbons, mousetraps, and bullseyes were sold. How well do I remember the little thirteenth-century church—white stone and stucco, and a wooden tower; the high-sided square pew and faded red curtains and cushions; the damp-smelling books of devotion; the music,[1] consisting of one or two preposterous wind-instruments—a concert divided against itself, but nothing could degrade the clear child voices: 'The Lord's my Shepherd, I'll not want.' In the churchyard a sheep or two were nibbling among the ill-kept graves; there were tombstones with uncouthly cut 'Hic jacets' and prophetic 'Resurgams,' milestones on life's highway, slowly passing into green obliteration, and therefore venerable; hard by was a pool where the swift dragon-fly glanced.

Since I left Yateley School the bell of that little

[1] In Church hymns the boldest metaphors of the Hebrew prophets and the most inscrutable dogmas of the Athanasian Creed are squeezed into the strait-waistcoat of English rhythm, to make them go glibly to such strains as 'Coventry New.'

church has tolled for more than one generation of peasant worshippers who had gone on patiently toiling

> Till the bell, which not in vain
> Had summoned them to weekly prayer,
> Called them, one by one, again
> To the church, and left them there.

I am sure Mr. Barnett was an absurd man, and that his ignorance was encyclopædic. Years afterwards, when I may have been about eighteen, he came to see my father at Greenwich, and I was amazed to think the person before me, old and *gauche*, and with a propitiatory grin, was that formidable savage who had once exercised so terrible a sway. We talked of past days, and as he was rather jocose, I ventured to say I still felt the tingling of the hazel switches. The miserable creature pretended that he had no recollection of the circumstance. 'It is strange, my dear young friend, but I have entirely forgotten it.' 'Perhaps *you* have forgotten it, sir; but then, as somebody else said, "you were at the other end of the switch."'[1] I never beheld him after that day. When he walked out of my father's library he walked out of my life.

From Mr. Barnett's I was sent, on March 21, 1831, to Mr. Elwell, of Clapham Common, not a

[1] Perhaps my child's imagination may have distorted some of the facts stated in these last pages. Perhaps—but who cares?

stone's-throw from the unloved Miss Griffin. Elwell was a kindly Calvinist; he wore a queer peruke, and in consequence was always called 'Old Rum Wig.' We were ill looked after, his wife seeming to think that salvation depended more upon predestination than soap. Dean Bradley, my schoolfellow there, tells me that Elwell subsided into the Irvingite faith and bankruptcy; that he migrated somewhere, and lived and died.

Elwell, like Miss Griffin, was the *protégé* of a Mrs. Shore,[1] who also dwelt at Clapham and domineered. His school consisted of some fourteen or more boys; and among them was the Dean of Westminster, as I have just said; also George Grove (now Sir George, an authority in music), and two sons of Sir Andrew Agnew. It was at Elwell's that I began to care for athletic games. We played at prisoner's base[2] in the lean strip of a playground at the rear of the house. I was considered formidable in a football scrimmage against the wall; and there was cricket once a week on the Common.

It was there that I bought 'parliament,' 'tom-trot,' and 'ginger-pop' of an old warrior with one eye and a *drôle de nez*, whose barrow of 'goodies' was

[1] See p. 42.

[2] A pastime referred to by Shakespeare, Spenser, Drayton, and Dekker.

our basis of such supplies. I sometimes think my chronic indigestion may have come out of that barrow!

As time went on I showed a further aptitude for games, and consequently became a more self-respecting person, and began to get quit of, or at any rate to control, my morbid feelings.

I had not been a year at Elwell's before my father and mother grew dissatisfied with my progress—as well they might be—and sent me (in 1832) to the Rev. Mr. Wight, vicar of Drearyboro', who advertised in 'The Record,' a Low Church newspaper. I have rather a misty recollection of this period of my life. However, I well remember the deadly temperature of my bedroom—freezing and cheerless—the thin blankets and scant white dimity hangings, the wintry sheets—

> The blankets were thin, and the sheets they were sma'—

and the water that turned to ice in my jug. In those days there were no hot-water cans. Hot water as a cosmetic rarely came my way. Talk of one's golden youth! At Wight's, as at Barnett's, I was a wretched little boy—shivery and chilblainy.

At this point I cannot help observing how little my father and mother seem to have known of the people to whose care they confided me. Mr. and Mrs. Wight they never even saw; and small blame to them, for they had gone to Italy for my father's health. It is different now—at least, my own experience makes me think so, and feel strongly on the subject. Only the other day I was describing to a friend the sort of qualities *I* thought absolutely necessary in a tutor for her son, and she replied pretty much in the words of Madame de Staël: 'Ma chère, si je trouve votre homme je l'épouse.'

Mr. Wight was a simple and kindly little man. My only recollection of Mrs. Wight is that she was remote from beautiful, and not quite aware of the distance, and that she had a rat-trap of a temper—at least, so said my fellow-pupil. But now I think on it, she may have suffered from bad health, and therefore was to be pitied.

I found Drearyboro' a very dull place—

> A little sleepy, lazy town,
> Begirt by daisied mead and down.

I knew no boys of my own age, and my sole recreation was gardening, for which I had no vocation. I used to sow pumpkin-seeds, and almost immediately afterwards dig them up, to see how they were getting on—and yet somehow they *did* get on.

Not very far from the house was a curiously shaped grass field, intersected by a stream and enclosed by high hedges and a little copse. It was called 'The Half-acre.' This field stimulated the fancy. I think if I could see it now I should recognise that it had a mediæval look. I used to fancy that perhaps some day or other I might go there and find St. George still fighting the dragon.

My dissipation was an occasional clerical meeting, where Biblical prophecy and the Apocalyptic number 666 were frantically discussed by a knot of what I now think must have been presumptuous jackasses, and in a way that then occasioned me cold, clammy terrors. I still suffer from their sinister predictions.

I did not carry away much classical accomplishment from Drearyboro'; but it was there that I mastered certain pedigrees in Genesis and the names of the mountains and rivers. There also I made my first acquaintance with the cuts in 'Tom Hood's Comic Annual;' they were then issued in sheets, and were indeed a revelation. I have always been true to this my early love.

There was only one other pupil. He was seven years older than myself, but I remember we both were desperately in love with the same lady—Miss Eleanor Orkney, a beautiful maiden, whose father lived in the town. I recall my high-flown admiration and reverence for her, and the shock of first seeing my schoolfellow kiss her. I wrung my hands. I am wiser now. By Jupiter! she was lovely. But think kindly of the infatuated young man, my rival; for though he patiently endured any amount of ill-treatment from that girl, she said he was a schoolboy—and so they parted. He afterwards came out as a Wrangler, and is now a dean. What has become of the young lady? If she is not dead, she is an old, old woman. The fuller recollection of these philanderings comes back to me as I write—*especially the kissing of Nell!*

I have said that as a child I suffered from religious tremors. It was about this time that I was more acutely persecuted by them. Thanks to early teaching and a constitutional melancholy, I was deeply impressed with a sense of my extreme wickedness and utterly lost condition, and as, alack! I have never done anything to justify a change of opinion, the impression has never left me, and I fear never will. The Biblical discussions at Wight's, founded on the works of 'blind' Frere, H. Raikes, Cooper ('Crisis'), &c., made my hair stand on end. It was the same, and yet different, with the creed and controversy of St. Athanasius, which once set Christians cutting each other's throats over a diphthong. I listened and trembled, but still I rejoiced in the resonant rhetoric and lyric splendour. The Christian religion as usually taught is a cruel religion.

> A moment's time, a narrow space,
> Divides me from that heavenly place,
> Or shuts me up in hell.

Surely this is too bad of Dr. Wesley. I left Wight's on December 20, 1832.

In the summer of 1888 I revisited Drearyboro', and, under the guidance of Mr. Good, a leading tradesman in the town, paid a visit to the fine church, and afterwards to the homely vicarage, where, nearly sixty years before, I had lived as Mr. Wight's pupil. I bought a photograph (now at Newhaven Court) which shows the lattice of my little bedroom, and I peered in at the window of the sitting-room, where I had conned my tasks. I also called on John Linton, the church clerk, who had blacked the Vicar's boots for forty years, and as a boy had worked in his garden—now a neglected precinct, full of burdocks, rubbish, and broken bottles. Dogs and fowls had established rights of way through the fences. Linton was six years my senior, kindly and pious. He remembered me as a thin-faced, delicate-looking boy, and he also well remembered my schoolfellow's flirtation, and told me its issue. Mr. Good spoke most highly of Mr. Wight, but he was less enthusiastic about Mrs. Wight. He pointed out to me a curious and interesting epitaph on the Vicar's monumental tablet, which the worthy man had composed for himself, and which was highly significant of his great humility:—

'A SINNER SAVED BY GRACE.'

I think Mr. Wight must have been something like Parson Adams; I am sure he had all his simplicity. When I got back to London I wrote a detailed account of my visit, but unfortunately it was lost, and this meagre paragraph is all I can give; however, the perfume of that day remains with me yet.

October, 1894.—I have again been at Dreary-boro', and have now seen the interior of the old vicarage. I measured my little bedroom; it is only about 9 feet by 11 feet 6 inches, and 6 feet 2 inches high, and it has no fireplace.

In January, 1833, Edward and I were sent to a huge unregenerate school at Greenwich. It had been a famous school. It was kept by Dr. Burney; he was the grandson of Johnson's friend.[1] I stayed there about a year. It was a bullying school.

> I have been kicked till I know not whether
> A shoe's of neat's or Spanish leather,

as may be gathered from the following more or less fanciful sketch, extracted from 'Patchwork,' of 'The Bully:'—

[1] Anthony and John Stirling; Mendizabal, a son of the Spanish Jew-patriot who made his fortune in London and became Prime Minister in Spain in 1835, and George Henry Lewes, were educated at this school. Lewes must have left just before I joined.

'At old Bliss's there was a big foul-mouthed bully, who tyrannised over the other boys; he held the lesser fellows in such abject subjection that long before the arrival of their plum-cakes they had been heavily mortgaged to propitiate him. A land pirate of a shameless type, he preyed upon our toffy and our tarts, confiscated our neckerchiefs and knives; he even made free with our pocket-money. I can see him now, pale and fat, with small eyes, a broad nose and face, and a poisonous smile. He would tear along the centre of the long dormitory when the younger ones were tucked up and asleep, and give a great yell as he dragged the bedclothes off each boy as he passed.

'There was no wickedness of which this young monster was not capable; and anybody might have supposed him to be utterly callous—incapacitated for remorse. Even now I hardly dare to say what I think of him, lest he should still be alive, and this should meet his eye! But, with all his beardless bluster, he was a coward: he would tempt other boys to mischief for which he himself had not the pluck. It was he who incited Wentworth to convey the bumble-bees to church in a whitey-brown paper bag, and then let them out, one by one, during the sermon.

'There was an old professor of pothooks and hangers (I call him old, but really I do not the least know whether he was thirty-six or sixty-three) whom we branded as "Gums" (like Mr. Barnett, he had an obnoxious way of grinning when he called us up to be punished). This usher was understood to be a monster of depravity and cunning, and he was a mysterious animal. I now think that probably the poor man was deadly poor, for there were the remains of thick worsted bell-ropes in his bedchamber, and grinning gossip whispered that when he hadn't any tobacco, he would cut off a piece of bell-rope, put it into his pipe, and smoke it. His position was shrouded in mystery; he remained, high and dry, up at the schoolhouse during the holidays. The only circumstance that I know to the credit of the Bully was, that he bought some mustard and cress (with another boy's money), and the day before the school broke up sowed "Gums" in gigantic characters under Gums's bedroom window. He would not have ventured to do this if it had not been his last half at the school. Yes, the Bully was an arrant coward. And now I will tell you why I have wasted so much of your time upon him. Remember, dear children, I am about to deal with a very serious subject, and I do so with all reverence. Pray remember this.

'There was a certain small apartment at the corner of the schoolroom which from time immemorial had been called the "Powdering Room," where the biggest boys washed their hands and brushed their hair. It was a darkish room, and one afternoon, when as a fag I chanced to be alone there, blacking boots, the Bully came up abruptly, and said, with a fright in his face: "I say, you fellow; look here, I say; I hope I haven't sinned against the Holy Ghost." This was all he said. He then grasped me by the arm—which had a Wellington boot on it—glared at me, and as I was taken aback, and did not instantly reply, gave me a vicious kick, which sent me flying.

'I afterwards found that there were a good many little boys to whom the poor wretch had, at some time or other, put the same question (and probably given the same kick), trying as it were to get comfort out of each. His name was ——'

It is remarkable how systems have changed as regards the treatment of boys. Burney's was not a cheap school: while there I cost my father 100*l*. a year—a large sum of money fifty years ago—and yet we were ill looked after and poorly fed. There were no cubicles; some of us slept two in a bed. We had tea, or milk and water, and huge hunches of bread spread with butter, for breakfast; for dinner, rice pudding and currant dumpling ('stickjaw') on alternate days, served on an unsavoury-smelling pewter platter, and before our meat; then our beef or mutton, served on the same plate as the pudding, and washed down with inferior 'swipes' in tin mugs; all this inaugurated by a lengthy Latin thanksgiving that could hardly be described as a transient act of adoration. The food was coarse in quality, and the washing arrangements, to make the best of them, were unpleasant. The system of punishment was a mistaken one: not much caning, and less flogging; but it was very often, 'Locker, copy out the Ten Commandments ten times,' or, for a neglected lesson or word forgotten, to write out, perhaps during the best part of a summer afternoon, that particular word a thousand times. I was not a royal captive, but, like Arthur, I could have said, 'So I were out of prison, and kept sheep, I should be as merry as the day is long.'

Edward stayed only a few weeks, and then left for Addiscombe, and as I made little or no progress in book-learning, and the school threatened to come to an end, I was sent on January 6, 1834, to a proprietary (day) school at Blackheath. There I remained two years, and had an inglorious time of it, nearly always at the bottom of my class, and often tearful about my tasks; rarely getting the *bene*, never the *ultra perbene*. There was a good deal of learning by heart, which was simply heartbreaking. What a misfortune it is that tuition cannot be suited to the peculiar capacities and tastes of children! The only thing that I did pretty well was original poetry. A subject was given us, and by a certain day we produced a poem. My mother wrote most of mine!

When I first went to this school I was under a Mr. Ellison, a rufous fellow, *grosso, rosso, e furioso*; very short, with an even shorter temper; as poor as Job, but not as patient, for sometimes, after he had caned one or two boys in the class, he would become drunk with fury, and hit out right and left till, being very fat, he was obliged to sit down, panting and exhausted, much to the enjoyment of the languid Tennant, the under-masters, and the boys of all the other classes. Mr. Hallam, the historian, recommended this school to my father because Tennant, his son Arthur's friend, had been appointed the principal.

The City and Old Times

It was about this time that my father and mother began to despair of me. What was the use of being clever at fives and fairly good at cricket, if I spelt abominably and could not construe a line of Latin? All their Oxford or Cambridge, Church or Bar aspirations and intentions, were abandoned. With some difficulty, and after considerable delay, on

September 18, 1837, they obtained for me a high stool as junior clerk in a colonial broker's [1] counting-house in Mincing Lane, where it seemed to be understood that I was, not speedily perhaps, but solidly and assuredly, to achieve my fortune. I did not receive pay; I was to 'learn the business.' I had to go to the Custom House and docks, was initiated into the mystery of invoices, warrants, and bills of lading. It was part of my duty to attend 'rummage' sales. Armed with a catalogue, I made a pretence of valuing cotton, rice, turmeric, indigo, shellac, and cochineal, to say nothing of salt water, damaged sugars, &c.; but in reality I learnt next to nothing. The recollection of it all is disagreeable and humiliating, for I turned out as inefficient at commerce as at everything else; besides, it was there that I gradually developed an unpleasant turn for quizzing, *l'esprit moqueur*—in itself fatal to success in life—together with certain

[1] What trivial circumstances linger in the memory, to the exclusion of that which is important! It is nigh fifty years since I paid this worthy gentleman a visit, and the following is all that I remember of it. I played at billiards with his boys, and while so engaged we were summoned to family prayer. The youngest son and I, with great reluctance, obeyed the mandate, the game the while being continued by the elder ones. The solemn function was held in a room immediately adjoining, and while we were on our knees we heard the delightful click of the shining ivory balls. I recall that after a very rapid click, click, my little fellow-worshipper turned, and whispered to me, eagerly but gravely: 'I think *that* was a cannon.' *Basta!* this is poor rubbish to set down here.

would-be-fine-gentlemen proclivities. I gave a good deal of my mind to the cut of my trousers. I was pensively sarcastic; but my wit was empty—a sneeze of the mind. I made fun of the clerks, and even of the kindly partners—and a duffer had no right to do that. Small wonder that my father was advised to remove me, which he did in December, 1838.

I have a lively recollection of Mincing Lane, for it was there that my real education began. It was a new world: every fresh acquaintance an event and every incident a discovery. The clerks were like clerks in all offices: there was the literary, and there was the sporting; there was the facetious and the ambitious, the clerk with a theatrical turn, and the unsatisfactory clerk. This last was a profligate dunce, a 'Trebonius,' who spelt sugar with two *g's*, and about whom there was a mystery. He used to make excursions to 'the West End,' and to us City birds this stepping westward seemed to be a kind of heavenly destiny. He was understood to spend the bulk of his leisure in places where, I fear, impropriety met with but slight discouragement. In fact he enjoyed the reputation of having run a-mok through every one of the Ten Commandments, which alone made him interesting. Lastly, there was the industrious clerk, whose writing was 'copper-plate.' He was curiously dexterous: he could design and execute a 'spread-eagle' composed entirely of pen-flourishes. He was specially interested in me because my name was *not* Cocker. The only clerk whom I can remember by name was Mr. Kindred, a valuable clerk: 'his head was an anthill of units and tens,' and his ears were stopped with cotton not of the finest quality! Mr. Kindred soon left us, for he had started a business for umbrellas. He owned the two large establishments dealing in those useful articles in Regent Street and Burlington Arcade, as you may still see by the trade legend over the windows. Mr. Kindred was very kind to me, and in return I tormented him by practical joking. I remember filling his umbrella (his own, not a portion of his stock-in-trade) with foolscap torn quite small, arranged in such a way that, when he afterwards opened it in the street, the paper descended in a white shower over his, at that moment, uncalculating head. Mr. Kindred had a thoroughly domestic bias, was uxorious withal. He made me the recipient of the most curious confidences. I can still call to mind his pale face, depressed and half-strangled manner, and rather superfine vocabulary.

Kindred is gone. He died quite lately; but, 'obedient to the Heavenly Will, his wife keeps on the business still.' Poor Mr. Kindred! I wonder, while you were yet alive, whether you ever thought of the F. L. of those days, an F. L. of whom I am ashamed.

From June 13th to 19th, 1840, Ellen and I joined the Hon. W. Cust, a Commissioner of Customs, and his family, old friends, in a cruise, in the Custom House cutter 'Vigilant,'[1] to the coast of France and Belgium, where I was very sea-sick. Between August 13 and October 14 of the same year I made a tour, partly walking, in France, Switzerland, and Italy, with John Templer, the friend and biographer of Rajah Brooke. I often met the Rajah. He wrote poetry, and could tweedle a guitar to songs of his own composing. I think he must have been very accomplished.

Times have mightily changed during the last sixty years. When I was preparing to enter the world, Napoleon was on the point of quitting it. The Act for the abolition of wager of battle had hardly come into force, and the 'Bride of Lammermoor' and the 'Isle of Greece' were not published. When I was a child Canning was at the Foreign Office; society still quoted Smollett; the prince-bishop of Durham had emoluments equivalent to 30,000*l.* a year; the right divine of kings was still an article of faith; the quartern loaf was con-

[1] In 1842 Thomas Carlyle made such a cruise, in the same craft, and possibly with a similar result.

sidered cheap at a shilling, and gas had not penetrated to Grosvenor Square.

As a very little boy I have played 'puss-in-the-corner' with that great sea-captain, Lord Exmouth. As a boy of nine, or even younger, I often heard my father tell of his interview with Buonaparte at Porto Ferrajo in 1814: of the strange nervous tremor that assailed him when he realised that in one minute more (only a curtain then separated them) he should be face to face with the most extraordinary human being that the world had ever seen. My father would graphically describe Buonaparte's appearance and bearing: his green and red uniform, his boots and spurs, his silver cross of the Legion of Honour, his pleasing voice, his snuff-box, his equine laugh, the alert but tranquil serenity of his demeanour, and his beautiful smile.[1]

Sir William Beatty, who was head of the medical staff at Greenwich Hospital, had been surgeon of the 'Victory' at Trafalgar, and had attended Nelson in his last hour. He carried a snuff-box in which he preserved the musket-ball that had given the hero his death-wound. I remember his carefully placing this unshapen piece of lead on my little outstretched palm. If my child's recollection is not at fault, there was a minute shining

[1] See p. 24.

thread of gold (torn from Nelson's epaulette) embedded in it.

I remember the haunting personality of Paganini and the diabolic laughter of his fiddle. I can recall Maria Malibran, beautiful in sandals and gigot sleeves, and my boyish enthusiasm about her, and her song:

> Thro' the wood, thro' the wood, follow and find me ;
>   Search every hollow, and dingle, and dell.
> I leave not the print of a footstep behind me,
>   So they that would see me must seek for me well.

When she died I bought one of the many prints that were exhibited in the shop-windows, and still have it. I only once heard her at the Opera, and that was as Amina. I have trembled under the eloquence of Edward Irving, the preacher, and respectfully admired the renowned Fuller Pilch as, in a tall hat, he 'played forward' to Lillywhite bowling,[1] also in a very tall hat!

London then-a-days, health and purse permitting, must have been a delightful little place to drive, dine, flirt, dance, and follow the fashions in; but there were few amusements for people of small means or young people. Nowadays the stateliness of high life may have declined, but refining

[1] 'I bowl the best ball of any man in England, and Mr. Harenc (the Harrovian who played for Kent) the next' (Lillywhite *loquitur*).

enjoyments have been enormously multiplied and diffused. I can just remember going to see Chunee, the elephant, at Cross's Menagerie, Exeter Change: he went mad with tusk-ache, and was shot by a file of soldiers under pathetic circumstances; his skeleton and diseased tusk may still be seen in the museum of the Royal College of Surgeons. Long after this came the Adelaide Gallery, its electrical eel and talking canary-bird, and the few and far between *fêtes* at Chiswick.

As I grew older I was taken to Vauxhall—to see Madame Sequi, the rope-dancer—which by that time had degenerated into rather a ghastly hole. Sham glowworms (variegated lamps) twinkled in painted canvas *bosquets*; the alcoves were altogether out of the question for Daphnis and Chloe; and there was a wizard with a sham beard and an Irish accent so racy that it seemed hardly genuine. There was usually a good deal of rain and slop, which put out the fireworks and damped the fun. There were bell-hatted, high-collared dandies, and frank and frisky shepherdesses. The orchestra wore cocked hats; there was the renowned Mrs. Bland, and a clown with his 'Houp la.'

I remember a balloon ascent there—my somehow getting into the inner circle of spectators, and being accosted by a very tall, rather stout gentleman, buttoned up in a frock-coat. He made one or two good-natured and appropriate remarks, as if he were interested in me, and then walked away. On this a bystander said, 'Do you know who that was? That was the great Mr. Gully.' This Gully was no other than the notorious John Gully, pugilist, publican, hell-keeper, and much-respected member of Parliament for Pontefract ('breaking the bridges of so many noses'), who seems to have succeeded in everything he undertook. He succeeded in pleasing me!

I remember the first omnibus (Shillibeer's) making its first trip between Greenwich and London; also the 'Sir William Joliffe' and the 'Sir Joseph Banks,' nearly the first steamers on the Thames. We were often rowed to London by 'Redriffe' in a wherry, and we always talked of 'shooting' London Bridge.[1]

I can call to mind certain poor Italians who carried heavy trays of plaster-casts on their heads. Also 'buy-a-broom' girls from Bavaria, in white mobcaps, tight bodices, and spreading pleated petticoats—perilously short—and well-darned stockings; they had little English, and even less soap, and offered you little brooms made of osier-sticks shaved in a peculiar fashion; they tripped little jigging dances to little jodling ditties.

Madame Vestris, and also Mrs. Waylett, each in

[1] See 'Travelling Fifty Years ago.'

her hour, sang a very popular ballad called 'Buy a broom; From Deutschland I come with my light wares all laden.' Such tuneful birds with such saucy graces were not to be heard from every bush.

I summon from the inner recesses of my memory the sensation caused by the Thurtell-Weare murder, for, though it happened as early as 1824, it was long talked about and shuddered over. Thurtell decoyed Weare (a worthless fellow) into the country, drove him down to Elstree in his gig ('gigmanity'), and there murdered him under circumstances of great horror and peculiar atrocity. As he passed Tyburn Gate he bought a sack, in which he intended to put Weare after he had killed him. Weare, cutting his jokes, sat comfortably on the sack as they drove. Thus, as we know, the object of the purchase was fulfilled.

I remember hearing Mr. J. W. Croker give my father and his guests a detailed account of this murder, and he quoted a Catnach ballad which ran:

They cut his throat from ear to ear,
His brains they battered in;
His name was Mr. William Weare,
And he lived in Lyons Inn.

Years afterwards I heard that this was written by Croker. It is said that Croker wrote the review of 'Endymion' in the 'Quarterly.' I would rather have written the ballad.

Wondrous social and other changes will have taken place when my great-grandson writes *his* recollections. He will then tell you that the Archbishop of Canterbury may occasionally be seen in Piccadilly on the roof of an omnibus; that Devonshire House, kept by one Cavendish, has been converted into a dry-goods store on the American plan—indeed, so completely will our fine old feudal system have been uprooted, that a tramway will actually have taken possession of patrician Pall Mall and the classic ascent of St. James's!

The change will soon be here; indeed, it is already at our doors. Only a few days ago I saw a deplorably dressed animal, diamonds and emeralds stuck in his *postiche* cravat, lounge up the steps of White's Club, and take his seat in the bow-window—the bow-window, mind you, of the Somersets, the Stanhopes, and the Fanes; then I recognised that he was my stockbroker, and in acknowledgment of my obeisance he gave me a calculated and reserved bow.

They now, no longer kept in awe
By Fashion's judges, or her law,
Sit in the window at their ease—
Sit with what looks and clothes they please.

The Admiralty

Although my father had always been a staunch Tory, he had influence with the Whiggish Lord Minto, son of his old friend, the Governor-General of India. In 1841 Lord Minto was First Lord of the Admiralty. Despite of politics, he gave me, on March 30, a temporary clerkship in Somerset House. This appointment was of small importance, for my chief occupation was the examination of Her Majesty's ships' muster-books under the authority of Mr. Stephen Garter, the senior clerk, a gentleman old and grizzled, gaunt, and hungry-looking as a wolf in winter; but he was not really formidable, and he soon took a fancy to me. He lived somewhere about Poplar, in a queer little detached cottage, bolted and barred, for he was suspicious of burglars; it was a tenement which the clerical imagination magnified into a grinning fortress. Mr. Garter always walked to and from the office. If he chanced to be late, he explained that, for the sake of other pedestrians, he had been detained on his way kicking pieces of orange-peel off the pavement and into the gutter.

The eccentric philanthropist did not make himself generally agreeable but he was always kind to me. However, I fear I was not always grateful. During the last few weeks of my service with him nearly the whole of my clerical work was the copying out of a long, long statement of his official service and clerical grievances—his defence when his enemies should openly assail him. He would stay on at the office till eight at night, 'religiously toiling,' or, like Ajax in his tent, raging against those who were preparing to attack him. He was very eccentric.

Poor Mr. Garter has been dead nigh half a century. I did not see him for the last two or three years of his life, but he had a friend who was at his bedside the day before he died. Stricken down with paralysis, the stern old man lay utterly helpless, unable to speak, or even to move, but conscious. There was an expression in his eyes as if he desired something. His friend pressed his hand, and then tears came into the old man's eyes—tears that he could not wipe away.

I and my fellow-clerks were ordinary fellows enough, and we recognised it. We were poor, some of us with a gloveless, an unbrushed poverty. Our messenger was a very tall, burly, and blustering fellow, called Joe Webb, who had been butler to an Under-Secretary of State, and who, naturally enough, despised us. We had no very exalted opinion of ourselves, *nous autres*; but *he* thoroughly despised us. Indeed, he made no secret of his contempt, for, as he walked leisurely along the passages to answer the thrice-pulled bell—he came unlooked for if he came at all—he was heard to bawl out, 'Ring away, my hearties, ring away; you've no bells to ring at home!' This Joe reminds me of the other Joe:—

> Would you see a man that's slow,
> Come and see our footman Joe.
> Would you his full merit know,
> Ring the bell—and wait for Joe!

Also of the impertinent serving-man who put his head in at the coffee-room door, and said, 'The more you rings, the more I won't come.' Joe Webb was not always insolent, but he was very often on the edge of it.

I made one or two friendships at the Pursery Office. John Bowles was a very pleasant young fellow. On looking back, it seems to me that he must have been refined and cultivated and good. He had a remarkable genius for music: he would accompany his sister on the pianoforte without seeing the score, simply guessing the harmonies; and after he had once gone through a piece he could play the whole, melody and harmony together, from memory. This seems incredible. He understood counterpoint. Bowles did not stay with us long. He joined the army in India, and died there, tragically, as I fear—a brief career. He introduced me to his beloved sister, whom Horatio Smith admired; or it may be her name suggested a rhyming compliment, for he had written something about 'the Graces.' and 'pretty faces,' but that 'whoever might happen to talk to Miss Bowles, would find that young ladies had also got souls.' He gave me an antique posy-ring, plain gold, '*Amor unit omnia*,' which I valued, but have lost. I have long survived poor Bowles, but I have not survived my affection for his memory; and I have not lost my belief in the motto on his ring. Those who knew him living, must deplore him dead.

Bowles was an interesting man. I have known men far more able than Bowles, but not half so interesting, which is quite a different thing.

There was another clerk who had a sort of reputation on his own little patch—a Pimlico 'Narcissus,' who gave himself ridiculous airs. He carried his nose in the air, as if he despised his official surroundings. Nature hath formed strange fellows in her time. This fellow's eccentricities beggar belief. He used to manufacture his own blacking, cut his own hair, and singe the ends; and he wore socks that were divided at the toes, like a glove. I never met him outside the office. Yes, once, years afterwards, I saw him in quite another sort of a place. I happened to be at St. Peter's with M. Jean-Jacques Ampère, and we beheld my quondam colleague stalking across the great nave, striking the stars with his sublime head; he had grown fat, was as bald as a peg-top, and evidently regarded the Basilica as a rather inferior Pursery Office. More than twenty years ago there was a fire at his lodgings, and he nearly lost his life in the vain endeavour to save a very precious umbrella and his favourite walking-sticks—a misfortune that calls to mind the fate of John Fletcher.[1]

At this time I was hopeless about my prospects. They were at their darkest. I disliked the department, but had begun to despair of ever escaping from it. However, 'there is a budding morrow in midnight,' and at last one day, on November 12, 1842—a memorable day—much to my joy, and, I may say, to my surprise, by the kindness of Lord Haddington I was transferred to the Admiralty, Whitehall, and placed as a junior in his private office, in constant communication with him and his private secretary. It was a precious and unexpected emancipation. I was a little like the horse that Homer described as breaking its tether and galloping, with loud neighings, to join the wild herd on the plain, for I rejoiced in my sudden freedom, and exaggerated the delights of my new

[1] He died of the plague. Aubrey says: 'Mr. Fletcher staying for a suit of cloathes before he retired into the country, death stopt his journey.'

surroundings. It was about this time, too, that I developed a faculty for making verses, quite independently of my mother's aid, and now and again I ventured to send such productions to Lord Haddington, which delighted him. Let me indulge myself in the remembrance of this good old man. I can see him now as I saw him on one occasion when, with a happy smile on his kind face, he was walking leisurely across the Parade at the back of the Admiralty to join a Cabinet Council, and I knew that at the moment he had William Peel's captain's commission in his pocket. Peel's father, Sir Robert, was then Prime Minister. I may add that William Peel had a passionate patriotism, a chivalrous daring, and an audacity of genius worthy of my grandfather's friend, Lord Nelson.

During the time I was in Lord Haddington's office, where his patronage was arranged, the list of the Navy was very much overcrowded. There were mates rising forty years, nay, fifty; and lieutenants, poor fellows! who would never see sixty-five again. Naturally these men were very much dissatisfied, and were constantly pleading for recognition, promotion, or employment; but as there were next to no vacancies, we could only give them a stereotyped reply. Indeed, many of them had grown so rusty that they were quite unfit for active service afloat. Among the most persevering, and I should think the rustiest, was a certain Lieutenant William Chesson. Regularly, once a week, this poor fellow wrote to Lord Haddington an official letter, which at last became an official joke. With Lord Haddington, as with all your true humorists, a small jest went a good long way. The dear old boy used to carefully refold these eloquent documents, and write 'Pressing,' or 'Immediate,' or both, on the outside, or 'This is important,' or 'Let me see Mr. Locker *at once* about this,' &c. On the strength of these notes, one day I wrote Lord Haddington a rhyming epistle, supposed to come from that oxidized and irrepressible mariner, which sent his Lordship into ecstasies. As far as I can remember it ran as follows :—

TO THE EARL OF HADDINGTON, K.T., &c.

I humbly beg but once again, Right Honourable Lord,
To crave your grace, and place my case before you and the Board.
Your Lordship knows I've written prose, but here's a rhyming fit,
And though it is a verse to you, don't be averse to it.

Your Lordship knows my griefs and woes—that I commenced the service
In Captain Noah's bark (the Ark)—I ended it with Jervis (St. Vincent);
I've seen blood spilled and people killed, but none can dare to say
That Billy Chesson ever ran, or tried to run, away.

Your answers to my humble prayers, my Lord, are always worded
Most cautiously. They "own receipt," and say "you are recorded;
To be considered, borne in mind—with those already noted—
As vacancies occur, in course, by officers promoted."

Excuse my lay; I beg to say it is not to annoy meant;
But if, my Lord, you can't reward, please give me some employment.
I'll serve your Lordship whilst aboard-ship with all my best endeavour,
And never more presume to bore your Lordship—no, not never.

It is my fate to have a mate and thirteen little Chessons;
Their cost, my Lord, for bed and board my income daily lessens;
So look with pity on my ditty, or William Chesson may
Be often found, in duty bound, to ever humbly pray.'

Lord Haddington was a high-bred gentleman of the old school; he was very courteous and kindly. He had been Canning's friend. He was an old man, and has been dead these many years—perhaps he is now forgotten.

'But I'll remember thee, Glencairn,
And a' that thou hast done for me.'

The fact of my having been appointed to Lord Haddington's private office, and afterwards selected to be deputy reader and précis writer, and without any serious catastrophe following, makes me suppose I must somehow have shown a slight departmental capacity; at any rate, I like to think so. I was many years in the Admiralty: my service extended through the reign of three successive chief clerks. It is not necessary to record their names; they were best known by their official sobriquets of 'Barabbas,' 'Judas,' and 'Ananias.' Chief clerks are usually detested by their juniors, especially graceless juniors; and, justly or not, each of these was execrated in turn. I doubt not but that they were thoroughly worthy men and valuable public servants; still, there was an impression, not reasoned out, that their nicknames were altogether appropriate.

One of the seniors at the Admiralty, whom I will call Hogan, was a festive but stupid fellow. To borrow one of his own homely similes, he had no more care for poetry, or literature generally, than 'a cow has for a clean shirt,' and he had no ear for music, though any amount of length of that organ for his asinine indulgences. Hogan had known Tom Campbell; they had often met at a dining-club—the Crown, called in ridicule the 'Five-shilling Club,' in Regent Street. He told me that Tom had a weak head, and would sometimes take too much wine; that on one occasion, after dinner, Campbell rose from his chair, and staggered towards the door; there were some providential pillars that supported the roof of the dining-room, and, having reached these with difficulty, he clung to one of them desperately, fearing to go farther, and afraid to return—and that he remained there! 'And,' said I, who worshipped Campbell with all a young verseman's enthusiasm, 'what did *you* do?' 'Oh!' says Hogan, 'we left him where he was, but every now and again, you know, we would flick a walnut at him!' He also told me—and this was interesting—

that Campbell, who was a fastidious writer, once took a six-mile walk to his printer (and six back again) to see a comma changed into a semicolon.

The first Lord Lytton had never met Campbell—had always avoided him, understanding that he was tiresome ; but one day, meeting him at the house of a friend, he found him extraordinarily humorous.

Tom rehearsed to him a highly dramatic, farcical, and outrageous dialogue, in which Tom's mortal enemy, Longman, the Potentate of Paternoster Row, was interviewed as to the copyright of the Sacred Writings ; the end of it all was that Longman, though greedy for a bargain, made up his terrestrial mind to have nothing on earth to do with the work in question.

Campbell, when he did himself justice, is known to have been an interesting converser : he rarely left you without having made some observation that was singularly suggestive, and which haunted the memory. Let us remember that it was Campbell who said—

> To live in hearts we leave behind
> Is not to die.

But the graceless Hogan kenned nothing of this ; he was only able to tell me that Campbell was a feeble little fellow, that he spoke with a broad Scottish accent, that he wore a wig. Poor Campbell! Poor Hogan! Hogan knew even less about

Campbell than Crabbe appeared to Moore to have known about Burke.

We knew Albert Smith. I remember dining with Dwarris, in Bolton Street, to meet Smith and the two Alfreds, d'Orsay and Mandeville. We had wines of the choicest *cru*, and a *plat* of which Dwarris was reasonably proud, and of which d'Orsay approved. D'Orsay (an Alcibiades of not really such very high life), as far as my recollection serves me, was quite simple and natural, and talked his broken English to 'Smeeth' and the rest of us very prettily. After dinner Albert Smith gave us that excellent legend, 'My Lord Tomnoddy;' he sang it very well. Mandeville has a sort of wit—the *à-propos* of the moment; he is a capital mimic. He used to personate the great Duke of Wellington, and talk like him, in spite of his stammer.

To realise its primitive condition, you must know that when I first joined the Admiralty it had no electric telegraph; there were only semaphores to the Ports—small structures built on an elevation, out of which sprang a mast with movable arms. These were clumsy and imperfect means of communication, for at night and in misty weather they were useless; however, the semaphores are sweet in my memory, for do not they recall the worthy naval officer who directed their working?

Lieutenant Squib, R.N., was tall and thin,

elderly and brush-headed, with a long nose, sparkling eyes, shaven face, and very bushy eyebrows, which projected like the antennæ of some insect. He always wore navy-blue, and a tall hat with a staring nap. Lieutenant Squib had a joyous aspect and the temperament of a boon companion, indigent but content, with a halcyon impecuniosity, the luck on which he ought to have been down (but was not) being the natural consequence of slender pay and a quiverful of bouncing daughters. However, the Lieutenant's was no haggard existence, and he would enter your presence radiant, but with a certain sinuosity of manner—a turn and a twist[1] —and with the airiest of bows; it was a salutation of his own conception—at least, I never saw any other quite like it. He would enter, rubbing his cheerful hands together, perhaps to announce some regrettable disaster, domestic or other. I remember on one occasion it was to tell us of his having just had a desperate physical encounter with a malignant turncock, who had cut off his water-supply —'and on the very morning, too—now, isn't it a curious coincidence?—you know,' when Mrs. Squib was presenting him with another daughter—Number nine, or ten, or eleven. We always spoke of her as 'The Fruitful Vine.' Lieutenant Squib was delightful.

[1] Like a sentimental harlequin.

There were people destitute of imagination, and as ill-conditioned as the turncock, who were indifferent to Lieutenant Squib. If he was a trifle vain, his vanity was a weakness, but it was an attractive weakness. He would don his regimentals on all possible occasions. He attended every Levée, and so many Drawing Rooms in succession, where he had no particular business, that at last his old messmate, William the Fourth, called out, 'Hullo, Squib! What! you here again?' This was one of the Lieutenant's interesting recollections.

Notwithstanding a disparity of years, Lieutenant Squib, R.N., was very friendly with some of the junior clerks, whom he treated with a jocose homage; and they, on their side, were affable and condescending, freely supplying him with pens and sealing-wax, and drawing him out. They set traps, into which the simple Lieutenant invariably walked. It was to their greedy ears that he confided the ins and outs of his domestic affairs—his triumphs, his chagrins, Mrs. Squib's prowess, and the admiration that her offspring inspired in the circles which they glorified.

There had been a dance at Deptford Victualling Yard, where a certain Viscount Lochinvar of Glenscar and the Isles, or some such rolling title, a tipsy mate, R.N., a heavy fellow, had danced the whole night through with sprightly Julia Squib, waltzing her after supper 'in a way that was exceedingly painful to Mrs. Squib.' The flirtation went on for months, and we had interesting intelligence of it through all its stages. The noble admirer continued to be particular in his attentions, the lady surrendered her affections, the pair became engaged. It was fairy Titania and a certain Athenian weaver, more or less, over again; then suddenly he altogether disappeared, and when, at last, Lieutenant Squib, R.N., ran him to earth at the old Hummums—it was on a Sunday afternoon—he found him in bed, in a dirty flannel jacket, tipsy, and quite insensible to the feelings natural to a nobleman. But, spite of the grievous disappointment, Lieutenant Squib continued to the bitter end to roll off the titles of this disreputable person. Now you have had enough of poor Lieutenant Squib, R.N., so we'll here bid him a very kindly good-bye.

Then there was Harris, our special messenger, who answered the bell, sealed the letters, pacified the duns, and turned up in a white waistcoat and white tie when Dwarris, or some other of us, gave a supper-party to our circle, constituting himself a sort of godfather to the whole concern. But if I once begin to talk of Harris—of his alertness, good temper, sagacity, imperturbability, and respectful-ness—a certain vague drollery in his eye—I shall never have done. Mrs. Harris, the sub-housekeeper, was almost worthy of her lord; she was an inspired coffee-maker, and had been very pretty.

It is the worst of these reminiscences that one is not able to relate the more racy portions of them.

The philosophy of life has always been my favourite cult, and I could tell you a good deal about people I have met—people whose names you know, and people whose names you don't know. But where should I begin, and when should I stop? There are the debts of friendship and hospitality, as well as of good feeling and decency, so I hold my hand.

The observation of my fellow-creatures—their fancies, their peculiarities, their virtues, and their foibles—has, almost unconsciously to myself, been one of my favourite diversions in life,[1] and one of my most remunerative, for I do not like my species the worse for it;[2] but it has also taught me that to

[1] '"Philosopher, sir," said Mr. Jingle.
'"An observer of human nature, sir," said Mr. Pickwick.'

[2] We like people with whom we are able to laugh; we do not so much care for people at whom we cannot laugh occasionally. There are people whom nobody laughs at without loving.

'O all ye men and women walking about in ordinary costume,
How comical you seem to me, and how I love you all!'

Some people, sinister or the contrary, inspire an interest which singles them out from their fellows; but the majority—such as A. or B. or C.—are not much more than the shining threads in a fine tapestry hanging. They get their importance from their association.

live comfortably with mankind one must not expect too much from them. Don Quixote loved Sancho, and Sancho was what is called devoted to his master; but still, when the knight was dying, the honest fellow ate and drank, and cherished his little carcase; and Don Quixote, if he could have known of it, would not have complained. I can understand the distraction that 'Melancholy' Burton got out of the ribald talk of the Oxford 'bargees;' I can also understand the pastime that the poet Cowper found in the simple chat and spiritual difficulties of gentle Mary of the Knitting Needles.

Whilst at the Admiralty I served under Lord Haddington, Sir James Graham, and Sir Charles Wood, and I will here give a brief sketch of the duties I performed; they were not unimportant.

As deputy reader to the assembled Board I read the principal despatches, and often had to decipher the telegrams. During the Inkermann fight, and afterwards during the Sepoy mutiny, when all England was held in painful suspense, this was no small responsibility, for on occasions—Sundays, for instance—I was often alone, had to act on my own judgment, and communicate with any Cabinet Minister who chanced to be in London and to whom I could get access. On ordinary occasions it was my duty to reach the office by 8.15 A.M. Arrived there, I found in a chamber contiguous to the board-room, on a large round table, the post of that morning, just come in. It was an immense heap, so large that I never attacked it without feeling it was utterly impossible that on *that* morning I could ever get through it; but somehow the irksome *corvée* was accomplished in about two hours. I literally tore through it. I placed the letters in separate packets, to be conveyed to the different departments—the more important ones for individual members of the Board—and afterwards, as far as time allowed, I mastered these more important letters. I should add that, among many other duties, I kept a folio book, posted up to the hour, which showed the station of every ship in the navy. Then the Board assembled, and the letters were read and discussed. Some hours later my duties were usually concluded for the day—that was about 3 P.M. When I was not deputy reader to the Board I was their deputy précis writer. I made a short abstract of all the papers which came before them, so that any member could at once see what business had been transacted during his absence.

I was appointed to these duties by Sir James Graham, a very powerful administrator, with an Olympian look that none durst gainsay. He was a portent—at least an Admiralty portent. Sir Charles Wood was a very able public servant, and of the quickest apprehension.

In course of time I was promoted by seniority to the second class among the clerks, and from increased rank was obliged to return to a department. In my case it was to the Pension branch, where the work was regulated by precedent. Soon after this my health gave way, and I retired. However, I am anticipating.

The official part of my career was not a success. I had few clerical triumphs—only one or two that I can call to mind; and when you hear how very pitiful they were, you will be the better able to appreciate what I have just been saying.

Scene: The Admiralty board-room, embellished with elaborate carvings by Grinling Gibbons. The portrait of Lord Nelson lackadaisically regarding us. The council is assembled. Picture to yourselves Sir Charles Wood enthroned, surrounded by his satellites—'sea-dogs' with tightly spliced pigtails and wide 'slops.' Lyons is at Balaclava, and Napier sharpening his cutlass in the Baltic. I am reading their despatches. Suddenly Sir Charles throws a leg over the arm of his chair, and turns to me in his quick way: 'Go to my room, Locker,' says he, 'and bring me the map of the Dardanelles; you'll find it on the round table.' I obey the command. The round table is covered with maps, but there is no chart of the Dardanelles, so I reluctantly return to say, with bated breath, that I cannot find it.

'Not find it?' exclaims Sir Charles with a 'humph.' 'It's there, if you'll only look; it is on the round table, by the fireplace, in the corner, close to the door.' Sir Charles was cruelly precise. Away I again went; and going, poor wretch that I was, I felt perfectly certain I should come back without the Dardanelles. And yet I went; I even lingered. On my return from this, my second unfruitful errand, Sir Charles jumps to his feet, hurries out of the room, and is back again before the first Sea Lord could pass the word, 'All hands to the for's'l;' and in his fist is a *map of the Piræus!* which he shakes at me reproachfully, amid the (also reproachful) silence of his 'old salts' of colleagues, in whose eyes glimmers a cold dismissal as they mentally masthead me. There the matter ended. No, it did not quite end there, for Admiral Sir David Milne, G.C.B., to whom I shall always feel grateful—but only a tempered gratitude—observed, *sotto voce*, to his neighbour, 'He'd ask'd for the Dardanelles!' Sir Charles did not hear this remark, or I am sure he would have done me full justice. No one had the temerity to tell him of his mistake.

People who know official life will comprehend what a snub this was to a sick, shy, sensitive young clerk on his promotion. I never wholly recovered from it. Though the pangs of the past are seldom more than a memory, even now, when I am languid and not feeling my best, the old despairing feeling comes back: Why was I born? Why was not I strangled at nurse? &c. If success in official life depends on comprehending it, I do not think anybody's career promised worse than mine did at that time. But enough of these empty lamentations.

You are thinking that what I have described was not altogether a triumph. I am coming to my triumphs presently; Sir Charles figures in one of them.

On a certain morning I found a slip of paper on my précis book on which Sir Charles had written these pregnant words: 'Extracts very creditable to the clerk.' I showed the precious little scrap to Algernon West, who happened to be in the room when the book came back from the Board. At that time he was a very ambitious young fellow, and he gazed at it with keen but not unkindly envy—nothing ignoble in it—and exclaimed, 'I only wish he had said the same about me.' Now, West is nearly the most successful Civil Servant on the permanent staff of the service—at least, I know no one who is more so. Everybody is the son of his own works, and the resolution to get on rarely fails to be its own fulfilment.

My other success was connected with a quarrel between a captain-superintendent of one of the naval yards and his storekeeper. I was deputed to make a précis of the correspondence. There were ridiculous circumstances, and I got interested in it. I afterwards heard that one or two members of the Board were so much amused by my paper that they said it was as good as a play. I am not sure that they ever knew who drew it up.

My Marriage

Dr. Johnson has asserted that ill-health makes every man a scoundrel. In 1849 I was especially scoundrelly, suffering from acute nervous depression. However, it was only the hag Dyspepsia, that beldame who waits upon grief and anxiety, and had always more or less tormented me. She now took entire possession of my being. I writhed in her accursed embraces. I was in that worst of prisons, the dungeon of myself, and all my desire was *libera me ab homine malo, a meipso.* Coleridge all his life suffered from severe internal discomfort, and took opium to allay it. When he died his body was examined, and nothing was found to account for these pains. The doctors attributed it to what is called nervous sympathy. Perhaps mine is a similar case. I hope his people were kind to him about it.

So ill was I that on May 23 I got long leave of absence from the office, and fled to the Continent. At Paris, one of my letters of introduction was to Lady Charlotte Bruce, at 29 Rue de Varennes, a grand old mansion, *entre cour et jardin* in the Faubourg St. Germain. I had not seen Lady Charlotte very often before I became much struck with her virtues and many charms, her humility, her deep feeling, and her gift of repartee. I saw a great deal of her in Paris. She was my beneficent angel, and when she left for England I followed her in spirit. I corresponded with her, and this continued when I returned to London at the end of August. At that time she was in Scotland, and then in the North of England.

Early in March 1850, when Lady Charlotte came back to London, we took a walk together in Hyde Park. It was a short walk, but it was one of the happiest that I have ever taken, for it was then that I proposed to her, and, in spite of the warning of the Sage of Bolt Court and all I could say, she accepted me.

This is how it came about. We had seated ourselves on a bench, and neither spoke. I took her hand. 'This is the prettiest hand in all the world,' said I. 'I happen to know of one that's quite as pretty,' said she. Another silence. Perhaps I was incredulous, but when she put the other pretty hand into mine I knew that we both were very happy.

In the first days of May she returned to Paris; I followed her in June, and we were married on July 4.

Lord and Lady Gray of Gray, the Duke and Duchess of Hamilton, my kinsman, George Cayley, Dick Edwardes, and others, were at my wedding. After the ceremony we drove to St. Germain, Mr. Thomas Erskine, of Linlathen, lending us his house. 'Dear Tom!' he was a most lovable person. But, alack! with a genius for goodness he had not a single redeeming vice; holy in all his ways, and with the aspect of one who sorrowed for his suffering fellow-creatures, his simplest greeting was a benediction. I have had many delightful walks and talks with Mr. Erskine. Yet his views were nebulous; like an angel, he spoke from a cloud, but also in a cloud. However, he did me good, and I am deeply grateful. He a little resembled his excellent friend, the Rev. F. D. Maurice, in this much, that *Viriliter age expectans Dominum* was the law of both their lives. Mr. Erskine was able to appreciate very different people; among others, Carlyle and Jowett, the Rev. Norman Macleod, Lord Rutherford, and Sterling of Keir. Indeed, his was a piety that many were able to apprehend, though but few could attain unto. He lived in the hearts of his friends, and when he died his funeral was a real apotheosis.

> We gave his body to the earth,
> And his pure soul unto his Captain, Christ,
> Under whose colours he had fought so long.

From St. Germain we went to Scotland. The wedding-tour ended, we returned to London, and set up our transitory Penates in King Street, St. James's, then in Albion Street, and then in Belgrave Street; but we soon bought the lease of 19 Chester Street.

The 'London Lyrics,' Rome

The Admiralty was not a genial soil for poesy, yet I continued to cultivate the laurel. If I was not a poet, it was not for lack of making believe; and if I had not the poet's temperament, I enjoyed the artist's endeavour. I think I had a true natural impulse, but it was almost an accident that I ever printed anything. However, in 1857 I published a thin volume—certain sparrow-flights of song, called 'London Lyrics.' Thackeray was fond of rhymes *galamment composé*, and about 1860, when he accepted the editorship of the 'Cornhill Magazine,' he surprised me by asking me to write, and I surprised myself by now and then sending him contributions. This encouraged me; but though sometimes I may have committed the venial mistake of posing as a man of letters, and the crime of being found out, I only hope that I have not been the lackey of merely fine phrases, and also that I have always borne in mind the narrowness of scope of my little pipe, which, I fear, may have often only reminded my readers of something better they have heard before.

My aim was humble. I used the ordinary metres and rhymes, the simplest language and ideas, I hope flavoured with an individuality. I strove, as at this moment I am striving, not to be obscure, not to be flat, and, above all, not to be tedious. How many important poets have failed in some of these laudable endeavours! Listen to even our great Boanerges themselves.

During these years I met many distinguished people. We used to stay at Frogmore with the Duchess of Kent. She liked whist; she would play a card, and take a transitory nap, and we were quite happy to wait till she woke and picked up the trick, which she did with dignity and very deftly. She was very kind. She used to pity me for having to inhale the 'fogues' (fogs) of London. I have a grateful remembrance of this exalted and benevolent lady.

While at Frogmore I very occasionally saw the

Queen's children, and Her Majesty once or twice. The Queen had a warm regard for Charlotte: rejoiced in her humour, honoured her by giving her her books, and commanded us to those select Courts which she decreed in the earlier years of her widowhood. I never felt much at my ease with Royalty, and I never shall, but I will tell you a funny little story of the Court. Sir George Cowper, an excellent administrator but an elderly valetudinarian, had charge of the Duchess of Kent's purse and the management and control of her household. One day little Prince Arthur questioned him: 'Sir George, are you the "Sir George" who killed the dragon?'

We were bidden to Windsor. Lord Palmerston was there, and the Prince Consort told that striking anecdote of the sleeping Windsor sentry and St. Paul's clock striking thirteen. This is all I can call to mind of that entertainment. I afterwards met Lord Palmerston at Lady William Russell's. He was not remarkably attractive—less so than Lord Granville, and, I should suppose, than Lord Melbourne, who, I have always been told, was especially so.

We paid a yearly visit to Lady Elgin in Paris. There, in the Rue de l'Université, I saw Lamartine, handsome and picturesque-looking, but with an over-refinement of manner. I object to the prurient chastity of his poetry. He was running, nay, galloping to seed in an atmosphere of twaddle and toadyism; his room was decorated with portraits of himself in the shape of medallions, pictures, and busts, one of them executed by Madame de Lamartine. I also knew Ary Scheffer, Barthélemy Saint-Hilaire, M. and Mme. Mohl, Le Duc de Broglie, Victor Hugo, Villemain, Ristori, Rémusat, Jenny Lind, M. and Mme. d'Haussonville, Prosper Mérimée, Tocqueville, Guizot, Thiers, Cousin, Mignet, T. de Lesseps, Comtesse de Castiglione, Duc de la Rochefoucauld, Sainte-Beuve, Odilon Barrot, Lanfrey; Loménie, Professor of Literature in the Ecole Polytechnique—very amusing; Prévost-Paradol, Montalembert, Renan, Tourgeneff, Paul de Kock,[1] and Gustave Doré. But why should I run through this string of names? Before fifty years have passed

[1] I find a note dated 'Paris, December 1, 1862.—To-day, much to Charlotte's amusement, I called on Paul de Kock, 8 Boul. St-Martin. He received me very amiably in a small inner room containing his bed, a rather untidy washing apparatus, and the remains of his breakfast. I told him that a sense of gratitude for the extreme pleasure his works had given me was the spring of my visit; that I believed His Holiness Pope Gregory and myself were his two most enthusiastic admirers. This pleased him. He is a plump little man, with a small moustache and humorous expression. His walls were covered with rows of his own blessed works. These appeared to be his only books—in fact, there was no room for anybody else's. He pointed out their large number with satisfaction, and gave me one of his songs in autograph. Though he said nothing that was specially interesting, I was much pleased with my visit; on parting we cordially shook hands, and he invited me to his house at Romainville.'

some of them will convey no idea to any one. Even now most of them are *les disparus.* However, they made their little fizz in the generation that they accompanied to oblivion. The people I should have best liked to know—namely, Balzac, Béranger, Musset, A. Dumas, G. Sand, and Heine—I did not even see. They were all, for some reason or other, *mésestimés.* Rachel Félix I saw several times on the stage in 'Phèdre' and 'Adrienne Lecouvreur;' also in 'Camille,' that wonderful scene with the soldier. Can I ever forget her thrilling tones and fateful gaze? Then, what a debt do not I owe to Ravel ('Le Caporal et la Payse'), and even more to Grassot, and others!

I think it was in London that I first made the acquaintance of Mr. and Mrs. Browning, at 13 Dorset Street, Portman Square. I afterwards met them in Paris. He used to come to the Rue de Lille to read John Keats's poetry to Lady Elgin. The good fellow never read his own. I knew but little of his wife; she died comparatively early. I never saw her in society, but at her own fireside she struck me as very pleasing and exceedingly sympathetic. Her physique was peculiar: curls like the pendent ears of a water-spaniel, and poor little hands—so thin that when she welcomed you she gave you something like the foot of a young bird; the Hand that made her great had not made her fair. But she had striking eyes, and we forgot any physical shortcomings—they were entirely lost sight of in what I may call her incomparable sweetness, I might almost say affectionateness; just as, while we are reading it, we lose sight of the incompleteness of her poetry—its lack of artistic control. She vanquishes by her genius and her charm. In reply to, I dare say, a not over-pertinent question of mine, she told me she preferred Hood's poetry to Gray's —'but then, I do not care very much for Gray.'

Browning has long been one of my kind friends. I saw a good deal of him when, as a widower, he was staying in Paris with his father and sister. I had much regard for all three.[1] Browning knew I was fond of scarce books, and he generously made me a present of nearly all the original editions of his earliest works, including 'Pauline,' not a few of them enriched with his manuscript corrections; and they are now in good company with W. Blake's, Burns's, Byron's, his own wife's, and 'Boxiana.'

We spent three delightful winters in Rome, arriving at the Piazza di Spagna, No. 31, on December 29, 1861; at No. 103 Via de' due Macelli on December 17, 1862; and, lastly, at No. 43 Via di Bocca di Leone, 2° p° (I specify it all with amorous precision), on November 17, 1866.

[1] I wrote a few lines about the elder Browning in Mrs. Orr's excellent memoir of his illustrious son.

Past times do not repeat themselves, but I often think wistfully of the days when Rome was garrisoned by priests and greedy for *baiocchi.* It was interesting in its picturesque dilapidation and the sprawling do-nothingness of a people whose speech is so sweet with its terminating vowels. I shall never again see Nemi, or Palestrina, or Castel Fusano; but I have the pleasant impression—the *et ego in Arcadia vixi.* Changed as I hear Rome now is—the Papal Principality shrunk to Vatican and garden—I presume it still possesses its leaping fountains, its ruined temples and shattered porticos, the weird desolation of the Campagna, the scattered tombs, the stretch of Claudian aqueduct, the baths of Caracalla thick with ilex and myrtle, the Coliseum, and the Basilica of St. Peter. I recall the musical functions at the Gesù, the Masses of Pier-Luigi da Palestrina, the Corso de' Barberi, the startling pastime of 'morra,' the 'novena' of the Pifferari; also the much garlic and little soap of the noisy Piazza Navona. Eleanor still has the blue majolica plate that I bought of Saturnino Innocenti, and which Mr. Gladstone greatly admired. But, body of Bacchus! where are Padre Garrucci and his *sozio*; Beppo of the Spanish Steps; Nabucco, our cook (a sort of Leporello—fancy having a cook called Nebuchadnezzar!); and, above all, where is the needlewoman, Lucia Fedeli, Lucia *del biondo crin?* Rome is more agreeably to be remembered by its Campagna than its cookery, by its women than its wine.

For a portion of the time that I was in Rome I filled the high office of warden to the Episcopal church immediately outside the Porta del Popolo.

We made the acquaintance, in some instances the friendship, of many people more or less pleasant and notable: of Mariano Fortuny, Friedrich Overbeck, and T. R. Tilton, painters; also of John Gibson, Miss Hosmer, and W. W. Story, sculptors. Story's fair daughter is referred to in the last couplet of my mediocre rhyme on Thackeray's admirable absurdity, 'The Rose and the Ring:' 'And you see there's a nice little *Story*.' Then there were J. J. Ampère and Franz 'Abbé' Liszt. The 'Canonico' unhesitatingly told me that Mozart was the most extraordinary musical genius that the world had ever seen. There was something magnetic in the Abbé Liszt; he was a *poseur*, but I think this was his real opinion. We knew Rosa, the amiable antiquary, and Cardinal Antonelli and di Luca; also Don Michele, il Duca di Sermoneta, a man who combined the wit and 'Pyrrhonism' of Poggio Bracciolini with the moral force of an ancient Roman. A geographical society had been started at Turin, and when asked to join, he replied in excellent English, 'No; I don't believe in geography.'

He was very grimly humorous. He made me a design for a brooch, which Castellani carried out. We were acquainted with Princess Corsini, Prince Massimo, Princess Rospigliosi, Prince Doria Pamphilj. We also knew Mrs. Gaskell (novelist), the Gladstones,[1] Cardwells, Clarendons, and others of mark who chanced to be in Rome.

I made Landor's acquaintance at the Villa Gherardesca, Fiesole. He was well known in Florence as 'il vecchio con quel bel canino' (giallo), also for the eccentricity of his opinions and the turbulence of his behaviour. He lived by himself, and solitude may have rendered him savage. His little villa was poor and bare, but there was enough for the exigencies of contentment and obscurity; and the situation was beautiful, looking down, over a breadth of olive, vine, and ilex wood, on Brunelleschi's dome and Arnolfo's tower, and here and there a stretch of the gleaming Arno.

I paid Landor only one visit, and that was 'a quattr' occhi.' I found him reading a Waverley novel, and congratulated him on having so pleasant a companion in his retirement. 'Yes,' said he, with a winning dignity, 'and there is another novelist whom I equally admire, my old friend [G. P. R.] James.' In the course of conversation he placed

[1] Just then Mr. Gladstone was enthusiastic about *bric-à-brac*, but, though he discoursed upon it eloquently, his judgment was faulty.

Southey on a level with Wordsworth! He was interesting about Addison: he said that an engaging simplicity shone through all that he wrote; that there was coyness in his style, the archness and shyness of a graceful and beautiful girl. This struck me as delightful criticism, and I felt glad that I had come to see Landor. Landor's face put me in mind of the portraits of Hogarth. He had a diabolical laugh—a prolonged mockery, with apparently no heart or happiness in it, and when you thought he had done he went on and on; perhaps his extreme age was the cause of its prolongation, but not of its *timbre*. He gave me an *aperçu* of his views on art, politics, and literature. I suppose he was a very wrong-headed man, and that his fierce individuality (Welsh choler) made his acquaintance as uncomfortable as his friendship was perilous. Every now and then the Tuscan States rang with his 'larum, and at one time he made Florence too hot to hold him. A paradoxical old Jacobin, it seemed to me that there was nothing really genial about the man Landor. Alfred Tennyson tells me he used to meet him at Mr. John Forster's[1] chambers in Lincoln's Inn Fields; that one day, while Landor was reciting some poetry, a member of the company tumbled downstairs and broke his leg, and that Landor the

[1] The biographer of Dickens. He was to Dickens what Ralpho was to Sir Hugh de Bras.

while went on spouting without showing any special concern.

In Florence I knew Baron Seymour Kirkup, the painter; he had been ennobled for good service connected with the discovery of a contemporary fresco portrait of Dante in the chapel of the Palazzo del Podestà (the Bargello).

Kirkup lived at the south end of the Ponte Vecchio, his *atelier* looking over the Arno; this room, like himself, was anything but commonplace. It was very large. Pictures, engravings, drawings, covered the distempered and time-stained walls, or were huddled together on the scantily carpeted floor. There were grimy plaster busts and bas-reliefs after Donatello and Michael Angelo, and coarse majolica, tattered old books, pipes and newspapers, scattered about in what is called picturesque confusion. Then there was a startling lay figure, dusty and distorted, which never changed its attitude; and last, but not least, two irrepressible parrots, swearing and flopping about, as is their wont. I do not think a housemaid's duster had been busy there since the Deluge.

At the time of which I am speaking poor Kirkup was more than half forgotten, given over to spiritualistic pietism, and a prey to quacks, male and female—the male by no manner of means the worse of them. Notwithstanding all this, I was fond of

Kirkup, and often went to see him. He discoursed delightfully about Italy and art; of Landor, the poet, and Blake, the painter; of Lady Orford and Lady Catherine Fleming, madams whom he knew, and of others, Cleopatra and Mrs. Jordan, whom he would have liked to meet.

We used to stroll and talk in the Boboli gardens or on the terraces of San Miniato. We were good friends. When I left for England we corresponded fitfully; but I never returned to Florence, never saw Kirkup again, and now that city of enchantment knows him no more.[1]

Several of the English we had met in Italy were friends of Arthur Stanley, and on our return to London we renewed our acquaintance, and made new ones at the Deanery and elsewhere. Among them have been Tyndall, Owen, Charles Kingsley, Huxley, J. G. Lockhart, the poet Barnes, A. Kinglake, W. H. Brookfield, Ralph Osborne, Lord Acton, Spedding (the admirable Spedding, who drew all good and great men unto him, but to converse with

[1] I liked Kirkup almost as much as, many years afterwards, I both liked and reverenced a very different man—the Reverend Dr. James Martineau. Many a time and oft have I walked through the forest from Rothiemurchus to the Polchar to sit at his feet, and rejoice in his sane and elevating spirituality. But why should I mention these two men on the same page? Perhaps from perversity. I might as well have compared Northcote, the painter and converser, with poet-priest Keble. I wish Kirkup could have known Dr. Martineau, whom it was a privilege to know and is a pleasure to remember.

whom, in consequence of his deliberate utterance, required an ampler leisure than even I, who am neither good nor great, found always practicable); also Herbert Spencer, the Grotes, Hayward, the Leckys, M. Arnold, J. A. Froude, Millais (who etched my portrait),[1] Fonblanque (a sickly-looking Mephistopheles), and Dr. Lushington. Dr. Lushington lived to be nearly ninety years old. He told me that as a boy he had seen a man whose father was present at the execution of Charles I. I must not forget my good friends L. Oliphant, H. Aïdé, and Leslie Stephen. I have had pleasant talk with many of the eminent Englishmen and Englishwomen of my day. I never had speech with Disraeli, though I once received a letter and a message from him.[2] His novels possess originality rare and peculiar, but as novels they are not of a very high order, and, in spite of their exquisite qualities and a wit and irony—I say it advisedly—worthy of Voltaire, I question their having a prolonged vitality. His philosophy of life was of the shallowest; and it is curious that a man who seemed to believe in nothing particular should have been so piously

[1] This was doing me high honour, for Millais, by his vigorous execution, is a worthy follower of Franz Hals. There are points where he almost surpasses the great Dutchman; but he wants charm, and I do not see in his faces that passing look, that exquisitely evanescent expression, which appears about to change even as we gaze. This I have seen in Hals's portraits. I have seen it in Hogarth's.

[2] Disraeli's father and mine were cordially acquainted.

believed in by his spouse and his party. But I knew nothing of Benjamin Disraeli, so you must not allow your estimate of him to be influenced by aught that I say here.[1] I had the honour of dedicating my 'Lyra Elegantiarum' to Dean Milman. I have met Tommaso Salvini, a most powerful Othello; and I often met Jenny Lind, a fair-haired and blue-eyed Puritan—an excellent woman, with serious enthusiasms and a plain but impressive personality. I remember her as Alice ('Roberto') and as Maria ('La Figlia'), two of her best impersonations. It is said that her first cry on coming into the world was F in alt.

I often dined with my dear Houghton, and once, at his house, took George Eliot in to dinner. The other guests were her Mr. George Lewes, Miss Thackeray, Dante Rossetti, Motley, his

[1] When I was about eighteen, my sister Ellen and I paid a flying visit to Boulogne, travelling by, I think, the 'Harlequin' or 'Magnet' steamer, which started from below London Bridge, and did the voyage in some ten hours. I seem to remember that there were no aft passengers excepting ourselves and a lady and gentlemen. He struck me as rather old and very odd, and she as much older and rather common-looking. He was dressed and adorned in the fashion of the Bond Street of that day—a tall hat, a queerly cut coat, and trousers that fitted over his boots like gaiters. His dress was highly peculiar, his air and manners still more so. He riveted my attention; I could not keep my eyes off him. He did not talk much, but stood and sat in a highly uncomfortable, shrug-shouldered, shivery, and exhausted manner. Years after this—I forget where—the man Disraeli was pointed out to me, and I instantly recognised my fellow-passenger in the steamer. Disraeli was married in 1839, and that was the year I met this pair. Were they Mr. and Mrs. Disraeli starting on their honeymoon?

daughter, Mrs. Ives (now Lady Harcourt), and one or two more, whose names I forget. On that occasion Rossetti seemed moody enough; every now and then, after dinner, he sat with his face buried in his hands, as if he were more than out of his element; but I am told he was very interesting when on his own text in his own territory.

I have been at Rossetti's house at Cheyne Walk, and he has been to me in Victoria Street. I liked him on both occasions, but from what I hear he could hardly have been a comfortable man to abide with. He collected Oriental china and *bric-à-brac*, and had a congregation of queer creatures—a raven, and marmots or wombats, &c.—all in the garden behind his house. I believe he once kept a gorilla. He was much self-absorbed. I never quite appreciated his pictures. 'Sister Helen' is his only poem that much impresses me, and it is not far from being repulsive. However, I suppose he draws inspiration from a world of his own. His pictures and his poems help each other. I like his poems least; but then I seldom see his pictures. I have a regard for his brother and his sister.

From what I say here it must not be supposed that I have not a high opinion, either as poet or painter, of this distinguished man; for he not only raised the quality of painting and changed its direction, but remarkable painters were content to learn from him. He brought us a new message in his poetry; but, with all his ornate ability and technical skill, for me it has little charm, and what is poetry—or painting either—without charm? I think he might have remembered Sidney's 'Look into thy heart, and write!' His 'I grudge Wordsworth every vote he gets' is significant.

Thanks to the friendship of that kind fellow, W—— A——, in 1865 I was elected a director of the Heart and Hand Insurance Company, that brotherhood which protects prudent people from the thriftless cruelty of Vulcan, and I am still on the direction. There are twelve of us; we meet every Tuesday at one o'clock. The fee is three pounds, and if a director is not in the room—if the whole of his body is not in the room—when the clock strikes one, he loses his fee. You, my dear children, who have so profound a knowledge of human nature, may be quite sure that very few of the directors arrive after that hour. We are perhaps the most punctual twelve men in all England. Our zeal is remarkable. Is it because we are able to recognise that a good thing should never be neglected unless a better offers itself?

Our society is an ancient one: it was founded in the reign of Dutch William, and there is a tradition that Daniel Defoe was a member of the board. Dear little Wag, if this be true of the ingenious author of 'Robinson Crusoe,' instead of meeting Tuesday, ought we not to meet Friday?

The board has a tacit understanding, an unwritten law of etiquette, that the subject of our fees should *never* be brought prominently forward. If ever there is a question on the subject, say, for instance, the increase of their amount—and that is anything but uninteresting—it is kept entirely in the background; it is merged in the general question—the welfare of the society. We are so sensitive on this point—at least, I am—and indeed on everything that regards our appointments, that I am sure it would be considered in the highest degree indecorous, not to say indelicate, in any director to chink the coin in taking his fee (3*l.*) out of the little canvas bag of fees that always lies on the centre of the board-room table. I have never chinked the sovereigns.

I ought to say that at the end of the year the fees of the absentee directors are divided among the entire body. One would therefore suppose that those who are least regular would be most popular, and doubtless they really are so; yet there is a formulated opinion kept up as to the great virtue of the directors who are the most regular attendants. As proof of this we used to have a certain old Mr. G—— P——, who had attended fifty-three Tuesdays in one particular twelvemonth. I do not know how he managed it. He was a very opulent person, and it was whispered, now and then when he got home at night he would lie down on his drawing-room carpet and roll in his accumulated fees. He died years ago, but he is still spoken of in our board-room as the most valuable and single-minded servant and friend that the society has ever had.

Our directors, as individuals, are exceedingly tough. Not long ago one of them, who must be between seventy and eighty, climbed upon his dining-room table to investigate an escape of gas. He had the temerity to do so with a lighted candle —remember, he is one of the most experienced members of our Fire Board. You may imagine what followed. There was a terrific explosion; our esteemed director was blown across the chamber, through the doorway, and into the passage, where his head crashed into a glazed case of stuffed birds. This was on a Sunday evening; and yet on the Tuesday morning following our exceeding tough director made his appearance at the board looking as if nothing particular had occurred! Indeed, the concussion seemed somehow to have vivified our respected colleague's mental constitution. It woke him up. He brought with him a claim for compensation for damages sustained, which, it is needless to say, was cheerfully recognised and promptly settled.

1893.—I am pleased to mention another matter, this time personal to myself. It is the unvarying consideration and kindness that I have met with from my co-directors, also from the staff, ever since I joined—that was twenty-eight years ago. Yes, for twenty-eight long years we directors for the time being (an elected twelve) have, one day in every week, been transacting business at a large green-baize table in the centre of a room where the portraits of many former directors still gaze down upon us.

I have seen so many changes since I first took my seat there, and so many men have come and gone, that I now begin to look at the portraits, silent as they are, with a feeling that perhaps we, and not the pictures, are the shadows.

'You admire that picture,' said an old Dominican to me at Padua, as I stood contemplating a 'Last Supper' in the refectory of the convent. The figures are as large as life. 'I have sat at my meals before it for seven-and-forty years; and such are the changes that have taken place among us—so many have come and gone in that time—that, when I look upon the company there—upon those who are sitting at that table—silent as they are, I am sometimes inclined to think that we, and not they, are the shadows.'[1]

[1] Note to Rogers's *Italy*: A Funeral.

My Mother-in-law

I must go back to relate my lamentable misadventure with Lady Elgin. I will begin by saying that the ethics of oaths has always had an interest for me. I devoted a page to it in 'Patchwork' (1879), to which I venture to refer you.

Although I am no better than I should be, I have never been much of a swearer; indeed, malediction offends my sense of the propriety of things. Quite lately, however—I suppose from a natural irritability, aggravated by failing nerve power and a young, very volatile, and irrepressible family of needless noise makers—I have sworn more than my wont. I mostly do it under my breath. Now, I should be glad to know what this swearing means, and what responsibility it carries with it. Is cursing a mere protest against things as they are, as compared with things as they ought to be. Is it a foible? Is it a sign of a deteriorated moral condition? Is it a recognition? [1]

[1] People of the present day do not know what mouth-filling swearing means. We know how the British army in Flanders swore in my Uncle Toby's time, and the sons of George III. all of them swore lustily; but I think the Duke of Cumberland was the only scion of royalty who habitually swore when conversing with the Archbishop of Canterbury.

There was a good deal of execration when I was a boy.

Curiously enough, in a bookcase at Frogmore there used to be a copy of Matthew Twogood's remarks on the 'Profane and Absurd Use of the Monosyllable "Damn"' (1746).

I hope that during all these years the spiritual part of my nature has not been quite starved. I want to go on growing. I should like to know whether this under-one's-breath Billingsgate is a good sign or a positively bad one. It may be a foible, but surely it implies a recognition. Perhaps, like a good many other things, it is not altogether one or the other.

Elizabeth Countess of Elgin was my mother-in-law. She was gifted, had many virtues, and a few oddities. She had a passion for cold air.

In 1850, not very long after my marriage, she honoured me with a visit at 19 Chester Street. You know that through all my life I have been more or less of a valetudinarian, a shivery animal. I have also been a person of gentle manners. Well, one unlucky winter afternoon, on returning from the Admiralty, I found my home desolate—cold, empty, and comfortless; the drawing-room was nearly pitch-dark, and very cheerless, for the fire had been allowed to go out, and though the curtains were drawn, a window was wide open. All this depressed me, and constrained me to heave a wholly languid and only half-audible malediction. I had an unlighted flat candlestick in my hand, and my first act was to drop out the candle. This produced another, a more audible imprecation. I rapped out a good round oath—an oath as round as possible.

However, having picked up and replaced the candle, I continued to grope my way to the writing-table for a match; but in doing so I stumbled badly over an abominable footstool, and dropped candlestick, candle, and extinguisher with a clatter on the carpet. This completely demoralised me. I broke into a storm of execration long, deep, and prolonged, but not launched at anything in particular. I again essayed to find the table, but, stretching forth my hand in the darkness, I laid it, not on the lucifers, but—can you conceive it?—on the upturned face of my respected mother-in-law, who all this time had been lying prostrate on the sofa. I do not know if she had been asleep—*that* I shall never know—but I should think not, for she said, in the most wide-awake, mellifluous tones of her very pleasing voice, 'Is that you, dear Mr. Locker?' This was all she said; she *never* said anything more. Heaven bless her!

Poetry—A Confession

There are not so many moments in our lives when we live entirely in the present and contentedly. We have far too many unfulfilled longings;

disappointment treads too closely upon the heels of joy. But I recall my first fine careless rapture when that kind fellow, Thackeray, as editor of the 'Cornhill Magazine,' sent me a proof of my verses 'On a Human Skull.' His daughters brought it to me. The flood of author's ecstasy has never since risen in me to the high-water mark of that moment. I also remember the first time I saw 'London Lyrics,' open at the title-page, in a conspicuous part of the window of a Piccadilly bookseller; but in that case it was a mixed feeling—the display was so painfully personal.

Adieu, ma Lyre, adieu, fillettes,
Jadis mes douces amourettes.

My rhyme-making has come to a not untimely end. I should be dull not to discern and ungrateful not to acknowledge that in spite of the specific levity, and lowly as is the aim, it has made its little mark. I do not know whether this mark still remains; but I do know that I have been a lucky fellow, and that some of my friends have been so injudicious as to overpraise it, and to urge me to go on writing. They forget that inferior work is a damaging commentary on that which is better, and they are not able to appreciate the old adage of 'Let well alone;' even authors themselves do not always perceive when their public has had enough of them. When I began writing I could not get into print; afterwards, when the periodicals were more open to me, I had smaller desire to make use of them. I once admired my little volume, and was inclined to be garrulous about it.[1] I am beginning to dislike the sight of a good deal of it. Such is the irony of destiny, and such are the revenges of time; so ought I to complain of the indifference of other people?

Dear children, I read but little poetry. My taste for it has always been imperfect, and my power of assimilation feeble, so that little has gone a good long way. There are more famous poems than I care to name which do not move me. Yet poetry has been one of the solaces of my life; and why should it not be as much to you?

There is surpassing melody and an unapproachable distinction in 'Lycidas;' perhaps it is the finest poem in the language; but there is a something in parts of it that to my ignorance sounds like pedantry, and I could well have spared the censorious Pilot of the Galilean lake. I admire Dryden's genial power, his sonorous and splendid diction, his manliness, and what Johnson calls his 'unexpectedness.' He is a glorious fellow. How

[1] I believe that nothing completely satisfies an imaginative writer but copious and continuous draughts of unmitigated praise, always provided it is accompanied by a large and increasing sale of his works. However, it is possible that even that might pall.

delightful are his translations from Chaucer and Boccaccio! But in 'Alexander's Feast' he makes Alexander a great fool. Heaven pardon me! I do not care much for Spenser. I admire not a little of Gray, and a good deal of Pope. The felicity of Pope's language and the energy seem to be the outcome of a vivid imagination. Read his portraits of Addison and Buckingham, his compliments to Cornbury, Walpole, and Bolingbroke ('great Dryden's friend before'). Read the 'Rape of the Lock.'

It is Wordsworth's meditative rapture, spiritual passion, sane imagination and serenity, his power of bringing the infinite into everyday life, that enthral me; but, for myself, all Wordsworth's best could be collected into a thin volume. I care little for his 'Laodamia.'

It almost puts one out of conceit of the saving gift of humour that Milton, Wordsworth, and Shelley, who do not appear to have had a spark of it, should have written such magnificent poetry. However, I am indebted to Wordsworth for these four lines on his doomed chamois-hunter:—

> Haply his child in fearful doubt may gaze,
> Passing his father's bones in future days;
> Start at the reliques of that very thigh [*thoi*, Cumbrian],
> On which so oft he prattled when a boy.

Alfred Tennyson has an exquisite grace, glorified by subtle harmonies. He is far more versatile than

Wordsworth. He has a more varied diction. He can give poetic expression to playful as well as to philosophic thought; he also has an eye for Nature; and I admire what Petronius might have called his 'careful luck.' A consummate artist, he is splendidly equipped. My selections from Alfred would make a much thicker volume than Wordsworth's, but would it be more precious?

Burns is one of the Immortals. What a fortunate thing for us that he was not educated, let us say at Eton and Balliol! There are many of Burns's poems (humorous and pathetic) which are superb. I can say much the same of short passages of Byron, though he is not a writer to be judged by selections. I could make a thin volume of either Burns or Byron, but the personality of Byron, apart from his persuasive rhetoric, inspires me with anything but regard. The region in which he usually moves is alien to my sympathies. I rank Byron with the very greatest, but he does not reach the cloistered sanctuaries of my heart. I grudge him the position I am constrained to give him.

Several of Cowper's short poems are inimitable. He writes so very like a gentleman.

I have read 'Rosalind and Helen,' and I have read 'Sally in our Alley,' and I prefer 'Sally.' I would rather have created the headlong drollery of the 'Lay of St. Nicholas' than written the 'Bride of Abydos,' and I would much rather have written 'The Solitary Reaper,' or

> I could not love thee, dear, so much,
> Loved I not Honour more,

than all the four.[1]

I immensely admire about eight or ten pages of Keats, the young Marcellus of our tongue. He instructs us by means of delight. He sees, as scarcely any other poet ever saw, the kinship of truth and beauty; as a young lady once remarked of him to me, 'He is enchantingly sensuous.' I dare say Keats liked little Jessica for saying 'I'm never merry when I hear sweet music.' Keats was a boy when he died, but he had the 'divinæ particula auræ.'

I care less for Shelley, who, for a great poet, seems to me to want substance (if Keats had lived, perhaps we should now be thinking that he also wanted it); and not more for Coleridge or Arnold, though there are admirable pieces in all of them. I am very fond of Hood, who is strongest on his whimsical side.

I greatly admire Coleridge's 'Youth and Age,' Arnold's 'Dover Beach' and 'Urania;' and have not we Andrew Lang's 'St. Andrews'? I like a few short pieces and passages of Mrs. Browning, and

[1] This is an idle comparison. I make it merely to show you how much I admire Dr. Barham at his best.

several minute but perfect poems of William Barnes. Austin Dobson has written some admirable little poems.

Three or four of Moore's melodies and verses leave little to be desired; and I can take up, and read, and like, Southey's 'Ode on the Death of the Princess Charlotte of Wales.'

Now I must say something of Praed. I once tried to write like him, and used often to talk about him to Ernest Lord Ailesbury, Chief Justice Alexander Cockburn, and Bishop Durnford (Chichester), and that accomplished scholar and amiable man, Dr. Hawtrey, the Provost of Eton, who specially delighted in him.[1] If Praed had been more of a colourist, he would have been our Watteau of the pen. I am not going to compare him with Prior, or Swift, or Cowper, or Thackeray, for their supreme merits are not his; but he is one of the brotherhood. I detect in him that ironic humour, very tersely and idiomatically expressed, which lies at the root of all their lighter work—which is rare, and which, I verily believe, disconcerts some two-thirds of their readers. Praed is quite on a level

[1] Dr. Hawtrey was very agreeable. I inherited his acquaintance from my father. We sometimes breakfasted together at the Athenæum Club. He was not handsome. His appearance was not attractive, but the way he condescended to my inferiority, without appearing to be aware that he was doing so, was very engaging, and his distinction and general accomplishment made me fully appreciate the value of that condescension.

with these—the very best of his school; indeed, he has a unique position, for in his narrower vein of whimsical wit, vernacular banter, and antithetical rhetoric, which may correctly be called *vers de société* in its most perfected form and its exactest sense, he has never been equalled. In spite of what Carlyle or Swinburne may say, let us be grateful to Praed and to Calverley, as we are to Watteau. They were perfect artists within their respective limits.

I admire Suckling's graceful audacity.

It is luckier to do a little thing surpassingly well than a larger thing indifferently so. There used to be a meritorious tragic actor who made a large income by his profession; he could also dance his fingers on a table to remind one of Taglioni. Where is that tragedian now? He is forgotten. But not so his imitation; at least, not by any one who had once seen a performance so consummate. We all know that Taglioni was at the very head of her profession; and yet, while poor Roscius was imitating her with his two fingers, you were almost deceived into thinking you were admiring the *ballerina*, whose chasteness of sentiment entirely secured her from Sallust's reproach, 'Saltabat melius quam necesse est probæ.'

I greatly appreciate a few pages of Browning: he has intellectual momentum and a subtle and spiritual energy; he is hopeful, and makes others hope. But Browning crushes me; as Shelley has too extravagant an imagination, and dwells in too rarefied an atmosphere, so is Browning too —— (I must leave it to you, my dear children, to here insert any words you think most appropriate and most kindly to Browning, even though it be at your father's expense.)

Perhaps as a writer he makes an excessive demand on the intellectual vigour of his reader. I hope this is the case, as, if so, the fault is mine, not Browning's. Poor poet! his hearth is desolate, so in age he still pursues that old, old coon, Society. Can it be that the fairest of his lyric offspring are strangled in his white ties?

Having said all this about poetry, and knowing, as I do, how difficult it is to write, and how easy it is not to write, and aspiring, as I do, to be something of a child of light, I wonder how I could have been so unconscionable as to print a volume of my own verses; but, strange as it may seem, there was a time when, rhyming dictionary in hand, I much overvalued myself and them. It was then that I regretted that my poetical lines had not fallen in more favourable places; that I was too much out and about, too often and too constantly distracted by petty cares and perpetually recurring domestic trivialities to be able to make a continuous effort.

Then there was my health. I may have made lamentation for *mes idées supprimées*—not by a white tie! Yet now, when I think of my small faculty and its attenuated thread, I feel satisfied that I have been less handicapped than other people, and that all is better, far better, as it is.[1]

Poetry is delightful, but what are we to say of the imaginative writers, the seers, the poets? 'Parler des poètes est toujours une chose bien délicate, et surtout quand on l'a été un peu soi-même!' Luckily for Shakespeare, he is in the dim twilight of Olympus; but what shall we say of Milton, and Byron, and a dozen others? Might not one or two of them have been a domestic handful? Would they have been the pleasantest people in the whole world to live with? I doubt it. The being who is gifted with genius does not possess it: it possesses him, and he and we have to pay the penalty.

Yes, there is still a good deal of human nature in mankind, and the genius is much like other folk. But he has a peculiar organisation, and a bent that is irresistible; he is more dependent than the ordinary man on the incense that comforts his immortal part—he must have it, or he withers.

[1] I have read that the Rev. R. C. Maturin, the poet, when in the throes of composition used to be seen with a red wafer stuck on his forehead, a sign to his numerous family that he was not to be spoken to.

Then, it is a misfortune for a poet that he should be compelled to capitalise his emotions, which often leaves the poor fellow with barely sufficient for even the conventional exigencies of everyday life. The poet is strong, but he is helpless; he may have a remarkable talent for expressing himself, and yet he may be vain and self-tormenting; he may have a delicate ear for metre and measure, and yet be irritable and capricious; he may even possess original thoughts and an extraordinary power of selecting and marshalling them, and yet be self-absorbed and very absurd:

> On this small matter speak I may,
> For, gifted less, I'm weak as they.

How admirably do our poets depict the virtues of domestic life—the heroic devotion of a husband to his wife, the self-denying solicitude of a father for his offspring! And yet, after all, with them it may be little more than affection in the abstract: not seldom the poet finds the absence of his adored one a positive boon.

The man of imagination enjoys the luxury of affection, but often as a fine art only; he shrinks from the sacrifices that go with the real thing. As I have said elsewhere, it is irksome for a poet to be always amiable to the same human being.

Read their biographies, and you will be struck by the manner in which many of our geniuses have put their comfortable trust in the ministering raven; have requited devotion with a perennial exaction, and sacrifice with a persistent dependence—neither of which cost them anything.

It is possibly an advantage for a genius, after his death, to have been disreputable. Think of Byron, Shelley, E. Poe, de Musset, even Goldsmith. There is, and always will be, an exceptional interest in them. Southey was far too reputable a man for curiosity to centre on him.

I believe that our best poets of this generation, the foolish fellows, have scrupulously paid their washing bills—they have washing bills—and have not paid too much attention to their neighbours' wives.

The poet is vastly imposing in his laurel crown, with his singing-garments about him; but be not surprised if, in the everyday concerns of life, when you get close to him, you find he is ordinary enough, and rarely so really agreeable as when encountered in homely cloth or a morocco jacket.

Genius, and the prestige that it brings with it, are impalpable essences, of little avail in our commonplace affairs. Put your poet into Parliament, or make him a peer, and he is marred—you will at once see the incongruity. But seek him out at odd times, and in his accustomed haunts, and 'he'll murmur to the running brooks a music sweeter than their own.'

To sum up all, what right have you to be disappointed that the man of imagination, who produces such beautiful verses, who has been so bountifully endowed on one side of his nature, should not be altogether superior? Rather be grateful for what he has done for you. Take my word for it that Sterne and Coleridge, and Campbell and Burns, were very seriously handicapped. It is curious that the very defects and foibles of some geniuses, like Steele, Goldsmith, Lamb, and Edward Fitzgerald, endear them to us.

Nur Lumpen sind bescheiden. I have met with not a few poets who were very delightful companions, but they were inferior poets. Poor fellows! let us hope that hereafter they may find a compensating Vale of Tempe of their own. Some day I will give you a list of poems for which I have a sneaking kindness, but which the literary world ignores.

Bric-à-brac

There was a time in my life when I was much taken up with art. Thanks to my father, I had always more or less lived in its atmosphere; but the taste waxed really active within me after my first marriage, and this was only natural. Bees do love their hives, and birds their nests; so, by the same instinct of Nature, I hungered for the Lares Urbani. I wished to adorn our dwelling, and collecting became my amiable madness. I bought ancient furniture, Louis-Seize gimcracks, china, and curiosities, also a few pieces of old silver—enough for decorative purposes—and I still have most of them. My tables smile with silver. The result was that my apartment was thought interesting; the affinity between the man and his dwelling-place was recognised. But its greatest attractions were the guests who from time to time found themselves under my roof. Nearly all were agreeable. There was no assumption, so there was no restraint; some talked, and the more silent took part in the conversation by their sympathy. It is a feat to talk agreeably, but it is a rarer merit to be attractively silent.

This curio-hunting brought me into communication with all sorts of people possessed with a kindred taste—the *conoscenti*: Franks, of the British Museum; Robinson, of the Kensington Museum; A. Castellani, of Rome; D'Azeglio, the Italian Minister; Bale, Felix Slade, John Malcolm, and William Mitchell (not a few of them old and valued friends), besides a host of others too numerous to mention. Among them, several of the de Rothschilds, Thiers, the Duc d'Aumale, Persigny, and other foreigners.

There are certain characteristics common to the whole of the collecting tribe—a tribe a good many of whom, I must own, are tolerably tiresome. They may be dullish fellows, but they are unmistakable. I think I could pick out your genuine collector from a crowd of any number of non-collecting beings.

Then there are collectors and collectors. I once met a divine who had a craze for the halters with which the more notorious malefactors had been hanged; and only a week ago another enthusiast showed me, with infinite glee, and as a great curiosity too—as something, in fact, to be piously preserved—a copy of the 'Times' newspaper of January 23, 1882, which contains a word that a malicious compositor had interpolated in a report of a speech, which some people might consider indelicate. *Parvum parva decent.* This was hardly decent, but it was a treasure.

You see, some collectors are less ambitious—do not fly so high as others: 'mais tous les goûts sont respectables.'

Mr. Matt. Dawson, the trainer, has a small piece of a chestnut horse's skin framed and glazed, a portion of the hide of the once famous racer, Eclipse. I think that may be considered a justifiable relic; it hangs underneath the picture which represents him to have been a heavily built animal—anything but a smasher.

It is not a misfortune to be born with a feeling for association. I seem nearer to Shakespeare when I have his volume of 'Sonnets' (edition 1609) open before me. I am nearer to Titian when I have one of his masterly sketches in my hand. This enjoyment is not given to everybody: Tennyson would not give a dam (a very small Indian copper coin) for a letter in Adam's handwriting, except from curiosity to know in what characters Adam had expressed himself. The influence of the associating principle is exemplified in the constant Penelope, when she shed tears over the bow of Ulysses.

Believe me, there is exhilaration in collecting. I would call it a perennial joy, if it were not so often pierced by despair.

My friends were mad about it; however, I hope with some discrimination. As regards myself, I had little money; but what with an abounding energy, chopping and changing, kind friends, and lucky chances, I acquired the few *objets d'art* which I possess—and even more, for I have sold some of them. We founded a Collectors' (Fine Arts) Club for the exhibition of our treasures at each other's houses. This was the *cunabula*

Romæ, the cradle of art-collectors, and developed into the Burlington Fine Arts Club, in Savile Row. I made several expeditions to Paris, the Low Countries—that 'land that rides at anchor'—and one or two to Germany; but, the ball having thus been set rolling, the collecting mania degenerated into a fashion, and genuine works of the Renaissance rose enormously in price.

There was a time when I was mad about Palissy ware, and possessed a reptile dish decorated with a large eel, dace, newts, crawfish, &c. I bought it in Paris for 40*l*. It was highly interesting, but, as I think now, exceedingly ugly. I had much anxiety and suffering in transporting this dish to London. It was too bulky for my portmanteau, so I carefully wrapped it in brown paper, and carried it under my arm. We had a long and very stormy passage in that perfidious barque, rigged with curses dark, the Dover Packet. I was exceedingly ill—horribly so—and what with nausea, chaos, and being banged about with this dreadful dish, which was not even a basin, I had a miserable time of it. I would cheerfully have flung my Palissy ware overboard if the doing so would have propitiated the sea-god; as it was, I as nearly as possible got it broken through the barbarity and brutality of my fellow-passengers.

When I reached London I had pretty well

recovered from my voyage, and hastened to the Museum to exhibit my acquisition and to get Franks's valued opinion. The Museum possessed a dish that had cost 80*l*., and which was manifestly superior to mine. The good Franks recognised this at once, but still he saw no reason for thinking my dish was not a genuine work by Palissy; and yet I detected that he did not feel quite comfortable about the coil of the eel in the centre. Now, if I had been a man wise in my generation, I should have rested satisfied with Franks's opinion, and enjoyed my dish; but I was not wise—I must needs take it to Bethnal Green Museum. The moment Harbottle Grimes set eyes on it he gave one of his laughs (you know his little withering laugh—we all know his little withering laugh). He said it was a nice dish, a very nice dish indeed; not by Bernard Palissy, not even of his time—at least two hundred and fifty years later! Then—and that was after closer examination—there was something very unusual in the glaze, which interested him extremely, and convinced him that it was altogether modern—in fact it was especially interesting on that account. Harbottle Grimes knew the place where my dish had been made, he had talked to the man who made it—somewhere in the Lot-et-Garonne country. He was able to give chapter and verse about it, everything about it, and he ended by sincerely congratulating me on my purchase. 'A very important acquisition, my dear fellah!' Grimes has always been kind to me—it was only his manner. This was heartrending; but I concealed my misery behind a merry smile, and betook myself to Stars, the dealer. Stars's rapacity is proverbial—he has no conscience, or else it is his accomplice. At any rate, Stars shook his head over my dish. However, just then he happened to know where to 'place it.' He had a customer who wanted a reptile dish—'which isn't everybody's money, you know.' Stars gave me in exchange a very ugly majolica tazza, lustred, signed in full by Maestro Giorgio, and with the magic date of 1623, which I afterwards resold for nearly forty pounds.

You see I had a good deal of worry about my dish; and yet, after all, I sincerely believe that it was an inferior but genuine work of the famous potter. I hope its present possessor is of the same mind. So much for Bernard Palissy and Co.

Art is a mighty mother, but at present we English people have little filial feeling. We cover our walls with pictures that narrow the soul, instead of expanding it—'des platitudes bourgeoises, des misères sans valeur et sans goût,' which make one despair for poor humanity. The fact is we do not care for fine art, and not generally for fine literature.

As a nation we are richer than any, and yet our most important possessions are gradually leaving the country, whether it be in the shape of a Rubens, a Botticelli, a choice Caxton, or a unique Shakespeare quarto. They find a home in Paris, or Berlin, or Chicago.

As I drive past the houses of palatial London I often think that, if their excellent and eminently practical occupants had really cared for rare and choice drawings, I should have secured none of mine. Many and many a time, even with my slender purse, I have outbid, unwittingly outbid, the British Museum. The unfortunate Museum is helpless, the Government is selfish and absorbed, the House of Commons is distracted, and the public are ignorant and indifferent.

It has been said that music thrives only where the grape ripens, and that Britons judge of it by the eye, as they do of painting by the ear. Now, of all the windy gospels that are preached, none is more empty and tiresome than that which pretends to explain the cause of our apathy and to provide a remedy. A nation's taste must grow up gradually. You cannot build it up; you might as well try to build up a forest-tree like the huge oak at Gunton:—

> Three centuries he grows, and three he stays
> Supreme in state and in three more decays.

We are a rude people, but just now house decoration attracts a great deal of attention; applied art has become a cult—it has its literature. Formerly any attempt to make an ordinary dwelling artistically pretty was thought eccentric, and therefore ridiculous, and was most uncommon. Now people ruin themselves to be fantastical. All houses should have their character stamped upon them by the people who inhabit them. This comes gradually, insensibly.

One of the most curious instances of a man stamping his individuality on his house was that of my old crony, Allerdyce. He had been an athlete, and was vain of his thews and sinews; so while in Rome he commissioned McDonald to take his full-length portrait in marble, colossal size, as Hercules, and therefore without a stitch of clothing, except a baby lion's skin fastened athwart his shoulders—a garment barely wider than the garment of our first parents. However, to make up for this startling nudity, he was armed with a tremendous club. It was a striking portrait, for McDonald was excellent at a likeness. The first object that greeted the coy visitor on entering Allerdyce's house was his lordship erect in the hall, in a decidedly threatening attitude, keeping watch and ward over the great-coats and umbrellas. A delirious *senex*, Allerdyce was very eccentric. He had all sorts of likes and dislikes. He went to church, but his devout spirit was easily disturbed: he could not say his prayers satisfactorily in a gallery pew. At the hotel in Paris he did not approve of the way in which the firewood was cut, so he bought himself a hatchet. Then he hated baronets: he always knew when there was a baronet in the room.

As time went on, my passion for *bibelots* grew cooler. Aiming higher, I gradually secured a few typical drawings by the great masters of the Renaissance, and three or four little oil-pictures which have been appreciated at Burlington House; also two or three fine illuminations and some rare sixteenth-century engravings. But, as I have already said, collectors with long purses crowded into the market, up went the prices, my innocent pleasures and pious excitements came to an end, my chance was gone, and I was obliged to retire from the unequal conflict. However, it was necessary to do something, so I turned to old books—little volumes of poetry and the drama from about 1590 to 1610. I haunted the secondhand bookshops in many a by-street of London, and studied the catalogues, giving out my heart in usury to such pastime. I was often unsuccessful; at other times my success was qualified, for I had to pay ruinous prices. But sometimes I have been lucky, and these shabby-looking little fellows now form a limited but curiously rare and highly interesting library of imaginative literature—a dukedom large enough for poor me.

Old poetry has also risen in value. What I once could secure for five pounds now costs five-and-twenty. Moreover, such books are rarely to be met with; so I am abandoning this pursuit also, and, having nothing to fall back upon except a wife and children, if I live three or four years longer I shall print my catalogue,[1] perhaps preparatory to selling the collection; then will I gather my virtuous old cloak about me, and beat a final retreat from the auction-room.

Mr. Bedford, the famous bookbinder, was an old and valued acquaintance of mine, a rare friend to the book-collecting race. A good deal of common sense (and uncommon sense) and uncommon kindliness lay funded in his little carcase.[2]

[1] It is now (1887) completed, but it is a failure as regards my original intention. I had hoped to make it a *catalogue raisonné*, and to give some amusing and curious information respecting many of the books—their vicissitudes, and how they came to me. This would have been interesting to my children, and would not have offended the public; but health and its accompanying despondency was the obstacle. I began to revive when the work was almost through the press, but then it was too late. I do not like to look too curiously into this catalogue. I fear it may be full of small errors. All such books are.

[2] My friend Mitchell has lately confided to me that Bedford, not long ago, said to him that I was 'cuttingly cynical;' that I 'shrivelled him up' with my 'sarcastic remarks.' This only shows how people may be misunderstood, for I was never in Bedford's company without having a real desire to please him.

There was nothing of the *durus arator* about this emperor of morocco—he appreciated tall copies; he respected half-titles and fly-leaves, especially the fly leaf A before the title; he venerated margins—and therefore we had many dealings. Bedford was of a cautious and furtive humour. He once sent me home a little binding which I considered unsatisfactory—the volume did not shut properly; it gaped! When I pointed out this grievous defect, his only remark was: 'Why, bless me, sir, you've been *reading* it!' The collector seldom condescends to become a student. I had not been reading it, and I told him so; but I understood the reasonableness of his reproach.

Mr. Bedford died, an old man, about a year ago. Though he did not display much fancy or originality, he was very skilful, had excellent taste, and was devoted to his craft. Death did not take him unawares: day by day, while he patiently waited for it, he tranquilly collated and prepared our shivering little innocents for their morocco jackets. This was a *non mihi sed aliis* and most piously bibliopegic of procedures. Bedford should be canonised.

Let me now tell you the adventures and fate of an old, old volume.

When I was at the height of my book-collecting mania I happened to meet a Mr. Anthony

Horneck, an elderly clergyman, who must have been mature in dulness from his tenderest years. This Horneck was a strong but tedious converser, and he gave me a very detailed account of a wonderful bargain he had once picked up, in the shape of a thin folio from the Pynson Press, the imprint: 'Lond.: In vico vulgacetor Flete Streete, 1510'—a beautiful specimen. It was quite perfect, and of curious rarity. My man described how, after much manœuvring, he had secured the prize for the small sum of one sovereign; that a little while afterwards, happening to take down his Pynson, he perceived it was 'infected with worms—alive with them.' This filled him with apprehension that they might defile his whole library, which, I should say in passing, was composed of modern and very ordinary volumes—'Only books to read, sir,' as the late Mr. Lilly used incisively to put it. 'But,' said Horneck, with a cunning look, 'I took prompt and effectual measures to prevent *that*: I buried the Pynson—I put him underground, sir. Perhaps you don't know that garden mould is a remarkable purifier.' 'What an excellent idea!' said I. This new method of treating a valuable book interested me exceedingly. 'And was it effectual?' 'Yes,' replied he, with increasing animation; 'I stopt all chance of the danger spreading.' 'Well,' continued I, 'and how long did you keep him buried?' 'Oh, he's still there!' 'Still there!' exclaimed I, in amazement; 'and when do you mean to dig it up?' 'Dig it up?' said he, with rather a puzzled air. 'I do not know that I shall ever dig it up! You remember, my dear,' turning with a complaisant air to his admiring wife, 'I buried it under the apple-tree, opposite your boudoir-window;' then, with increasing animation, 'You know it was that spring when the Persian cat kittened in my sermon-box. It's curious how time flies! It must be six or eight years since I buried that Pynson.' *Habent et sua fata libelli*, as the Latin grammar has it.

Lady Charlotte Locker's Death

It was after our last visit to Rome (1866–67) that Lady Charlotte's health began perceptibly to fail; but it was in the spring of 1872 that her decline grew more decided and our anxiety deepened. Her mode of life was straitened; she became a confirmed invalid, and, though she said very little to me, and less to others, I saw that she was preparing for the 'great change,' and with a serene mind.[1] The crisis

[1] Cowper, the poet, said: 'It is well for those who can stand on the mountain-top of life, and, while gazing down with something akin to

came while we were in Victoria Street: she had a much more violent seizure, and died two days afterwards, on April 26, 1872. She was buried at Kensal Green.

I will say nothing here of her winning manners, her genial spirit, of her fresh and sparkling wit. She was not a worse woman for being a witty one. I never knew a sweeter temper or more dignity of character united to so much real humility. The garment of piety did not obscure the vesture of daily life, for she walked gaily among us, the unassuming servant of God. Her conversation was a human delight, her extreme lovableness a perpetual surprise.

There was an enlarged humanity about Charlotte. She never forgot those who had depended upon her, and all such instinctively felt she was their friend, as well as the friend of human nature. Hers was the memory of the heart.

She saw things and she saw people as they really were, and yet to her nobody appeared base. She found large redeeming qualities in every one, for all who came within her influence could not but exhibit themselves under their most favourable aspects. She got much happiness through this

pleasure at the green valleys through which they have passed, can stretch their wings in joyful expectation of a flight into eternity.'

appreciation of the good qualities of those immediately about her. She drew out the best that was in them, and then unconsciously formed an estimate which was nearly always a just one. There are not so very many monsters in the world; there is a fair proportion of good in most people. Some favoured beings are born with a sweetness which naturally impels people to love them, and that through no effort of their own:

> Glad hearts, without reproach or blot,
> Who do God's work and know it not.

Of such was my dear Charlotte.

Her thoughts were for her fellow-creatures—for her suffering fellow-creatures. As I have said, she was the friend of the unfriended poor. This went on to the end of her beneficent life. Her last faltering words, uttered only a few minutes before that seizure from which she never rallied, referred to her anxiety about a poor girl, Kate Gibbs, who was in a decline.

There is a memorial window to Lady Charlotte in Hallingbury Church. It is within sight of the pew where she had so often offered up her prayers and thanksgivings.

The following lines are on a monument erected in Dunfermline Abbey.

Her worth, her wit, her loving smile,
Were with me but a little while.
She came, she went—yet, tho' that voice
Is hushed that made the heart rejoice,
And tho' the grave is dark and chill,
Her memory is fragrant still—
She stands on the Eternal Hill.
Here pause, kind soul, whoe'er you be,
And weep for her, and pray for me.

Re-marriage

In the autumn of 1873 I renewed the slight acquaintance I had made the previous year with Sir Curtis and Lady Lampson, and it ended in my becoming engaged to Hannah Jane, their only daughter. We were married at Rowfant on July 6, 1874, by Arthur Stanley, Dean of Westminster. Amongst those present at the wedding were William Mitchell, my best man, my brother Arthur, Alfred Tennyson, Wilfred and Lady Anne Blunt, and Annie Thackeray.

I believe Janie's married life has not been an unhappy one. But this is small credit to me—it is mainly due to her absolute uprightness, her affectionate nature, and—long, long may she retain them!—her never-failing animal spirits. However, I am not going to praise the living.

A young friend of mine has a favourite cat. It grew old, extremely old, but it retained its vivacity to the last: it ran after its own tail only ten minutes before it died. What an example to the whole human race! It has been observed that those whom the gods love die young, and there never was a truer saying; so I hope all of you will remember this tale of a cat, and 'preserve a lamb's young heart among the full-grown flock.'

The Shakespeare Folio

I will tell you another story about a book.

The Shakespeare folio of 1623 is the most important volume in all Shakespearean literature; for, besides being the first authorised edition, it contains *editiones principes* of no less than twenty plays. It is not really a scarce book—one or two copies come into the market every season. But in a perfect and fine state it is a very rare book, not above four or five really satisfactory copies having turned up since the beginning of the century; for it is almost invariably defective in the first two leaves, viz. the title which has the portrait, and the leaf with Ben Jonson's verses. The rarest leaf of all is the verses, probably because it is nearly blank, and therefore has been less cared for. I know of one or two copies that have the title, more or less damaged, without the verses; I know of several which have neither; but I only know of one copy (of which more anon) which has the verses and no title. The page with the verses is, I repeat, the most difficult page to get.

Some years ago I was offered a splendid example of this folio Shakespeare (1623); it was one of the tallest, largest, and cleanest copies in existence, but it lacked the verses. The owner guaranteed that if I would buy it he would before very long get me the missing leaf, and it was upon this assurance that I closed with him.

Since that time five or six copies have been sold. One was to all intents and purposes perfect, and ultimately fetched (I think) either 1,000*l.* or 1,200*l.*; others had no title and no verses. I heard of several which had neither, and one which had a rag of a title and no verses. But none had the verses without the title. A book so defective might, if it turned up at all, be got for 150*l.*, or less, and this would have been my opportunity, for the possession of it would have enabled me to make my own copy perfect. One day—a day to be well remembered—I heard that a bucolic, Mr. Zachary Dene, living in the West of England, 'an illiterate booby,' had such a copy. Just then the possession of the Ben Jonson leaf was the absorbing ambition of my book-collecting soul; so this was indeed news, and at once set me scheming. I had no sort of acquaintance with Mr. Dene, but after inquiry I found that the brother (a great man) of one of my friends was his neighbour, and knew him well. I immediately got my friend to write to his big brother, and it ended in the owner of the precious book very civilly proposing either to send it to London, or that I should run down and see it at his house. I should have much preferred the former course—very much preferred it—but I hardly liked the responsibility of having the book in my possession; so I determined to go and see it. I own I was encouraged to take this trouble by hearing that Mr. Dene was exceedingly needy—that half his farms were thrown on his hands, and that he did not know which way to turn in his extremity. This news was delightful.

When I left London it was a dark, chill morning, defaced by angry storm-gusts and a threatening sky—

> With low hung clouds that dipt themselves in rain,
> To shake their fleeces on the earth again;

and three hours afterwards, when the train reached Mr. Dene's station, it was raining. While I was inquiring about a conveyance, a roughish-looking person, who from his appearance might have been a farm-bailiff or a depressed tenant-farmer, came up to me, and, to my surprise, and, I may say, satisfaction, informed me that he was the Mr. Dene of whom I was in search. He at once picked up my portmanteau and lifted it into a very high gig with a tall, big-boned, sprig-tailed, sinister-eyed horse in the shafts—altogether the sort of conveyance you would not care to climb into unless you had a spare neck in your pocket, for if you were pitched out of it you would certainly be shot into a neighbouring county. Mr. Dene then took his seat, and invited me to climb up, which, after a struggle, I succeeded in doing. He then informed me that we were six miles from his house; and as it was now raining hard, I recognised that I was in for it. My companion was clownish but kindly. We talked of all sorts of people, always excepting William Shakespeare, and the poor fellow said: 'You must not expect much at my place. Like many another landowner, I am suffering from bad times, but I have taken the bull by the horns and sent away all my men-servants—I've only two or three maids.' 'Dear me!' said I, 'I'm very, very sorry.' However—though it sounds brutal to say so—this was about the best news I had heard yet, and I began to think that the folio (1623) was as much mine as if it were safe in my portmanteau. I required this consolation, for it was raining hard.

I was getting very cold indeed, and beginning to be exceedingly damp.

Mr. Dene then expressed a hope that I took an interest in heraldic archæology; that for himself he did not care for novels—'story-books, you know' (this was indirect, but it was his first allusion to Shakespeare); and when I mentioned the name of Walter Scott, he strained the privilege of country squires to be unlettered, for he had not read a line of him! Here was a good fellow! Of course I happened to be 'interested in heraldic archæology—particularly so,' and if he had not been quite so dripping, I could have hugged him. At this point a gate barred our path, which I had to descend from the lofty gig to open, and from that time to the end of our drive, some two miles farther on, I had nothing but gates to open! I had to clamber up and down in the rain and mud to open gates—the mud was everywhere; sloppy meadows, watery expanses, a universe of slush. And these abominable gates followed each other in the most senseless manner; there was a gate about every three hundred yards or so. All this would have been simply intolerable but for the certainty which I now felt as to the successful issue of my expedition.

At last we arrived at his house. It was an interesting, a noble mansion, a good deal obscured by ivy, the nimble luxuriance of which had almost reached the tops of the tall chimneys. There was a spacious cortile, an arched cloister, and the ruins of a beautiful mediæval wall. This was tumble-down, like everything else—and no wonder, seeing that all the owner could do was to keep his roof weather-tight. The rain had ceased, the sun was in the sky, and the breezy rooks were garrulous on the tall tree-tops. The door into the yard was open, but there was no one to greet us; so down he jumped, telling me to carry my portmanteau into the house, where I should 'find somebody,' while he looked after the 'trap.' In I went, and soon found myself in the presence of Mrs. Dene, a refined and amiable person with a French *tournure* and a pretty, appealing French accent, a certain timidity of manner, but an appreciation of the echoes from our outer world. We got on famously. If she had been young, beautiful, and bewitching, I could not have exerted myself more.

She told me *en tête-à-tête* everything about herself, her narrow joys, and her chilling sorrows; and after dinner, also *en tête-à-tête*—for her husband, grimy Gibeonite that he was, busied himself in getting wood up from the shed—I had the whole history of how she had been wooed, and why she had been won. I fancy it had been a question of single-blessedness or this ill-washed Briton, and that matrimony had carried the day. Poor soul! she had not had so sympathetic a listener for many a long day, perhaps not since the love-making time, even if then. Her life, beyond the superintendence of certain domestic trivialities, must have been a very uneventful one.

Goethe says that women value order more than freedom. I have observed that they resent neglect more than positive ill-usage. The only one of her husbands that the wife of Bath really cared for was the fifth, who, on her well-thumped ribs, left tokens of his love in black and blue.

We dined—a hospitable board. The good fellow actually offered me Madeira from his cellar; but I would have none of it, and preferred his unsophisticated cowslip. Our *pièce de résistance* was a pasty composed of some of the lately mentioned rooks and a juicy pudding. They encouraged me to eat in the spirit, if not in the letter, of

> This pudding's good, this cowslip's healing.
> Pray dip your whiskers and your tail in.

The meal finished, we adjourned to the drawing-room, an apartment telling a tale of vanished stateliness, and fairly comfortable; the rest of the house was a lengthy series of lumber-rooms. Bellerophon was entertained for several days by Prœtus before the latter's ideas of hospitality permitted him to approach business; anyhow, I toasted my toes at the fire, sipped my coffee, braced myself for the all-important moment, and determined to make the plunge. It had come—now or never! It was curious, as I got nearer to the inevitable, and sanguine as I felt too, how nervous I became. My spirits had gradually fallen, like wind at sundown; but it was necessary to begin with something, so I observed: 'I think you must now show me your very interesting book—your Shakespeare.' The sound of the great enchanter's name, uttered for the first time inside these walls, seemed to my highly strung nerves to vibrate, and linger, and echo, and pass away into space with a strange significance. Mr. Dene responded with alacrity, passed into the adjoining room, and speedily returned with the envied volume under his arm. I placed it before me; I carefully examined it. Yes, sure enough, there was the leaf of verses—the real thing, and not—*not* a facsimile, as, after all, I feared it might prove to be. I was also glad to find the book was a poorish copy: some pages were slightly injured, and the title, with its famous portrait, was wanting; the leaf of verses was *doublée.*

All this promised well. The critical moment had arrived. 'Now,' said I genially—'now, I've a copy I should like to show you; you shall see my folio.' I left the room, brought it down from my bedroom, and placed it gently before him.

It did not interest him: he merely glanced at it, though he seemed to comprehend what I was saying. I continued talking, serious but self-possessed, and at last, putting the two volumes side by side, I exclaimed, 'What a pity it is that two such books should be imperfect! Yours is wofully so: it has been cut down, it wants the magnificent title that contains the precious portrait; mine is less so, but it lacks the verses which yours has. I really think I ought to show my magnanimity—take out my title, and make you a handsome present of it!' He laughed with a brutal frankness. 'Or perhaps,' continued I waggishly, 'you might cut out your verses and give them to me.' Then, the ice being broken, I went on, and spoke gravely, earnestly. I said that his copy was fatally, almost irremediably damaged; that he would never be able to get that most important leaf of all—the title—and that he had much better sell his verses, from a printer's point of view the least important leaf in the whole volume. But he interrupted me at once. He said that nothing would persuade him to injure his book. 'Not,' said I, rendered desperate—'not if I gave you an *exact facsimile* of that leaf and 80*l.* into the bargain?' At this his wife nearly jumped out of her chair, out of her linsey-woolsey gown, out of her skin! I saw at once I had an ally in his wife. 'No,' said he, slapping down his coffee-cup on Hemming and Condell's dedication—his precious folio was open at that page—'I won't spoil my book for any one!' 'Spoil your book? Why, you blockhead,' shouted I, 'your precious book is utterly spoiled already. It is cropped, it is incomplete, and can never be perfected unless you pay some 200*l.* or 300*l.* for the missing leaf.' This was the substance of what I said, but clothed in the most guarded and courteous language.

Well, at this point I was completely *au bout de mon latin.* The game was up, and it seemed to me that Mr. Dene was an ignorant and obstinate idiot, and no wonder his farms were tenantless, and that he had to cut and carry his firewood. However, with dulness and a sound digestion a man may endure much. I saw there was nothing more to be done—that I had better be off. But no! then—then began the misery. They insisted on my remaining two nights. I protested. I had to yield, and to smile and talk, and to make myself agreeable. I had to listen to Crispinus's long-winded histories of his antiquarian exploits. He had published an account of a certain dreadful ruin, which he exhibited to me, and with me went through its elevations and all its measurements. There was St. Nynyan's from the east, and St. Nynyan's from the west, and from the N.N.W., and from the W. by N., and from all the points of the compass. Then we had the crypt, and the clerestory, and the Lady Chapel. Then came the heraldry. 'Ah!' says Mrs. Dene sportively, dropping her head a little on one side, 'if you are to be up the genealogical tree together, I shall beg to say good-night!' The thing dragged on. I heard his voice—I smiled—my thoughts wandered—I was absent, but, alas! without being anywhere else.[1] I appeared cheerful, but I nearly died of it—and I had brought it all upon myself! At last—

Time and the hour runs through the roughest day—

I escaped to a penitential pillow.

A martyrdom awaited me in the guise of a very bleak chamber, small and low; there was no fire in the grate, but in its stead a powerful down draught of icy air mingled with smoke; and through the ill joinery of the door there also came in a zephyr that blew my boots off. A strip of drugget partially concealed the brick floor. The drawers of the only chest in the room were filled with curtains and their rings, and some more favoured person's raiment and rags. This is the sort of treatment that a self-respecting guest should resent. Then the bed! The mattress was on a steep incline from one side to the other and from the wall; the bolster a mere

[1] 'Dieu me fait quelquefois la grâce de ne pas les écouter.'

fistful of cock-and-hen feathers at either end, and none in the centre; the crevices in the window-frame were much too wide, and the cotton bed-clothes a great deal too narrow; 'the blankets were thin and the sheets they were sma'' [1]—quite untuckable. I had a comfortless night of it, with no hope for the morrow.

I have not spared Mr. Dene in this description, and I will swear that I have not immensely exaggerated the incompleteness of himself and his establishment; if so, and it is so, you must take into account my grievous disappointment.

I am thankful to say that I never broke down. I retained my native amiability of manner to the bitter end, and we parted the best of friends. I think both husband and wife were sorry to bid me 'good-bye,' and I murmured something about 'seeing you again.' Since then I have occasionally written to her. I hope they think kindly of me. I now think most kindly of them. Indeed, I remember them as I believe they would wish to be remembered.

I recollect as I drove away from Mr. Dene's I had one cause for satisfaction, and only one. I felt I had done my very best to gain my point; that I had not said *too much*,[2] and that I could not blame

[1] I see I have said this at p. 109.

[2] La Bruyère says that nobody regrets having said *too little*.

myself for any diplomatic slip or for the manner in which I had conducted the negotiations.

Was not my square-headed squire a queer fellow? He had not the slightest literary interest in his Shakespeare; to him the volume on his shelf was a folio book and nothing more—it was nothing beyond the bare fact of possession. Perhaps so; but he was not an 'illiterate booby.' I do not take the same view of the matter now as I did then, at any rate not in the same degree.

Some years after the dealer who sold me my Shakespeare (1623) was at a print sale, and he chanced to hear a man in the crowd of buyers say that a friend of his had the precious leaf of verses—it was pasted into an old scrapbook!—and that he had been told it was worth 80*l*. or 100*l*. It has ended in my becoming the possessor of this leaf for the larger sum. So I suppose I may now consider my Shakespeare is perfect.[1]

Here comes the moral of a very long story. 1. If ever you want a perfect copy of the folio (1623), do not buy one which has not the leaf of verses with the hope of getting it afterwards. 2. What right had I to scheme to get Mr. Dene's leaf out of him; and, having failed, what right have I to abuse him in

[1] One hundred pounds seems a large sum for a single mutilated leaf, but sensible people have paid more than that for a black tulip or a blue ribbon.

revenge for my disappointment and chagrin? Was not I rightly served? *Adieu paniers, vendanges sont faites.*

The Philobiblon

I have been for many years a member of the Philobiblon. It is a small and select breakfasting society, and it has an object. Half a dozen times during the London season we meet at each other's houses and admire each other's illuminated books and ancient manuscripts. On these occasions I have seen and handled the most priceless volumes, bindings glowing with the arms of Mazarin or the cypher of Mary Queen of Scots, or the skilled needles of those apparently overworked virgins, the nuns of Little Gidding—books so rare that the individual copy was almost the species. The mere remembrance of such treasures must have a benign influence on the soul of the true book-lover; indeed, it can emolliently affect the nervous system of people who have no real sensibility. However, I may remark that it is a mistake to suppose that your book-collector is much of a reader. Your true bibliophile rarely reads anything—he contemplates, he examines bindings, criticises illustrations, and scrutinises title-pages or pagination.

He does not read; but still, when he shall have passed away into bookless ether, at least let the lingering scholar drop a flower, or flyleaf, on the turf where his once book-collecting body is laid.

These books and manuscripts are the ostensible interest of our meetings, but there is another and a more pressing, a far deeper interest, of which I will speak to you presently.

The Prince Consort was our patron, and he was succeeded by the Duc d'Aumale, who, while he lived in England, entertained the Society most royally, and with a captivating *bonhomie*. Among our thirty-five members are, or were, the Prince Consort, the Duke of Albany, Robert Curzon, the Dukes of Hamilton and Newcastle, Richard Ford, Evelyn Shirley, Deans Stanley and Milman, Stirling-Maxwell, H. Hucks Gibbs, Silvain Van de Weyer (and his widow after him), Bishop Wilberforce, 'Big' Higgins, Lords Ellesmere, Acton, Dufferin, Salisbury, and Houghton, Henry Ruffe, and Hildebrand Buggins.

[1] Van de Weyer was much regarded by the Society, and with reason, so when he died his wife was elected in his place. Her name appears in vol. xiv. among the list of members. Vicomte de Tharon, of the Affaires Etrangères, told me that in the French war with England a French commanding officer had blown up his ship (and himself) to prevent its being taken, and that his Government had recognised his heroism by entering his sister's (his only surviving relative) name in the place in the French Navy List which his name had occupied, where it remained till her death.

The last is the widely known vinegar merchant and virtuoso, and he would thereby be well qualified for membership but for his bearing and conversation, which are noisy and arrogant—so much so that the man and his manners have become almost ridiculous.

I do not think I ever remember a Philobiblon breakfast at which Mr. Buggins did not very much assist. He is now exceedingly old, but he has yet to learn that an occasional absence has a charm.

During the first year of my membership we happened to be breakfasting, I think, with Lord Powis. I was seated between Messrs. Ruffe and Buggins, and I complained to the former of the way in which the guests were packed: 'Seven or eight lords huddled together, and we two or three ignoble ones' (ignoble because untitled) 'left out in the cold.' 'Oh!' says Ruffe, in a grave and nervous whisper, 'that's not it—that isn't it. Haven't you observed as we walked in to breakfast how everybody tries to get away from that brute Buggins?—that's how it is that we get "packed," as you facetiously put it. I assure you there is no sort of notion of exclusiveness, *altro!*'

Ruffe may have been right; but, as a new member, this extreme unpopularity of Mr. Buggins had not come entirely home to me, for we are much too polite a society to even hint at such a thing.

However, certainly on reflection I called to mind, and it sank pretty deep into my soul, that hitherto, for the few times that I had breakfasted, somehow or other I had always been seated in Mr. Buggins's pocket!

Since that morning in Berkeley Square I have greatly hardened my heart, have frantically struggled, and have generally succeeded in escaping from Mr. Buggins. It requires alertness, added to considerable presence of mind, to do this decently and decisively. However, it is practicable, for providentially we have two much-valued members, both of distinguished rank, one of whom is exceedingly inert, while the other is as meek as he is long-suffering; and I observe that the unconscious Mr. Buggins almost invariably sits by one or other. I can assure you that the fifteen seconds of time during which we are passing from the library to the dining-room is an ordeal. When the company is assembled and seated, the first thing that everybody does is to glance round the table furtively, to find out which of the party have fallen a prey to Mr. Buggins.

Now you know the supreme interest of our breakfasts: the might-and-main, the hammer-and-tongs struggle to escape from Mr. Buggins.

Perhaps Ruffe expressed himself intemperately when he called Buggins 'a brute,' but, poor fellow!

he had suffered. He is large and unwieldy; added to that, he has terrific attacks of gout, and after one of these he is completely at the mercy of this uncouth person. He does his best to escape. He hobbles—for his heart is good; could he go faster than he could?—he hobbles, but sometimes he is headed; whereas I can slip through and away like a lizard.

Hildebrand Buggins is an extraordinary animal, *seul de son espèce.* He is entirely destitute of social tact; he curiously combines the foibles of youth with the frailties of age; he bawls, he brags, he domineers; he grossly exaggerates about his biddings, his pictures, his china—the prices he has paid for them—and his exploits generally. His flights of fancy are not calculated mendacity—they are merely a mental mirage.

Mr. Buggins's philobiblical ego is enormously developed.

The Duc d'Aumale, for instance, will be unaffectedly exhibiting a copy of that very rare volume, Frans Rabelais's 'Plaisante et joyeuse Histoyre du grand géant Gargantua,' on vellum, bound by Antoine Padeloup, perhaps with the arms of Renault César Louis de Choiseul, duc de Praslin, in gold, on the side, which he has just had the astounding good fortune to secure in Paris, or The Hague, or on a bookstall in Pekin. Well, above the gentle *susurrus* of polite conversation you hear Mr. Buggins's detestable *staccato*, 'Yes, sir, I've two copies of that book, and mine are taller and finer. One of them is with the cancelled leaves, which apparently your Royal Highness's don't possess,' &c. The Duke is not the least annoyed, and talks of 'ce cher Buggins;' but his Royal Highness does not sit next to him at breakfast.

If I were asked whether Buggins was always disagreeable, I should say he is always as disagreeable as the special circumstances admit of. You see, he would go out of his way (if he had any such to go out of) to be unpleasant. Perhaps there are people in the world more annoying than Mr. Buggins, who more need our prayers, but they are not Philobiblons.

Is it fair to gibbet anybody as a social scarecrow? Is it kindly to be merciless to the absurd? Certainly not. And now, my children, I tremble, for is it not well known that a man never betrays his own character more completely than when he laughs at that of somebody else? However, I hope I hardly ever laugh at any one unless I like them—just a little.

My dear children, let me whisper in your ears: make up your minds that there is no such person as Mr. Hildebrand Buggins.

Mr. Doo

'On the 15th instant, at his residence in Eaton Square, deeply regretted by all who knew him, John Doo, Esq., F.S.A., F.G.S., F.R.G.S., J.P., in the 80th year of his age. Friends are requested,' &c.

A propos of this announcement, I must tell you another long story of a little book, a volume of extraordinary rarity, and of which at one time I greatly coveted the possession. It had the scarce title-page without the date; there is only one other copy known with this peculiarity, and that copy is locked up at Sion College.

This little book is curiously connected in my mind with the above-named Mr. Doo, a consequential old gentleman whom I used frequently to meet at the club. I fancy I see him. He would stand before the fire with a pinch of snuff between his finger and thumb, his coat-tails and the 'Art Journal' in the other hand. He had a slow, a deliberate cough, a pug nose, and long hairy ears—ears as long and as hairy as the ears of a jackass—which he was. He had eyes with scarlet rims, and a prodigious quantity of white whiskers; but there was nothing venerable about Mr. Doo.[1] To look at him, it seemed impossible that he could ever have

[1] Extracted from *Patchwork*.

been dandled in a fond mother's embraces; but people do change considerably. Mr. Doo was a patron of the fine arts, a person whose conversation was pompous and empty—in fact, so extremely tiresome that his fellow-creatures, myself included, gave him the widest possible berth. He had once beguiled me into seeing his collection in Eaton Square, and had often pressed me to go there again, or, as he phrased it, to 'overhaul his portfolios.'

One day, while he was holding forth on art revival and the decay of literature, and I was meditating how it would be possible to give him the slip, he mentioned the title of the rare little book at Sion College. I instantly pricked up my ears. But when he casually let drop that he possessed a copy of it, and without the date on the title, I was indeed surprised, and at once became interested in everything concerning him—his collection, his conversation, and even his cough! I am ashamed, too, to confess it, but from that moment I was a deal more attentive to him than I had hitherto been. I sought him out, and listened respectfully while he expatiated on what was exploded, enlarged on what was trivial, and bragged of his influence in the art world. I stultified myself by defending him behind his back. After this, when we met, our talk somehow always got round to the rare little book.

One day—it was a memorable day for me—Mr. Doo cleared his throat, and said, in his usual humdrum tones: 'I have been thinking about that shabby little book of mine. It is tossing about somewhere in my town house; I begin to think it's quite wrong for me to keep the little fellow all to myself—it's much more in your way now;' and then he paid me one or two rancid compliments about my 'Lyrics' which I should be ashamed to detail here, and which I am more ashamed to have half swallowed then.

I ought to have suspected that Mr. Doo was acting a part, for he exaggerated it. He overstepped the modesty of nature.

'I wish,' said he, with a glittering grin which was as false as what it revealed, 'you would just name a day, and come and have a good overhauling of my portfolios.' Then he added, 'And you know, about that book—now, I really don't think I ought to keep such a gem all to myself. When you come, you will find it on the corner of the table, and you'll slip it into your pocket without saying anything to anybody, and that will be all about it—eh? You know it has got the scarce title without the date, &c.' Conceive my feelings! I at once, there and then, fixed a day—I nailed him to it. 'Yes, to-morrow, at eleven o'clock,' would 'suit me down to the ground.'

The next morning, punctual to the minute, I found myself in Mr. Doo's library.

When I entered this 'chamber of horrors' (interesting because everything was so exquisitely in keeping), I naturally looked at all the corners of the tables. I did not see the book, but I made up my mind that it would be forthcoming at the right time, and I was quite cheerful. We again went through his pictures, this time thoroughly—his Haydons, his Hiltons, his Fuselis (masters that I detest), a smirking Romney or two, very flagrant specimens of what may be called 'the roguish school.' Mr. Doo had one oil-picture that was extremely interesting. I am reluctant to mention it, as its possession was a credit to him.[1] Mr. Doo had a long, long history about each, and all to his own glorification. At first I listened with interest, and then with politeness and patience; but, as has been well remarked, tediousness has a peculiar power of propagating itself, and I began to be very stupid, for there was no end to the stories and no mention of the precious little book. It was then that, to my horror, he brought out his 'folios.' These were a caution to snakes!—heaps and heaps of seventeenth-century prints, worn-out impressions after Goltzius and the schools of M. Angelo and Rubens—the sort of rubbish one used to see exposed for sale in an old umbrella in the New Cut. I feigned as deep an interest as I

[1] Michel, le Sieur de Montaigne, observes that it is not wrong to say of a thief that he has a handsome leg.

could, but my nerves were fast giving way under the strain. I was very weary. I began to suffer from a queer sensation, as if I were being nibbled to death by ducks—in other words, I had an acute attack of the fidgets, and should have liked to kick Doo's shins under the table. Twelve o'clock had struck—one o'clock had struck; I wished old Doo at the deuce, and began to perceive an ominous something in his manner that made me suspect he was beginning to have much the same sort of feeling about myself. It was getting on for two o'clock; I was bored through and through, and, as we turned over the last Goltzius, I yawned cavernously in his face, and murmured something about its being 'time to go,' and of 'an appointment at the Zoological Gardens.' I thanked him; I spoke with effusion of his 'extreme kindness;' I begged he would excuse me: 'I must be off—due at the Monkey House at two o'clock.' Not a word about my precious little volume! 'But you have not yet seen my folio of Everdingens. Great creator, Everdingen, *malo cum Platone errare*—eh?' said Doo. 'Oh, hang your Everdingens!' I mentally ejaculated, 'where's my book?' Not a word was uttered about it. I again said, 'I fear I must go,' and for the twentieth time I glanced at all the corners of all the tables. I did it, and yet I knew it was quite useless. And old Doo saw me doing it! In vain I sought it, for it was not there. We shook hands. I moved to go—I went; but as I grasped the handle of the door I turned round, and, with a cadaverous smile, a smile so sickly that the hand of death was upon it, I said: 'By the bye, Mr. Doo' (sprightlily, just as if it was occurring to me for the first time), 'I haven't seen that little book of yours.' 'Oh!—oh!' says Doo, in his exasperatingly deliberate way—'the book, eh? Yes, I've been considering about that little fellow. He's a gem, and really—I don't know—but the fact is, you see, I've been thinking I ought to consult my relatives' (mind, he was not far from eighty years of age) 'before I proceed further in that matter. Good morning.'

I never felt in such a rage in my life; I nearly bawled out, 'You and your relations may go to glory, sir, for aught I care, and be blest to you!' I was furious—I had been so completely bamboozled and made such a fool of. But I stifled my wrath; I kept silence, though it was a pain and grief to me, got out of the room and out of the house as quickly as I could, and banged the door behind me.

I banged the door with such a slam
It sounded like a wooden d——n.[1]

All this occurred three years ago, and even now

[1] Poor Sganarelle and his 'Ah mes gages! mes gages! tout le monde est content; il n'y a que moi seul de malheureux.' My book! my book! my book!

I am in doubt as to the exact object of that miserable old man; but I am inclined to think that from beginning to end it was an artfully devised plot to humiliate me, a scheme carried out with deliberate malice and consummate cunning. I doubt if he ever had the book at all. However, I shall go to the sale of his library.

The whole affair, like unto Gil Blas's legacy, is only another instance of the deplorable uncertainty of human hopes and expectations.

Unfortunate old man! I do not say that he was a humbug and a traitor, but he had that order of mind that inclines its possessor to villainous courses. I suppose he could not help it.[1]

The Barbarians

I have paid many a pleasant visit in my day, some to smart people in smart houses, one or two to Lord and Lady Tadcaster at Babram, formerly Babraham, near Bosworth, the land of Robert Burton and George Eliot; but Burton and George

[1] This sketch appeared in *Patchwork*. That work was issued to the public on a Wednesday, and, curiously enough, old Doo died on the Friday following. My friends pretend that he read it and instantly took to his bed.

Eliot are prophet and prophetess about whom Babram does not mightily concern itself. I have been to them at The Hut.

The Tadcasters are addicted to the turf, and their surroundings somewhat, and not unpleasantly, savour of that fancy. I made their acquaintance at Doncaster. Lady Tadcaster was a Blois, and I venture to assert that she is still divinely beautiful. 'Sérieusement, c'est une chose surprenante que sa beauté!' She is connected with the Cavendishes, Cecils, &c.

Babram Hall is stately and imposing, and the demesne is perfection. We know that God Almighty planted the first garden; those of Babram were laid out by a Reverend Sir Hilary Jinks—brilliant parterres, somewhat in the Dutch style, and enchanting lawnlets. Lady Tadcaster has a passion for her flowers—a passion that Lenôtre would have respected—and the flowers requite her affection. The park is very fine. There is a scarcity of water that would satisfy even a Dutchman.

These, however, were not my principal attractions to Babram. My attractions were Lady Tadcaster herself and the interesting library. You see, I unhesitatingly place the fair lady first.

Among many important and desirable volumes —quaint Bibles, patristic folios, choice old county histories, and solemn jest-books—are one or two of Shakespeare's quartos of extraordinary rarity, *rarissima*! Can you conceive it?—they have the four Shakespeare folios; the 'Sonnets' (1609); 'Romeo and Juliet' (1599); 'Richard II.' (1598); 'Richard III.' (1597); 'Midsummer Night's Dream' (Fisher, 1600), and the 'Hamlet' of 1604; to say nothing of Anthony Munday's 'Banquet of Daintie Conceits' (1558) and Edmund Spenser's 'Shepherd's Calendar,' first edition.

Now, in cold blood, I ask myself why, in the name of all that's wonderful, have I not appropriated a few of these little old books? Why? oh, why? They would never have been missed, and there would have been some chique in adding the 'Hamlet' of 1604 to one's starved little treasure-house at home—that is to say, if it had been stolen!

In those days we used to sit a good deal in the library, where the beautiful old bindings are in perfect harmony with all that female taste and refinement can devise for the adornment of such a room. However, during the talk, which now and again indicated a slackening of mental activity (there are such *lacunæ* in the most refined circles), 'poor old Bibliophile' could not help sometimes saying to himself (the gay and frivolous scene before him glittering, as it were, through the passing grimness of the thought), 'By Jupiter! and all this time there are those disregarded quartos within a few yards of all our heads!'

You now know why I specially speak of Babram. Yes, it is those priceless books—and a pair of beautiful blue eyes. I would call them eyes of *watchet* hue if I were quite sure what 'watchet' means. Would that we had a Latour or a Cosway to do justice to the eyes!

> The power that she has o'er me lies,
> Not in her BOOKS, but in her eyes.

As a child of the epoch, Lady Tadcaster is graciously exclusive and captivatingly matter of fact; her style is so excellent that it seems something very like impertinence to praise her.

Did I write the following lines in her visitors' book? If so, it must have been a long, long time ago.

A WORD THAT MAKES US LINGER.

Fair hostess mine, who raised the latch,
And welcomed me beneath your thatch,
Who makes me here forget the pain
And all the pleasures of Cockaigne.
Now, pen in hand, and pierced with woe,
I'll write one word before I go—

'A word that dies upon my lips
While thus you kiss your finger-tips.

When 'Black-eyed Sue' was rowed to land,
That word she cried, and waved her hand—
Her lily hand!
It seems absurd,
But I *can't* write that dreadful word.

There is a good deal that is exhilarating in the society of the 'Barbarian.' I could be eloquent about it. The men are so manly, the women so womanly; and both are so good-looking, so plucky, and so natural—they are nearly always that. They cultivate what John Dryden calls 'the sweet civilities of life,' which make life so smooth and which, like grace and beauty, beget love at first sight. It is these that open the door and let the stranger in.

Then in their bearing there is a charming unceremoniousness, a polished off-handedness, and an easy unconcern that go straight to the point. These qualities, rare as they are, come to them insensibly in the air which they breathe, being not much else than the result of one, or, it may be, even two generations of an assured position. I must not be thought ungrateful if I now confess that unadulterated barbarism has its drawbacks and (I brace my resolution to say so) its drearier side.

The truth is that there is more than the probability of the Barbarians missing nearly everything that is finest in literature and art, and possibly in life itself. This is a discredit, seeing that they have abundance of capabilities and opportunities, and, if they would but determine it, a luxury of leisure.

With tastes and instincts that are excellent,

they do themselves scant justice, for they give themselves no time for that which is the outcome of simple living—and of that only. Not that they are indolent; on the contrary, there is a self-reliance, an energy about them that is remarkable. They dress, and dance, and shoot, and ride, and please themselves; they are passionately fond of pleasure; new frocks, love-letters, and many other good things gush forth at their feet in increasing streams. And no wonder they indulge. They are often inconsequent and capricious, but not specially selfish or insincere; but in everyday life they are apt to be governed by the humour of the moment, and to be influenced by the chance sympathy of any one who attracts them, or whom they may desire to attract. Indeed, their admirations often betray them into the very strangest company. Nor are they incapable of sacrifices. They are capable of much; for they would battle for a form of faith the spirit of which they do not understand and the precepts of which they habitually disregard. Indeed, I believe, if the necessity arose, they would part, heroically part, with their diamond shoe-buckles, and take cheerfully to primitive shoe-ties.

I suppose they think that they discharge their duty to their fellow-creatures by simply existing; that intellectual pursuits are no special concern of theirs; that such properly belong to the working classes—Darwin, G. Stephenson, C. Dickens, Faraday, Wordsworth, Hallam, &c.—for the working classes to cultivate, and for them to enjoy.

It is thus they spend their careless hours. Time flies, my pretty one! These precious hours are very sweet to thee; make the most of them. Now, even now, as thou twinest that brown curl on thy finger—see! it grows grey.

Dear children, our life is a shadow dance. I say this, and yet my common sense keeps telling me that while we are here we should be content to do our best for ourselves as well as for our fellow-creatures: to do our duty without worrying about the 'great hereafter.' But as I get older the magnitude of the unknown oppresses me, overpowers me; and this, perhaps, may account for the rather fleeting view I take of life, and may have unduly influenced these remarks. How should I feel, and what should I do, if I were young—again young and active and buoyant as those about me?

All nature seems at work:
The bees are stirring, birds are on the wing,
And I the while, the sole unbusy thing,
Nor honey make, nor pair, nor build, nor sing.

Society

Dear children, I told you in a former chapter how much pleasure I found in the company of the Barbarian; but writing as I now do, far away in the Rowfant woods, I venture to hint that the sort of existence these attractive savages make for themselves is not altogether satisfying. One values the privilege of *entrée*, but it must be indulged in with moderation, for they lose it that do buy it with overmuch care.

The more estimable of the people who compose smart society (what will it be called in the next generation?) are courteous, obliging, and hospitable. I admire their simple manners and good breeding, their frank self-reliance and tempered reserve, their graceful negligence; sometimes a certain freemasonry of refined clownishness—a tone which cannot be acquired, and which is the inheritance of a privileged class that, for many a long day, has not been disturbed by the feeling of social insecurity, and has breathed an atmosphere of more or less refinement.

I especially recognise this agreeable negligence, this freedom of demeanour, in royal personages. I observed its dawn in the young princes and princesses (the Queen's children) as they grew up. Its possession is small credit, for by reason of their being placed in such an exalted condition they can be perfectly unaffected, and say exactly what they choose without jeopardising their status; they can afford to be merciful to the absurd and indulgent to even the presuming.

Consider what an advantage it gives a royal, or even a titled converser, to be sure of a deferential and appreciative audience! He can talk when he pleases, and change the subject when he so decrees it. He can skulk behind his title.

At a state ball at Buckingham Palace I was struck with the demeanour of the Shah of Persia. He sat enthroned, and gazed at the dancers as at an anthill; he looked material and stolid enough, and his manner and gloomy stare gave one the idea of indolent indifference; but it was indifference engendered by a supreme will, the result of power that had never been challenged.

However, to return, I see in these exclusives who consider themselves of the 'haute volée, ce qu'il y a de mieux au monde' (they ignore some three-quarters of the Peerage because it does not happen to be in their set), the same weakness that is to be discovered in all coteries. They think they have the monopoly of everything which is of any real importance; that those who are not in their sacrosanct circle are nowhere. They may be wrong, but when people who have a powerful position have made up their minds, it becomes embarrassing.

As regards the least gifted and most trifling, if they ever reflect, if they are ever mindful of the outside world, it is with a careless curiosity, perhaps with a good-natured contempt; and yet, if you took your brainless Alcibiades, or vapid Lady Clara, away from their special babblement, their futile pleasures, and the fineries and impertinences of life, you would discover they had just as much to say for themselves as, and not more than, any other gabies. Their little lives are rounded by the vision of eligible lovers, becoming costumes, luxurious upholstery, and all the other exigencies of a frivolous existence; and from that, as time overtakes them, they pass easily and by slow degrees to small scandal, conventional prayers, and a serene or acrimonious nothingness.[1]

Consider the opulence of their surroundings and the penury of their talk! It is indeed small, it is humiliating—the iniquities of a cook or a governess, the naming of a thoroughbred, social *tracasseries*, poor political intrigues, the last *on dit*, or the general question of the distractions of yesterday, to-day, and to-morrow.

[1] An old, old woman who was asked how she contrived to get through her day, replied: 'Well, you see, I coughs a bit, and I scolds a bit, and I prays a bit, and it all helps to pass the time.'

Like Mary Wollstonecraft's baby,[1] they are passionately fond of material enjoyments, and they pursue them (without always overtaking them) with an ostentatious candour which, in people of less assured position, would be thought almost shocking.

On the other hand, there are your *bourgeois* acquaintance, some of whom may have become suddenly opulent, and are pretty sure not to have been improved thereby. The wealth of these people is apt to rot into luxury and extravagance. Material enjoyment is much more expensive than intellectual: reading costs little, thinking and conversation cost nothing at all. Yes, matter is more expensive than mind, so I cannot help contrasting such people, to their disadvantage, with persons of birth and breeding, and maybe even larger possessions, who conduct themselves with dignity, moderation, and decency. Such are greatly to be admired.

There is something almost ludicrous in the arrogance of many of the suddenly enriched. Pride was not made for Adam's posterity, especially placed as they are in a corner of a fussy and very inferior planet.

My children, I have been speaking of the delightful characteristics of persons of rank and

[1] Mary Wollstonecraft said of her baby: 'Besides looking at me, there are three other things that delight her—to ride in a coach, to look at a scarlet waistcoat, and to hear loud music.'

fashion, and I will add that these are the qualities which their satellites are apt to imitate, distort, and even defile. Persons not naturally belonging to exclusive circles, but who obtain admittance to them and habitually haunt them, are apt to develop into what have been brutally called toadies and flunkeys. These are men and women not necessarily base, but upon whom Nature has bestowed an abnormally flexible spine.

Who fetch and carry nonsense for my lord.

These people are often affectionate, sometimes intelligent, not seldom cultivated and agreeable, and not to be despised. However, they are not to be admired, much less to be imitated. I have known many such people. And there will ever be a certain demand for the parasite, who begins by being tolerated, then grows useful, and often ends by becoming contemptibly indispensable. The 'Rambler' says that few can be assiduous without servility, and none can be servile without corruption. Such is poor human nature! 'Fuge magna . . . dulcis inexpertis cultura potentis amici; expertus metuit.' There is force in these words of warning, coming to us as they do across the ages, and uttered as they were by a satirist whose father had been a serf. I would have my children lay them to heart. However, I think the tone of criticism on this subject usually indulged in by people not the best qualified to judge is crude and misleading.

I know people who are under no special obligation to the aristocracy of their country, but who are curiously dependent on them. For example, there is S——, a kindly, a domestic fellow—a tame cat—and, in what he calls his own set, rather looked up to than not. Quite lately he and I were spending the evening at Mrs. R——'s, whom we all like so well. There were eight or ten guests, but not one of them had any social vogue, and, as they kept arriving, S—— became languid—more languid—almost plaintive. This continued and increased till Lady G—— arrived—not the young and clever, observe you, but the aged and dull. However, with this addition to our party S—— soon got back all his sprightliness. He was completely braced up by the serene vacuity, in itself almost regal, of kindly old Lady G——.

It had been the entire absence of patrician oxygen in our social atmosphere which had disturbed him. Mrs. R—— was hurt, and spoke to me about it. 'Didn't you notice him?' 'Yes,' said I; 'indeed I did, and be hanged to him!' 'I like you for that,' quoth she; 'but just now I pointed out the idiotic way he was going on to Molly F——, and she was so taken up with that pretty new lilac *négligé* of hers that she hadn't noticed it. Is that because she is so stupid?' 'No,' I replied; 'I think it is because you and I are more sensitive—may I say, more in sympathy with S—— ?'

A worldling, a boudoir Diogenes,[1] has observed that it is advisable to associate with the highest, not because the highest are the best, but because, if you become disgusted with them, you can at any time descend; but that if you begin with the lower, woe unto you, for the ascent is wellnigh impossible. In the grand theatre of human life a box-ticket carries one all over the house.

Our aristocracy is fast becoming a plutocracy, and we know that each section of society has its besetting virtues and its characteristic frailties; but in the great essentials the various ranks are more alike than the observer who spends his time in contemplating the surface of things would imagine. However, all are not equally pleasant to live with.

I dare say nearly all I have been saying here has been said before, and much better said; but it is the result of my personal experience, and I repeat it because I would have my children retain their independence of character, and at the same time keep clear of cant. Traditional class prejudice is the bondage of unreason.

[1] The Rev. Caleb Cotton, author of *Lacon*.

My Guardian Angel

'Abra was ready when I called her name,
And, tho' I called another, Abra came.'

I will here describe a ridiculous misfortune that happened to me about fifteen years ago, and record my obligations to my guardian angel.

I was calling on some friends in Pentonville (I do not care to reveal the exact address). It was in June, and they were not at home; however, as I had come a long distance, and really wished to see them, I asked the servant to let me wait their return. This handmaid was past her giddy youth, but had not nearly arrived at middle age. She was of haughty eye and serene countenance. Some people might have called her comely, some attractive. I found her anything but cordial; in fact, she had a slightly chilling manner, as if she was not overjoyed to see me, and would not break her heart if she never saw me again. However, in I walked, and was taken to a drawing-room on the ground-floor with French windows (open) to the garden.

The apartment was gorgeously furnished—gold wall-paper, sumptuous hangings, and an aggressive crimson and orange carpet. It was quite new, of the kind which, I think, is called 'velvet pile.' There were books on the inlaid tables—depressing books, books of beauty, illuminated volumes of devotion, views in the Holy Land, and gems from our poets, all elaborately bound. Humming-birds were stifling under glass shades; there were gimcrack ornaments, frail, carved ivory absurdities, only waiting for someone to smash them, and magnificent paper-knives, smelling-bottles, and all the rest of it, in velvet cases. This was not cosy, not even homelike, for there was no inkstand in the room, and no writing materials.[1]

I resented this. Fifteen years ago—alas! I was fifteen years younger than I am now—rhymes were more often trotting in my head. It happened that such became the case as I sat waiting for my friends, and I felt if I did not at once secure them they might be lost to me and for ever. I had no pencil, and only the back of a letter. So, rather cautiously—for I felt ashamed of what I was doing—I opened the door and stole across the passage to the library. There I found pens and a gigantic glass inkstand. It was somewhat this shape:

[1] However, I am bound to say that there was compensation, for a garden-chair was drawn to the open window; also a small table, on which a fan and a few freshly gathered roses were laid. A pair of pearl-tinted kid gloves, lying light as fallen leaves, and an open book, were on the chair, just as the fair owner had left them. She had actually been reading that delightful prose idyll of 'Old Cheeseman'!

I had never seen the form before, and I am not ambitious of beholding it again. I bore it across the hall as far as the centre of the drawing-room; then, all of a sudden, without any warning, the lower portion (till that moment I had supposed the bloated monster to be one piece of glass) detached itself from that which I held in my hand, and to which it had hitherto clung corroded, and fell to the floor, rolling over and over along the wretched crimson and orange velvet pile, and emptying its ample contents as it rolled.

Can you conceive my feelings? I spun round the room in an agony. I tore at the bell, then at the other bell, then at both the bells; then I dashed into the library, and rang the bells there, and then back again to the drawing-room. The maid who had admitted me came up almost immediately, looking as calm as possible, and when she saw the mischief she seemed all at once to rise to the gravity of the occasion. She did not say a word, she did not even look dismayed, but in answer to my frenzied appeal she smiled, and vanished. 'In the twinkling of a bedpost,' however, she was back again with a pail of hot water, soap, sponge, &c., and was soon mopping up the copious stains with a damp flannel, kneeling, and looking beautiful as she knelt.

Then did I throw myself into an easy chair, exhausted with excitement, and, I may say, agony of mind, and I swore to myself: 'Good heavens, if this blessed creature should really help me in this frightful imbroglio I will give her a sovereign. It will be cheap at a sovereign. Yes, she shall have her 20*s.*!'

Well, what with sponging and dabbing, the great black stain began gradually to wax fainter, and my spirit revived in proportion; and all the while this angelic being spoke so cheerfully, and had altogether such a delightful air, that I longed to assure her how profoundly I respected her.

> Old as I am, for ladies' love unfit,
> The power of beauty I remember yet.

However, at this juncture—I am almost ashamed to confess it—I began to revolve in my mind whether ten shillings might not be a sufficient recompense, for, after all, she had not been much more than ten minutes about the whole affair. Well, the scrubbing went on; then she took to her brush, and in certainly less than twenty minutes the stains had entirely disappeared, and my guardian angel rose to her feet and asked me, with a quiet little smile, as though it were all the most natural thing in the world, if I should like to have a cup of tea. I accepted her pious offer with joy and gratitude; and there I sat me down, and gazed complacently at the again gorgeous crimson and orange velvet pile, and sipped my tea, and by the time I had finished it (and my rhyme) my esteemed friends made their appearance.

You may suppose that at first I felt a little uncomfortable; especially so when, in something less than ten seconds, my good and demonstrative friend bawled to his fascinating wife, who had become at once occupied with her roses, 'Millicent! Millicent! look here! Now, isn't this too bad? Just look at my carpet!' My soul died within me. I had my back to him. He was not far from the window; he seemed close to the spot where the catastrophe had happened. 'Yes,' said he, 'they will leave the windows open, and your brute of a pug has brought all this filthy gravel in on his paws.' I breathed again, and, feeling constrained to say something, I observed, with a sickly smile: 'So our friend Edgar is very particular about his carpet, eh?' 'Particular!' says the little woman; 'I should think he was particular—and awfully so just now, for this is a *new* purchase, don't you know; it was only laid down yesterday. You can't conceive how awfully fidgety Edgar is about his carpets—it's perfectly ghastly! Won't you have some tea?' All this tumbled out of her pretty mouth with enviable ingenuousness, of which she alone had the secret. But it was not reassuring. I lost heart; I became completely demoralised. I am ashamed to say I made a hurried excuse, bolted out of the room, and out of the house, without telling my friends a word of what had occurred. On my honour, I had intended to tell them, but could not muster up courage to begin; indeed, they never gave me the chance.

As I journeyed home I speculated whether that dreadful stain, like the crimson traces of a foul murder, might not reappear next day; or—horrid thought!—whether my beloved parlourmaid might not betray me. I feared she might do so; therefore, and before I went to bed, I wrote my friends a penitential, I might almost say a pitiful, letter, giving a full and true account of what had happened. I threw myself on their mercy. I posted this letter —I posted it myself—but——

I do not say that anybody is bound to reply to a letter, unless it is greatly to his interest to do so.

I have almost forgotten to say that I presented my guardian angel with a handsome donation of five shillings! This is the end of a true story.

Mrs. Branaghan

Four or five years ago Frank Grant and I were on our way to Great Russell Street, to call upon Miss Sylvia Robinson, the Euterpe of Bloomsbury.

Perhaps you never heard of that forgotten district, for it is remote and out of fashion, as it is dingy and desolate; indeed, our genteel novelists make use of humdrum old Bloomsbury when they want to point a moral of social degradation. The man who is completely undone, the man who has married his cook, is relegated to that *bourgeois* region. However, as Miss Sylvia is its muse, and her mission is to delight us, I had put on my best hat the more completely to do her honour.

Great Russell is a very long street, and it began to rain hard while we had still some distance to go; so out of consideration to my hat we ran a few undignified paces, and then, as it came on still heavier, I took refuge on a doorstep which afforded a narrow verge of shelter, while Grant made the best of his way to the maiden's bower.

Whilst I was leaning with my back against the front door an errand-boy arrived from the chemist's, and in answer to his summons a strapping, short-nosed, black-browed hussy of a servant-girl suddenly opened it behind me, which caused me to stagger backwards on to the mat. The girl took no sort of notice of me, received the physic from the boy, automatically slammed the street-door on his retiring form, whisked past me, and flitted down the kitchen stairs. This was all done before you could say Sylvia Robinson; and thus, to my surprise, and, let me say, perplexity, I found myself completely sheltered from the storm, but standing in the hall of an entirely strange house!

Then, immediately, and ere I could make any arrangement for absence of body, let alone presence of mind, a rather tall, ample, and majestic-looking lady emerged from the 'front parlour' and sailed into the passage.

She looked about forty; she was dressed in a light-coloured and voluminous dressing, or rather tea robe; her hair, although no doubt it had been scrupulously *coiffée*, was curiously dishevelled, almost standing on end. I have seen children's dolls, neglected dolls (dolls which, after being subjected to the most frightful ill-usage, have been thrust away into an untidy nursery-cupboard), peeping out with just such heads of hair as had this lady. Madame Mohl, of the Rue du Bac, had such.

This startling apparition made me a sweeping curtsey, and when I began, in abject fashion, to apologise for the way in which I, an entire stranger, found myself in her house, she exclaimed: 'Oh! never mind, sir; I'm delighted to see you!' (with a slight Irish accent). 'It's raining hard; would you like to sit awhile?' I said I could not think of such a thing; that I could not possibly trespass further on her indulgence. But the gracious lady insisted, and in less than no time I found myself seated by her side in the dining-room.

I was bewildered ; I could not make it out. I thought she might be a little eccentric. I did not know what to think. I am not naturally bashful, but I behaved as if I had left my tongue in the hall, where I should have left my umbrella—if I had brought one. However, I concealed my trepidation, and she soon began to tell me about herself, her ailments, her prolonged agonies—neuralgia, or some other obscure malady. Poor soul ! seated in that unlovely chamber, it seemed to do her good to talk to me—to pour her tale of suffering into my ear. I think I was not a bad listener, for her kindness and courtesy had quite won me.

It seemed she was a lonely spirit hungering for human fellowship, and that she had made up her mind that I, for one short half-hour at least, was harmless, possibly sympathetic. *Enfin !*

After a while I again proposed to relieve her of my presence ; but she would have none of it, and reiterated and insisted that she was delighted to see me. She even, kind lady that she was, asked me if I would take anything. I was overcome by her hospitable offers ; but I must confess that the situation was a novel one—so strange, indeed, that all my old landmarks of convention seemed fast crumbling away. I declined the tea, and fell to talking of the prints on the walls. We brightened up, we discussed; we even argued—we took sides. She was for Jones, I was for Brown.[1] However, at last, saying, and indeed feeling, that I must not trespass further on her great kindness, and Sunday hat in hand, I made her a bow—my most deferential salutation. But before going out I mustered up courage—or rather, without the courage I couldn't muster, I murmured something as to not knowing to whom I was so deeply indebted for such genuine hospitality. 'Perhaps you may know or may have heard of Patrick Branaghan, the member of Parliament. He is my husband.' 'Indeed,' said I, with fervour—'indeed, I have not the honour of a personal acquaintance with that distinguished person; but I know his writings, I have read his speeches, and, what is more, I have a copy of his son's—of *your* son's essay, which your son was so obliging as to give me.' ''Deed,' cried Mrs. Branaghan with enthusiasm, 'this *is* remarkable!' But when I told her my name the good soul threw up her arms with an appearance of transport. 'Now, this is wonderful, this is indeed a privilege, Mr. Cocker! I never could have expected such a thing. What! *the* Mr. Cocker who wrote the *pomes* that I've heard of so often? They say we sometimes entertain angels unawares. 'Deed now,' &c.

[1] At that time there were two accomplished painters so named.

All this was exceedingly pleasant. Many and more compliments passed from either side; and then I effected my escape. But, after such real kindness, it would not be gracious, indeed it would not be correct, so to characterise my leave-taking.

I found Grant waiting for me at Miss Sylvia's door—on the damp side of the door; so the faithful fellow had not stolen a perfidious march on me.

It appeared that the world was getting smaller and rounder; for when I spoke to the fair Sylvia of her benevolent neighbour, she exclaimed, 'Oh dear! how like good, kind Mrs. Branaghan!' She knew her quite well.

That evening I happened to dine with Arthur and Augusta Stanley, and they were much interested in my Bloomsbury adventure. Arthur affected to be diverted by it, and said that such could only have befallen a *sentimental* rover; whereas it seems to me that, under the circumstances, I could have done nothing different from that I did. He added that he had just had the pleasure and profit of reading Mr. Branaghan's book, and, in consequence of what I told him, he should venture to ask him to dinner. Would I meet him?

I did meet him, and we had a very agreeable repast; but I am sorry to say that a very short time afterwards I received a black-bordered card conveying the sad tidings of the death of poor Mrs.

Branaghan. She had suddenly exchanged the narrow little home of a suffering body for the limitless and unknown. Her brittle life, with all its aches and ecstasies, was shivered within a month. However, although I never again saw her kind face, her memory is very fragrant to me. I had so long lived in a region of conventionality and artifice, that when I was brought face to face with simple cordiality and kindliness I did not at first recognise them.

How much pleasanter and happier and wiser our petty world would be if there were more people like Mrs. Branaghan!

Two Suburban Graves

Five years ago, for the first time in my life, and on a mournful occasion too—the funeral of Mr. G. H. Lewes—I found myself in Highgate Cemetery. I was alone, so for lack of better occupation I fell to talk with the custodian of the ground, a civil fellow. He spoke with pardonable complacency of the many distinguished people who had been buried within its precincts; amongst others, of that good and illustrious man, Michael Faraday, the blacksmith's son, the bookbinder's apprentice, the humble-minded seeker after truth, the greatest experimentalist the world has yet seen. 'And then,' said he, 'we have another that used to be a deal talked about. You've heard, I suppose, of Tom Sayers, the fightin' man?' This interested me. I *had* heard of Tom, and before I left the ground I found my way to his last resting-place. It was not difficult to identify; for, although the inscription was almost effaced by time and weather, and the imagery was fast mouldering away, the grave was recognisable by a rather coarsely chiselled bas-relief which claimed to be the portrait of Tom himself, and by the sculptured effigy of his favourite mastiff, Lion.

I should have liked, there and then, to have sent for a monumental sculptor and had the inscription recut; but the custodian told me this was impossible. Litigation as to the possession of the grave was in progress, and while that went on the stones could not be interfered with. In fact, a battle-royal was at that very moment raging over Fighting Tom's remains.

I have no idea what kind of an animal Thomas Sayers may have really been in familiar and pacific life, but I had seen enough of him to recognise a remarkable simplicity and steadfastness, and the sight of those weather-worn effigies carried my thoughts back to a memorable spring morning some twenty years ago, and to a merry 'mill' in a

Hampshire meadow, near a stream, not half a mile from Farnborough railway station.

In imagination I am again at the London Bridge terminus,[1] with a 'there and back' ticket in my pocket. The hour is about four in the morning. There is a motley crowd, a huge gathering. There are butchers from Newgate Market; fish-porters from Billingsgate, bringing their vernacular with them; there are pugilists and poets, statesmen and publicans, dandies, men of letters, and even divines, elbowing each other in the semi-darkness.

We have taken our seats. There is considerable delay, but at last a bell rings, there is a snort, and then the monster train glides slowly out of the dimly lighted shed. Once beyond the station we quicken up. Away we tear in a gale of our own creation—a Faust flight on the devil's mantle, over the roofs of the houses, through market-gardens; and, leaving the steepled city behind us, we are soon hissing and snorting through the quiet country; then before very long we find ourselves in a willow-fringed and sunny little field.

For several months I had been confined to London pavement and the dead timber of the official desk. How well I remember the strange delightfulness of the green trees, the fresh grass, cool beneath my feet, and the gracious April air as

[1] In those days the station for Farnborough.

it played upon my face! A lark is soaring and singing far above our heads, rejoicing in his glorious privacy of light; yokels and costermongers are clambering over fences and leaping dykes. And there, the observed of all observers, is the veteran Tom Oliver, superintending the erection of a twenty-four-foot arena.

Sayers was the first to make his appearance in the ring; but when his opponent, Heenan, threw his hat within the ropes, followed it, and stripped, there was a murmur of admiration. He was at once recognised as the most magnificent athlete that had ever been seen in such a place. He was five inches taller than Sayers—who, strictly speaking, was only a middle-weight—some two or three stone heavier, and (no small matter) he was eight years younger; while his length of reach was remarkable for even so tall a man.

Then, shall I ever forget the look of perfect self-possession and calm courage, mingled with curiosity, with which Sayers faced, gazed up, and smiled at, his terrible antagonist? He had never set eyes on him before. Having lost the toss, he was obliged to accept the lower ground. But there he stood, his enormous shoulders shining in the sun, in his well-known and faultless attitude, tapping the ground lightly with his left foot, his arms well down, his head thrown back, ready for a shoot or a jump, and a smile of confidence on his open but not classical countenance.

Still—and no wonder—there was a pretty general opinion among outsiders, expressed in the flowery but forcible vernacular of the 'fancy,' that the match was 'a horse to a hen'—that 'Heenan would knock Sayers into a cocked hat in ten minutes;' for how was Sayers to get at him? I could not but feel the force of this opinion, and that Bob Brettle's observation was an apposite one: 'Well, Tom may beat him, but may I, etc., if he can eat him!' However, as it turned out, Sayers had no difficulty in getting over Heenan's guard, for he punished him frightfully.[1]

I recollect my strange tremor as the men stood up, advanced, shook hands, and took up their positions. The fight began about half-past seven, and finished soon after ten. I am not going to describe it. Has it not been already described in the racy columns of our revered old chronicler, 'Bell's Life'? We have had enough of the 'rib-benders' and 'pile-drivers.' I will say, however, that never in the annals of the ring were courage, science,

[1] He was more remarkable as a fighter than as a sparrer. I have seen boxers quicker than Sayers. Nat Langham and Ned Donally were quicker, and so was Charley Buller; but in force of hitting, either with right or left, and in his extraordinary skill of timing his man, he had no equal. Like Entellus, he defended himself by the movement of his body.

temper, judgment, and staying qualities combined and displayed in such a marvellous measure as by Tom Sayers on this memorable day. He fulfilled to the uttermost Livy's *facere et pati fortiter.* At the beginning of the encounter Heenan was both out-generalled and out-fought; but as early as the fourth round Sayers had his right arm completely disabled, and from that time he defended himself and attacked his gigantic adversary with only his left. The battle ended in a disgraceful scene of riot and blackguardism, especially among the backers of Sayers, who, as soon as they saw that their money was in extreme peril, broke into the ring. It ended by the umpire wisely deciding that it was a draw.

Volenti non fit injuria may be barbarous Latin, but it is sound sense. A boxing-match is a voluntary exhibition of pluck and endurance; there is no malice; and it proves to the uttermost the stuff of which a man is made. There was something in this great fight which the whole nation recognised, for it appealed to a very universal sympathy. It affected all classes, in a way that boys and men always will be affected when they hear of the exploits of a Peterborough or a Grenville. It was magnetic—and why should it not continue to move us? Though, when I recall this battle, and Heenan's face, out of which all that was human had been pommelled, I cry, 'Heaven forbid that the prize-ring should ever be revived in all its hideous and loathsome degradation!'

So long as manly sentiments and sheer English pluck are valued, so long shall the name of Thomas Sayers, the Polydeuces of our country, be held in honour.

Dear reader, one of these days make a pilgrimage to Highgate, climb its steep ascent, and enter the rueful-looking, the lonely burial-ground. The custodian will be pleased to see you; he will greet you as he did me, and pilot you to the green resting-place of Michael Faraday, of whom a distinguished man of science well said, 'He was too good a man for me to estimate him, and he was too great a philosopher for me to understand him thoroughly.' Michael Faraday had the true spirit of a philosopher and a Christian. He was, indeed, one of England's worthiest sons, so it will do you no harm to muse awhile beside his grave.

Then, if by chance you should come upon another grave—a monument of mouldering stones, a forlorn *hic jacet* (it will not be far to seek; you will surely recognise it), you may at once pass on. You need not stay; but at least have a kindly thought for the plucky Englishman who lies buried there.

The grass on Tom's grave is also very green; and

you will be as like to see the lark soaring, and to hear him rejoicing at heaven's gate, from the one grave as from the other.

Alas, poor Tom! Like most of his calling, he died a young man. I happened to meet him on Hampstead Heath shortly after the battle, and not very long before his death. He was walking alone where John Keats had once liked to walk, in

> A melodious plot
> Of beechen green and shadows numberless.

We saluted as we passed, and I had the honour of grasping his hand—that fist which had so often administered his terrible blow, 'the auctioneer.'

Heenan died much about the same time as Sayers. There is a spice of romance in the story of the gallant Benicia Boy. He was the husband of Ada Menken, a handsome actress with dark blue eyes—glorious eyes. She was the 'Infelicia' whose love poems Mr. Dickens introduced to the reading public in 1868.

I remember seeing Ada at Astley's Amphitheatre in 'Mazeppa;' and, from what I have heard, I am inclined to think that, like some other splendid women, she may have been a handful as well as an armful.

NINE MINUTES AND A HALF

The fashion of women walking about unattended is a feature of the present day, and I hope it is a sign of that higher civilisation which is nothing more than the progressive development of our faculties. This license has made prodigious strides during the last forty years. I can recall when Belgravian virgins were first permitted to pay their Belgravian visits alone; and Sydney Smith insisted, in consequence, that—at least in that Arcadian quarter—all the women were brave and all the men were virtuous.

Let us be thankful that in these latter days an audience would recognise very little point in such a scene as that in Vanbrugh's 'Relapse' where, on the arrival of Tom Fashion at his house, the Knight bawls out, 'Let loose the watchdog, and lock up Miss Hoyden.'[1]

Years ago, as a young man, travelling by railway I occasionally had an opposite neighbour in the shape of a young lady; and if I chanced to address her, she would look scared—perhaps sidle

[1] According to the printed copies of *The Relapse* and *A Trip to Scarborough*, this is not strictly correct; but I have read somewhere that Mr. Gatty, who impersonated the knight, so gave it with applause.

away to the other end of the seat, and feign to look out of the window. It is different now. As an elderly gentleman, I find that if I now hazard a remark under precisely similar circumstances, my young lady jumps up from her comfortably padded corner, comes and seats herself beside me, and makes herself very agreeable for the remainder of the journey. All this she does—and yet, am I altogether satisfied?

I have given a slight outline of some years of my life, and with this preamble I now venture to give you a more detailed account of nine minutes and a half of it.

Not so very long ago I took a train at Three Bridges to go to Rowfant; and, perhaps because at the moment I was especially under the influence of my beneficent *daimon*, I contented myself with a third-class ticket.

There were no elbow-rests in the carriage, but, as it turned out, there was something a good deal better—there was a young lady. This maiden did not look distinguished, but she had the greatest of natural attractions—she had youth! However, it seemed to me that, except for her little kitten face, she hadn't very much else to boast of. She wore, perched on the top of her head, a self-asserting straw hat, trimmed with light-blue ribbon, and round her neck was a double row of rather aggressive light-blue glass beads, a trumpery ornament that must have but meagrely ministered to her vanity. She looked as if she might be the daughter of a small shopkeeper in a small country town; and so, as it turned out, she was.

When I entered the carriage this young lady was reading a letter, and, without peeping over her shoulder, I could have almost told what it was all about, for her countenance betrayed every passing emotion: it expressed lively satisfaction and sorrowful concern; it was pleased, indignant, sentimental, and tender by turns. It was delightful to watch her. I never saw a more transparent face. Her changing feelings were faithfully reflected as in a mirror.

The train started and the engine snorted. My companion had dropped her railway ticket—it was lying at her feet—so I picked it up and ceremoniously presented it to her. It was then, for the first time, that she seemed to be aware of my existence. She thanked me, but with a bashful gravity. Not discouraged by this, I hazarded a remark or two about the weather. These were acknowledged in monosyllabic fashion. But we were more in sympathy when I spoke of the country; for then all at once she woke up, she became communicative—the words began to tumble out of her little mouth. She told me of her home, of her parents. She had four brothers and sisters—only four; she wished she had a dozen! She told me her christian name. What could her godfather and godmother be thinking of? It was 'Pomona'!—and it was 'too hidjus.' She enlightened me as to which was her favourite name, though she and Fanny Privett didn't 'a bit agree about names.'[1] She even asked me which was my favourite colour. I should state that all this was done with an appealing, an infantine simplicity, but with a mixture of frankness and bashfulness difficult to conceive of.

Miss Pomona further informed me that quite lately, while climbing a stile, she had sprained her ankle. Upon this I assumed my most paternal air. I said that her companion could hardly have been sufficiently attentive at the stiles, for, if he had been so, she would have been spared that sorrow.

This at once set her off; she became confidential, extremely so. She bridled—she had not climbed that stile with a 'young man.' *Her* young man—or rather the young man, one of the many who just then appeared to be making life a burden to her, and who, I suspected, was the writer of the letter—was not what she altogether cared for. She rather disliked him than otherwise; she was not

[1] She quoted this lady as if *I* knew all about her. I presume she was her bosom friend, such a one as was Miss Anna Howe to Clarissa.

quite sure she should have anything more to say to him. He was a 'tall, dark, military young man, of old family.' He was Irish. Fanny Privett always said it was much better to have nothing to say to Irishmen. What did *I* think?

She described their last interview; she described it gravely, minutely. And she was tender, almost tearful, as she did so, for it appeared that she had been cool and sarcastic; and even now she slightly projected her pretty under lip and jerked her head about at the recollection of each telling point of their conversation. She was irresistible when she did that. It was this mixture of contrasting feelings that made her so fascinating; and it was evident that she had more than a sneaking kindness for her young Milesian—that she was proud of him: of his tallness, of his darkness, also of his ancient lineage.

'J'aime encore à retrouver mon cœur.' I was satisfied to be vanquished by this damsel. Her childlike candour, her sprightly simplicity, and her naïve self-betrayal captivated me, as did also the many-coloured flowers of half-conscious coquetry that blossomed in her prattle. Like to my Dear Lady Disdain, there was little of the melancholy quality in Pomona. She had been born in a merry hour. If she was incomplete, it seemed an incompleteness that was well worthy of being completed, and I thought to myself, What a nice little wife you would make to that lucky young trooper!

> Heureux qui mettra la cocarde
> Au bonnet de Mimi Pinson.

As thus I meditated—for by this time I had become very much attached to her—the engine began to slacken its speed, and in an instant came the sobering reflection that there is a parting at the root of all our joys. We had arrived at Rowfant Station.

I placed her little satchel and umbrella by her side. Her eyes met mine, and fell, and again rose with a glance of trustful goodwill. All the lively flutter of the last few minutes was at an end. We seemed to have known each other for I don't know how many years; we were serious, we were good friends. There was a brief silence, a sudden handshaking, and then an everlasting Farewell!

Each generation of children begins the history of the world anew; those of to-day are the wives and mothers of to-morrow. What has become of this young, this interesting, this confiding little companion of mine, my dear friend during a journey that had occupied nine minutes and a half?

Ghost of Dick Steele, shades of Charles Dickens and Charles Lamb! these few lines are but the dry bones out of which either of you could have fashioned a very pretty essay.

The Story of a Postage-stamp

When Lionel Tennyson was first plighted to Eleanor, he lived at 3 St. James's Street. One afternoon I had occasion to write to him. I stamped my letter, intending to have it posted. However, something unexpected decided that I must go to the Travellers' Club, so I sent for a four-wheeler, meaning to drop my letter at his lodgings on my way to Pall Mall, and thus to save a penny.

As I rattled up St. James's Street it was raining. It was so dark, and rained so hard, that I could hardly distinguish the shops, and I fancied that we were passing No. 3; so I clapped down the glass, thrust my head out into the storm, and bawled to the driver to pull up. I shouted frantically, as is my custom; but cabby took no notice of me. I shouted again—we were close to the kerb; and this time I opened wide the door, to be prepared to spring out the instant he stopped, as is also my invariable custom.

I was in a state of extreme irritation; but this was quenched by the cab suddenly striking against a stone post, which in one instant whipped the cab-door off its hinges and hurled it into the gutter. Upon this the cab stopped, and after a struggle with my watch and chain, which had caught in something or other, I floundered helplessly out into the lashing rain.

The driver was already waiting for me on the pavement—a weather-beaten old pilot of the causeway with fog in his throat. He said nothing, but he stooped and picked the door out of the swollen gutter, and placed it carefully, I might say tenderly, against the seat which I had that moment vacated. He did this as if he had been in the habit of doing it every day of his life. Then he turned to me. And it was then that I discovered that we had only just reached No. 3. So you see I was in the wrong in every respect. We faced each other; and as it seemed necessary that some one should say something, I ventured the not very original remark, 'This is a bad look-out.' 'Yes, it is,' replied Jarvey, deliberately; then he took off his hat with both hands, so that he might arrive at a cool-headed opinion as to the whole affair; then he scratched his head. But he did not seem inclined to enlarge on the idea, so I could not help pointing out, in an aggrieved tone, that if he had only obeyed my directions, and had stopped when I told him, the accident would not have happened. 'Ah!' said the dripping cabby, 'I read you as one o' them gents as be werry fond of argufying; now, if you wants to argufy'—shaking the rain off the brim of his hat, and planting himself against the guilty post—'I'll argufy with you as long as you likes.' Then he added that he did not know how much it wouldn't cost to repair his cab—'Not my conweyance, you know: my proprietor's'—for, as he pointed out with a ruthless perspicacity, the door had not been simply wrenched off its hinges, but a portion of the framework had been torn away with it.

It further appeared—and this made matters worse—that he had only just come on the rank, and must be paid for his time, for he could do nothing more that night; and, to use his own words, he'd 'just like to see the colour of my money.'

By this time an almost preternatural calmness had come over me, and, thanks to the rain and the excitement, what may be called a damp resignation. I gave the man my address and ten shillings, and, like Pope Pius the Sixth in *assez mauvais état* (I was almost wet through), with my watch in my hand—for it had fallen out of my pocket on to the pavement—I took another cab home.

A day or two afterwards I received the estimate for repairs, preposterous, and couched in brutally peremptory terms; then close upon it there came a second letter, illiterate and insolent, threatening to 'County Court' me if I did not instantly pay up.

This was humiliating, and it revealed a seamy side of life, a glimpse of something very unsavoury.

The proprietor of the cab treated me with complete distrust. He had at once made up his mind that I was a scamp, thus showing the sort of people with whom he was in the habit of doing business.

The affair altogether cost me five or six pounds. One of them was for the mending of my watch. My hat was damaged, and my temper !—and, after all, I had spoiled the postage-stamp in trying to get it off Lionel's letter.

I do not bear that cabman any ill-will. Some time afterwards I came across him at the door of a public-house. He had been assuaging the asperities of existence by gratifying his natural taste for beer. He looked rather shabby, and had a shirt which, under more auspicious circumstances, might have been white. I saw no cab. He was shod in wooden clogs, and his ankles were enveloped in haybands, so I presume he had left 'the rank' and turned waterman. He may have come down in the world, but there was contentment in his old face. Evidently he was a superior man, a man of few wants (he who wants least is most like the gods, who want nothing), and seemed to view his altered condition with a philosophy that Zeno himself might have envied. Peace be with him !

A Charity Breakfast

I am rarely asked out to breakfast, but when the bidding comes I am not sorry to accept. It is now some three or four years since I received a very cordially worded invitation from the Patagonian Church Extension Society to take that meal with them, and as it was summer-time I did not object to the primitive hour of half-past eight.

The repast was spread in a very large room. Numbers of men in black coats and white ties (cleric and servitor) were hovering about, and with them was Sir Bonamy Veroles, who had been advertised to take the chair. I knew Sir Bonamy.

There were huge metal tea and coffee pots, capacious cups and saucers, and plates of ham and tongue, flanked by thick toast and hot rolls. These refreshments repeated themselves at regular intervals all down the tables, looking homely but inviting; for, what with my walk and the early rising, I felt uncommonly hungry.

I was directed to a seat beside a clerical gentleman of colour, tropical and strange, but not especially Patagonian in build. People were talking in all parts of the room, but when silence had been obtained there came a murmur from the further end. This turned out to be a far-away benediction,[1] quickly to be followed by the renewed clatter of conversation and crockery.

The teapots were being pushed about briskly and jovially, and while I was helping myself to tongue and toast, thereby committing myself to the breakfast, a busybody of a fellow in a white tie, waiter or cleric, came bustling up, and with ostentatious assurance slapped down a blank cheque, a lead pencil, and the eulogy of the charity by my plate, looking significantly at me and my substantial slice of tongue as he did so. It was then, and not till then, that I apprehended the whole force of the affair—why I had been invited, and to what I had rendered myself liable. It was a snare, a pitfall. I understood it as well as if the clerical exotic at my elbow had held a cannibal knife at my throat.

A great revulsion of feeling at once overtook me. I was wounded, I was indignant at this flagrant breach of hospitality; *ventre affamé*, a hungry man is an angry man. I should have liked to know what the Patagonians and their Church Extension were to me. But how was I to save myself? The eyes of Sir Bonamy and of everybody else in the room were fixed upon me—or seemed so. But save myself I would, and it struck me there

[1] 'Then, breaking their chats off,
Say Grace with their hats off.'—JOHN GAY.

was only one way of doing so, and that that was to fly! I resolved, but I hesitated—I lingered on my unfulfilled resolve. However, knowing that time was everything, and procrastination would be fatal, and mustering up all my courage, I slowly and with great apparent difficulty raised myself from my chair. I bent myself nearly double, my right hand pressed just below the spot where my waistcoat ends. Every eye seemed to be upon me; but I got clear of my chair, and staggered away between the narrow tables to the door. By worse luck I had to pass Sir Bonamy, and as I caught his cold, inquiring gaze fixed upon me I made a rueful face. However, by that time I was close to the principal entrance, and, once there, I leaped into a cab and drove home, with no better escort than an uneasy conscience. Strange to say, I was so much affected by the dramatic force of my impersonation that I kept my hand where I had placed it till I reached my own door!

I arrived just in time for a much better repast than that from which I had severed myself.

Anatomists insist that the heart is very near the stomach, and singularly dependent upon it. Whether or no, this was my first and last charity breakfast, and it only shows how necessary it is for a man to be on his guard in London. It also shows how innocent I was. I may add that next morning, impelled by promptings of a weak compunction, I sent a guinea to the Patagonians, and in due course received a long list of the society's benefactors, in which my name (quite wrongly spelt, and therefore unrecognisable) duly figured. Altogether it was an unfortunate affair.

The Royal Academy Banquet

It is a distinction to be invited.

I used to be acquainted with Mr. W. E. Frost, the accomplished and unassuming Academician. As a youngster I had often seen his pictures exhibited—undraped nymphs engaged in doing nothing in particular; compromises between Stothard and Etty, but really not much like either. As nymphs they were perfectly well-conducted young persons, their nudity being one of their attractions:

> Induitur, formosa est: exuitur,
> Ipsa forma est.

As Frost got into years he lost vogue, grew exceedingly deaf, and exhibited only fitfully. However, he solaced an enforced leisure, which practically was a solitude, by hunting up old prints; and he showed his excellent taste by making an almost complete collection of book-plates after Stothard—

that admirable Stothard! It was these that had encouraged me to seek his acquaintance. We met several times, and he gave me many valuable hints; for which, in spite of his extreme hardness of hearing, I succeeded in making him aware that I was grateful.

A year or two after my first meeting with Frost I received a card to dine at the annual banquet of the Royal Academy on May 3, 1873. As Sir Francis Grant, the president, was my distant connection, I thought I might be indebted to him for the honour, and joyfully accepted the invitation.

When the day and hour arrived I found, a little to my surprise, that my name was between a knife and fork on Frost's dexter hand. Our chairs were in a corner near the door, as far from the President as could well be.

There is no doubt that Frost was exceedingly deaf; but still, for the sake of his own great obligingness and the incomparable Thomas Stothard, I was satisfied to be where I found myself—between Frost and a gap—though now and then I looked wistfully (a humble foible) at my friends and acquaintances gathered around Frank Grant.

Many months after this dinner I fell in with Quintin Carver, the Academician. Among other matters he spoke of Frost as being seriously out of health, and asked me if I had seen him lately. He went on to say that perhaps it would interest me to know that, at one of the Royal Academy meetings, the diffident, deaf, and, to all practical intents and purposes, dumb Frost had got on his legs and proposed that I should be invited to the next dinner; and, said Carver, 'you will be gratified to hear that there was not a single dissentient voice; his motion was carried *nem. con.*' Carver is a candid fellow, and he showed by his voice and manner that he thought this an extraordinary circumstance—extraordinary that Frost, a very retiring man, should have proposed me or anybody else, but more extraordinary still that his motion in my favour should have been so unanimously carried.

When I heard Carver say this, I remembered how dull and silent I had been at dinner, how little attention I had paid the good Frost; and I thought to myself, Poor painter! but for you I should never have assisted at that banquet. At least let me hope you were aware that I did not know to whom I was indebted for my invitation.

The next day I called on Frost,[1] but he was ill. A few days afterwards I again called, and he was

[1] On these visits to Frost I would sometimes pass 7 Buckingham Street—the house with a tablet to the memory of John Flaxman, who had once lived and worked there. My first sight of that tablet had been a surprise and a pleasure. It seemed to give sunshine to an otherwise shady place.

worse; and then he died. So I was never able to make my peace with my conscience by thanking him.

Whenever I pass through Fitzroy Street I look up at a window of No. 46, and the shadow of an unpleasant thought oppresses me.

Now was not Frost a kind fellow? I only wish that he could have known that I thought so, and that I was really pleased to sit by him at dinner, and to talk about Stothard. I like his memory none the worse that he never told me how it all came about.

I have a long letter from Frost, dated January 1876, in which he gives reasons for his retirement as an active Royal Academician—ill-health and ill-fortune.

> I fill up a place which may be better supplied
> When I have made it empty

is the burden of it; it is written under great depression of spirit.

I trust that his last days were not embittered by poverty; that, at any rate, he had enough for the exigencies of his self-imposed obscurity.

In 1885 I was again invited to the dinner; but Sir Curtis Lampson had died hardly three weeks before, so I declined. I think that good fellow Leighton may have proposed me this second time, and I hope there were not so very many dissentient voices; but I shall know all about that when next I see Academician Carver.

Travelling Fifty Years agone

In the good old coaching days there was an idea that our stage-coachmen were reputable in proportion to the number of miles they drove us, and there was something in it; certainly our interest in them, and I hope theirs in us, was usually increased by the length of the time that we continued in company. This remark is *à propos* of what I shall say later on.

Are the 'Bull and Mouth' (Boulogne harbour), the 'Spread Eagle,' the 'Swan with Two Necks' (nicks), and 'Green Man and Still,' yet in existence? In Greenwich Hospital days, when I went back to school I was obliged to journey up to one or other of these queer places of entertainment to meet the mail, and at a very early hour. On looking back, it would seem that these mornings were almost invariably misty and raw, and sometimes nearly pitch-dark. I often felt cold and squeamish, and sometimes, for what seemed hours, had nothing to do but grope about the deserted innyard, where one or two deserted coaches were standing and a 'helper' might now and then pass with a horn lantern. Feeble lights the while would flicker and disappear in the ghostly galleries above. Very occasionally a tinkling wagon, fresh from the country, and perhaps covered with snow, came rumbling in. At last—and it was a long-deferred at last—the morning began to break, the house woke up, and I was able to distinguish all which till then had been dim and uncertain and mysterious.

I have a recollection of many expeditions made as long ago as when George, or Billy the Fourth, was King, made no matter whither—to Brundusium or to Birmingham; of the humours of the road, and the conveyances and inns. I have more than once travelled in that commodious vehicle which had a round sort of basket behind the body, and comfortably accommodated six full-sized passengers.

What an agreeable and edifying companion was the stage-coachman! How complete his winter costume, how sufficing; how garish his summer!—a wonderful coat, hat, cravat, and bright flowers in his buttonhole. So decorated, he tooled along his four bloods with glancing harness and ring-snaffles, their hoofs clattering merrily along the road, and entertained the occupant of the box-seat—a throne to which I very seldom aspired—with appropriate talk of Sir 'Vincent' Cotton, Dick Brackenbury, and many another hero and highflier. Let me recall his tone of superiority when, in hovering fashion, he condescended to the politics of the day. I can remember many coachmen of that time, but I can remember only one observation, exactly as it was made, by any one of them. We were on our way to Clare, and were in the suburbs of London, when a child trotted out into the road, right in front of the horses, and was nearly run over. The coachman was equal to the emergency, superbly equal to it; he pulled up in time, and then turned coolly to his 'box-seat' with this pithy and laconic remark: 'They does it a purpose!' This was all he said, and this I have never forgotten. Separated as it is from the being who uttered it and the occasion that prompted it, it may not appear striking, but I know we passengers were much impressed by it. However, although he was the hero of my fancy, then—even then I had a lurking impression that he was not an altogether educated man, like my father; but how interesting!

The guards often wore scarlet coats, and were on curiously genial terms with everybody, male and female, along the road—that is, with everybody worth being on such terms with. There was a delivery of parcels going on, and a receiving of them—some of a confidential character. Part of their duty was releasing the skid and rehanging it. I remember I used to long for yet one flourish more of gallant good-bye from his cheery key-bugle, or 'yard of tin,' which was always consigned to a funnel-shaped wicker sheath when we were well started for over the hills and far away.

I remember the old yellow post-chaises, their musty perfume and their many pockets ; the white, fluffy, beaver-hatted little postboys, their legs encased in worn white cords and mahogany tops, their elbows well turned out, and the gait which is peculiar to their calling ; the halt for changing horses, and the cheery bustle. A bell rang, and 'First turn-out' was called. Then would follow the interesting speculation as to the number on the approaching milestone, or the colour of the next boy's jacket.

It was interesting, as the post-chaise drew up at the door of the roomy and comfortable hostel where we were to dine or sleep, to see Boniface and his better half smilingly awaiting us—*Us in particular!*—waiter and chamber-lasses grouped behind them. The landlady advances to the carriage-window with a cordial, with a self-respecting, 'Will you please to alight?' I remember that the landlord, who announced dinner, sometimes entered with the first dish, and placed it on the table, bowing as he retired. Why, it all seems as if it were but yesterday! now it is gone for ever. This is how the genial Prior described it in 1723 :

'Come here, my sweet landlady! How do you do?
Where's Sisley so cleanly, and Prudence, and Sue?
And where is the widow that lived here below?
And the ostler that sang about eight years ago?
And where is your sister, so mild and so dear,
Whose voice to her maids like a trumpet was clear?'

. . . .

'By my troth,' she replies, 'you grow younger, I think.
And pray, sir, what wine does the gentleman drink?
But now, let me die, sir, or live upon trust,
If I know to which question to answer you first,
For things since I saw you most strangely have varied—
The ostler is hanged, and the widow is married;
And as to my sister, so mild and so dear,
She has lain in the churchyard full many a year.'

. . . .

There is just a something in Hogarth's Country Innyard that reminds me of it all.

I have a remembrance of the Thames below Woolwich, and of certain queer old bankside alehouses, the resort of smugglers and, we were assured and convinced, of pirates; also of a pair of below-bridge watermen, who now and again pulled me and one or two others, in a clinker-built wherry, or rather skiff, with a buff bow and flared rowlocks, to and fro between Greenwich Hospital, Redriffe, and London Bridge, that being the only means of public conveyance excepting the three-horsed coach. We used to skim along in mid stream if the tide was favourable, but hugged the shore when it was adverse. The Pool required careful navigation. I have often shot the most critical arch of *old* London Bridge.

We knew a good deal about our two watermen and their domestic concerns. We had been acquainted ever since they had been out of their time. They had an interesting way of dealing with the letter *v*: they sometimes used it as though it were a *w*. At that time the 'Venus' was an important river steamer; they always called her the 'Wenus,' and referred to her as a 'wessel.' The man who pulled stroke had come in second for Doggett's coat and badge. In winter he worked as a pilot, and in rough weather wore a *fantail* or sou'wester.

Here I return to the thought which prompted the opening paragraph of this reminiscence.

Last week I got into an omnibus at Liverpool Street railway station, and had not long been seated before I cheerfully observed to the conductor that the fare all the way to Charing Cross was only a penny; that I had never done the entire journey before, but that I was going to do it to-day; and that I had thought I should make a good thing out of him! His reply was not gratifying: 'That's nothin'; why, I've an old bloke as goes it every day;' and it was delivered in so callous and languid a manner that it set me thinking out the moral of the situation. It was merely this. In the eyes of that conductor there was nothing remarkable about me; *I was an old bloke* who represented a very hardly earned penny, and that only. Yes, suppose every one of the thousands who entered that omnibus had given the man as much extra trouble as I had done by my unnecessary remark, why—his life would have been a burden to him. How slender was our interest in each other! What on earth could he possibly care about his passengers!

I should be curious to know the extent to which the London and General Omnibus Company had profited by my patronage. I should have thought that my extra weight, the pausing to pick me up, the getting quit of me, the effort of getting under way again, and all the wear and tear, must have deteriorated that 'bus and those two horses to the extent of much more than a penny.

I ought not to have made the remark. I might as well have asked a ticket collector on the Underground Railway, say at Baker Street station, for his views on bimetallism or the doctrine of free will.

I have had the same sort of experience at the enormous Paris and London hotels. It is there that you are known by a number (which you yourself with difficulty remember), and by that number only; and it is there that the bill you have run up—an important item to you—would hardly defray the cost of the caravanserai toothpicks for twelve hours.

The inhabitants of the United Kingdom are now better fed, better housed, better dressed, better educated, and better mannered than they were when I was a youth; but the increase of wealth, the increase of the population, the huge inflation in all directions, the spirit of the age, are overflowing and swamping everything, and conspire to entirely obliterate the individual, as well as those humble associations and homely incidents which used to sweeten our somewhat contracted and sleepy daily life. They are pleasant to look back upon, but, like the country innyard as depicted by Hogarth, they are gone, and gone for ever!

On a Coloured Caricature by James Gillray

1893.

When George the Third was king there was a scurrility, a ferocity in the work of our political and other caricaturists which it is now difficult to understand. The good Gillray himself was not the most urbane artist of his generation.

In spite of this I often turn, and always with renewed pleasure, to a homely little coloured print which hangs in my dressing-room. It is by Gillray. He introduces us to five human beings: an army officer, two old gentlemen, and two ladies, one aged, and the other quite young. They are seated at a very small round table, in a room the furniture of which is curiously scanty. One of the old gentlemen, whom I make out to be the host, for he is seated in the elbow-chair with a decanter before him, is telling an anecdote. Opposite to him is the young lady. She has a glass of wine in her fair hand, and on her left is the not altogether youthful soldier, whose attention is mainly directed to her, though, like herself, he is listening to the story. On the soldier's left is the old lady; and opposite to both is a clergyman (probably her husband) in a well-powdered wig, and with an exquisite grin on his venerable profile. These two are also listening to the story. The whole party, with the exception of the young lady, are hugely enjoying what their genial host is confiding to them—they are revelling in it. But it is easy to see that she is not altogether at her ease: she is bashful; she looks as if she does not quite know what may not be coming next. Her military neighbour, who is also her adorer, is in raptures with the story, but he watches her furtively, evidently being afraid of wounding her susceptibilities by a too delighted and too open appreciation. Such is the subject of my little old print, and this is its title:

'A DECENT STORY.'

Examine this little work of art, and you will see

how entirely the artist has depended on the humanity of his characters: he has not taken refuge in elaborate upholstery or *à la mode* toilets to hide the poverty of a jest. The piece depends on its Hogarthian quality. I am very fond of it. And in this I am not singular, for my housemaids gaze at it, leaning on their early brooms, and they giggle as they gaze. It amuses my children. Oliver laughs aloud, and cries, 'What is the story about, papa?' My excellent and dear old sister, seventy-four years old July 3 next, and just come back from the Antipodes, is in ecstasies over it, and she goes so far as to wish she could have heard the story. Now, what does all this enjoyment mean? Surely there are seasons when even the mirth that resembles the crackling of thorns under a pot may be salutary. I ask the question because I have been told by superior people that my 'Decent Story' is not a 'nice' thing to hang up. P. says he would like to turn it with its face to the wall. Q. (a lady-moralist), to whom I had said it was worth its weight in gold, advises me by all means to sell it.

I am a rusty old poet, so, by way of trying to satisfy everybody, I have written under the title three abortive but well-intentioned lines, and they run thus:

> In a roomy old house that I wot of there's *one* room
> Where merry folk meet, and they call it the *fun*-room
> —This story he's telling is 'Grouse in the gun-room.'

Is the pleasure that I and mine experience in this print within the limits of becoming mirth? Is it a harmless pleasure, or has the fiend anything to say to it?

Where is the ghost of old Gillray? I wish we could ask him something about it. He would be certain to know. If the Divine Ruler of the universe permitted the fiend to incite the gifted Gillray (Heaven bless him!) to invent this naïve little conversation-piece—an invention worthy of Honoré Daumier—I do not see why, after all, there may not be a beneficent intention at the root of the matter.

Silvio's Complaint

This is a tentative essay—an attempt at an attempt. I call it tentative because I do not know how far the feelings which impel me to write it can be understood by even a very small minority of mankind.

It may be that my pen is swayed by a unique idiosyncrasy. Anyhow, I crave your indulgence and will state my position.

I am prosperously married. I have a rich, young, and affectionate helpmate. She has excellent abilities, and, being sincerely religious, it is not necessary for me to say she has irreproachable principles. She is not a vegetarian; she is not a Plymouth Sister; she does not even wear the divided skirt. Indeed, she is just such a woman as the poet was thinking of when he exclaimed, 'A wife is the peculiar gift of Heaven.' On the other hand, I am poor, and old, and testy, and no longer comely to look upon. As regards my own virtues, you will be the more able to gauge them when you have read these few pages. Marcus Aurelius was a better man than I am; but somehow I have a much better wife.

After this preamble you may be surprised to learn that I am not satisfied—that I want less than I have got, and yet, Heaven be praised! that I still want something.

I want a possible 'she,' and I want to be let alone.

There are times when solitude would be a paradise. Where is the man who really cares for the caressing voice of the adoring one if he has a grain of cinder in his eye? It is for this reason that I am yearning for a creature who would be willing to be my devoted friend; content to yield me everything, and to expect nothing; and who would set herself to fulfil the duty of making me happy in my own way. My legitimate helpmate expresses solicitude at seasons when I do not care for solicitude being expressed. For instance, when I am going out for the day, her parting injunctions invariably are—she has always been a timid creature—'Now, mind how you get in and out of trains, and pray take care of mad dogs and thunderstorms.'

To speak plainly, I am in search of a self-denying creature—an animal who will talk and be lively when it pleases me, and be satisfied to be silent and subdued if I so desire it. I want a companion who will rejoice to be with me, but will remain out of the room, and cheerfully too, when—from what shall I call it?—when, from a nervous, excitable organisation, I may have just kicked her out of it.

Such a being could make herself attractive in a thousand different ways. She could do so by showing an interest in all that concerns me—a regard for my comforts, especially my *small* comforts.

She should lend a greedy ear when I dilate—as I fain would occasionally dilate—on my fancies, my caprices, and my foibles. She should not seldom express astonishment at the amount of knowledge I have accumulated, at the consideration in which I am held; and if she praises me with an air as if she cannot possibly help praising me, she may do so to my face. Hitherto my natural inclination has been to efface, I now wish to assert myself. The behaviour I describe would soon embolden me to brag of my achievements. I never brag now.

I want a good listener. I have conversed with women who, the while that I did so, regarded me with ecstasy, and yet, a moment afterwards, I found that they had not the remotest idea of what I had been saying to them! The woman I seek must be a really good listener. Then there should be something timid and tentative in her bearing and movements. I shall be pleased if she furtively watches me. She should especially do so, and with solicitude and concern, when she sees me moody or self-absorbed. I shall be flattered if she chooses those dishes which she may have observed that I prefer, or takes but little food when I am disinclined to eat.

I have long felt the want of a real companion. I shall need it the more as I grow old, and as the world drops away from me.[1] How I shall value a long-suffering soul like the person I am attempting to portray! I should become exceedingly attached

[1] Oh, my crutch! Is it not spring when the cuckoo passes through the air, when the foam sparkles on the sea? The flowers, are they not shining? The young corn, is it not springing?

Ah, my crutch! The young maidens no longer love me.
Ah, my crutch! The sight of thy handle makes me wroth.

LLYWARCH HEN, Bard of Argoed.

to her; and I do not despair of finding such a being.

However, I am not a conceited jackass—*senem verecundum esse decet*, so I moderate my pretensions. I do not the least insist that this companion of mine should be rich. I do not expect her to have any great affluence of charms, much less that *grata protervitas* which is irresistible to both young and old. I can hardly hope that one who would regard me as I have described would be very youthful; indeed, I have lately experienced a sharp lesson in this respect. I had selected quite a young lady, not pretty, but interesting, whom I hoped to educate for the position. Not very long after our correspondence began I discovered that she showed my letters to her mother.

I speak with sincerity, and acknowledge that I may have to be content with a 'half-worn' woman —*nec bella, nec puella.* However, there is one thing which is absolutely necessary. This precious soul, whoever and wherever she may be, must not only be devoted to me, but she must be *really* a vassal to my poetry. It must move her to tender thoughts, and occasionally to even emotional transport.

This necessity is an anxious consideration; and it is embarrassing, because there are very few people indeed who have been deeply affected by my verse. Hitherto I have not been spoilt in that respect.

It is possible that the companion I am in search of will have had her disappointments, her trials. Likely enough she may have led a life of dependence, and therefore of prolonged self-denial. If so, she will probably be a grateful being. The friend I seek ought to be a very grateful being.

No woman can be extremely attractive without some personal vanity. Let my possible 'she' be vain to that degree. She need not be pretty, but I wish her to be interesting-looking. She may be weak, but she must not be stupid; sensitive, but not exacting; impulsive, but not too negligent; and not opinionated, excepting in her opinion of me.

It is also important that, if ever she should desire to improve the occasion, she should do so by example. She must *never* do it by precept—understand this; and her religious opinions should be in complete harmony with my own. We ought to find mutual comfort and support in theological conversation and discussion. She must not be a prude; and she should always know the day of the month.

I am now sixty years old. I think I should prefer that this amiable friend did not live under my roof, for sometimes I should like to be quit of her altogether. However, she might abide in my immediate neighbourhood, perhaps with a querulous grandmother. My dear wife will advise and help me in this matter.

I am told that Felix Carroll, the lyric poet, who is threescore years and ten, has a consolation of the nature I describe; indeed, that in his case there has been a succession of them. He finds it exhausting to be amiable every day to the same human being. A flower out of place is a weed—so his present adorer lives near at hand, with a fat valetudinarian aunt. She writes to him continually. There is a confiding softness and whispering charm in her punctual letters. She knows a good deal of Felix Carroll's poetry by heart; she treasures his autograph; she is sentimental or sportive over his spectacles and lampshade. She is tolerant when he is testy. She is devoted to his wife. She goes to him every day, sometimes twice, whether it be wet or fine, whether she be ill or well. She sits at his feet; or, if he wills it, she ebbs noiselessly away. Felix Carroll's life is sheltered from disturbing episodes: wild roses fill his hedgerows, and fragrant woodbine clambers everywhere; his woods are vocal with rooks and pairing birds; the clamour of the great city comes mellowed from afar; he can say, as another has said:

> Thoughts which at Hyde Park Corner I forgot
> Meet and rejoin me in the pensive grot.

He finds Tusculan repose in a creeper-covered combination of rusticity and refinement. In summer he loafs, and invites his soul in shady walks, shadowy verandahs, cool alcoves, and a wealth of mignonette, jasmine, stephanotis. In winter he has a perfectly regulated temperature, cheerful fires, a complete system of hot-water piping, and, of course, the most modern appliances. With these and all the latest periodicals and papers, and, to crown all, with the radiant reflex of his companion's youth, his old age is lapped in simple luxury ; he is handsomely hedged about, lighted up, tucked in, and provided for. He secures comfort by being comfortable. Can any arrangement be more satisfactory ?

I am not acquainted with the Chinese language, but I have read that it possesses a word which has three different meanings—at least, they seem different to me—a towel, a comb, and a woman ! What a language ! What a people ! I have heard it maintained that woman is a fair defect of Nature, and that she is at the core of all our troubles ; that she is a necessary evil, a natural temptation, a desirable commodity, a domestic peril, a deadly fascination, and a painted ill. *Cherchez la femme !* It may be so. I suppose it always will be said to be so ; but I do not believe it. Such notions are shocking to me. Woman is a beautiful, romantic animal, to be adored and doated upon. I honour women, and have resolved that my happiness shall be cradled in the smiles of a devoted woman.

Montaigne had such a friend (Marie de Gournay); so had V. Hugo in Juliette Drouet; so had—— But need I run through the names of all the men illustrious in imaginative literature who have been so courted and consoled? Biography is rich with them, and why, I say—why should I be left out?

> What joy to wind along the cool retreat;
> To stop and gaze on Delia as I go;
> To mingle sweet discourse with homage sweet,
> And teach my lovely scholar all I know!

I hope the spirit of this paper will not be misunderstood. It is pure fun, and those who know me will recognise that the person most quizzed is myself.

SOME BIOGRAPHICAL SKETCHES

Mr. Thackeray

I had a sincere regard for Thackeray. I well remember his striking personality—striking to those who had the ability to recognise it: the look of the man, the latent power, and the occasional keenness of his remarks on men and their actions, as if he saw through and through them. Thackeray drew many unto him, for he had engaging as well as fine qualities. He was open-handed and kind-hearted. He had not an overweening opinion of his literary consequence, and he was generous as regarded the people whom the world chose to call his rivals.

I made Thackeray's acquaintance at the British Embassy, Paris. Events are liable to get confused in the refracting medium of one's memory, but I think it was about 1852 or 1853. From that time to the end of his life we often found ourselves together, and were always good friends.

Thackeray, though he was not so subtle a critic as some of the present day (1883), was an excellent judge of poetry, and when Tennyson's 'Grandmother' first appeared in 'Once a Week' he was greatly struck by it. 'I wish I could have got that poem for my "Cornhill"—I would have paid 50*l*. for it; but I would have given 500*l*. to have been able to write it.' Nobody knew better than Thackeray that, though Mercury is a pleasant fellow, Apollo, to say the least of him, has the larger following. Still he was duly impressed with the difficulty of reaching excellence in writing even *light* poetry; he often spoke to me about it. Lady Blessington once sent him an Album print of a boy and girl fishing, with a request that he would make some verses for it. 'And,' said he, 'I liked the idea, and set about it at once. I was two entire days at it—was so occupied with it, so engrossed by it, that I did not shave during the whole time!' These lines may be found among his ballads, under the title of 'Piscator and Piscatrix.' I remember his words: 'It is easy enough to knock off that nonsense of "Policeman X.," but to be able to write really good *occasional* verse is a rare intellectual feat.' Now it appears to me that it would be indeed a triumph to write anything half so good as 'Policeman X.'

What an admirable gift had Thackeray! Who is so genial, tender, and humorous? Why, the very negligence of his verse has its charm! Read his Horatian 'Wait till you come to Forty Year.'

Thackeray greatly admired George Cruikshank, but only in his quite early works. When Cruikshank was engaged on the 'Omnibus' he asked Thackeray to contribute. Thackeray sent him a fairly long contribution, I forget on what subject, and Cruikshank returned him a sovereign in full satisfaction. Thackeray laughed good-naturedly as he told me this, and added, 'You may suppose after that I did not trouble George with any more of my poems.'

He once pointed out to me an illustration in the 'Comic Almanac'—'The Marriage Breakfast; or, the Happiest Day of my Life'—an old gentleman in barnacles, his arms folded, with difficulty keeping back his tears. This figure, something like the late Mr. John Forster, gave Thackeray infinite delight.

He also much admired the work of John Leech. 'Leech is the sort of man who appears once in a century.'

Thackeray had hardly any personal acquaintance with Hood. I think he only met him once, at a City feast. He told me that Hood was a 'pallid, thin, melancholy-looking man.' He did not care for a great deal that Hood wrote; but just at the time when Thackeray's 'Roundabout Paper,' 'On a Joke by Thomas Hood,' appeared, he said to me: 'What a vigorous fellow Hood is; what a swing there is in his verse!' I agreed with him, and then said something about Thackeray's own poetry. 'Yes,' he replied—'yes, I have a sixpenny talent (or gift), and so have you; ours is small-beer, but, you see, it is the right tap.' He said other things about my verses, both to me and behind my back, which I am pleased to remember, but not pleased to repeat.

I will now give a reminiscence of Thackeray which certainly, for my own sake, I mention with reluctance; but I wish to give you a true idea of the man, and this will show you he was very sensitive. I happened to meet him as I was leaving the Travellers' Club. Even now I think I could point out the particular flagstone on which the dear fellow was standing, as he gazed down on me through his spectacles with that dreamy expression of his which his friends knew so well. He said: 'What do you think of the last number?' (Number 2 or 3 of 'The Newcomes'). He himself was evidently not quite satisfied with it. 'I like it immensely' was my cordial rejoinder. A word or two more passed respecting the illustrations, which had been sharply criticised, and just as we parted I was tactless idiot enough to add, 'But, my dear fellow, perhaps there may be some kind people who will say that *you* did the cuts and Doyle the letterpress.' On this Thackeray's jaw dropped, and he exclaimed bitterly, 'Oh! really, that's your opinion, is it?' I saw at once what a mistake I had made; but I could only reply, 'I spoke in fun, pure fun; you know perfectly well how much I admire your writings, and also Doyle's cuts.' But Thackeray would have none of it, and turned wrathfully away in the direction of Pimlico. However, his wrath, I presume, died away in the large and charitable air of the Green Park, for when I met him the day after he was as amiable as ever.

The fact is, I had so exalted an opinion of Thackeray and of his writings that it seemed impossible such a demi-god should care for aught anybody said; whereas, like Tennyson, he felt everything that everybody said.

I remember another, a more agreeable meeting, in Pall Mall, close to Marlborough House. He was on his way to Kensington across the Green Park. He told me that I must not turn with him, as there were some rhymes trotting in his head, and he wanted to finish them. I quite understood the situation, and he continued his solitary walk. When we met a few days afterwards, he said: 'I finished those verses, and they are very nearly being very good. I call them *Miss Katharine's Lantern*; I did them for Dickens's daughter.'

He spoke with a lisp, as if his teeth were defective, and ended by, 'I am now on my way from the dentist.' You will remember that towards the end of that little poem he refers to his toothless condition.

I admire Thackeray's style, and the pathetic quality in his writings; in this he never faltered. I like his sardonic melancholy. Thackeray, in a passing mood, might quite well have said: 'Who breathes must suffer, and who thinks must mourn, and he alone is blest who ne'er was born.'

He shows knowledge of human nature and much acquaintance with life—not a wide acquaintance, but complete within its limits. The vernacular of his Fokers and his Fred Bayhams is classical, and so is their slang.

Some years ago I met a man somewhere—I forget where, or who he was—who told me that in past times he used to pay annual visits to Paris; that he often looked into Galignani's reading-room (now defunct), and there was to be seen a very tall young man, with black hair and spectacles, who used to *rôder autour de la chambre*, with his hands in his pockets and his shoulders up to his ears, in a shivery, restless, uncomfortable sort of way. This young man occasionally would take up a paper, glance at it, and then fling it back on the table, over the heads of the readers. He often saw this man, who never addressed any one, and whom no one ever spoke to; and my informant wondered, in a languid sort of way, who the deuce he could be. One day he happened to enter Frascati's. The first person he saw there was the tall spectacled man, prowling about, standing behind the punters—observing, not playing. He did not seem to speak to any one. And now my informant became interested to know who on earth the man could be.

Some time after this, on a Sunday, he was walking in Hyde Park, and met his very tall spectacled hero, still alone, his black hair beginning to be grizzled. From time to time during the next six or eight years he encountered the same man in the Park and in the streets; once or twice with a man even taller than himself—an amiable, handsome, and complacent-looking giant; and now my informant was seized with a consuming curiosity to know who, in Heaven's name, this person could possibly be.

One afternoon, long afterwards, he chanced to be in King Street, Covent Garden, and as he passed the Garrick Club (the original house) his spectacled *incognito*, grown portly and almost white, came sedately forth. Here was an opportunity. He saw him descend the *perron* and well away; then in he slipped and says he to the porter: 'Can you kindly tell me who that very tall white-haired gentleman is who has just left the club?'

When every one knows how a story will end, the

story is ended. It is not necessary, dear children, that I should tell you what that porter said.

You may gather from this little account that though at times and seasons Thackeray enjoyed society, and was always valued by it, he was not what is called a very social being. Tennyson in this respect is something like him.

Some people thank God that they do not set store by the smaller refinements and civilisations of life. Let me tell them that they are thanking God for a very small mercy. Such boons gave Thackeray a keen satisfaction. He was a man of sensibility: he delighted in luxuriously furnished and well-lighted rooms, good music, excellent wines and cookery, exhilarating talk, gay and airy gossip, pretty women and their toilettes, and refined and noble manners, *le bon goût, le ris, l'aimable liberté.* The amenities of life and the traditions stimulated his imagination.

On the other hand, his writings show how he equally enjoyed Bohemianism, and how diverted he could be by those happy-go-lucky fellows of the Foker and Fred Bayham type.

Thackeray expanded in the society of such people, and with them he was excellent company. But, if I am not much mistaken, the man Thackeray was melancholy—he had known tribulation, he had suffered. He was not a light-hearted wag or a gay-natured rover, but a sorrowing man. He could make you a jest, or propound some jovial or outrageous sentiment, and imply, 'Let us be festive,' but the jollity rarely came. However, I ought to say that though Thackeray was not cheerily, he was at times grotesquely, humorous. Indeed, he had a weakness for buffoonery. I have seen him pirouette, wave his arm majestically, and declaim in burlesque—an intentionally awkward imitation of the ridiculous manner that is sometimes met with in French opera.

I remember calling in Palace Gardens, and, while talking with all gravity to Thackeray's daughters, I noticed that they seemed more than necessarily amused. On looking round, I discovered that their father had put on my hat, and, having picked my pocket of my handkerchief, was strutting about, flourishing it in the old Lord Cardigan style. As I was thin-faced, and he, as a hatter once remarked of Thomas Bruce, was 'a gent. as could carry a large body o' 'at,' you may suppose he looked sufficiently funny.

Thackeray could be very amusing about the malice of kind and the perfidy of honest people; but still, in everyday life, and in spite of his *flair de cynique*, he was naturally inclined to believe that gossip false which ought not to be true.

One day I happened to speak with admiration

of Sydney Smith, and Thackeray looked surprised, and said, 'Ah, Sydney! he was a poor creature, a very poor creature.' He said it twice, and I think he was about to give his reasons for holding so crushing an opinion, when some idiot came up, and, to my very great regret, carried him off. I hope the time may come and place be appointed when certain small mysteries connected with our sojourn here below may be made plain; if so, I shall indeed be glad to know why Thackeray did not approve of the plucky, the buoyant, the inimitable Sydney Smith.

During the last three or four years of Thackeray's life he suffered from bad health, depressing bad health. He lived with his daughters and his intimates, and almost entirely gave up general society—and he was a wise man to do so. My dear reader, whoever you are, think of this illustrious man with tenderness; think of his upright nature, of his affectionate heart, his domestic affliction. These are enough—you need not trouble for his genius.

Dear Thackeray! his happiness and his comfort were fragile charges to be entrusted to any one. His dutiful and gifted daughters were their best guardians.

Most of us have some sort of belief, some ideal as to the end and object of life. Thackeray was a good man. He had a strong sense of religion: he recognised that the human soul requires such a sanctuary and would starve without it. It was Thackeray who spoke sorrowfully of his little Ethel Newcome as going prayerless to bed.

I knew Thackeray for years, and had very many talks with him—and this is all I have to tell you about him. What a wonderful fellow was James Boswell!

George Eliot and Mr. G. H. Lewes

Nature had disguised George Eliot's apparently stoical, yet really vehement and sensitive, spirit, and her soaring genius, in a homely and insignificant form. Her countenance was equine—she was rather like a horse; and her head had been intended for a much longer body—she was not a tall woman. She wore her hair in not pleasing, out-of-fashion loops, coming down on either side of her face, so hiding her ears; and her garments concealed her outline—they gave her a waist like a milestone. You will see her at her very best in the portrait by Sir Frederic Burton. To my mind George Eliot was a plain woman.

She had a measured way of conversing; restrained, but impressive. When I happened to call she was nearly always seated in the chimney corner on a low chair, and she bent forward when she spoke. As she often discussed abstract subjects, she might have been thought pedantic, especially as her language was sprinkled with a scientific terminology; but I do not think she was a bit of a pedant. Then, though she had a very gentle voice and manner, there was, every now and then, just a suspicion of meek satire in her talk.

Her sentences unwound themselves very neatly and completely, leaving the impression of past reflection and present readiness; she spoke exceedingly well, but not with all the simplicity and *verve*, the happy *abandon* of certain practised women of the world; however, it was in a way that was far more interesting. I have been told she was most agreeable *en tête-à-tête;* that when surrounded by admirers she was apt to become oratorical—a different woman. She did not strike me as witty or markedly humorous; she was too much in earnest: she spoke as if with a sense of responsibility, and one cannot be exactly captivating when one is doing that. Madame de Sablé might have said of her, 'elle s'écouta en parlant.' She was a good listener.

I ought to say that during all the time I knew her, George Eliot appeared to be suffering from feeble health, and without doubt this affected her whole bearing.

When we first became acquainted we were told that she and Lewes had been married in Germany, and that they were reluctant to move out of their own immediate circle, or to enlarge it; however, when I ventured to ask them to dine with me, to meet Arthur and Augusta Stanley, they came.

The Stanleys appreciated the dinner; they did not think Mr. Lewes attractive, but they were interested in *her*. I think they and I afterwards met both Mr. Lewes and George Eliot at Lord Mount-Temple's, and at Jowett's; but these subsequent meetings did not deepen Arthur's first favourable impression, and then he was considerably taken aback when he found that Mrs. Lewes was in no way Mr. Lewes's wife.

I saw George Eliot only two or three times after Lewes's death: on the first occasion she was shrouded with much weed, so I talked to her with bated breath, hardly venturing to initiate a subject; however, as I was leaving the room, I chanced to say something about Mrs. Langtry, just then sailing with supreme dominion on the buoyant wings of her beauty; upon this George Eliot pricked up her ears, and asked about her. I said that I had lately met Mrs. Langtry at Mrs. Millais's, and had had an amiable little letter from her about some verses which afterwards got into the *World*. On this George Eliot became more and much more interested, and laughed, and asked me to repeat the lines.

This was one of the few occasions on which I had seen George Eliot entirely alone; it enabled me to know her better, and it made me feel sorry that she had not more sprightly and natural people about her—indeed, that she did not breathe a more healthy atmosphere; for unless Du Maurier sang, or W. K. Clifford talked, or Vivier, the horn-blower, gave one of his impersonations, her *réunions* had somewhat of the solemnity of religious functions, with the religion cut out. Her intimates were mostly composed of her admirers, of scientific people, *littérateurs*, and the disciples of that grotesque sophist, Auguste Comte.

Sir Charles Bowen, the distinguished judge, told me that he had known George Eliot during the last twelve or fifteen years of her life. He knew her very well, and often went to see her. Bowen thought her exceedingly agreeable, and Bowen is an excellent judge. She once confided to him a manuscript of considerable length, the skeleton of, or memoranda for, a novel, which had a legal *dénoûment.* Bowen read it carefully, and felt that it would not do, that it was too thin, and he wrote and told her so. She did not resent this frankly expressed opinion, for when next he saw her she referred to the manuscript, and said she had made up her mind not to use it, and I believe she never did.

She told a friend of mine that, when she was arranging for a new novel, she first sketched in the characters, and then they gradually and naturally fell into certain positions in life and evolved the story. George Eliot had this questionable advantage over novelists like Bulwer and Miss Braddon: her stories, as stories, are not so artfully constructed that the reader is apt to sacrifice appreciation of the beauty of the thoughts and style in eager pursuit of the agonising plot.

At Keir, many years ago, I met Mrs. Norton,[1] afterwards Lady Stirling-Maxwell; she told me that she had reviewed 'Adam Bede' in the 'Edinburgh Review,' and that she thought it the finest of George Eliot's novels. She especially spoke of the first volume. I agreed with her that, if the third volume[2] had been equal to the first, the work might take rank with the best by Walter Scott, which nearly always improve as they advance. George

[1] Mrs. Norton at the same time told me what now (1883) seems almost incredible: that she had seen Benjamin D'Israeli in St. James's Street in black velvet trousers, lace ruffles, and with high scarlet heels to his boots. He tried that sort of thing for a short time, found it was not a success, and discontinued it. Mrs. Norton mentioned this not as a proof of his curious ignorance and want of taste, but of his good sense. May not Mrs. Norton have exaggerated?

[2] Shakespeare even could not make the fifth act of *Julius Cæsar* so interesting as the third.

Eliot has none of Scott's animal spirits, but, like Scott, her humour is the humour of truth, and not of exaggeration. George Eliot is most happy in describing the middle class.

Mr. Lewes was very clever, acute and vivacious, with an essentially all-round intelligence; a ready man, able to turn the talent that was in him to full and immediate account.

There are special types, as there are different degrees, of ugliness; there is the ugliness of Sir ——, who is so grotesquely featured that he looks as if he were walking about doing it for fun. On the other hand, there was the plainness of Mr. George Lewes, but that was of a less comic character, and yet he was credited with having been a Lothario, who could have boasted 'personne ne connaît la puissance de ma belle laideur'—it was suggested that George Eliot, or time, had tamed him—however, anybody, judging by his appearance and manners, would have been justified in thinking that the number of his conquests might have been represented by a vanishing quantity. He had long hair, and his dress was an unlovely compromise between morning and evening costume, combining the less pleasing points of both.

His adverse critics said that he was literary among men of science, and scientific among literary men. It struck me that he had a reprehensible delight in ridiculing the dogmas of revealed religion, which displeased me. I believe (a word that did not go for very much in his vocabulary) he was a good-tempered, and I dare say a benevolently inclined, person, and nothing could have exceeded his devotion to George Eliot; for he was ever on the alert to shield her from worries and annoyance, and keen to get her good terms from the publishers, but somehow it seemed an incongruous partnership.

I did not find him very agreeable; but he once made Tennyson and me laugh heartily by his description of a certain 'noble lord' of his acquaintance, an effete and preposterous personage, going, under the guidance of Mulready, the well-known genre painter, to see a collection of pictures, and how the 'noble lord' talked the whole time, never stopped, and yet never once committed himself to an opinion. Lewes had been an actor, and he imitated the voice and gesture.[1]

[1] *Noble Lord.* 'Haw, yes, you've a great many pictures here, Mr. Mulready—a great many pictures. Now this picture—the Old Masters, you know (*with his double eyeglass between his finger and thumb*). Let me see now, to whom shall we give this picture, eh?'

Mr. Mulready. 'This, my lord, is by Cuyp.'

Noble Lord. 'Haw, yes, of course. This picture's by Cuyp, you know: and this, Mr. Mulready, what shall we say to this picture?'

Mr. Mulready. 'This picture, my lord, is also by Cuyp.'

Noble Lord. 'By Cuyp, eh! Haw, yes, of course (*always with his eyeglass*). This picture is also by Cuyp. The Old Masters, you know, and this. Mr. Mulready, you've a great many pictures here; to whom shall we give this picture? an Old Master, eh?'

Mr. Lewes had known Charlotte Brontë; he admired her writings, but complained that she spoke of Catholics and the Catholic Church with acrimony, reviling the incense-pots, and such like, which offended the little Comtist, who, in spite of his impieties, was by way of being contemptuously tolerant. I doubt, however, if it was much more than a sceptical indifference; for only touch him where he did believe—and sceptics are very credulous—wound his self-love, and he was all beak, claws, and bitterness. Lewes was considered very amusing in a sort of way, and it was understood that he had anything but deteriorated by his association with George Eliot.

I once took Major Lawrence Lockhart (John Gibson Lockhart's nephew and the author of 'Fair to see'), to call on George Eliot. She was attracted by manly beauty, and Lockhart was very good-looking; he was also a clever, rollicking writer—the sporting novel in the style of Surtees—a species indigenous to England, and he had considerable conversational powers; but in appearance and bearing he was the typical horsey dragoon, the

Mr. Mulready. 'Why, curiously enough, my lord, this is also by Cuyp.'

Noble Lord. 'Indeed! Haw, really now, this is remarkable (*looking about him, always with his eyeglass*). This is also by Cuyp, you know. Why, bless my soul, Mulready, we've a monstrous number of pictures by that fellow Cuyp,' &c., &c.

plunger. I at once introduced him to Lewes, who (and this was very generous on Lewes's part) presented him to his wife, and then, taking him aside almost immediately, began to talk about horses, the racehorse of the present day, and of a curious circumstance that had been mentioned in the papers about laying the odds; and then he (Lewes) passed on, and talked to somebody else. However, he soon returned to Lockhart, who evidently much interested him.

> As inward love breeds outward talk,
> The hound some praise, and some the hawk,

so this time the subject was canine, from the Anubis of the Egyptians down to the last dog-show. All this surprised poor Lockhart. 'What the deuce did he mean by talking to me about his horses and dogs, and nothing else?' I did not care to tell him that I thought Lewes was entirely justified in supposing a warrior of his appearance and manner could not possibly think of anything else, but I ventured to say his doing so was a proof that he thought a good deal of him. Lockhart's amused and simple unconsciousness pleased me exceedingly.[1]

[1] Lockhart was a very agreeable companion; a diverting and interesting paper might be written about him, his writings, his adventures, his faculty for friendship, his breezy rhetoric, and his marvellous practical jokes. An account of one of these last will be found among my papers. Mrs. Rudd, his beloved sister, is more than worthy of him.

When I attended Mr. Lewes's funeral in Highgate Cemetery, we were a very small party in the mortuary chapel, not more than twelve persons. I never before had seen so many out-and-out rationalists in so confined a space. A brief discourse was delivered by a Unitarian clergyman, who half apologised for suggesting the possible immortality of some of our souls.

George Eliot's funeral was also at Highgate; snow and slush, and a bitter wind blowing, but still there was a remarkable gathering from all parts of England. I took Tyndall there, and brought him back, and had great pleasure in the philosopher and his conversation. He is full of imagination and I may say of affection.

George Eliot's more transcendental friends never forgave her for marrying. In a morally immoral manner they washed their virtuous hands of her. I could not help thinking it was the most natural thing for the poor woman to do. She was a heavily laden but interesting derelict, tossing among the breakers, without oars or rudder, and all at once the brave Cross arrives, throws her a rope, and gallantly tows her into harbour.

I am sure that she was very sensitive, and must have had many a painful half-hour as the helpmate of Mr. Lewes. By accepting the position, she had placed herself in opposition to the moral instincts of most of those whom she held most dear. Though intellectually self-contained, I believe she was singularly dependent on the emotional side of her nature. With her, as with nearly all women, she needed a something to lean upon. Though her conduct was socially indefensible, it would have been cruel, it would be stupid, to judge her exactly as one would judge an ordinary offender. What a genius she must have had to have been able to draw so many high-minded people to her! I have an impression that she felt her position acutely, and was unhappy.

George Eliot was much to be pitied. I think she knew that I felt for her and would have been glad to do her a good turn; for more than once, when I was taking leave, she said, 'Come and see me soon, Mr. Locker; don't lose sight of us.' And this to an outsider, a nobody, and not in her set! She wrote me two or three interesting letters which should be read in connection with this paper.

I framed that exquisite little Rembrandt etching, the 'Funeral of Jesus,' and gave it to her. She was pleased, but I dare say she did not appreciate its merit. I do not know whether she had any instinct for pictorial art.

Those who saw more of George Eliot than I did, tell me that as Mrs. Cross she seemed a changed woman; she was more natural, more cheerful, happier.

I have given a very meagre and cold-blooded account of this brilliant, unfortunate, and, I may say, noble-natured woman, and now I have done so, will my children have a better idea of the sort of person she was? However, they can learn that from her books and letters, and the biographies. These few pages are written that they should better understand the impression she made upon their father.

I must re-read one of her least prolix and most powerful—one of her earlier stories. I have not read any of them for years; and then, with the enthusiasm fresh and full upon me, I may perhaps add a postscript.

Mr. Charles Dickens

I think it was on July 1, 1841, that I first saw Mr. Charles Dickens; it was at a charity bazaar, in the Painted Hall of Greenwich Hospital, where my mother had a stall. Mr. Dickens was there with two friends, Mr. Clarkson Stanfield, the painter, being one of them. I remember we young people gazed at the visitors with intense interest. Dickens at that time was a handsome, vivacious-looking young man of rather low stature; he favoured the redundant locks and elaborate costume which you see in his portrait by Maclise, and which were the fashion of the period.

The next time I saw Dickens was in 1843 or 1844, at an Odd Fellows' club dinner, held in the vicinity of Lincoln's Inn Fields. I was the guest of Mr. Crofton Croker, an interesting writer and an Admiralty clerk, and—proud moment!—he introduced me to Dickens.

About ten members of the club were present—they seemed commonplace as well as *odd fellows*; punsters, somewhat inclined to dilate on what was tedious, and insist on what was obvious; but I was proud to meet them. Dickens struck me as altogether different: he spoke to the point, listened well, and now and then made a sprightly remark. Mr. Henry Hope's house in Piccadilly, at present the Junior Athenæum Club, had just been built; the introduction of flat slabs of polished red granite between the windows was a novelty in domestic architecture, and therefore disturbed the Odd Fellows. Dickens, I suppose to please them, said the house looked as if it had had its face scratched and then covered with strips of sticking-plaister. This was not a brilliant *mot*, but it comforted the

Odd Fellows, and we made the most of it. As it was the first I had heard from Dickens's lips, and it sounded exceedingly well, I venture to record it on my poor little page.

After this dinner I did not see Dickens for several years, but I did my best. I feasted on his greencoated numbers as they came out, and chewed the cud of my recollections. At last I encountered him at the Athenæum Club—it must have been in 1848, soon after my election. I was entering the club, and a man was standing on the threshold opposite to me, talking to one of the members; the bright sunlight shone full on his face, on his dancing blue eyes and arching brows, and it struck me as the most animated countenance I had ever seen. It did not seem altogether strange to me—at any rate, I was so impressed by it, that I asked the porter who the gentleman was. 'It's Mr. Dickens, sir,' says the porter; 'one of our members, sir.'

Dickens sometimes came into the club for luncheon; he did not care to stop and talk; perhaps he did not know many members, and there were few in the room at that hour. He had forgotten me. He used to eat his sandwich standing at the centre table, or striding about.

After that I was often in company with Dickens. I once heard him make a speech at Covent Garden Theatre, on Administrative Reform; there was no gush or rhetoric; it was a most telling speech. I saw him and Mr. Charles Knight (the publisher, my father's old friend) and other amateurs act Lord Lytton's play, 'Not so bad as we seem;' they seemed pretty bad. I heard Dickens read two or three times.

I met him at Charles Knight's house, and at Lord Houghton's. It was there that I ventured to talk of the Greenwich Hospital bazaar and the Odd Fellows' dinner, and he remembered all about them.

A long time afterwards, probably in 1869, I met him at the house of my hospitable acquaintance, Mr. Routledge, the publisher, in Russell Square, at a banquet to Mr. Longfellow, and then Dickens was very friendly; his hearty manner was exceedingly attractive. In March, 1870, we again met at a very pleasant dinner given by my friend, Colonel Hamley, at the Army and Navy Club. Mr. Secretary Walpole, Motley, afterwards United States Minister in London, and Russell Sturgis completed the party. I sat by Dickens. He was remarkably agreeable; his conversation was so affluent, so delightfully alive, so unaffected. When Dickens was in congenial company—and he had the happy faculty of making it congenial to himself—he talked like a demon of delightfulness. At this repast Motley, who was very fond of Dickens, poked a good deal of pleasant fun at him, especially about his 'American Sketches,' pretending to be Mark Tapley; much to Dickens's joy, who gave it him back with interest. This was the more diverting as we knew how sensitive Motley usually was as regards America and the Americans, and certainly Dickens had tried him.

I recollect everything about that memorable banquet. I even recall a wonderful chicken *écharpé*, with béchamel sauce. We know the ingredients that compose a *plat*: the incantation that accompanies its preparation is the mystery.

A short time before or after this, Alfred Tennyson happening to be in London, and expressing a desire to see Dickens, I invited them to meet at dinner. Just then, however, Dickens was engaged on his readings, and was obliged to decline. About the same time I had been talking to Arthur Stanley of the burials in the Abbey, and he told me that there were certain people who he sincerely hoped would survive him, as, if not, however much their friends might desire it, he should be obliged to refuse them burial in the Abbey. The names of one or two distinguished people were mentioned, such as Carlyle and Mill. Then Dickens's name came up, and the Dean said, 'Oddly enough, I have only once met Dickens. I do not know him; I have read hardly any of his writings; I should like to meet Dickens.' To gratify this pious wish, I asked Dickens and his daughter to dine, to meet the Dean and Augusta. This was on February 2. As the Dean entered the room, he whispered, 'We are late; I have been finishing "Pickwick."'

My dinner went off excellently. Arthur said he had had a delightful time, and had found Dickens 'most agreeable.'

I afterwards dined *en garçon* with Dickens, Lady Charlotte being out of town, and met the Stanhopes, Edward Hamley, Darnley (his neighbour at Gad's Hill), Costa, the composer, Strzelecki, and others whose names I forget.

Dickens had much social tact; he was genial and manly; he had a strong personality; he could say 'No,' but I should think he had infinitely greater pleasure in saying 'Yes.' He was a jovial fellow, with a most elastic spirit, and apparently an exhaustless vitality. I am told he was an adept at brewing stiff punch, but sparing in his own libations. He favoured convivial philanthropy—indeed, he was the first person to preach the deep spiritual significance of the Christmas goose. He boiled the hot water and potatoes at picnics, was adroit at conjuring and otherwise amusing the young people. Indeed, Dickens entered heart and soul into everything he did; he was a keen man of business, active and practical. He told me that genuine appreciation of his works was as fresh and precious to him then (1869) as it had been thirty years before; indeed, he was still so sensitive to neglect that, in a railway carriage, if his opposite neighbour were reading one of his novels, he did not dare to watch him, lest he should see the book thrown aside with indifference.

His appearance was attractive; he was not conventionally gentlemanlike-looking—I should have been disappointed if he had been so: he was something better. I shall not quickly forget him at Macaulay's funeral, as he walked among the subdued-looking clericals and staid men of mark; there was a stride in his gait and a roll; he had a seafaring complexion and air, and a huge white tie.

Dickens was fond of dress; he owned that he had the primeval savage's love for bright positive colours. I consoled him with the assurance that it was the poet side of his nature that was so gratified.

Dickens had, as indeed I have already remarked, a wonderfully animated countenance. There was an eager look in his bright eyes, and his manners were as free from *mauvaise honte* as from unseasonable familiarity. He told stories with real dramatic effect; he gave one at my table, as related by Rogers (who made story-telling a fine art), of the English and French duellists who agreed to fight with pistols, the candles being extinguished, in a small room. The brave but humane Englishman, unwilling to shed blood, gropes his way to the fire-place, and discharges his weapon up the chimney; when, lo and behold! whom should he bring down but the dastardly Frenchman, who had crept thither for safety! Dickens said that Rogers's postscript was not the worst part of the story—'When I tell that in Paris, I always put the Englishman up the chimney!' Dickens mimicked Rogers's calm, low-pitched, drawling voice and dry biting manner very comically.

Dickens admired Smollett; he considered 'Humphrey Clinker' a highly humorous story, and very originally told. He christened one of his sons Henry Fielding. He did not unduly appreciate Miss Jane Austen's novels, for Mrs. B—— met him at a dinner party where they were discussed. She enthusiastically admired them: said so, and silently appealed to Dickens, who shook his head as much as to say, 'Do not ask me.' Soon afterwards the company appealed to Dickens, when he excused himself thus: 'I have already told Mrs. B—— my opinion: I must refer you to her.'[1]

[1] Dickens was hardly capable of appreciating her peculiar genius, at once delicate and strong; her truth to nature, with all its little harmonies and discords, her fine humour and exquisite restraint. Miss Austen's scope is limited, but it is the completeness—the perfection of art. My children, if you do not realise the force of what I say, read the story of Frederick Wentworth and Anne Elliot.

Dickens told me two or three excellent stories. One was an account of his reporting the late Lord Derby's (then Lord Stanley) speech on Ireland; another of President Lincoln's last dream; and another of his meeting a monk in an Italian monastery, who talked English fluently, but with a cockney accent, a dialect curiously familiar to him, and that he found out that the monk had taught himself English by reading the Sam Weller chapters in 'Pickwick.' I think all these stories have appeared in print, but no written account can give an idea of the racy vigour with which Dickens told them.

Dickens had a wonderful memory, ready and tenacious. He happened to call on Mrs. B—— soon after her husband had been presented with a living—I think in Lincolnshire—and he asked what sort of a neighbourhood they would have. She told him that there would not be a soul to speak to, excepting an old friend, a Mr. Maddison, and there the talk ended. A year or two after this conversation, Mrs. B—— met Dickens in a crowded London drawing-room; he smiled at her (I should have said she was a clever and remarkably handsome woman), then made his way to her, shook her warmly by the hand, and said, 'How's Tomkinson?'

A young poet, Mr. Laman Blanchard, sent

Dickens a metrical contribution for 'Household Words,' entitled 'Orient Pearls at random strung;' but Dickens returned them with 'Dear Blanchard, too much string,—Yours, C. D.' At or about the same time I sent 'the Editor' my little verses called 'Beggars.' These were also declined, but politely. You see I have full and sufficing reason for questioning Dickens's fine taste in literature.

I think the last time I saw Dickens was late in May, 1870, at Arthur Stanley's. The party consisted of Lord and Lady Russell, the Clarendons, Nisbet Hamilton, Mary and Constance, Thirlwall, Bishop of St. David's, Arthur Helps, and other distinguished persons whose names I cannot recall.

In June, 1870, I was staying with Tennyson at Aldworth, and heard of Dickens's sudden death. I read the account of it in the train, and on my arrival at 91 Victoria Street I found a note waiting me from Arthur Stanley, thanking me for having made him acquainted with Charles Dickens 'while there was yet time,' and adding that he was 'prepared to receive any communication from the family respecting the burial.' I at once sent his note on to Charles Dickens, junior, then at Gad's Hill, whom up to that time I had never seen. The family knew how anxious the public were that Dickens should be laid in Westminster Abbey; but the terms of the will were so binding that they had decided the funeral ought to be at Rochester. Indeed, I believe the grave was dug before my letter—which had got overlooked—was opened. However, young Mr. Charles Dickens and Mr. Forster came at once to London, saw Arthur, and received his assurance that the funeral could be as quietly and privately performed at Westminster Abbey as anywhere else. This decided them.

The morning of the funeral was very fine. Eleanor and I left 91 Victoria Street at twenty minutes past nine. As we reached the entrance to Dean's Yard, and as St. Stephen's clock chimed the half-hour, a hearse and mourning coaches swept round the Broad Sanctuary; they seemed to bring with them an unusual stillness; then, as they drove under the archway into Dean's Yard, the great bell began to toll. There was hardly a creature in the street or in the Abbey, that 'Temple of Silence and Reconciliation,' and no one but ourselves knew whose funeral had passed, or for whom the big bell was tolling. Later in the day we saw the coffin in the grave, covered with flowers, and then there was an immense crowd of excited and sympathetic mourners.

Dickens was a very good fellow, a delightful companion, warm-hearted, gay-natured, with plenty of light-in-hand fun, and a great capacity for friendship. He was the devoted lifelong servant of the public, and in my opinion, to say the least of him, he was the most laughter-provoking writer that the world has ever known.[1]

Character-painting depends for its vitality on the amount of wisdom that it veils. The wit of Cervantes and Shakespeare veils a good deal: there is not much wisdom in Dickens, but through the farcical oddity and cockney burlesque of Dick Swiveller we recognise a lovable human soul. Still, class characteristics and local peculiarities are always changing; so, in spite of the opulence of his fun, the vigour of his style, and the wonders and delights of his genius, a time may come when Dickens will have found a grave in short memories, when he will be as remote from the taste of the day as Jonson is in his comedies, or Pope in his 'Dunciad.' However, he will be read till the world, with its insatiable maw, will have got from him all that it wants to get—all that he has to give. I think Charles Dickens will continue a remarkable

[1] There is a witty rogue who loved sack in Shakespeare's *Henry IV.*, before whom, as a humorous creation, Dickens's characters wax pale; however, Dickens's best, in one important respect, are at least as Shakespearian as those of any other English writer of the century. They are essentially *ideal*, but he puts so much vitality into them that we are able to accept them as real human beings. We can take a real interest in them, although, all the time, we know they can never have had a prototype in nature. We can conceive of a Major Pendennis, we may even have had the luck to know him; but can we ever hope to meet that ideal, but delightfully human, Mr. Wilkins Micawber?

name in English literature—who knows for how many generations? Perhaps, just now (1883), Thackeray may be a little in the ascendant, especially with the rising generation; but the fashion of things passes away, the ebb and flow of opinion as regards literature is one of its laws. So Dickens will again have his turn, and enjoy that impalpable reward which is vouchsafed to the ghosts of genius. Poor fellow! he was prosperous in his life, and I may say not unfortunate in the opportunity of his death; for perhaps his powers were failing him, and it is said that he was aware of it. It would be sad indeed if Charles Dickens ever lost his hold on the affection of his readers, and should ever come to be talked of as we now speak of Tobias Smollett.

This is all I have to say about Charles Dickens, all I knew of him, and it is far too little. I have said nothing which will be an addition to Dickens literature; but still it may interest some of mine who come after me, and so I leave it.

In 1870 I was to have paid him a visit at Gad's Hill, but I was too late. I shall always think of him with affection for the immense delight his earlier books gave and give me, and with gratitude for his extreme kindness.

ANTHONY TROLLOPE

Tallyhoiser, the Norman, came over to England with William the Conqueror, and one morning in the New Forest, while a-hunting with that monarch, the gallant fellow was lucky enough to kill three enormous wolves; so ever afterwards, in memory of that great achievement, he was called Troisloups, which name, in the course of centuries of change and corruption, has become Trollope.

This exploit is not mentioned by the novelist in his autobiography, but it is the account he gave of his name and ancestor when he himself was a very unlicked cub at Harrow. The late Sidney Herbert, at that time the *Nereus formosus* of the school, whose distinction it is not for common men to criticise, has the credit of having handed down the tradition.

Anthony Trollope, like his ancestor of old, was combative, and he was boisterous, but good-naturedly so. He was abrupt in manners and speech; he was ebullient, and therefore he sometimes offended people. I suppose he was a wilful man, and we know that such men are always in the right; but he was a good fellow.

Some of Trollope's acquaintance used to wonder how so commonplace a person could have written such excellent novels; but I maintain that so honourable and interesting a man could not be commonplace.

Hirsute and taurine of aspect, he would glare at you from behind fierce spectacles. His ordinary tones had the penetrative capacity of two people quarrelling, and his voice would ring through and through you, and shake the windows in their frames, while all the time he was most amiably disposed towards you under his waistcoat. To me his *viso sciolto* and bluff geniality were very attractive, and so were his gusty denunciations, but most attractive of all was his unselfish nature. Literary men might make him their exemplar, as I make him my theme; for he may quite well have been the most generous man of letters, of mark, since Walter Scott.

I used to encounter Trollope at the Cosmopolitan, at the Athenæum, and at the meetings of the Royal Literary Fund (where he was amusingly combative). I have dined with him, and he has dined with me. I hope we had a mutual regard. He gave me the bulky manuscript of his 'Small House at Allington,' which I much value. Bound in dark morocco it has the aspect of our Family Bible.

Trollope had a furious hatred of shams and toadyism, and he sometimes recognised and resented these weaknesses where they would hardly have been detected by an ordinary observer.[1] He could not be said to be quarrelsome, but he was crotchety. It would have been as well if sometimes he had borne in mind Talleyrand's advice, 'Surtout point de zèle.'

Trollope told me that he was a great reader, omnivorous as regards old plays and other-day romances. However, unlike many bookworms, he was anything but a mere absorbent, for he was always giving out, always writing, and he could do it anywhere. Erasmus's 'Encomium' was composed on horseback, and Trollope did some of the chapters of 'Barchester Towers' on the 'knife-board' of a 'bus. Fecundity in itself is a distinction, and he told me that he had written more books than any Englishman that had ever lived, but that if Mrs. Oliphant (so much admired by Kinglake) survived him, she would soon surpass him. There was none of the sterility of genius about my friend Anthony.

It is a law of literature that every generation should be industrious in burying its own, especially novels. What has become of Smollett and Mackenzie—the cockpit of the 'Thunder,' or the sentimental Harley? Where is the shadowy Mr. G. P. R.

[1] Le grand Prince de Ligne, after making strenuous but almost fruitless endeavours to create a piece of water in his demesne, was told that a man had drowned himself in it. 'Bah!' exclaimed he, 'c'était un flatteur.'

James, and where is that witty old ghost of the Silver Fork school, Mrs. Gore? Is there anybody under sixty who has heard of 'Tremaine' or 'Doriforth'? Yet all these had vogue. I hold that the best of Trollope's stories are excellent reading. He has admirable qualities as a writer of fiction; indeed he has helped to ameliorate the asperities of our middle-class existence. He gives us enough, sometimes more than enough; but still he has a happy tact of omission. Trollope's chief excellence is in the portrayal of character; the dialogue is what people naturally use; it is even more than that—they could not well use any other. I am fond of his heroines;[1] they are affectionate and true; one knows pretty well what they are going to do next, one always feels safe with them. His young people are not discouraged by the tedium of *la grâce* or bezique, or other equally mild amusements: they smile and dance and whisper themselves into each other's hearts, and, what is so very agreeable about them, they are generally content to remain there. Trollope's ideal of happiness has nothing in it of the unattainable. We know he had not the distinction of Thackeray, the exuberant genius of Dickens, or the vivid and vehement force of Charles Reade; but not seldom he is worthy of their company; and his tone can compare favour-

[1] Some people say they are not *ladies*, but they satisfy me.

ably with that of any of his illustrious contemporaries, from Bulwer and Disraeli to the geniuses just mentioned. Trollope has a fund of common sense and hearty good nature. It is the tone of a gentleman of the middle class, who is able to esteem and do justice to all classes. A novelist should deal with fancies and feelings that are natural without being obvious; perhaps Trollope did not sufficiently recognise this distinction; however, he did his best, and thus I hope the intention of his being was achieved.

Classicism was defunct when Trollope began to write, and the novel of romance was moribund. The maiden in white and the wooer in steel—tourney and revel—buff jerkins and misericordes—sack, jesters, nuns and oubliettes—cowl and crucifix 'et tout le tremblement'—were all being huddled away. They are gone, as cashmere shawls have gone, but of course some of these days they will all come back again.

Trollope was a warm admirer of Thackeray, and he appreciated Miss Brontë; he said that one or two scenes in 'Jane Eyre'—for instance, that in which Rochester gives Jane the wine—were better than anything by almost anybody.

I told him that Mrs. Norton thought 'Adam Blair' a first-rate novel, and he agreed. He insisted that 'Caleb Williams' is as bad as 'Uncle Tom's

Cabin.' He did not much care for Dickens or Smollett; he cared less for Disraeli—'"Vivian Grey" is his best.' Strange to say, he did not think highly of the 'Bride of Lammermoor.' You see he was a better writer than critic. He considered the 'Antiquary' and 'Old Mortality' to be Scott's happiest, and that the last and 'Robinson Crusoe' and 'Esmond' were the finest novels in our literature. He said nothing of Sterne, whose Toby Shandy is one of the finest compliments ever paid to human nature.

I think that a few of Trollope's excellent novels ought to live. I say this remembering that some of them are already beginning to fade away—to be forgotten; reputation seems as much an accident as popularity.

Not the worst part of a distinguished man's reputation is the esteem in which he is held by his friends, and in this Trollope was rich.[1] He indulged in no professional jealousies; indeed, he had none to indulge in. He only had much nobility of nature; he worked hard for wellnigh seventy years, and when the end was near he awaited it with becoming fortitude and resignation, and so gave up his honest ghost, which, as Montaigne says, proved what is

[1] I remember that Thackeray spoke to me with delight of passages in *The Three Clerks*, and that I felt I was qualified to tell him that he was right in admiring them.

at the bottom of the vessel. I think Trollope must have been able to sing his 'Nunc dimittis' without much faltering.

Mr. Leigh Hunt

There are not a few misty portraits hanging in the gallery of my failing memory: Mr. Leigh Hunt's is one of them. I made his acquaintance in 1859 at No. 7 Cornwall Road, Hammersmith, where he lived, not wholly in the busy world, not quite beyond it. I walked thither with Mr. Joseph Severn, the painter friend of John Keats, and we found the man of letters seated in the corner of his poorly furnished parlour. It was a small room, in a small house, looking out on patches of small back gardens. There were one or two busts, and on the walls a few prints. Mr. Hunt had a book in his hand, and many books were lying about, on the table and under the table; there were books (shaggy books) and papers everywhere. By his side was a common white jug filled with yellow flowers.

Mr. Hunt was striking in appearance—tall, dark, grizzled, bright-eyed, and rather fantastically dressed in a sacerdotal-looking garment.

He received us with cordiality tinged with ceremony. He had just been reading Horace

Walpole, and he related in an animated manner that funny little story of the desperate lovers whose course of true love would always run so provokingly smooth that they never had the chance of writing any of those long letters which carry with them a long pleasure, for they were never separated; so at last, in despair, they arranged to sit on different sides of a tall screen, and toss their sighs (square, oblong, or three-cornered, carefully addressed and sealed) over it!

Mr. Hunt was most amiable: he discoursed about poetry as exhilaratingly as Ruskin does about art. He spoke of his own writings, and quite unaffectedly. It appeared to give him pleasure to do so. Perhaps if he had talked less about them it would have been because he thought the more.

He seemed proud of his old age, speaking with a smile of his *soixante et mille ans.* He gave me the impression of being rich in the milk of amiability and optimism. I do not think this was feigned, for I often heard of him as a benevolently minded man.

I could hardly realise that this was the Mr. Hunt who had written that underbred book about 'Byron and his Contemporaries.' I suppose age and experience had mellowed him. I wish I had asked him about Byron; there is no doubt that he had been sorely tried by that unhappy creature.

He spoke kindly of Tom Moore, the subject of whose verse was 'The love of one's country—the wine of other countries—and the women of all countries.'

Shortly after this visit, and encouraged by it, I inflicted (this is an excellent part of speech to describe the act)—I inflicted some of my verses upon him; he acknowledged them with gusto and criticised them with tenderness. He had actually read some of them! I think I paid him three or four visits in all, and each time I liked him better. He was remarkably cheerful, even buoyant, which, considering his age and what I have since read of his surroundings, was remarkable.

On one of these occasions I had tea with him. The meal was presided over by a nimble-fingered little nymph of a daughter in a stuff frock imperfectly hooked and eyed. She had not even had the coquetry to pin her collar straight! I can still hear his 'Jacintha, give Mr. Locker another cup of tea,' delivered in a suave, almost stately manner, and in silvery tones.

I have observed that the surroundings of your especially interesting people are generally commonplace. Their intimates are nearly always dull fellows.[1] While saying this I am not in any way

[1] A man of original mind is best able to discover the latent good qualities in those about him, and he is more easily satisfied. Un-

reflecting on the little Jacintha, who, if she had condescended, might have proved a very agreeable companion. She was not exactly pretty, but, as the gallant Frenchman said of somebody else, 'she had a particular sweet expression in some of her eyes.' Her tea was excellent. Mr. Hunt was amused with my story of a Scot who said in praise of his wife's tea, 'Eh, sir, it takes a graat grip o' the third watter.'

He told me a wonderful story of Charles Lamb and his smile. It appears that a certain Mr. Thomas Allsop, the sentimental assassin, was speaking to Coleridge of the peculiar sweetness of Mr. Charles Lamb's smile. 'And,' said he, 'there is still one man living, a stockbroker, who has that smile.' 'And,' added Allsop, 'to those who wish to see the only thing left on earth of Lamb, his best and most beautiful remain—His Smile—I will indicate its possessor: it is Mr. ——, of Throgmorton Street, City.'[1] Leigh Hunt's concluding remark was: 'How the original possessor of this apparently assignable security would have wished to feel Mr. Allsop's bumps!'

imaginative people are the most quickly bored, and certainly most keen to resent the intellectual and other shortcomings of their acquaintances.

[1] [See *Letters, Conversations, and Recollections of S. T. Coleridge* (Moxon, 1836), vol. i. p. 36. Harman was the name of the lucky stockbroker.—Ed.]

When I got home I sent Mr. Hunt some curious and rare tea, which Elgin had lately despatched from China, and he thanked me in a delightful letter. His handwriting was as beautiful as Tennyson's. After that I sent him a few flowers; then I went abroad, and never saw him again, for he died soon afterwards.

Leigh Hunt had a delicate palate for poetry, and, as far as an amateur like myself can judge, was its admirable critic. *Imagination and Fancy* is delightful reading, but I wish he had been a more downright, a more masculine writer. He had the less robust virtues, which are sometimes regarded as weaknesses. From among his poetical associates, men more gifted than himself, he appeals to us as a picturesque exotic; but I think Abou ben Adhem will not be soon forgotten.

Poor poet! I like to think of thee as I saw thee on those two or three occasions, and not engulfed in draggle-tailed impecuniosity.

> And the thyme it is withered and rue is in prime.

It is said that an author is the reverse of all other objects—that he magnifies at a distance and diminishes as you approach him. I have no right to say this of Mr. Hunt, and it would not apply to him; but people said that he would have been a happier man if he had not introduced disturbing forces into his lyrical life;[1] that he had an incapacity for dealing with the ordinary affairs of existence, such as arithmetic and matrimony; but that he had a beautiful reliance on providence—which word in this connection I venture to spell with a little 'p.'

My children may find some of Hunt's letters to me in the correspondence edited by his son.

As I have spoken of Mr. Joseph Severn, I will just add that he was a jaunty, fresh-natured, irresponsible sort of elderly being, leading a facile, slipshod, dressing-gowny, artistic existence in Pimlico. Like his friend Hunt he was not rich, but he never seemed to be in actual want of anything, unless perhaps it might be a brush or a comb.

I afterwards knew him in Rome at the Palazzo Pali, where he was British Consul. Then he was all that I have said, and more besides, for he had the opportunity of being, and was especially, amiable and obliging.

Mr. Severn was the most buoyant of Britons, a man of cheerful yesterdays and confident tomorrows. He had a prosperous laugh and coruscated with cheerfulness. Then he had a jovial way of grossly flattering one which did not seem to carry the slightest degradation with it. I remem-

[1] We know that a poet filled the vestibule of his Gehenna with squalling children; and a prose philosopher says, 'Avant de se marier il faut avoir au moins disséqué une femme.'

ber as we walked to Leigh Hunt's, he said, and with a certain fervour which at once raised it far above the region of banter, 'Hunt asked a good deal about you and your *immortalities*.' Severn was especially amusing when he indulged in the melancholy looking-back vein. 'Ah! Mr. Locker, our youth! that was the time when Hope and Fruition went hand in hand—*altri tempi, altri tempi*. What is left to us? Vain anxieties, delusive hopes, unexpected issues!' The good Severn lived to be a deal over seventy, and, I believe, continued *cet adorable ci-devant jeune homme* to the very last.

Whilst I was in Rome Mr. Severn introduced me to M. and Mme. Valentine de Llanos, a kindly couple. He was a Spaniard, lean, silent, dusky, and literary, the author of *Don Estehan* and *Sandoval*. She was fat, blonde, and lymphatic, and both were elderly. *She was John Keats's sister!* I had a good deal of talk with her, or rather *at* her, for she was not very responsive. I was disappointed, for I remember that my sprightliness made her yawn; she seemed inert and had nothing to tell me of her wizard brother of whom she spoke as of a mystery—with a vague admiration but a genuine affection. She was simple and natural—I believe she is a very worthy woman. She most kindly gave me one of her brother's letters addressed to herself which I now have, and which I believe may be found in Mr. Buxton Forman's 'Life' of the poet.

The story of Keats's life and death is very interesting and very sad. No one had a truer and more self-sacrificing friend than John Keats found in Joseph Severn. Wherever the poet John Keats shall be tenderly remembered, the name of Joseph Severn ought not to be forgotten. Mr. George Richmond, the R.A., has a beautiful little picture by Severn of the Roman Campagna.

Arthur Stanley, Dean of Westminster

I have spoken of Edward Stanley, Bishop of Norwich, and I will now say a few words about his son Arthur, late Dean of Westminster. My acquaintance with Arthur began from the day after his engagement to Lady Augusta Bruce, and lasted to the end of his life. I was at his bedside when he died.

How shall I describe this illustrious man? He was thin, he was small, but, like Cæsar, he was not insignificant. Though his features were not strictly handsome, he had a refined, an intellectual, a most interesting countenance. He was endowed with high personal courage and a chivalrous nature, I should like to say a buoyant pluck; and there was an eager sweetness in his address that was very winning. Occasionally he had a dreamy expression. His intellectual alertness a little reminded me of Monsieur Thiers.

Arthur was pure-minded and simple-mannered; and though he happened to be curiously indifferent to what is called small talk, his powers of conversation were remarkable. We constantly met, and in divers places, and he was a valued member of every society in which I found him.

Arthur was a thoroughly amiable man, and entirely destitute of personal or other vanity. He had the unmistakable air of good-breeding. He was a man of the world and a courtier, in the very best sense of that word; but he was a courtier through circumstances and not by choice. His marriage had brought him much in communication with the Royal Family, who held him in honour; but, though loyal, and indeed devoted, I know he always had the courage of his opinions. He took an unflagging interest in public affairs, and did not fear opposition, or even abuse, when his sense of justice was aroused, as witness his manly support of Voysey, Mill, Colenso, and Père Hyacinthe.

There is a peculiarity in some earnest-minded and well-meaning people, which I venture to call cussedness, which peculiarity qualifies them for the *rôle* of religious martyrs; but there was nothing of this in Stanley.

He had a happy metrical gift, and a very picturesque sensibility, yet I think his poetical insight was limited. It is possible that he did not fully appreciate the difference between rhetoric, in which he was much skilled, and pure poetry. I am not sure that he greatly valued poetry for its own sake. He was fond of it, and of art also, but chiefly where they entered the domain of and illustrated history; for he had a keen historical imagination, and was able to vivify the past without distorting it. I have heard good judges say that he was a master of historical narrative. I believe in his heart he preferred Southey to Burns, Scott to Wordsworth, and Macaulay to Keats. He much admired Shakespeare's 'Tired of all these, for restful death I cry.' One of his special admirations was Bunyan's 'Pilgrim's Progress;' he twice read me the account of Christian climbing to the Celestial Gate, after passing through Death's River.

Arthur had no soul for music: its pathetic passions and harmonious despairs did not move him. However, as he was a good man, he was patient; for him it was not impertinent noise!

After his wife's death he became better acquainted with my daughter Eleanor, and more drawn to her. She was able to enter into his intellectual life, and grasp a new subject with intelligence, and he appreciated this. He was very kind to my child, and those who at that time were kind to her were very kind to me.[1] Though he was fond of having young people about him, he never seemed to regret that he was not a father.

Arthur Stanley's position as Dean of Westminster did not in itself require any special administrative capacity, but he more than once told me that he had serious responsibilities as regarded the finances of the Abbey, and that, from time to time, this weighed on his mind. Indeed, he confessed that he had moments of extreme anxiety as to how fiscal and official matters might be going, and whether some day or other there might not be a catastrophe. I am certain he had no real ground for these tremors. Dr. Bradley, his friend and successor at the Deanery, assures me that at Rugby he was not so very bad an accountant, and yet the following story is characteristic.

I was telling him the story of composer Hallé's cook, who had won a good round sum in a lottery with the number twenty-three. Hallé, being glad to hear it, had asked how it was she happened to fix on so lucky a number. 'I had a dream, sir,' said she; 'I dreamt of number seven; I dreamt of it three times, sir, and as three times seven makes twenty-three, I chose that number.' When I had concluded my story, I observed a wistful expression

[1] 'Whoever loves Plato cannot be altogether a stranger.'

on Arthur's countenance, as if he were ready, nay, anxious to be amused, but could not, for the life of him, quite manage it. Then suddenly—for he was very quick—his face brightened, and he said, but not without a shadow of dejection, 'Ah, yes, I see, yes; I suppose three times seven is *not* twenty-three.'

Though they often met, and in a cordial way, I do not think Stanley had a deal of sympathy with Mr. Gladstone. He complained that, much as he had seen of him, and often as he had talked with him and differed with him, he did not think he had ever influenced him in anything. 'Yes,' said Arthur, recollecting himself, 'I influenced him in one matter; I told him he ought never to use the word RELIABLE, and I gave him my reasons. Some time afterwards I met Mr. Gladstone in the street, and he said, as we parted: "I have never used that wretched word *reliable* since you spoke to me about it."'

Arthur did not know one kind of porcelain from another, but he was much attracted by my two busts, in very old Dresden china, delicately coloured, of a baby boy and a baby girl. They are the larger-sized pair, well known from the modern copies, and are said to have been modelled at Meissen in honour of George III. and his sister, who were children at the time. When he came to see me he would often take notice of these busts, for he much admired them. A dealer once offered me 100*l.* for the pair, but, much for love of Stanley, I would not accept it. Arthur had also a great fancy for my Joshua Reynolds's 'Strawberry Girl.' It is a good impression of the mezzotint engraving. He said it was a novel in three volumes; I suppose he meant that it arrested him as a work of imagination, and he was right.

I think it was in 1870 or 1871 that Charlotte and I spent a few weeks at Hastings (in Robertson Terrace). Augusta and Arthur came down from London to see us, and Lord and Lady Arthur Russell came at the same time. Augusta used to keep her husband very neat and trim, his black suit and boots being always carefully brushed. One afternoon he, Russell, and I made an expedition to Fairlight. The soil in those parts is a bright sandy clay, and that day it happened to be particularly wet and slippery. We had not got far before poor Arthur slid gently down on the flat of his back. Not long afterwards he again slipped and fell, this time face foremost. Then his goloshes got unfastened and full of clay and water, and, as he was rather helpless, we aided in taking them off. All these misfortunes did not in the least impair Arthur Stanley's serenity, and hardly interrupted the flow of his delightful conversation. However, the figure he cut was indescribably funny. There is no greater leveller than *mud.* Arthur was a bright brown from the soles of his feet to the crown of his hat, and yet it did not discompose him. He walked complacently between Russell and myself, each of us carrying a golosh, which, with its mud, was a considerable weight. Augusta met us a short distance from home, and her mingled amazement and amusement and pride were very delightful.

On this expedition he told us a story which I think he had read in Martineau's 'Society in America,' where it was given to illustrate the kind of quizzing which went on about the Germans. It was at the time that the political contest between Adams and Jackson was at its height.

I quote from memory. A supporter of Adams complained that somebody had been telling the Pennsylvanians that Adams had married a daughter of George III., an untruth which, he averred, would lose Adams every one of their votes. 'If that is the case,' said Miss Martineau, 'why do you not at once contradict it?' 'Oh!' replied the partisan, 'that would not be of the slightest use; you don't know these Germans—*tête carrée.* They will believe anything, and *unbelieve nothing.* No, we must not contradict this wicked lie; we must allow that Adams *did* marry a daughter of George III., but we must swear that Jackson married *two* of his daughters!'

The second time that Stanley fell down he was in the middle of this story, and I never heard him tell it better.

I have had five or six friends who have been so sympathetic that I have had no difficulty in forgiving them all their faults, if they had any. I do not think I have ever been more drawn to any of them than to Arthur. Yet he never had any taste for sport, or the *ludi circenses*, or for much else that greatly interested me. Unlike my beloved and gifted and many-sided Whitwell Elwin,[1] Stanley cared for none of these things. He was neither so witty as Rosslyn, nor so humorous as James Gibbs, nor so many-sided as Tennyson, and perhaps William Stirling and Richard Milnes were in a degree his superiors in these qualities; but there was a peculiar attractiveness about Arthur: he had a lambent fancy, a bright and felicitous personality, a charm, an unconscious purity, a genius for goodness, which none of my other friends, warmly as I regarded them, possessed, or possess, in anything like the same degree. The Ten Commandments were written on Stanley's face.

Each had his distinguishing merit, and all were affectionate, or, at any rate, kindly. Rosslyn is witty, and Gibbs is humorous, but both are influenced by class foibles. Stirling was the most

[1] Rector of Booton.

quaint and comical, but his spirit often flagged; and Tennyson suffers in the same way, even to a greater degree. However, when Alfred is quite at his best, there is no one like him.[1]

I was constantly in Arthur's house, and he not seldom in mine. It was there that from time to time he met Ruskin, Froude, Browning, M. Arnold, George Eliot, Dickens, Lecky, Alfred Tennyson, and others whose society gave him great pleasure. His death was a severe loss to me, for whenever or wherever we met there was always something which he seemed anxious to tell me, or to discuss, and, occasionally, on which he wished to consult me. I think I see him now as I have often seen him after a short separation; he would meet me with two cordial hands extended, and would instantly enter on the conversation of the previous meeting, and at the exact point, too, where we had broken off. I am proud that I was able to acquire so much of Arthur's confidence. We had many likes and a few dislikes in common; some-

[1] It has been said that a good listener provides half the conversation, and it is no mean accomplishment to maintain a graceful and agreeable silence. What constitutes an agreeable companion? I have often met people who puzzled me. Were they reserved? No! Were they shy? No! Were they uncivil? No! Then why were they disappointing? At last I discovered that they were well bred and stupid. Women who appear to be very much taken up with one are especially agreeable. They receive your remarks with an air of mental reserve, as much as to say, 'I shall think of that when you are gone!'

how, when I think of him, Cowley's fine couplet comes into my mind. I only wish it could have been at all appropriate :

> He was my friend, the truest friend on earth ;
> A great and mighty influence joined our birth.

Arthur's leading characteristic was joy in *light* and his power to spread joy.

He was not unhappy in the opportunity of his death, for I am told he had begun to feel his failing powers, and the harassment of ignoble men. I might say with Benignus Bossuet, 'Là, où je vois un grand regret, j'éprouve une vive consolation.'

I have received much and peculiar kindness at the Deanery since Stanley died, but it is painful to return thither. The house is the same, the view from the house is the same—all is so familiar, so mournful, yet different.

Arthur and Augusta were well—perhaps too well—mated ; they had much mental and moral vigour, they abetted and stimulated each other ; but the strain was perpetual, and she wore herself out.

When I first knew Augusta, she was bright and frolicsome, for she had her adorers, and though her best friends could not have said she was beautiful, if she had any foes, they would not have denied that she was charming. However, as time ran on, the 'bow was too seldom unbent.' Referring to this, Arthur more than once said of her:—

Whene'er she chose to sport and play,
No dolphin ever was so gay
Upon the tropic sea.

Augusta was always sacrificing herself for those about her, and even for those afar off, and she never allowed any one to discover that she was doing so. She was compounded of superior clay, yet you were never given to understand that she thought herself a 'superior woman.' She had an untameable energy, but nature at last gave way. Augusta had been my affectionate sister for nearly thirty years.[1]

Her death was an irreparable blow to Arthur. She seemed to have woven herself into the very fabric of his life. May we hope that warp and woof are now reunited!

Had she defects? If so, it is only a proof that she was human; and these defects were so controlled, so kept under, that one could only surmise them. She gave one the impression that she was suppressing herself; except on rare occasions, she did not allow her individuality—her charm—free

[1] She thought I made her sister happy. I am not going to conjecture how far her affection for me was a reflected affection.

My dear children, you will gradually find out how much of the affection which you inspire is *reflected*. Indeed, people who do not love you for anybody else's sake, may love you for their own.

play, and this rather impaired the pleasure of free intercourse with her. I mention all this, not to exhibit, but to prove how slight were, her defects. Perhaps her foibles were her extreme discretion and her extreme self-repression, and these, as virtues, are not altogether to be despised.

'In life nothing is better or more beautiful than when a man and woman dwell together in one house, being one of heart.' Ulysses might have said this of Arthur and Augusta, for they led beneficent lives in their memorable abode, a house precious in the memory of all who knew and were capable of appreciating its inmates. 'What shame or limit can there be to our affection for so dear a couple?'

Mr. Carlyle

Although we had many friends in common, I seldom had speech with Mr. Carlyle. *Vidi tantum*: I first met him at Mr. Thomas Erskine's (of Linlathen), and afterwards at Louisa Lady Ashburton's (Lochluichart). I saw him at his house; once or twice with Tennyson, who honoured his character and valued his opinion. He gave Eleanor his essays on 'Johnson' and on 'Burns.' I met Mrs. Carlyle two or three times, perhaps oftener; she must have been nearly fifty when I first saw her; as far as I recollect, she had a pair of bright eyes, but no other remains of beauty. I have seen her in a crimson gown, and I remember some babbler told me she was fond of smart clothes and smart people, as most intelligent people are. She was supposed not to utter when Carlyle was within hearing, but she gave me the impression that she might be keen and sarcastic. The following is all that I can now recollect of her conversation. Her husband had 'just returned from Paris,' where he had been maddened by the ticking of a clock in his bedroom; 'instead of banishing it to the passage, or tilting, and so stopping it, as anybody else would have done, he dashed it down and broke it—so like him!'

Carlyle was a master of vituperation, and if he had merely spoken a good deal of what he has left behind him in writing, it would not have appeared offensive; for often and often after a volley thereof, delivered with a strong Dumfriesshire accent, he would burst into a roar of laughter, partly at himself and partly at the situation—and this toned down the savagery. It was well remarked that he mixed so much that was picturesque and grotesque in his abuse, that it seemed more like an utterance in a vision than vulgar invective. He had many faults, and they were not all pleasant ones; he was a man of many wants; he was extraordinarily tenacious, and weakly unreasonable as to his personal comforts, and this became a terrible tyranny for those who lived with him. Then people did not appreciate his intellectual scorn or sinister and furious vaticinations. He abused his knack of caricature and power of saying bitter things, and was remarkable for the impartiality with which he exercised that power; he may have been scornful and perhaps envious; but remember he was a Scot, peasant born, peasant bred—and dyspeptic. It was unfortunate that his wife, by reason of her caustic temper, was not qualified to influence the softer side of his character.

How entirely out of place is all this acrid stricture! What is the use of it? What are the foibles and failings of half a century ago? We have enjoyed the writer, let us now think kindly of the man, and of his biographer, and be grateful for what they both have given us. Well may I say this, as you, kind reader, will think, when you have read this paper to its end.

The Queen had never set eyes on Carlyle, Grote, or Browning, who were making her reign illustrious, till, as elderly subjects, they were presented to their elderly monarch at the Deanery. Eleanor was there when the first was presented, and she tells me that when Carlyle was brought forward, he almost immediately said, 'I am an old man, and, with your Majesty's leave, I will sit down,' or words to that effect, and that he forthwith drew himself a chair, and sat down, and Her Majesty was fain to do likewise. Eleanor could only catch a few words of their conversation, but she was amused by Carlyle's rugged tone and uncompromising manner (I take it that his predictions as regarded her dynasty were not assuring and far from palatable), also by Augusta's sweet words and nervous urbanity, and by the surprised dignity of Her Majesty.

This account of Carlyle and the Queen reminds me of a small dinner at Richmond, at which Eleanor, and Tennyson, and Mr. Gladstone were present.

At that time Tennyson was a political admirer of Mr. Gladstone; but even then he had a vague apprehension as to what the grand old man might possibly be going to do next.

Eleanor drove back to London with these two eminent personages, and on her arrival at home she gave an amusing account of the drive, and of the many searching inquiries that Tennyson had addressed to Mr. Gladstone on the most delicate matters of Cabinet policy, questions civil and religious, domestic and foreign.

The child, seated in her dark corner, was greatly

diverted with the simple and startlingly direct way in which Alfred put his questions, and the amiable and wary manner in which Mr. Gladstone parried them. Mr. Gladstone has always had a real respect and admiration for Tennyson, both as poet and man.

Mr. Carlyle was a man of imperfect sympathies. I am told he did not care for art, and that he did not care for poetry or fiction, perhaps because he had failed in them. For aught I know, he may have been that inclement and identical Scot whom Charles Lamb would have been willing to consign to the most 'Caledonian corner in hell.' I should say that generally he was not quite understood. Let us try and think of him as a comic Ezekiel, and then we shall be better able to do him justice.

Carlyle may have been wanting in magnanimity, but he was pure-minded and honest—a mystic with a great spiritual force, and, in spite of his style, a remarkable literary artist. He cannot help you to conclusions about many things, but he waylays and startles; he stimulates as only a genius can do. A fiery-tongued delineator of men, he has the devouring eye and the unerring hand—and then what a power of pathos! His was a noble life lived nobly to a noble end, and they commit the crime who call him base.

What is my object in writing this paper? Is it to place before my children, and those who may come after them, the following letter addressed by Thomas Carlyle to 'Mr. James Munro'? This letter is interesting in itself, but I think it will much more concern them when I tell them that 'James Munro' was not the real name of the writer of the letter to which that name was attached; the real writer was an insignificant person, a miserable poacher after the autographs of eminent men, and he wrote this letter in order that he might get a reply from Thomas Carlyle. The said writer is a person of whom, as he was then, I am now exceedingly ashamed, and I have gibbeted him on this page, as I wish that he should do penance for the sins of his early manhood.

This expiator well remembers his poignant regret when Mr. Carlyle's letter, penetrated as it is with simple sincerity and good faith, reached him; for it was *then* that, for the first time, the gracelessness of his own letter came fully home to him.

Yes, this very inadequate paper is written to show my children what a sterling good man was Thomas Carlyle, and it also shows how much their father did *not* know of the great Thomas Carlyle.

Copy.

The Grange, Hants (for Chelsea, London):
September 22, 1848.

Sir,—I rather apprehend there must be some mistake in this matter of the gardener, concerning which I first received your note this morning.

I never had any servant specifically doing duty as a gardener, nor for many years back have I had anything that could at all deserve the name of garden to employ one upon. It occurs to me, after reflection, that I did once, about twenty years ago, lay out a piece of new ground among the mountains of Dumfriesshire, and fashioned it into a small garden, with lawns, &c., on a very humble scale, to correspond, and that there worked for me, on that occasion, for perhaps six weeks or so, a man by regular profession a gardener, from Dumfries, whose figure and performance I remember very well, but whose name I either never knew or have now quite lost. Perhaps this was Andrew Leitch? If so, he is (or was) a trim man of middle size, with slightly aquiline countenance, much marked by small-pox, grey-eyed, with Anglified-Scotch manner, and must now be about fifty years of age. This man was one of the expertest workers with gardener's tools I ever saw, full of invention, promptitude, impetuosity, indeed of extraordinary vigour and diligence, and skilful beyond common at whatever he put hand to, in gardening, or otherwise; for the rest, a perfectly respectable man, so far as I knew, and fit, I should think, to be a most useful servant, had it not been (as I heard, and could partly observe) that his temper was apt to be a little hot and uncertain, and his humour capricious, so that he was said to be often changing his master, and not quite easy to command, in those years. In this latter respect age may have done much to amend him, and I knew nothing else to his disadvantage, but all else as I describe it.

Possibly enough, however, this is not your man at all; possibly your man alludes to another 'T. Carlyle, Esq.,' also of Dumfriesshire, with whom I am sometimes confounded, who is now, I think, called 'Rev. T. Carlyle,' and lives at Albury in Surrey for most part, joined in some kind of clerical function with Hy. Drummond, Esq., M.P., of that place.

Craigenputtock was the name of my residence in Dumfriesshire, and the gardener came to me from a Mr. Kennedy, (?) nurseryman in Dumfries, who must know a good deal more about him than I.

I remain yours very truly,

T. Carlyle.

James Munro, Esq.; Jermyn Street, London.[1]

[1] [I rather deprecated the telling of this story, but Mr. Locker insisted on 'doing penance.'—Editor.]

Mr. Hayward and Mr. Kinglake

I have been reading a notice of Mr. Abraham Hayward in this month's (March, 1884) 'Fortnightly.' It does not give a very correct idea of the little man; at any rate, he is not my Mr. Hayward. I think the editor could have only known him slightly. From that article, a stranger would judge that Hayward was a personage of prodigious importance, whereas he was merely a man of mark—not a man of great mark. He was not a genius, or a distinguished scholar, nor was he politically eminent, but he had an assured position in the great literary and social world. His aspirations were not lofty, but still they must have been difficult of attainment. It was his desire to live with the great, and at the same time to be a thorough man of letters; and he succeeded in both ambitions. We were acquainted, though not intimately, for some thirty years. I will say a few words about him.

I need not describe his personality—any day you like you may study his elderly effigy as cartooned in 'Vanity Fair.' He was the Mr. Flam of 'Mrs. Perkins's Ball.' Like that exquisite, he had curling locks, a neat little foot, a lip vermilion, and an Abra'm nose.

Most people have heard of Hayward's meritorious prose translation of 'Faust,' [1] and everybody has read his 'Art of Dining' and other articles, excellent within their limits, in the 'Quarterly Review.' The best of these are light enough, but they are notable for their clear-cut vigour, critical acumen, and anecdotal brightness. Though Hayward was not so merciless as Croker, not so entirely given up to destructive criticism, he exemplified the saying that its exercise often robs the critic of the satisfaction of being pleased.

Hayward had a vigorous, but not an original, mind. He had little wit and less humour; but he had much mental energy, a great faculty in the use of his very powerful memory, a marked individuality, and last, not least, a passion for society. Then he had some fine qualities: he was a plucky little fellow; he showed this in his squabble with Ranelagh, and indeed in his many quarrels. He was honourable to his opponents, and faithful to his party and friends. Perhaps his most attached ally was poor Kinglake.[2]

[1] I do not know if it was Hayward who spoke of Goethe's 'scrutinising wisdom,' and said 'His was the most splendid specimen of cultivated intellect that ever manifested itself to the world.'

[2] I call Kinglake poor because he is old, blind, and deaf, has survived most of his contemporaries, and because I like him, even with his deafness. The old are always surviving the young, and Kinglake, like the rest of us, has discovered that *vieillir est encore le seul moyen qu'on ait trouvé de vivre;* but, old as he is, I am never for a quarter

I have heard Hayward spoken of as a *toady*. There never was a more misleading description of any one. I allow that he exerted himself a good deal for society. He read for it, he wrote for it, talked for it, he lived for it. He delighted in the society of the socially powerful; but if he kept good company, he was always one of the number. In quite a legitimate though not a very refined way, indeed with a persistent hardihood, he made the most of his opportunities of enjoying and influencing it; he took great pains, but wherever he went he also took with him an independent, even *cassant*, manner, an aggressive self-assertion, and these were aggravated by a rasping voice. He had a real pride in and respect for literature, he spared no pains in cultivating it, and he was a sincere and laborious seeker after accuracy.[1] Hayward was intrepid, he did not mind saying unpleasant things;

of an hour in his society without his telling me something worth carrying away. His voice is clear and low, not fitted to dominate a dinner-party; but one recognised a peculiar, a personal charm even in his general utterances, as if they were more especially addressed to oneself; he has other gifts of a more serious and sterling character. He gave me a copy of *Eothen*, composed of the rough proof sheets, and a concluding chapter, never published, and wrote my name in it. *Eothen* is a delightful itinerary; it is humorous, with a Voltairian wit, and is the truthfullest of books of travel. Its author has considerable sensibility, but, at the same time, makes no pretence of more than he possesses. I much admire his *Quarterly Review* article on 'The Rights of Women.'

[1] Always excepting the Byron controversy, when I think, perhaps from a good motive, he exercised a good deal of special pleading.

it pleased him now and again to be 'the devil's advocate.' He once felt it his duty (I suspect, not very much against his will) to tell me that my lyrics were a good deal overrated. I had suspected this, but still I was sorry to hear him say so; I had a respect for his opinion, and had sense enough to know that an acquaintance has a keener eye for defects than a friend. Happy are they that hear their own detraction, and can put them to mending! I think his remark did me good. He had been encouraging when I first sent him my book. I had written with it, telling him how little hope I had of recognition. In his reply he said something of my idiomatic style, and finished with 'Wir heissen euch hoffen.'[1]

With the ordinary equipment of a professional diner-out (story-relating, joke-retailing, and scandal-mongering), Hayward had also some of the defects: he was overbearing and yet not over-agreeable. His talk was good, but almost incessant; when on his mettle he would put words into your mouth, for the satisfaction of contradicting you.

Hayward was not without his foibles; and who is? You might have gathered from his conversation

[1] He did not approve of my traversing his special domain in my poor little *Patchwork*. He abused it roundly; but, even at that time, knowing the temper of the man, I did not much resent his doing so, and I had no right, for I now remember that I spoke with huge contempt of *his* lyrics.

that he was an ardent worshipper of female beauty, especially of aristocratic female beauty—that he had suffered; also that he had had his substantial consolations. As a sardonic and senile Adonis, he spoke mysteriously of 'Caroline Norton' and other fair ones, not forgetting Mrs. Langtry; the latter lady flourished during an emotional epoch of his career, when he was not quite eighty.[1] This reminds me that he had an idea that in London mere literary distinction was no passport to good society, and he enforced his opinion with a reference to himself. 'I am now in the best society, but it was only by breaking one of the Ten Commandments that I got there.'

In one respect Hayward and I were alike—we both wrote middling poetry, which we honestly thought was not so bad in its way, and which we both presented to our friends. I dare say he thought his better than mine; I know that I thought mine a great deal better than his; so we were both satisfied. He gave me his two little volumes, 'although,' said he with easy sarcasm, 'you are *not* a pretty woman.'

Hayward was disliked by the bulk of the members of the Athenæum Club. Their rancour displayed itself rather amusingly in a ballot for Costa, the much-respected conductor and composer.

[1] 'Difficile est longum subito deponere amorem.'

The club wiseacres had been a little in doubt whether Costa ought to be admitted within the sacred temple. They had pretty well decided against him, but when they discovered that Hayward was especially bent on keeping him out, they turned round and voted him in with acclamation.

Unless he was dining out, Hayward always favoured the 'Athenæum,' and often in the same coign of vantage ('temperance corner'), which had been affected by Theodore Hook, or, now and again, by Tom Moore. There his convives were Strzelecki, or Henry Rawlinson, or Drummond Wolff, or the Duke of Newcastle, or Kinglake, and at times myself or any member or foreigner of whom he approved, who happened to come in.

It is difficult not to be drawn to a person who is generally abused. There is no doubt that Hayward was sometimes as unattractive as his imperfect condition here below permitted him to be; yet I really liked him, when he allowed me to do so, and his friends liked him. However, he was an acquaintance whose good qualities it was necessary to keep pretty constantly in mind, if one wished to render him justice, which of course one wished.

As I have already said, puny little Hayward showed a good deal of pluck on more than one occasion, and this made many people exceedingly angry. Nothing annoys us so much as to hear of a fine trait in any one whom we cordially dislike.

Though I had known Hayward so long, and we had met so often, we were never really intimate. I dare say he did not think me worth much of his powder and shot, and felt, as I felt instinctively, that we were not quite in sympathy. However, I called upon him two or three times during his last illness. I found him solitary, the lamp of life burning very low; he was curled up in an easy-chair with his old figurehead at the top of a grey dressing-gown. The plucky little fellow gazed at me with faded eyes, and, though weak as a baby, seemed glad to see me. During my last visit he said, 'Do not introduce a subject; I am too weak; you need not talk, but I like to have you there—stay there.' Poor fellow, at that moment he might have exclaimed with Faust, 'Give me, give me back my youth.' He may have appreciated that dissolution is our destiny, and oblivion our portion, but he did not seem resigned, or to recognise that there is something ignoble in living unless you have an object in view besides mere existence: that years long drawn out to what one's acquaintance might call an inconsiderate longevity are sure to be weighted, if not with contempt, at least with a salutary neglect; but Hayward was masterful. As I sat there I thought admiringly of the old pagan in antique story, and his 'Proserpine, I come.' I should have liked to say that it was to eternity we both, we all were hastening, that this life was only a short link in a very long chain.

It was just at this time that Hamley had seen and told him a funny anecdote, which Dicky Doyle had related only a few hours before his death (he predeceased Hayward some five or six weeks), and Hayward had growled out with feeble raucity, 'What the devil did Doyle mean by going about spoiling my stories?' The story was of Nelson and Lady Hamilton. When Hamley mentioned this to Kinglake, the latter remarked quite gravely, 'Ah! poor fellow, I'm glad to hear that. I feared he was losing his masterfulness, and that would indeed be a bad sign.'

During this illness, Kinglake was one of his ministering angels. Torrington was equally so; both were as benevolent as women, and as tender. Is it on such beneficent wings that saint and sinner are carried heavenward? At the end of my last visit, as I waved my hand at the door, I said, 'Wir heissen euch hoffen;' his reply was 'God bless you!' I think of this with pleasure.

[1] Since writing the above I have heard that some time ago Hayward met his friend Gladstone (Mr. Gladstone had a high opinion of Hayward, or acted as if he had) and Sir Andrew Clark at P. Ralli's, in Belgrave Square, and that after dinner there was a lively argument between Hayward and Clark as to a future state, in which Clark

Lady William Russell

When Charlotte and I were in Rome, I think in 1866, we made the acquaintance of Lady William Russell; this ripened into a friendship which lasted till Charlotte died in 1872, and which I was more or less able to keep up and enjoy till Lady William's death in August 1874.

She had been Elizabeth Rawdon, niece to the first Marquis of Hastings, and was born about 1792. Lady William could quite well recall the time when Buonaparte was a growing terror to Europe, when the name of Byron carried no significancy with it, and when the square of Russell was only a cabbage garden, within easy reach of the entirely rural Islington.

took the orthodox view. Ralli had said but little, and Gladstone had said nothing. This was the first time that Hayward and Clark had met, for on rising from the table each asked Ralli who the other was. Some little time afterwards, Hayward met Ralli in St. James's Street, and the former referred to the dinner, and showed Ralli a letter of I do not know how many pages on the subject of their discussion, that he had just received from Gladstone, and in which Gladstone took the orthodox side. It was an eloquent disquisition, and had been written in the full swing of a fierce parliamentary debate.

When Hayward fell ill, when he was dying, he sent for Sir Andrew Clark, but Clark was out of town, and could not go to him. Hayward expressed disappointment, and among his last words to his attached and devoted sister, who came to town to nurse him, were: 'Tell Clark I die a believer.'

I do not know how far this account is correct, but as it is not discreditable to any concerned, for I am sure Ralli provided a dinner of an orthodox quality, I venture to give it.

Lady William had been a beauty. There was a tradition that her face would have been entirely faultless if she had had a more decided chin: however, as compensation for that slight physical shortcoming, Nature had possessed her of a resolute character and a powerful understanding, a striking individuality. She was exceeding wise, fair-spoken and persuading, and took a keen interest in the most important questions that concern poor humanity. Her conversation was spirited, agreeable, and instructive, and she had an extensive knowledge of literature—indeed, altogether she was bountifully equipped.

When we were first introduced to Lady William, she was confined to her couch; she had just been cruelly knocked down by a *legno d'affito*, while crossing the Piazza di Spagna to the Europa, which accident caused the dislocation of her hip joint; a grievous misfortune, for during the whole time that we knew her she was a confirmed invalid and a cripple. However, this calamity did not quench her spirit or fetter her intellectual ardour; she submitted to a prisoned existence with fortitude and even cheerfulness. When she was sufficiently recovered, and had moved to her house in South Audley Street,[1] she continued her studies,

[1] Her journey home, accompanied by Lord Rosslyn, was painful and very exhausting. When they reached the hotel at Marseilles, he

leading a life of apparently satisfied aspiration, and surrounding herself with and governing (she had a genius for command) a varied society of distinguished and pleasant people: for, though of advanced age, she retained a keen interest in many things, more especially in such as appertained to her *monde*—her politics, her books, her china, her pearls, her *causerie*, her religion, and her cats: not forgetting the babble of the great world about and beyond her. Lady William's rule was a despotism, but it was agreeable, for it was tempered by refined and cordial feeling; lion and lamb were content to converse amicably on her couches. We recognised her sovereignty, and she accepted our homage.

As Lady William had an imperious volition, she decreed that her acquaintances should share her enthusiasms.

Lady William never left South Audley Street after she had been conveyed thither, but she received every evening that she was equal to doing so. The woman was always ailing, but the hostess was rarely ill. I was often under her roof. I had a sincere regard for her, and also for her sons, Hastings, Arthur, and Odo. They were clever, and, what is better, they were high-minded, amiable, and

feared she was sinking: she lay silent and prostrate; at length she made a slight sign for him to approach his ear to her mouth. She whispered only one word, but that encouraged him to hope. It was 'Bouillabaisse.'

affectionate. They were attractive, either in isolation or association; for each was unlike the other, and all three were an interesting contrast to their mother.[1]

Lady William, at home and abroad, had always lived in the great world. She had a boundless pleasure in her friendships. She knew everybody, which means she was acquainted with those whom everybody desired to know. In former days she had acquitted herself creditably in conversational fence with Madame de Staël; the Emperor Alexander was understood to have admired her, and that remarkable woman, the late Queen of Holland, was one of her intimates. Lord William Russell had been equerry to the Duke of Wellington, both at Paris and Cambray, and Lady William saw much of the Duke's family circle. This was not all: Byron, of whom more hereafter, had referred to her, rhetorically, as 'a charming woman,' and he had immortalised the fleeting bloom of her cheek in two stanzas of Beppo.

Towards the close of Lady William's career,

[1] They were most dutiful children. The lovable and learned Arthur is still spared to his many friends, but the equally beloved Odo has passed away—gone—cut off in his prime! The Duke, whom I liked so cordially, is only buried, somewhere in the Bloomsbury district. He spends laborious days in an office (often gas-lit, I am told) surrounded by myrmidons casting up columns of figures. *Crescentem sequitur cura pecuniam*, as impecunious people, quoting a prudent man, are so fond of saying. [This note is no longer accurate. The three brothers are now all dead.—Ed.]

all the distinguished foreigners regarded her as *la doyenne des diplomates*, which indeed she well may have been called, though she never quite mastered the party politics that surged around her; for her eldest son, a most dutiful son, was once constrained to say to her, 'My dear mother, you never seem to understand that the Russells are Whigs.' Lady William's real reputation lay in the region that never carried her actually beyond the limits of private life. She valued genius, but never seemed to covet its crowns. She and Lady Jersey, though they gazed from hostile (political) camps, had a mutual respect and esteem; they aspired to and made the same friendships, nay intimacies, with crowned heads, and they also resembled each other in their intrepidity and masterfulness, and in a remarkable skill in drawing out the people with whom they conversed. But Lady William had too wide and searching a mind to carry to an extremity and to be content with that systematised exclusiveness which swayed and satisfied her more conventional and less intellectual neighbours. She was far too eclectic; she cultivated society with selection, but without exclusion: she was *grande dame*, if ever there was one.

Lady William, as a girl, had known Byron, and I will here set down a very few notes[1] of her con-

[1] There was much that I do not care to quote.

versation, which was copious: she prided herself, and with reason, on her tenacious and accurate memory. Some of these scraps are tinctured with scandal; but, after all, they are only social utterances—the impressions of a woman who, although she had a great deal of real kindness, had also a capacity for polite hatred.

'*London, October*, 1869.—To-day I dined with Lady William Russell; Lady Westminster and Arthur were the only other guests. Lady William told us that Lady Westmorland had had entire possession, for six weeks or more, of Byron's Journal, and found it very amusing. That Lord John Russell, on the contrary, did not much care for it; indeed, he never considered that the public were great losers by its destruction. Some half-dozen pages were very *déréglé*, so if the journal had been spared, these passages must have been suppressed. Lady Westmorland had copied out a few pages, which described the poet's life at Eton, but even these she was obliged to burn, Tom Moore being present. This holocaust took place in Albemarle Street, when John Murray paid the 2,000*l.*'

Lady William, who I need hardly say was a woman of rare intelligence, thought Byron a bad-hearted fellow, and others, even better qualified to judge, were of much the same opinion.

Lady Melbourne was the person who had encouraged Byron to propose to Miss Milbanke. Although he was nettled that she should have refused him, they continued to correspond; for one day Byron said rather abruptly to Miss Rawdon, 'Have you seen Miss Milbanke lately? I wish when next you see her you would be so kind as to give her a hint not to send me any more of her foolish little rhymes: she is charming, but I wish she would not send me her foolish little rhymes.' After this, as we all know, he again proposed and was accepted.

November 24, 1869.—To-day I dined *tête-à-tête* with Lady William; she again spoke of Lord Byron. She said, 'We were all fascinated by him—his conversation and his bearing. He was not natural, but I was struck with his remarkable shrewdness. I often met him in London, and also at Cheltenham, where he had gone for his health. This must have been about 1809. I was a girl at the time—I was much interested in him—all the women adored him—I adored him, and partly on that account, and partly because his manners were affected, the men hated him.

'He had a magnificent head, a melodious voice, and a very curious and "dangerous underlook" with his beautiful eyes; but his shoulders sloped, and altogether he had a mean figure, rather below the middle height. As he entered the room his feet made a clump, clump, on the floor, as if he wore very heavy shoes; they looked like peasants' shoes. He wore loose nankeen trousers, while everybody else was attired in knee-breeches—tights.

'These nankeens were strapped over his feet; his coat was peculiar in cut, and while it was universally the fashion to wear a high cravat, he walked about with his throat bare. He always seized the first opportunity of sitting down.

'I remember Lord Byron talked with pleasure of "Sandford and Merton," and said, "I wish Day had lived to make men of them!" He also praised Knolles's "History of the Turks."'

This is a meagre sketch of the poet, but it exhibits the intelligent girl as only half fascinated.

Lady William went on to say that, though Lord Aberdeen, the 'Travelled Thane,' was not handsome, he in a way reminded her of Byron. I said that the eleventh Duke of Hamilton had reminded me of Byron's portraits. She could not see this; however, *I* did; and, curiously enough, they also remind me of a little engraved profile medallion of Beckford,[1] the author of 'Vathek,' (1884).

. . . .

[1] Beckford was the Duke's grandfather.

Lady William thought Sir James Macintosh one of the most agreeable talkers she had ever met. I have heard my father express the same opinion; he used often to meet Macintosh at the Literary Club; but my father would have put Walter Scott (Walter Scott at home—at Abbotsford) on a level with him. Lady William spoke of Lord Melbourne, Henry Luttrell, Dudley Ward, and Sydney Smith, as carrying weight by their conversational powers; also of Tom Moore, though not in the same degree—'he was more like a clever little gnat singing about.' She said that Speaker Denison, and Lords Clarendon and Granville, most strikingly reminded her of what she had most admired in the talkers of the older generation.

Major G. J. Whyte-Melville, and Others

'On December 5, 1878, killed by a fall from his horse while hunting with the V. W. H. Hounds, near Tetbury, George Whyte-Melville, late Coldstream Guards (soldier, sportsman, author), only son of the late John Whyte-Melville, of Bennock and Strathkinness, and Lady Catherine Whyte-Melville, aged 57, deeply mourned by his daughter and only child, the last of the race. (In loving memory.)'

It is the sight of this notice in the 'Times' of December 4, 1886, which recalls George Whyte-Melville to my mind, so I place it at the head of a very brief and imperfect sketch that I wrote in 1883.

Read 'Kate Coventry.' If you have not read it, you will be delighted with it; if you have already done so, you will not be sorry to read it again. Its author, Major George Whyte-Melville, was as worthy of his books as of his social popularity. He was one of the pleasantest people I ever met; almost as good company as his friend George Payne, the owner of Musket, but of course in a different way.[1]

[1] George Payne, of Sulby, also had the social gift and faculty of quick reply, and he had much worldly experience; he may be said to have read the Book of Life very attentively, and other books a little, but, after all, none of them to much serious profit. However, he fascinated all sorts and conditions of men, and women, and children—by his genial bearing—his generous spirit—his refined gaiety—his quaint sayings—the twinkle of his eye—his imperturbable countenance—his black and white linen cravat (the Payne tartan)—and by something beyond all these, something always felt but never describable. How fragrant is the memory!

Payne was one of a party at a country-house when the gratifying news arrived that Sir John Macgregor, who was very poor and very popular, had been appointed Lieutenant-Governor of the Virgin Islands; atlases were immediately got out, but nobody could discover the whereabouts of those islands; however, Payne seemed pretty certain that they could not be in the neighbourhood of the Isle of Man.

There are humourists still living who remember with keen amusement his billiard contests, *à outrance*, with his old friend Admiral

I used often to meet Whyte-Melville in Fifeshire, and have dined in his company at Anthony Froude's (the historian). I sometimes saw him at Stirling Crawford's, Langton Hall ('Old Craw,' the owner of Sefton, who won the Derby in 1878, and Thebais, and the husband of the Duchess of Montrose), with whom, years ago, I spent some time in Italy, especially a memorable week in Venice. I have met him at Market Harborough.[1]

If Whyte-Melville had a weakness, it was a singular one. He appeared to undervalue his literary faculty; he held it cheap; he gave you to understand that it was of no importance, at most an amusement to while away an idle hour, or to replenish a lean purse; but if he really thought so, why did he assert that his objects in life were the pen and pigskin?

This notion of the smallness of his gift may have been fostered by his never having been a really needy man; he could always afford to hunt the fox, so the excitement of the *chasse aux pièces*

Rous, their method of contention, and of calculated exasperation, each to put the other off his play, so highly characteristic of both.

[1] I was very fond of Crawford. He gave me a beautiful Greek onyx, a scarabæus of Hercules floating on amphoræ. He was opulent of impulses, many of them most praiseworthy. He was exceedingly good-looking, his nose a very little on one side, probably from a fall in the hunting-field. Crawford has gone from us, but I should like to meet him in another world, and should prefer him with his nose still a very little on one side.

de cent sous, which stimulates most authors, was denied to him.

Whyte-Melville ignored literary society: he almost exclusively cultivated the sporting; and I think he was wrong in so doing. I have always objected to cliques, and therefore it has especially pleased me to seek the society of pleasant people with various tastes, and wherever I could find them. I am very glad I have been so pleased, as otherwise I might not have known Fred Archer, the jockey; or Hanlan, the sculler, whose *avatar* made an epoch and founded a tradition in the art of sculling; or Captain Webb, the swimmer; or Tom Sayers, the bruiser; or George Hazael, the pedestrian, who ran six hundred miles in 141¼ consecutive hours; or Mr. Brookes, who jumped six feet two inches high; or J. E. Barre, the tennis champion; or Grace, the cricketer; or Kentfield[1] or Roberts, the billiard players—not to speak of

[1] Kentfield's Brighton Subscription Room was very pleasant; there I first learnt to 'go back game,' and met many good hazard strikers, from Lord Eglintoun, of tournay renown, to 'Ginger' Stubbs, the turfite. The latter, to the uninitiated eye, in his knowingly cut black cloth suit, and white neckcloth marvellously folded, looked like a clean-shaved and rather austere ecclesiast. Nobody could fathom how Mr. Stubbs lived. He used to say, 'I should be quite satisfied to have two thousand a year *clear*, and all my expenses paid;' and then, —and this was much more interesting—nobody could fathom how he tied his cravat. It has been suggested that he lay at full length on his back while his wife ironed it on. 'Mrs. Ginger' was very pretty.

Pellegrini and Ada Menken, or Whyte-Melville himself.

Any company cultivated exclusively is apt to become tiresome. I have known literary men whose talk was as wearing as an earache. I have encountered sportsmen who bored me to that degree that I could have jumped from a steeple to be quit of them. Still the conversation of intelligent literary or sporting men, like George Boyle[1] and George Payne, is delightful. I do not care so much for the sportsman's poet, who may be said to be inspired by a tenth muse, but his artist is very agreeable, as seen in the works of Stubbs, Sartorius, Aiken, and Ferneley.[2]

The turf and covert sides are battlefields where mankind is equal. On the turf, or under the turf, it is all one; there is no pride of place, there are no distinctions, yet, in a sort of way, the turf is more exclusive than the hunting-field. Its votaries, too, have the credit of being even narrower in their sympathies, and of more completely ignoring letters,

[1] The Dean of Salisbury.

[2] 'C'est beau comme *Le Cid*' was a fine literary compliment for a great nation to pay to one of its dramatists. My dear children, your grandfather has a celebrity—a small one. The other day I was looking at an atlas, and recognised a Cape Locker in the north-west corner of Australia, lat. 21·20° S., long. 114·41° E. This promontory was called after my father, I am not sure by what navigator, but I think by the distinguished Captain George F. Lyon, R.N. The names of certain old friends, Lord Exmouth, John Wilson Croker, Sir John Burrow, &c., are given to contiguous regions.

which is something to be vain of; so it would particularly please me to hear that London Lyrics had just won the Derby! That would be fame.

However, we are forgetting Whyte-Melville. I have read very few of his books, and think I prefer 'Kate Coventry,' though I do not say it is at all his best. His verse does not greatly move me; but, taken with the novels, it is another very green leaf in the chaplet.

Whyte-Melville wrote about horses, and the men who live for and by them, and he wrote as a man of the world; while describing the stable he had an eye on the drawing-room, and he did it with literary skill. When he treats of rogues and demireps, he always does it like a gentleman. He thought the not refined Mr. Jorrocks one of the most lifelike characters in English fiction. Considered in that way, can the unattractive Jorrocks take his place with the Baron of Bradwardine, Major Pendennis, or Mrs. Poyser?

I once encountered Whyte-Melville as he was ringing the Q——s bell. We exchanged a word or two, and on parting I said, 'You like the Q——s?' 'Yes,' said he, and his answer was characteristic: 'yes, very much. I like *him* better than she does, and I like *her* better than he does.'

His father is still (1883) living at St. Andrews, and though he is nearly ninety, no one ever heard him make reference to his 'time of life.' He still plays a resolute round at golf, and he still has a more jaunty air than George ever had.

There was a serious, even a sad, side to Whyte-Melville's character, which, his friends tell me, made him the more interesting; besides this he had much practical benevolence and a kind heart.

It is not every day that the covert-side breeds an imaginative writer, so when Whyte-Melville met his death in the hunting-field, there were not a few regrets. Many tears have flowed round the laureate hearse where Lycidas is laid.

Sir Curtis Miranda Lampson

Sir Curtis Miranda Lampson, the father of Mrs. Locker, was born at New Haven, Vermont, on September 21, 1806. He came to England in 1829. I am told that as a youth he was wise beyond his years and intelligent in advance of his experience; that he was confided in for counsel by people old enough to be his father. He has foresight, judgment, a clear apprehension of men and affairs, a strong will and a sweet temper, and his success in life may be attributed to his own and sole exertions —*Sapientia duce, fortuna permittente.* He is a simple and unassuming person, but no one takes a liberty with him, and though disappointments have come, I have never heard him complain.

Sir Curtis is cheerfuller than I. He is a breeder of shorthorns now, when shorthorns are at their excessive price. He has a valuable herd, and he had a young bull said to be the most promising for its age in all England. It was understood that Allsopp (Lord Hindlip) desired to possess it, and that 5,000*l.* was its value.

One afternoon Sir Curtis arrived by his usual train from London, was cheery at dinner, afterwards played whist, and was especially keen over the game. He has wonderful spirits, and when he won the ultimate rubber he could no longer contain himself; he sprang to his feet and shouted for joy, more like seventeen than seventy-one; then he said, gravely enough, 'Now I'll tell you all a piece of news—MY BULL'S DEAD!'

The splendid beast had been ailing. Pure-bred shorthorns are always delicate; however, no serious anxiety had been felt about him, but on Sir Curtis's return from London, his stock-bailiff had intercepted him at the station, and had said, 'The bull is dead.'

Sir Curtis is now an old man, but still one of his chief characteristics is a manly cheerfulness, and with the manliness there is something tender and womanly; you see it in his countenance, in the delicate curves of his mouth, in the grave but frank and affectionate firmness of his eyes. He is seventy-eight years old, but he is still an excellent shot, and still very handsome. He reminds me of Lord Herbert of Lee. People have stopped him in the street under the impression that he was Lord Herbert. He has the same frank and thoroughbred manner. I knew Lord Herbert, and like to think that he was as loyal, just, and upright a gentleman as Sir Curtis Lampson. Norman Lampson inherits one or two of his father's most admirable qualities.

(1890) Sir Curtis Lampson may be said to have been a distinguished member of the Athenæum Club, for the day before he died he was elected a member without ballot in consideration of his public services. See 'National Dictionary of Biography,' &c.

Mr. James Gibbs

'I was born on January 10, 1804, in a court that was called Old Round Court. It no longer exists. It ought to have been called Roneval Court. As far as I can remember, it was nearly opposite Buckingham Street in the Strand, and it was pulled down to make way for King William Street, Agar Street, &c. There was a long narrow lane on the north side of St. Martin's Church called Porridge Island; its real name was Church Lane, and at the end of this lane was a little narrow court, called Church Court, or Church Lane.

'My father was a Baptist: he worked for Jackson, a bookbinder in Villiers Street, Strand. My parents afterwards had lodgings in the neighbourhood. At the age of fourteen I was apprenticed to young Jackson. I was about twenty-six when I married Mary Hillier, and about thirty-two when I opened my shop (bookbinding and printselling) in May's Buildings.

'I lived for about two years in May's Buildings. I then moved to Lisle Street, Leicester Square, and was there for two or three more years. My second wife was Anne Bennett. Her mother nursed my first wife. From Lisle Street I removed to 8 Great Newport Street.'[1]

This is the succinct account of himself that my old friend, James Gibbs, gave me on February 10, 1870. When I first knew him, about twenty-five years ago, he still lived in that dingy, decaying, and disorderly centre, and he is there now. I made

[1] As a boy he remembered seeing Mrs. David Garrick walking on the Adelphi Terrace, a neat little old figure, dressed like one of Hogarth's dames in a blue gown caught up over a dark petticoat, and carrying a small basket on her arm.

his acquaintance while collecting engravings by Hogarth, and at once found his company and conversation most exhilarating. Although we have had serious differences, we have been fairly good friends ever since.

I wish I could describe Gibbs's personal appearance. I have several photographs of him: I think the most satisfactory is that inserted at the end of the folio memoir of Captain Locker, which Gibbs inlaid, illustrated, and bound. He was short and thick-set, had soft brown eyes, and a shock of hair, now white. He had many attractions, but he had many prejudices. He could not endure people who were bald, who stammered, or who were deaf; he himself is now very deaf. He despised footmen, clergymen, tailors, and teetotallers: he was not intemperate, but, like many another, he had a vague notion that tippling, in some sort of way, pertained to good-fellowship: you see he was ignorant, wrong-headed, and had little toleration.

Gibbs's parents were Baptists; his father was a journeyman bookbinder; they rented a roomy but dark and black-beetley parlour-kitchen in Old Round Court, and had a pet starling that whistled the 'Black Joke.' The mother was comely, but had an imperious temper, and when under baleful influence, she would lose her self-control, and shy the furniture about. To use her own words of homely vigour, she combed her husband's head with a three-legged stool. You see she did not hold with the poet who sings didactically that

> Whatever brawls disturb the street,
> There should be peace at home.

Gibbs says that he was spoilt by this mother of his; for when, as a child, he would not take his physic, to encourage him she would halve the senna-tea with him. Gibbs's absorbing passion was 'collecting,' whether it were books or prints or cuttings, and this lust asserted itself early; for his mother told him that while he was yet a babe in arms, he would instinctively clutch at any print or drawing that came within his reach: indeed he may be said to have been doing this, and not much else, all his life. As the boy grew older, and the taste developed, his not especially artistic father, by way of inducement, would now and again bring home an engraving, with a 'Here, Jim, here's a nice dark one for you.'

Gibbs's crowning triumph was an interleaved and profusely illustrated Bible, in more than sixty volumes folio, each so thick that he could hardly lift it from the counter. It became the property of an American enthusiast, who evidently appreciated quantity at least as much as quality; or he may have felt with the Stoic that *multitudo librorum* distracts the mind, and therefore piously restricted himself and his library to one work. I have often wondered what that American is now doing with his big Bible: does he ever look for anything in it? Does he ever find it? Does not all lie buried in overpowering accumulation? I hope he finds solace in and room for it: if so, he must be living in one of the larger States. Gibbs, in his time, has illustrated a great number of books; amongst others, several copies of Chambers's 'Book of Days,' besides making enormous collections about 'barbers,' 'Jews,' the 'cries of London,' and anything else that has taken his fancy. I fear he has ruthlessly sacrificed, mutilated, and broken up many a rare but probably imperfect work. The number of Bibles he has cut up or destroyed would have satisfied Mr. Tom Paine.

Uncompromising book-collectors have branded my poor friend as a book ghoul, a reptile who regards title-page and colophon as his natural prey, for in a sort of way he has sacrificed everything to this obscene passion. What were wife or children to him if it were the question of a portrait or a 'cutting' that would illustrate anything? I mean, what was their Sunday dinner to him? Gibbs was clever and original, frugal and hardworking, and yet, after all, if he lives long enough, in all probability—and probability is the guide of life—he will die in the workhouse, and only because he has all his life been governed by crotchets, aversions, and passions.

I am anxious to give an idea of the man Gibbs, but it seems impossible. His aspect, the tones of his voice, his pronunciation, cynicism, sensibility, and irritability; his extreme rudeness, his gusto, humour, simplicity, causticity, and vanity; the touch of unconscious poetry in his talk, and, to me, his exquisite attractiveness, all these should be rendered to make my sketch a finished portrait.

Gibbs was sceptical as regards revelations, but he had religious instincts. He felt, in a half-articulate manner, that certain mysteries which his natural intelligence (an intelligence that came from the Eternal) could not accept, had better be left alone.

I remember his saying to me quite gravely: 'I wonder what the Almighty does with Himself: how He gets through His day. It must all seem so flat: He can have no pleasant surprises.'

He was a Radical, fond of reading, and, as he hardly ever talked to educated people, he used a good many words without any idea as to their correct pronunciation, which sometimes was comical enough. There was much agreement, but also much disputation, in our talk. I remember our discussing the well-worn subject of rich and poor; he did it in a crude, ignorant, and very annoying manner, but with a certain force, and I should have been irritated if throughout the argument he had not pronounced the name of Dives as if it were a rhyme to knives. He insisted that, if there were perfect harmony of taste and temperament between, say, one of our princesses and Calcraft's (the hangman) son, they ought to be encouraged to marry each other.

A very queer temper had Gibbs. Of an afternoon he drank his tea and read his book in the parlour behind the shop, but he left the glazed door of communication open, in case a customer should come in, as very occasionally one would. I've been told that, if any one arrived whose looks he did not like, he would call out in a not conciliatory voice, 'I don't know what you want, but I've not got it in stock,' and then would go on with his tea and his book.

He attracted many and different people unto him.

Gibbs had several distinguished patrons. I introduced him to Thackeray, and to Lady Lovaine, afterwards Duchess of Northumberland (Mr. Henry Drummond's daughter). Rogers the poet had bought of him, so had Mario de Candia, the singer. He also had a very valuable customer, a dentist, who was mad about old drawings. This man's name was Hall (not a bad name for a tooth drawer): I used to tell Gibbs that Hall lost quite as much as he gained by his drawings! Hall would give almost any price Gibbs chose to ask, provided the works came out of a celebrated collection, if they had the stamp, such as 'B.W.' (Benjamin West), or 'M.' (Mariette), or 'P.S.' (Paul Sandby) in the corner, and even if they had only the mark of a former collector: but such drawings as these are not plentiful, and Gibbs had none of them.

One day he was expecting his dentist, and had baited the counter with a folio of old drawings, when all at once it occurred to him, 'Why should not I manufacture a mark?' No sooner thought of than done; he stuck one of his brass bookbinding tools into the flame of the candle to blacken it, and then stamped it in the corner of each of the drawings: it was a little twiddle like this ~~~~, nothing more! He had just finished the last Cuyp or Rembrandt, and actually had the stamp in his hand, when Hall glided in: Gibbs, nothing abashed, pushed the folio towards him with an air of triumph: 'The Snake collection!' He boasted that by this artifice he had made a hundred per cent. more than he would otherwise have done. The amateur often called, as often asked him for drawings out of 'that Snake collection,' and Gibbs occasionally humoured him. Gibbs was a needy man, and, referring to himself and others, would often say, 'It's hard for an empty sack to stand upright.' However, in this instance he entirely justified his conduct, maintaining that the drawings were worth much more than he got for them—in fact, that he had been Hall's benefactor.

There is a romance in all our lives. Gibbs has given me delightful accounts of his first meeting with Mary Hillier. As an artisan it was his custom to buy a chop of mutton, and take it to the public-house where he got his beer, and cook it at the bar fire. One summer day he was returning from such a frugal meal, when his future wife suddenly appeared before him. She had just come out of the door of the poor lodging-house where she was general servant. She was dressed in a gay-coloured cotton frock, and had a flower stuck in her bosom, and, said Gibbs—and the way he said it made it an original remark—'I could have lighted my pipe at her eyes!' He was intoxicated on the spot; what with her frock and her flower she 'seemed like a being from another world.' From that moment he was in a heaven of content. She was his first and only love. Mary was good and virtuous; she had the gift of innocence; indeed she was passionately virginal: but the modesty of an attractive young woman in her rank of life is often sorely wounded, and apt to become bloomless.

Gibbs has often spoken to me of their courtship, their meetings at the cannie hour at e'en, of the few simple presents that he bought for her, and of which he and she were so proud, of the very many scrapbooks he made for her—of their wedding in the early summer of 1830, and honeymoon of twenty-four hours. He told me of the drive to Dulwich, at that time a quiet little village, with his reluctant and consenting bride, his delicious Mary; of the sweet sense of possession, the feeling of rest from hard manual labour, the feeling of liberty, the incomparable day and its deep tranquillity—a day that saw nature and human nature in complete harmony. He described the cosy nooks and well-to-do homesteads, the bye-lanes and their green hedges that wound on and vanished, but were still present to the imagination; the loitering men and women, chubby children and lazy dogs, cattle in the sleepy meadows; the fresh grass and trees, the flowers wherewith the bountiful season had filled their laps; the full song of the finches piping their 'Marry, maidens, marry,' as well as *Gloria in excelsis*, and a blue sky over all.

This was their outing! The amatory, the humorous, the familiar, the kindly but homely all prettily combined. However, at the tavern where they dined, all this was much marred by a rapacious and cloudy-shirted waiter, in a black alpaca jacket; a gaunt fellow with a rasping voice, and an aspect menacing and predatory, who cringed and swaggered and showed off his paltry serving-man skill in folding his unclean napkin into twenty different shapes, and then ended it all by sneering at Gibbs's modest orders and abusing him for his niggardliness; and this, too, before his angel bride. Poor people are very sensitive to such insults. Gibbs partially relieved his feelings (probably she did not require consolation) by entering a good pastrycook's shop and devouring four twopenny 'three-corners;' however, he still writhes under the recollection of that waiter.[1]

[1] Gibbs's grudge against waiters made him appreciate the following. It appears that there is a *pipe-and-pewter* room attached to some of the old-fashioned public-houses where clubs meet. These societies are *free-and-easys*. The tradesmen of the neighbourhood consort there of a night. They 'blow clouds,' tipple, gossip, prose, and warble songs, and there is a strict etiquette as regards the waiter. One of the party volunteers a song; the vice-chairman bawls out, 'Silence, gentlemen, pray silence, Mr. So-and-so is about to favour us with a song—your 'ealth, sir;' then there is a 'Hear, hear,' and banging of tumblers; but perhaps, just before the songster begins, one of the party starts on his legs and says, 'Mr. Vice, perhaps you are not aware, sir, that there is a waiter in the apartment, sir?' On which the Vice looks suspiciously about him, and calls out sternly 'Waiter! leave the apartment, sir, instantly.' Whereupon the wretched waiter tucks his not over-clean napkin under his arm, and shuffles out of the room. Then begins the *tol de rol lol*, but not till then.

Apropos of waiters, Percy Fitzgerald, in his interesting memoirs, speaks of an entry in the visitors' book at the George Hotel, Lichfield, perchance written by himself:—

I came for change and rest.
The waiter took the change,
And the landlord took the rest.

I fear that all was not quite so rosy after marriage; Gibbs, with sensibility and much real kindness, carefully concealed, had a cranky temper; he was difficult to live with, and the wife-and-weans instinct was never strong within him. He has described to me, with sorrow in his eyes and contrition in his voice, how he would sometimes hardly speak to Mary for days; that even on their Sunday excursions he would walk ahead, with his pipe in his mouth, and let her follow with her suckling and brats.

However, all the real and exquisite romance of his life was connected with Mary. I have not forgotten his ditty, sung in the quavering treble of an old man, and full of feeling:—

> And I will luv thee still, my dear,
> Till a' the seas gang dry—
> Till a' the seas gang dry.

The recollection of her drew passionate grief from the man whose philosophy was not to grieve at all. She died of consumption.

Gibbs was about forty when he married his second wife; she was entirely uninteresting—an incapacity for good, an incapacity for evil, a bad seamstress, a worse cook, given over to do-nothingism, but I believe faithful. She died about 1870, and was buried from her old mother's cottage at Barnstead. I was at the funeral. Her relations were labouring people who cultivated their glebe, but let themselves lie fallow. They were quite unlike your peasants *à la Watteau*; for them there were no flowery kirtles and canary-coloured small-clothes, there was no guitar strumming. They did not say :—

> Content and sweet cheerfulness open our door,
> They smile with the simple and feed with the poor.
> The happiest of folk are the guileless and free,
> For who are so happy, so guileless as we?

They were not even round-frocked swains and rosy shepherdesses; with no guile in their hearts, but plenty of honeysuckle at their porch. They were real peasants. Life for them was a hard and sordid reality.[1]

It was a walking funeral, about a quarter of a mile to the churchyard. I was paired off with a slim niece, who was general servant to the apothecary—a taciturn little girl, with an obliquity of vision—a 'silent nymph, with curious eye,' who made a curtsey every time I spoke to her. She was very meanly clad; her old and soiled garments skimpy yet baggy, and looking all the shabbier from their admixture and contrast with crisply new crape trimmings. She carried a prayerbook bound in some faded stuff, a clean and neatly folded pocket

[1] There is something dreadful in grinding poverty, and theirs was the next thing to it—wealth does not make happiness, but it contributes a good deal to it.

handkerchief, and a broken parasol, which she would have been glad to use, but that it would not open. I remember the handle was roughly carved into the effigy of a very beaky bird. As we passed slowly along the dusty lane, a pair of thrushes were singing their hearts out, and I whispered, pointing to her parasol handle, 'A bird in the hand is not worth two in the bush.' She looked up at me, made her little *bob*, and her grave young face relaxed at once; she smiled with timorous archness, as any little princess might have smiled, but she betrayed her cockney bringing-up when she murmured something about the *sparrars*. This was not nearly all; for a day or two afterwards I received a small box packed with hay, containing a little old earthenware mug of the most primitive manufacture, decorated in colours with a picture of a country inn, and the sign, 'The Bird in the Hand.' You may suppose I was much pleased with her little present. If the next Sunday happened to be her Sunday out and a bright day, she need not have suffered from the glare. It has not been my lot to share the same dog's-eared hymnal with so many lasses that I do not feel a little sentimental about this poor girl.[1]

[1] Soon afterwards this mug and a much-valued clock were simultaneously smashed by a newly imported and very heavy-handed housemaid with a bold plain face. She had those very points that made the timepiece so precious.

Two or three of the nearest relations came up to me in the churchyard as I stood looking down at the coffin, before and while the earth was shovelled in, and said, as if it were a small mercy, 'It's a nice dry grave.'[1] Each said this with what was probably a *congenital* stodginess, nobody said anything more. Gibbs had but little sympathy with any of his people; the *adscripti glebæ*, their hidebound natures, and inconclusive grumbling troubled him. He was or had been one of them, and yet he clung to me. Poor fellow! I wish I had the pen of Charles Lamb, whose works he so much admired, to describe him. He was sad, and yet somehow he was almost comical. I have known people who mourned jovially; he jested ruefully. Like all persons with sensibility, he was stricken with remorse, contrition that he had not been kinder. As we sat in the room with the corpse, waiting for the undertaker to screw down the coffin, he said, 'She might have married a younger man—I don't forget that. I thought I should have been able to make something of her, more of her than I did. I thought she was a flower, but she was only a weed.' He then got up, softly approached the coffin, gazed at her poor withered face, and kissed it, and looking up sadly said, 'I don't think I

[1] The grave's a fine and private place,
But none methinks do there embrace.

shall ever marry again.' At that time he must have been about sixty. He was perfectly plain-spoken. He is the 'J. G.' of my 'To Postumus,' and though he has changed since those lines were written, they do not jar as I now read them.

Their midday repast—the funeral baked meats—was interesting, for it exhibited the family in their bare, simple, almost pitiful rusticity. They did their best to be hospitable: a boiled leg of mutton, enormous and of a peculiar pallor; after that, a very ruddy cheese cut into little squares, without bread, and with no plates; and the beer in a jug, with one glass tumbler passed from hand to hand. A russet-coated episode!

About 1858, I offered to take Gibbs abroad for a week's holiday. He had never travelled, and he was sufficiently intelligent to jump at his opportunity—*un voyage à faire, et Paris au bout!* I have long forgotten the ridiculous circumstances connected with our visit, but there were plenty of them. Among the people whom we went to see was Capet, the celebrated bibliopegist. Gibbs was much struck with his work *à petits fers*, as well he might be! In fact, Capet considerably extended his bookbinding horizon. He was interested in all that he saw, and thoroughly enjoyed himself, though he had not a single word of the language wherewith to bless his entertainers; even the sparkle and *abandon* of Ollendorff was denied to him. Perhaps this may account for his returning home with a poorish opinion of the French as a people. Their cafés! Their language! which has been called Neo-Latin. 'What can you expect of a waiter who's called *Alcibiade*? It's a good enough language, you know, for people who have no business to do, but,' &c. It was a surprise to him to find that the French have the same natural feelings as ourselves.

At one time it was Gibbs's pleasure to spend a Sunday afternoon at our *pied-à-terre* in Victoria Street. At the time of which I am specially thinking it so happened that our parlourmaid fell ill, and Gibbs's second daughter, Margaret, being just then out of place, we agreed to take her temporarily. She was a good girl, a good servant (never in and never out of the way), and it was edifying to see her dear father seated before the fire in my dressing-room, his feet on the hobs, smoking my cigarettes, and leading the conversation in a delightful manner, while I was ringing the bell and commanding Margaret to coal the fire.

An appreciation of the humorous is a great leveller. It was in this sort of way that, for a long time, we let the world slide, and tried, without *gêne*, to bridge the social gulf.

It is characteristic of Gibbs that when I was

preparing for my first tour with Tennyson, Arthur Locker happened to call on him, and told him of the projected expedition. Gibbs instantly remarked, 'I wonder what Tennyson sees in your brother to make him want to take him about with him.' I can understand why Gibbs thought less of me than I of him—that is, if he did think less; after all, perhaps it may have been that I admired him, and he was capable of enduring me.

Gibbs was cynical, and yet even late in life he had an unusual power of enjoyment. He nourished an idea that he cared for nothing but his 'book and fireside,' yet whenever we got him to the theatre he laughed so hilariously that we were ashamed of him.

He was piously sceptical and pessimistically jovial.

My children, it is a mistake to cultivate friendships with people decidedly inferior to yourselves in social status. I used not to realise this, and I have suffered. The inferior either settles down into a parasite, or groans under the burden of obligations conferred, and which must increase; in either case he is likely to be on the look out for slights and neglect. This is my advice to you and your offspring: 'Find your acquaintance among people more liberally educated, more able, more socially powerful, and more high-minded than yourselves; keep good company, and be *one of the number*, and let your friendships form themselves on the simple intercourse of everyday life; do not hurry into them, but when you have made them, do your best to keep them. Grapple them to thy soul with hoops of steel. Quarrelling and making it up is decidedly unsatisfactory. The Latin grammar says, *æqualem uxorem quære*. I do not think you will go far wrong if, when forming your friendships, you bear this in mind; and remember that much of our happiness in this world depends on the amount of affection we are able to inspire and hive up.'

I had and have a sincere friendship for Gibbs, and though he has tried he has not lost me. I am sure I have sorely tried him. We have had numberless money transactions. I was and am very rich compared with him. He is not a bit of a tuft-hunter; he is less of a toady; indeed, he has been occasionally what in an educated man would have been called wanting in courtesy, and I have suffered. Gibbs is now very old, so old that I have occasionally referred to him in the past tense, so old that he has outlived nearly all his friends. I hope he has forgiven all his enemies.[1]

[1] The Spanish patriot, Ramon Narvaez, on his death-bed, when exhorted by the priest to forgive his enemies, exclaimed feebly, 'My father, I have no enemies; I have shot them all.'

I trust I have not spoken unkindly of him; I ought not to have done so.

I should not have given this account of Gibbs, inadequate as it is, if I had not felt a real regard, and indeed admiration, for him. Last week I met one of his very few remaining friends, and as we spoke of the poor old cynic and his grand *peut-être*, we were both nigh shedding tears—*rideat ille nos, si sciat dolore.*

The Last Chapter

Dear Children,—On re-reading these fragmentary chapters your father thinks that, without intending it, he has given a not altogether correct impression of himself. Yes, I have talked so persistently of the people I have known and the company I have kept that you might naturally infer you have had a very social being for your progenitor; but you must understand that great sociability is not in my nature. In truth, a very large part of my life has been spent in my own society, and much of it with my own reflections. I have borne the burden of solitude, but often, as I once expressed it, with

> That best of company—
> Those graver thoughts . . .
> Which hold us fast and never pall.

Indisposition has, in a measure, been the cause of this. It has made me languid, and nervous, and restless; it has made me impatient. I often weary of 'the subject under discussion,' and therefore have but little ease of manner. I hope I have some moral courage—that I have not been an impostor, or the dupe of impostors. But I never had the frank dignity of bearing which I have always so much admired, or even that buoyancy which not seldom is only the offspring of health and impudence.

I confess, too, that I have not been so popular as I should like to have been, especially with some of my connections.[1]

There is little more to be added to these fading memories. I am fast growing old. The inevitable is upon me. General society was always an effort, and will soon be an ordeal; so it is as well, if I *must* shed my friends, that the bulk of my acquaintance should drop away with them.

I speak thus because a generation has grown up with ideas which, if not new, are less familiar to me. Names once honoured are now wellnigh forgotten. There are new men, strange faces, other minds. People and things are drifting from me.

[1] Not very long ago my daughter Eleanor said a true thing. I wish I could have laid it to heart when I was thirty years younger. It might have saved a good deal of trouble, and me some chagrin. 'You make a great mistake, papa. You are always taking pains about people who by disposition and tastes are no way akin to you. You can never make them really congenial, however much you may efface yourself. You do not really sympathise with them, and they think less of you for the effacement and for the very trouble you are always taking about them.' I have made up for it in this volume. There is no self-effacement here. And perhaps you may have observed that there is a good deal of mock modesty in my humility.

The old order is passing; all is changing—but is not it also improving?

Then, sad to say, though I still retain the local regard, the catlike affection for London, its streets and neighbourhoods, its National Gallery and museums, its mental atmosphere—and I shall always retain it, for London is very dear to me—I am losing my keenest pleasure in it. I have become declimatised: its winter fogs and beloved smoke are now an alloyed satisfaction.[1]

I used to think that, for a thorough appreciation of the country, it was necessary to make one's home in the capital. But I begin to feel that a prolonged sojourn under green leaves, in sunny pastures and a transparent atmosphere, is not so entirely insupportable, and that redeeming points may even be found in miry lanes, dripping eaves, and leafless and songless groves. Indeed, the time has come when I must rest satisfied with that retirement which is an irreproachable obscurity.

The scents and sounds, the unpolluted air, the pastoral pleasures of the country, are an anodyne to the enfeebled spirit. Stagnant, it is not stupid; and it is not even unsocial, for I have already established affectionate relations with some of the

[1] And yet I can quite sympathise with Charles Lamb and the ham and beef shop in St. Martin's Lane, and Mme de Sévigné's *ruisseau* in the Rue du Bac.

children of its glebe. I watch the return of the seasons, can recognise the notes of several of its birds, and am on pleasant terms with not a few of its trees and flowers.[1] As I write the beeches are budding and the fans of the horse-chestnuts are broadening, a signal to the blackbird and the thrush. Very soon the whole family of finches will be in full chorus.

We have drained, and we are planting, and it is a new interest to mark the growth of our young trees, at present *haut comme ça*. We vegetate together.[2]

I like to see the squirrels and voles about me, and approve of the poet who remarked to much-persecuted bunny:—

> Farmer I, and landlord thou—
> I for thee must sow and plough.

However, all this must soon be an Arcadia where there will be more necessity for a staff than a crook: it is already a valetudinarian's pastoral. And yet, though I do not expect to realise the delight with liberty which belonged to butterfly hours, superfluous joys having slipped away, I hope to have as much peace as an average terrestrial sojourner has

[1] You see I am a cockney.

[2] At Newhaven Court, Cromer, in the interests of posterity, I have planted slow-growing but sturdy trees—oak and ilex. and some hardy pines (1890).

any right to expect, with perhaps now and again a thrill of sexagenarian rapture.

Then there are my precious drawings and rare books; also those very few writers to whom I can again and again return. They still hold me by their vivid truth, their earnestness, their serene beauty. And have not I my children and my grandchildren shooting up about me, or near me, and becoming more interesting and—although they do not know it—growing dearer every day? They open their mouths, and the prettiest pearls drop from their lips. Dear ones! I could fill pages with your amusing and edifying little remarks.

Then my friends and my affectionate acquaintance! Some of the most valued are not even mentioned here: it would still require Nicolò Pisano's pulpit to hold this dwindling company. And though hereafter I shall *see* but little of them, I hope that something of the sweeter part of friendship will remain to me—the certain knowledge that the feeling thrives in spite of separation.

> I count myself in nothing else so happy
> As in a soul remembering my good friends.

I think I have understood what friendship means, though I have but ill cultivated it. I have not asked much of my fellow-creatures, and they have requited me more than I have given. My fellow-creatures have been very kind to me. I could go some way with the old Roman when he said:

> In all my life
> I found no man but he was true to me.

However, I have run away from them, and it is not their business to follow me. I am grateful for their toleration.[1]

Why am I satisfied to forego my social London? Am I sick of it? Has it had enough of me? I do not know, but somehow, age and health duly considered, I seem to have had enough. It might jar. The streets and sights, the great wave of life, the indescribable attractiveness, are still there, but there are also a good many well-meaning but harassing people. (The divine wisdom of democracies! 'We are all descended from apes! Hell yawns for us!' &c.) To me the questions of What is life? What does it all mean? are daily becoming more importunate; and this is what London—intellectual, superficial London, with all its fascinations—cannot aid me to solve. And,

[1] On the other hand, very occasionally my acquaintances have been wanting in manners to me or mine, probably from infirmity of temper, or an ignorance of how to behave; and instead of frankly forgiving them, I have nursed a passive recollection of their behaviour. People who wish to be comfortable in this world should learn betimes to forgive a great deal.

besides all this, I have a duty elsewhere.[1] The names of my younger children are Godfrey and Dorothy, Oliver and Maud; and with these darlings I have their mother—dear always, dearest of all, happiest of the happy—'whose hours dance away with down upon their feet.' Long, long may they continue to do so! My dear wife, who has been indulgent to my many shortcomings, light-hearted under crosses of my own creating, who has ever been so faithful a wife, the dutiful daughter of a most worthy father! If any love me, they ought indeed to love Janie.

There are drawbacks to age. It brings its weariness with it, and it encourages the contempt of the less thoughtful; so I think that the best possessions that an old man can hope for are the respect and affection of his family, and it behoves him to make himself as little disagreeable as possible. And now—and I say it again—this old age is immediately in front of me.

I do not know that there is a great deal to be said for this world, or our sojourn here upon it; but it has pleased God so to place us, and it must please me also. I ask you, What is human life? Is not it a maimed happiness—care and weariness, weariness

[1] But a trouble did importune
And perplex him night and morn,
With the burden of a fortune
Unto which he was not born.

and care, with the baseless expectation, the strange cozenage of a brighter to-morrow? At best it is but a froward child, that must be played with and humoured, to keep it quiet till it falls asleep, and then the care is over.

Then there is the tenure, which is precarious, and its end, which is certain; the foreboding of disaster which might be irreparable; too much misery, too much sin; the conflict of creeds, and only a clouded hope. And yet, strange to say, the greatest real good that has come to me has come in the guise of sorrow and tribulation—a veiled blessing.

I love the past, am wistful as to the future; and as for the present, if I had robust health and high spirits, it might be more enjoyable, but perhaps only a little more so.

As it is, I have a craving for that repose which never comes, that peace which does not seem compatible with our condition here on earth. We groan, waiting for the redemption of our body. The desire for rest grows upon me. It never comes; and those I most love seem most lovingly to conspire against me.

I am so far resigned to my lot that I feel small pain at the thought of having to part from what has been called the pleasant habit of existence, the sweet fable of life. I would not care to live my wasted life over again, and so to prolong my span.

Strange to say, I have but little wish to be younger. I submit with a chill at my heart. I humbly submit because it is the Divine Will and my appointed destiny. I dread the increase of infirmities that will make me a burden to those around me, those dear to me. No! let me slip away as quietly and comfortably as I can. Let the end come, if peace come with it.

I am not a very old man—I am still nearer sixty than seventy, and still active; yet I often feel, and have an inclination to act, like a being about to take wing into another state of existence.

I have grieved for those who have passed away, but do not grieve when I go. Be occupied, be cheerful, be gay; nourish a tender recollection. Do not grieve, or only for a very little while. Children, love one another—that will be your best remembrance of me.

On the first pages of this Apology I have spoken of a Moral, have wished I could point an edifying one—and have not I done so? *However, try and think kindly of Pierrot.* You must take him for what he is, and was; and remember 'que ce pauvre Pierrot serait content s'il avait l'art de vous plaire.' As he looks around him and above him, he feels that the *sunt aliquid manes* is no chimera of antiquity, no fantasy of the present—but it is a mystery. 'We shall not all sleep, but we shall all be changed.' 'We are in God's hands, brother'—let us trust in God.

It is time that I should bring this memoir to a close; it is already five times as long as I originally intended it to be.

There will be nothing to record in the future, for while I sit and listen to the spectral voices, the far-away music of the past, do not I see signs that the end is not far off—signs on earth, and the gathering in of the heavens?

I know that all things come to an end. Now and again, during a passing sickness, a shadowy hand seems stretched forth, and then withdrawn. I am only waiting for it to beckon me away. And yet I, even I, may, after all, be surprised when it comes.

FAREWELL, DEAR PEOPLE.

APPENDIX A

RELATING TO

MR. LOCKER'S GREAT-GRANDFATHER AND GRANDFATHER

From Nichols's 'Literary Anecdotes of the Eighteenth Century,' Vol. V

John Locker, Esq., barrister-at-law, Commissioner of Bankrupts, and clerk of the companies of Leathersellers and Clockmakers, was the son of Mr. Locker, a scrivener in the Old Jewry. He is styled by Dr. Ward, 'a gentleman much esteemed for his knowledge of polite literature;' and by Dr. Johnson, 'a gentleman eminent for curiosity and literature.' He was remarkable for his skill in the Greek language, particularly the *modern*, of which he became master by accident. Coming home late one evening, he was addressed in modern Greek by a poor Greek priest, a man of literature, from the Archipelago, who had lost his way in the streets of London. He took him to his house, where he and Dr. Mead jointly maintained him some years, and by him was perfected in that language so as to write it fluently, and had translated a part, if not the whole, of one of Congreve's comedies into Greek. He married Elizabeth, eldest daughter of Dr. Stillingfleet, and died a widower, much respected, May 29, 1760, aged sixty-seven. In the preface to the complete

E E

edition of Bacon's works by Dr. Birch and Mr. Mallet, in five volumes, 4to, 1765, the advantages of that edition above all the preceding ones are said to be 'chiefly owing to two gentlemen, now deceased—Robert Stephens, Esq., Historiographer Royal, and John Locker, Esq., Fellow of the Society of Antiquaries—both of whom had made a particular study of Lord Bacon's writings, and a great object of their industry the correcting from original or authentic manuscripts and the earliest and best editions whatever of his works had been already published, and adding to them such as could be recovered that had never seen the light.' Mr. Stephens dying in November 1732, his papers came into the hands of Mr. Locker, whose death prevented the world from enjoying the fruits of his labours; though he had actually finished his correction of the fourth volume of Mr. Blackburne's edition, containing the law tracts, letters, &c. After his decease his collections, including those of Mr. Stephens, were purchased by Dr. Birch.

William Locker, Esq., eldest son of Mr. John Locker, entered early into the Royal Navy. The spotless excellence of this gentleman's character would alone entitle him to the notice of the biographer. While distinguished by good natural parts, by the highest sense of honour, by an enlarged intercourse with the world, and by that inartificial politeness which had been contracted in the highest society, his conduct uniformly displayed the innocence of a child, and the humility as well as the piety of a saint. His personal courage was equalled only by his kindness, and his general benevolence only by the warmth of his private friendships. As a son, a father, a brother, and a master, he stood unrivalled. Such were the excellences by which his private station was adorned. Nor was his professional life less admirable. It is difficult to say whether his prudence, his bravery, his humanity, his zeal for the service, or his discipline, were the most remarkable. This is the uniform account given by those who had the happiness to serve with him; for not a word ever fell from himself on these subjects. His virtues, if we may venture so to say, receive their last polish from his perfect modesty. He was appointed a lieutenant in 1756, and holding that station on board the 'Experiment' in 1758, was wounded in a very gallant action with the 'Télémaque.' He was appointed a master and a commander in 1763, a post-captain in 1768; in the American war commanded the 'Lowestoffe' on the Jamaica station, and had with him at that time young *Nelson*, the future gallant 'hero of the Nile,' to whom he had the honour of being nautical tutor. In February 1793 (being then Commodore at the Nore) he succeeded Captain James Ferguson as Lieutenant-Governor of Greenwich Hospital. He married Lucy, daughter of William Parry, Esq., by whom he left three sons and two daughters. Of the sons, (1) William is a captain of a troop of dragoons; (2) John, Deputy Judge-Advocate in the Island of Malta; and (3) Edward, just now returned from the East Indies, where he has for some years been secretary to Sir Edward Pellew, our admiral on that station. The daughters are Lucy and Eliza, both of whom are unmarried.

This noble-hearted officer died at Greenwich, December 26, 1800, at the age of seventy; and his funeral was attended by his sons, his noble pupil, Lord Nelson, and two old private friends.

Bred as it were in the lap of literature, under the immediate superintendence of his father and of Mr. Stillingfleet, it is not at all surprising that he imbibed an early attachment to literature, which he retained to the close of his life. . . . The Lieutenant-Governor had a good collection of books and pictures; and among the latter, particularly, a considerable number of portraits of naval officers, many of whom, with honest exultation, he generally styled his 'younkers.' A good portrait of him, from a painting by Abbott, was engraved soon after his death by Heath, at the expense of the family, as a private plate, to be presented to his intimates in lieu of the customary gift of mourning-rings—an example worthy of imitation, and infinitely to be preferred in every case where the person deceased has acquired a right to be perpetuated.

APPENDIX B

[The following account of Mr. Locker's grandfather was written by his father, Edward Hawke Locker, and was first published in 1823 in 'The Plain Englishman,' one of Charles Knight's earliest miscellanies, and was subsequently reprinted in his 'Half-hours with the Best Authors.]

TWO-AND-TWENTY years have this day expired since the decease of my much-honoured father. The retrospect presents to me the lively image of this excellent man, and carries me back to a distant period, when I was a daily witness of his benevolence. It is natural that I should dwell with affection upon this portrait, and I cannot refuse myself the pleasure of thinking that it may interest my readers also. The earliest of my impressions represents him as coming to see my little sister and me, when we were but five or six years old, residing in an obscure village under the care of a maiden aunt. Nor should I, perhaps, have remembered the occasion but for my taking a violent fancy to a rude sketch of a stag which he drew to amuse us on the fragment of one of our playthings. So whimsical are the records of our childish days! Only a few years before he had the grievous misfortune to lose my mother in childbirth in the flower of her age, leaving him, with an infant family, almost heartbroken under this severe privation. I have often heard him say that, but for our sakes, he would gladly have been then released; and, indeed, he had every prospect of soon following her. He had recently returned in ill-health from Jamaica, and the violence of his grief so much augmented his malady that the physicians at one time despaired of his recovery. A firm reliance upon the goodness of Providence, and the strength of a powerful constitution, carried him through all his sufferings. He was by nature of a cheerful disposition; but though his spirits recovered with his health, the remembrance of his beloved wife, however mellowed by time, was indelibly expressed by the fondest affection. He never mentioned her name without a sigh, or handled any trifle which had once been hers without betraying the yearnings of a wounded heart. He attached a sanctity to everything allied to her memory. Her ornaments, her portrait, her letters, her sentiments, were objects of his constant regard. When he spoke of her, his tremulous voice proved the unabated interest with which he remembered their happy union. When alone, her image was continually present to his thoughts. In his walks he delighted to hum the airs she was accustomed to play; and I remember the vibration of an old guitar, which had been preserved as one of her reliques, immediately drew tears from his eyes, while he described to us the skill with which she accompanied her own melody.

From all I have heard of her she must have been a woman of very superior merit. With many personal charms, she was accomplished in a degree which rendered her society highly attractive. She had accompanied her father to the West Indies, where he held the chief command, and during that period she had abundant occasions of showing the sweetness of her disposition and the steadiness of her resolution. Her father was an admiral of the old *régime*; and I believe it sometimes required all her discretion to steer her light bark amidst the stormy seas she had to navigate.

My father was no ordinary character. One of the most remarkable features of his mind was simplicity. He was the most natural person I ever knew, and this gave a very agreeable tone to all he said and did. I verily believe he hated nothing but *hypocrisy*. He was blessed, moreover, with a sound understanding, an intrepid spirit, a benevolent heart. From his father, who was a man of distinguished learning, and from his mother, who (as a Stillingfleet) inherited much of the same spirit, he derived a taste for literature which, though thwarted by the rough duties of a sea life, was never quenched, and afterwards broke forth amidst the leisure of more gentle associations on shore. He had been taken from a public school too early to secure a classical education; but such was the diligence with which he repaired this defect, that few men of his profession could be found so well acquainted with books and their authors. In the retirement of his later years he was enabled to cultivate this taste with every advantage, and numbered among his familiar friends some of the most eminent persons of his own time. Saturday was devoted to receiving men of literature and science at his table. On these occasions we were always permitted to be present, and looked forward with delight to this weekly festival, which contributed essentially to our improvement as well as to our amusement. He lost no opportunity of affording us instruction. All departments of literature had attractions for him; and, without the science of a proficient, he had a genuine love of knowledge, wherever it was to be found. He was a great reader. I think Shakespeare was his favourite amusement; and he read his plays with a native eloquence and feeling which sometimes drew tears from our eyes, and still oftener from his own.

He always considered himself a fortunate man in his naval career, although he persevered through a long and arduous course of service before he attained the honours of his profession. Having greatly distinguished himself in boarding a French man-of-war, his conduct at length attracted the notice of Sir Edward Hawke, to whom he ascribed all his subsequent success. My father often said that it was that great officer who first weaned him from the vulgar habits of a cockpit; and he considered him as the founder of the more gentlemanly spirit which has gradually been gaining ground in the navy. At the period when he first went to sea, a man-of-war was characterised by the coarseness so graphically described in the novels of Smollett. Tobacco and a check shirt were associated with lace and a cockade; and the manners of a British admiral partook of the language and demeanour of a boatswain's mate. My father accompanied his distinguished patron to the Mediterranean in the year 1757, when he was despatched to relieve the unfortunate Admiral Byng in the command, with orders to send him a close prisoner to England. I stop to relate a curious anecdote regarding that affair, which I have often heard from my father's lips.

When Sir Edward reached Gibraltar, he found Byng, with his fleet, lying at anchor in the bay. On communicating the nature of his instructions, he forbore to place the Admiral in arrest, and conducted the affair with so much delicacy that none else suspected the serious nature of his orders. The two admirals met at the table of Lord Tyrawley, then Governor of Gibraltar, who, after dinner, withdrew with Byng to another apartment, where he assured him that, by private letters just then received, he was convinced the Ministry meant to sacrifice him to the popular fury, advising him to take this opportunity of escaping to Spain, as the only chance of saving his life. Byng, in reply, confided to his Lordship the generous conduct of Hawke, declaring that no personal consideration could induce him to betray that honourable man; adding, that he was determined to meet his fate, whatever might be the consequence of his return to England. This transaction, which does equal honour to both admirals, shows the generous nature of Hawke, who found in my father a kindred spirit, worthy of his future friendship and protection. Under the auspices of this patron he shared in the glory of the fight with the French fleet, under Marshal Conflans, off Quiberon in 1759, and being preferred after the action to the post of first-lieutenant of the 'Royal George,' bearing Sir Edward's flag, he advanced him through the successive stages of his subsequent promotion, their mutual attachment only ceasing with the life of that illustrious commander.

A reputation so well earned was rewarded not only with preferment, but by the esteem and affection both of officers and men. The sailors respected him for his gallantry and loved him for his humanity—virtues in which he emulated the brilliant example of his patron. In the selection of his earliest naval friends he had shown great discernment, for they subsequently became the most distinguished officers in the service. When, in his turn, he became a patron, his example as a commander, aided by the high integrity of his character and the native benevolence of his disposition, drew around him a number of young officers, whose brilliant career richly repaid the obligations they received from him. Several of them, who rose to distinction, afterwards presented him with their portraits. These were hung round his room, and he took an honest pride in showing to his visitors these memorials of his 'younkers,' relating some honourable trait of each of them in succession. Among these was Horatio Nelson, who, to the last hour of his life, regarded him with the affection of a son and with the respect of a pupil.

While Nelson was yet a private captain, and his merits unknown beyond the limits of his own immediate friends, my father always spoke of him with a prophetic anticipation of his future greatness, such was the sagacity with which he penetrated the character of that extraordinary man. When, at length, Nelson returned to England, his old friend was rapidly sinking into the grave; yet the desire to behold once more the hero whom he still regarded with the affection of a parent, occupied his thoughts during the last days of his life. But this wish was not gratified. He never saw him again. Nelson, when informed of his death, hastened to pay the last tribute of respect to his remains; and though on that occasion I was deeply engaged with my own sorrows, I could not be insensible to the unequivocal proofs of grateful attachment which he then showed to his early patron.

The principles of my father's character are perhaps better understood by viewing him in the retirement of domestic life than in his professional relations, for it is only in private that the more delicate traits of disposition are to be observed. There is a certain exterior, worn by most men in their intercourse with the world, which produces a general resemblance; but this is thrown aside upon their return home, and the nicer peculiarities of character, hidden from the public eye, are disclosed without reserve in the bosom of their own families. Thus it was with my father. The playfulness of his disposition never appeared to such advantage as at his own fireside; and though the warmth of his benevolence, which beamed on his venerable countenance, diffused itself wherever he came, it glowed with peculiar ardour towards those more closely connected with him. He was no party man. Though cordially attached to his Church and King, he was neither a bigot in religion nor in politics. He had great reluctance to controversy, and enjoyed the friendship of men of worth of all parties. His father, indeed, was a staunch Jacobite, and he thus inherited Tory principles.

He used to relate that, when a boy, he was often sent with presents to relieve the poor Highlanders confined in the Tower after the Rebellion of 1745. One of these poor fellows (who deserved a better fate) gave him his leathern belt as a keepsake a few days before his execution; and in treasuring up this simple relic he fostered the political opinions with which it was associated. With all this partiality, he reprobated the heartless ingratitude of Prince Charles; and among the honourable distinctions of his late sovereign's character, he most of all admired his tenderness to the last of the Stuarts.

The remembrance of any considerable act of kindness became a part of my father's constitution. It cost him no effort to retain it in his memory. He never seemed to feel the *burden* of an obligation, and it arose to his mind whenever he had an opportunity to requite it. The child, the friend, nay, even the dog of any one to whom he was obliged, was sure to receive some acknowledgment. I shall never forget a visit to the tomb of his naval patron in the little village of Swatheling, which called up all his gratitude at the distance of twenty years. A rough old admiral, who accompanied us, struggled hard to hide his emotion; but my father gave free course to his feelings, while the tears stole down their rugged cheeks in sympathy.

Good breeding is said to be the daughter of good nature. There was an unaffected cordiality in my father's hospitality, a frank familiarity towards an old friend, a respect and tenderness to women of all ranks and ages and complexions, which marked the generous spirit of an English gentleman of the old school. Towards young persons he had none of the chilliness and austerity of age. He treated them on equal terms; and they learned many a valuable lesson from his conversation, while they fancied themselves only amused. He had an excellent library, which before his death was nearly exhausted in presents to his youthful friends. Of this I had, some years ago, a very gratifying proof on visiting a Spanish gentleman in the island of Majorca, who, unexpectedly to me, opened a little cabinet filled with the best English authors, which my father had given him when a student in London.

The fireside, on a winter evening, was a scene highly picturesque, and worthy of the pencil of Wilkie. The veteran sat in his easy-chair, surrounded by his children. A few grey hairs peeped from beneath his hat, worn somewhat awry, which gave an arch turn to the head, which it seldom quitted. The anchor button, and scarlet waistcoat trimmed with gold, marked the fashion of former times. Before him lay his book, and at his side a glass prepared by the careful hand of a daughter, who devoted herself to him with a tenderness peculiarly delightful to the infirmities of age. The benevolent features of the old man were slightly obscured by the incense of a 'cigarre' (the last remnant of a cockpit education), which spread its fragrance in long wreaths of smoke around himself and the whole apartment. A footstool supported his wounded leg, beneath which lay the old and faithful Newfoundland dog stretched on the hearth. Portraits of King Charles the First and Van Tromp (indicating the characteristic turn of his mind) appeared above the chimney-piece; and a multitude of prints of British heroes covered the rest of the wainscot. A knot of antique swords and Indian weapons garnished the old-fashioned pediment of the door; a green curtain was extended across the room, to fence off the cold air, to which an old sailor's constitution is particularly sensitive. Such was the picture.

The servants, who reverenced his peculiarities, served him with earnest affection. Even his horse confided in his benevolence as much as the rest of the household; for when he was of opinion that the morning ride was sufficiently extended, he commonly faced about, and as my father generally rode in gambadoes (not the most convenient armour for a conflict with a self-willed steed), he generally yielded to the caprice of his horse. The chief personage in his confidence was old Boswell, the self-invested minister of the extraordinaries of the family, who looked upon the footman as a jackanapes, and on the female servants as incapable of 'understanding his honour.' Boswell had been in his time a smart young seaman, and formerly rowed the stroke oar in the captain's barge. After many a hard gale and long separation, the association was renewed in old age, and to a bystander had more of the familiarity of ancient friendship than of the relation of master and servant. 'Has your honour any further commands?' said Boswell, as he used to enter the parlour in the evening, while, throwing his body into an angle, he made his reverence, and shut the door with his opposite extremity at the same time. 'No, Boswell, I think not; unless, indeed, you are disposed for a glass of grog before you go.' 'As your honour pleases,' was the established reply. A word from my father soon produced the beverage, at the approach of which the old sailor was seen to slide a quid into his cuff and prepare for action. 'Does your honour remember when we were up the Mississippi, in the "Nautilus" sloop of war?' 'Ay, my old friend, I shall never forget it; 'twas a happy trip—the poor Indians won all our hearts.' 'Ah! but, your honour, there was worse company than they in the woods there. Mayhap you recollect the great black snake that clung about the sergeant of Marines, and had wellnigh throttled him?' 'I do, I do; and the poor fellow was obliged to beat its head to pieces against his own thigh. I remember it as though it was but yesterday.' 'And the rattlesnake, too, that your honour killed with your cane, five-and-forty feet?' 'Avast, Boswell!' cried my father; 'mind your reckoning there;

'twas but twelve, you rogue, and that's long enough in all conscience.' These scenes were highly amusing to our occasional visitors, and are still remembered with delight by those of his familiar friends who yet survive him.

If benevolence was the striking feature of his disposition, religion was the guide of his conduct, the anchor of his hope, the stay of all his confidence. There was an habitual energy in his private devotions which proved the firm hold which Christianity had obtained over his mind. Whether in reading or in conversation, at the name of God he instantly uncovered his head, by a spontaneous movement of religious feeling. Nothing but illness ever kept him from church. His example there was a silent reproof to the idle and indifferent. I see him still, in imagination, kneeling, unconscious of all around him, absorbed in earnest prayer, and though his features were concealed, the agitation of his venerable head indicated the fervour of his supplications. The recollection has often quickened my own indolence.

Such was the man whose memory was endeared to all who knew his worth, affording us a beautiful example of a true old English officer.

December 26, 1822.

INDEX

Spottiswoode & Co. Printers, New-street Square, London

www.ingramcontent.com/pod-product-compliance
Lightning Source LLC
Chambersburg PA
CBHW031051110726
47900CB00003B/884
* 9 7 8 3 3 3 7 0 1 0 8 4 3 *